P9-DDO-827

A Final Judgment

A Final Judgment

A Ron Shade Novel

Michael A. Black

Five Star • Waterville, Maine

This novel is a work of fiction. Names, characters, places and incidents are either the product of the author's imagination, or, if real, used fictitiously.

First Edition
First Printing: September 2006

Published in 2006 in conjunction with Tekno Books and Ed Gorman.

Set in 11 pt. Plantin by Myrna S. Raven

Printed in the United States on permanent paper.

Library of Congress Cataloging-in-Publication Data

Black, Michael A., 1949–
A final judgment : a Ron Shade novel / Michael A. Black —1st ed.
p. cm.
ISBN 1-59414-426-5 (hc : alk. paper)
1. Shade, Ron (Fictitious character)—Fiction. 2. Private investigators—Illinois—Chicago—Fiction. 3. Chicago (Ill.) —fiction. I. Title.
PS3602.L325F56 2006
813′.6—dc22 2006013785

To Andrew Vachss

Thanks, Brother.

Acknowledgments

Once again, there are many people to whom I owe a debt of gratitude. I would like to thank my "big brother," Andrew Vachss, for pushing me to be the best writer I could be, and for telling me, in his own inimitable style, that I'd better do another Shade novel. (The two other members of our "Chicago Wolf Pack," Mike McNamara and Zak Mucha, are included in this.) A special thanks to Debbie (D.C.) Brod, who agreed to come out of "editing retirement" to edit this book and find out if Shade does fight for the title this time. Another special thanks to Julie A. Hyzy, my special friend and writing partner, who helped me build this one, step by step, and always told me when I was going wrong. Thanks to my buddies and peerless first readers, J. Michael Major and Len Jellema, both of whom are talented writers in their own right. Thanks to Ray Lovato, my brother and best friend since we both ran up that dirt hill so many years ago. Thanks to my cop-writer buddies, who never let me down when I needed support or advice, Jim Born, Dave Case, Paul Doyle, John Lamb, and Rick McMahan. Thanks to Mr. Stephen Marlowe, whose work inspired me and whose kind words of support gave me faith in myself. Thanks to Tiffany Schofield, Mary Smith, Myrna Raven, and all the rest of the wonderful people at Five Star who had faith in my ability as a writer. Thanks to Martin Greenberg and the great staff at Tekno Books, John Helfers and Denise Little, for their faith in me as well. Thanks to the members of my writers' groups who listened and gave me their honest opinions. There are so many more, too numerous to mention, who have helped me realize my dream of being a writer, who may not be mentioned here, but hold a special place in my heart. Thanks to you all.

Chapter 1

I usually try to avoid lawyers unless it becomes a case of absolute necessity. This one wasn't, but it had all the earmarks of coming real close. It started with a message from my service that Rick Walters wanted me to call him as soon as possible. I'd known Rick from the days when he was an Assistant State's Attorney, and I was a cop. He'd always impressed me as an honest and likeable guy. I often wondered if he had too many of those qualities to be a really effective lawyer.

I looked out the plate-glass window of the restaurant, swallowed a bit of my coffee, and took out my cell phone. Outside, the traffic was backing up along Western Avenue, and my buddy George, who was supposed to be meeting me here this morning, still hadn't shown up. Yet it was a beautiful spring day, full of bright sunshine, cool temperatures, and the promise of things to come. In a few hours I'd be enjoying an afternoon run before my workout. The message from my service loomed in my memory again.

I dialed the number and got connected to his secretary.

"This is Ron Shade," I said, "returning Mr. Walters's call."

"Oh, yes, Mr. Shade, hold on, please."

She'd called me "mister." Always a positive sign.

I waited about thirty seconds, and Rick came on the line.

"Ron, thanks for calling back."

"My pleasure," I said. Mentally I conjured up how he'd looked when I'd last seen him. Curly brown hair, fleshy cheeks, solid build.

"Are you available?" he asked. "I mean for hire. You still have your private investigating business, don't you?"

"Unless the state's planning on revoking my license. And hopefully that won't happen anytime soon."

"Good, good," he said, adding a nervous-sounding chuckle. "When could you come over to talk? I want to hire you."

A red flag went up. Now that Rick was in private practice, that meant I'd be working for the defense. Something I wasn't sure I really wanted to do if the client was some scumbag. He must have sensed my hesitation when I asked about it, because he sprang in with all kinds of assurances.

"This isn't a criminal case, Ron," he said. "In fact, it's just the opposite. A wrongful death suit. The family's hired me to go after the guy the state couldn't put away."

"I see. What are the circumstances?"

"An ugly divorce," he said. "Got real ugly when the wife turned up dead. Husband was arrested and charged, but acquitted. Now we got one last shot to try and get some justice."

"That's in short supply these days." I glanced at my watch. "Okay, I'll drop by this afternoon, if that's all right."

"That'd be great," he said. There was something else; I could tell in his tone. When he spoke again his words were rapid. "There's a little more to it than that, but we can go over it when you get here, okay?"

I told him it was, and that I'd be there at one-thirty. But after we hung up, I couldn't shake the vague uneasiness I was feeling in the pit of my stomach.

Suddenly I saw George's big form passing in front of the window. His head swiveled and our eyes met. He grinned and gave a small wave. I figured he was on his way into work from the way he was dressed: a gray sports jacket that looked like it'd barely made it out of the last century intact, and dark slacks. I could see the outline of his gun, in its pancake holster on his hip, and his shining Chicago star right in front of it. His white shirt was tight around his gut, and made me realize he'd gained weight, which worried me. He was in his early fifties, and spent way too much time sitting behind a desk, drinking way too much coffee, and eating way too much greasy food.

He pulled open the door and headed over toward my table. There seemed to be a bit more gray in his dark hair, too. Like he'd had it frosted, or something. And that wasn't likely.

"Hiya," he said, sliding into the booth opposite me. "Sorry I'm late."

"You seem out of breath," I said. "You had a physical lately?"

"Huh?" His mouth stayed open, and bundles of crow's feet gathered at the corners of his eyes. "What are you talking about?"

"A physical. You know, been checked out by a doctor lately?"

His mouth closed, drawing into a semi-scowl.

"Yeah, right. Who the hell has the time?" He took a deep breath, and looked out the window. "It's a great-looking morning, ain't it?"

The waitress came over with a second cup and the pot of coffee. She set the cup in front of George and asked if he wanted some.

"Absolutely," he said.

"Maybe you should switch to tea," I said.

"Tea?" His brow furrowed, and when the waitress stepped away, he added, "What the fuck is wrong with you today?"

"With me? Nothing. I'm just . . ." I let the sentence dangle. "Concerned that you're not taking good enough care of yourself, that's all."

He snorted as he brought the cup to his lips.

"You trying to make me choke, or what?" he asked. After a long sip, he set it down and looked across the table at me.

I'd always thought George looked like a young Robert Mitchum, but recently he'd begun to take on the more pouchy look that Mitch had developed in his later years. Still, he was a big guy and carried the extra weight well.

"Anyway," he said, "if you're through insulting me, I got some very interesting news for you."

His smile, from across the table, was damn near infectious. Almost gleeful.

"What might that be?" I asked, cocking my head. This could be either real good, or real bad. From his grin, I figured it must be good.

"I got a job for you," he said.

"A job?"

He nodded. "And you'll never guess who the client is."

"Then there's no sense trying."

He smirked again, like a teenager who could barely conceal news of his first sexual conquest.

"Lieutenant Bielmaster," he said.

I felt my jaw drop. The name stunned me. Bielmaster had made it very clear that he had no use for me on many occasions. In fact, he'd made official complaints to the state licensing committee several times, trying to get my PI license revoked.

George sat across from me, watching my reaction, with that Cheshire cat's smile still plastered on his face.

"You're kidding, right?" I said.

He shook his head and waved for the waitress.

"Come on," I said. "This is the same Lieutenant Bielmaster that I've known and loved for so long?"

"The one and only." He took another sip of coffee and turned to the waitress, keeping me in suspense while he ordered his customary eggs sunny-side up, bacon, toast, and orange juice. She turned to me.

"Scrambled," I said weakly. "Skip the bacon, and make my toast whole wheat, no butter."

When she left, I stared at him.

"Suppose you tell me what this is all about?"

The grin again. "Of course, but let me at least have a little fun first."

I stared directly at him.

"The lieutenant wants to hire your services," he said.

"Bullshit."

That got another smirk out of him.

"No, it's true." A furrow appeared between his eyebrows. "You heard he's in the hospital, right?"

I hadn't. I asked what the problem was.

"Ticker," he said, pointing to his own chest. "Gotta have a bypass."

I raised my eyebrows. "That sounds serious. Any idea what he wants from me?"

George took a swig of his coffee.

"Just that he made a point of calling me last night and being real secretive about it." He set the cup down. "And, he said something else that you might find interesting."

The wide grin again. He was either enjoying this more than he should, or what he was about to tell me was extremely shocking.

"He mentioned that if you help him," George said, still grinning, "that he might be able to speak to somebody to get you reinstated on the PD."

I was stunned. I'd lost my job with the police department after a botched HBT/SWAT operation, and my appeal had evolved into an endless series of continuances. Bielmaster himself had always taken a hard line with me, giving George a lot of grief because we were close friends.

"You're kidding, right?" I asked.

He shook his head slowly, still grinning.

I looked down at the table, unsure of what to think.

George reached over and tapped my hand with his fingers.

"Hey, Ron, this is your big chance here. You could get back on the job, full pay and bennies, not to mention back pay." He paused. "Then you could take the detective exam . . . Hell, we could be working together in no time."

"I don't know," I said slowly, shaking my head.

"You don't know what? You want back in, don't you?"

I took a deep breath, uncertain of the answer. Sure, it was something I'd sought for several years, but I'd been able to build up my own business fairly well, and wasn't handcuffed by a lot of rules. Still, I'd be working for the right side, and not have to worry about owing loyalty to some unsavory client. But regardless, it would have been nice to leave on my own terms.

"How come you ain't saying something?" he asked, the lines appearing between his brows again.

"I'm just kind of used to working for myself. Being my own boss . . ."

The waitress came carrying a tray with our plates. George moved his cup and smiled at me.

"Yeah," he said, chuckling, "but remember what you always tell me. If you work for yourself, you got no one to blame if your boss is an asshole."

That brought a smile to my lips, but the strangeness of the whole situation still hung over me.

"Seriously, you got any idea what this is all about?" I asked.

He waited until she'd finished setting down our plates, and then dipped a corner of his toast into a bright yolk and popped it into his mouth. Before replying, he shifted his food to his cheek.

"Bielmaster's got a daughter," he said. "Gonna be eighteen in another month or so. Set to graduate from Mother Maria's."

I watched him dab the yolk again.

"A couple of years ago she got . . . in trouble."

"What kind of trouble?"

He shot me a lips-only smile and stuck his hand in front of his stomach, mimicking a swollen belly.

"You know . . . *Trouble.* Bielmaster got her an abortion and had the boy arrested for aggravated criminal sexual abuse, on account of him being five years older and her being less than fifteen." He reached for his coffee and washed down whatever he'd been chewing.

I nodded.

"So boyfriend went away for three to five, and Bielmaster does everything in his power to see that the kid does the max." He soaked up some more yolk with another piece of toast, then smeared some strawberry jam on top. "You gonna eat, or what?"

I still hadn't touched my food, which had cooled off substantially.

"I'm on pins and needles listening to your story," I said.

He shrugged, shoved the toast into his mouth, and took a long drink of juice.

"The kid's out now," he said. "Parole."

I considered this. "So what does he want me to do?"

George shrugged again. "Considering what a big, strapping boy you are, maybe he wants you to run the little shit outta town." He grinned.

I poked into the yellow fluff of eggs, suddenly without any appetite whatsoever, thinking about all the indignities that had been heaped upon me by Bielmaster. . . . His smug expression as he stared at me during my dismissal hearing, saying that my recklessness and lack of leadership had brought disgrace upon the department . . . His sarcastic and biting comments whenever I'd come to visit George at Area One . . . The threats of what he'd do if he ever caught George bending the rules to help me on a case . . . And now, the thought that he could use me to bend those rules to suit his own private purpose.

"Just tell him to go to hell," I said.

George looked up, his fork full of fried egg halfway to his mouth.

"What? Are you nuts?" he asked. "You been listening to what I been saying at all?"

We locked eyes momentarily.

"This is your chance to really turn things around for yourself," he said. "At least go see the man. Listen to what he has to say."

I compressed my lips, considering this.

"Besides, he's still my boss," he added. "I already told him you'd be by this afternoon at three o'clock. He's at Christ Hospital."

I stared at him and sighed.

He smirked, shoveled some more eggs into his mouth, and grinned.

"You know," I said, picking up a piece of my unbuttered toast, "I used to dream of having a gorgeous redheaded secretary to set things up for me, but I don't need one with you around." I waited until he'd just started sipping more coffee before adding, "Ever think of shaving your legs?"

I stood and watched George pull the unmarked out into traffic and give me a wave. The crispness of the March morning was almost, but not quite, mild enough to be actually warm. But it flirted with the promise of spring, just the same. Turning, I went down the alley and through the lot to my red Pontiac Firebird and pressed the alarm button. The car beeped in response. It had been part of a payment for one of my previous cases, and I enjoyed the hell out of driving it. The whisper of power as I pressed the accelerator pedal was enough to send goosebumps down the back of most red-blooded American males, and it seemed to have a similar effect on the ladies as well.

Still, the car carried a lot of memories, some good, some bad, and it set me thinking about George's preordained certainty that I'd be bending over to kiss Bielmaster's ass and take the case. *Considering what a big, strapping boy you are, maybe he wants you to run the little shit outta town.*

Ironically, a little more than a decade or so before, I'd been in a similar situation, but not as the irate father. I pondered the effect it had had on my life at the time, and was suddenly grateful that I'd ended up in the army and not in prison. But, still, there had to be more of an age difference between Bielmaster's daughter and this guy. He wouldn't have served time unless he was what? Five years older? I'd have to look up the statute to see what the exact requirements were. But then again, I really wasn't planning on taking the case anyway. No, I'd go to the hospital, partly out of loyalty to George, who was sort of like a surrogate big brother to me, but more so just to see Bielmaster's face when I told him what he could do with his request. The asshole had a lot of nerve expecting me to do something for him after the way he'd treated me. What goes around, comes around, they always say. Except most of the time, it doesn't come around quick enough. Maybe this time it would.

As I slid into the low seat of the Firebird I slowed my movement and checked how my left knee felt. No strain or pain gripped me, and for that I was thankful. I'd hurt myself three weeks ago in a fight in Atlantic City. After trying unsuccessfully to win the heavyweight title in the World Kickboxing Association twice, missing both chances due to last-minute injuries, my manager and I had accepted two back-to-back fights in two short months. But these were no bum-of-the-month affairs, and I probably shouldn't have taken the second one. It was with the number one contender of a different organization than the one I usually fight in. This one, the Professional Kickboxing Council, followed a different set of rules and allowed leg kicks. My opponent had shins like fence posts and used them to punish me through six grueling rounds before I caught him with a left hook as he was coming in and put him down for the count.

To offset the leg kicks, the PKC didn't have a minimum kick requirement per round, which made it a little easier. Except that I was used to building up points that way by jamming my opponents. When all was said and done, running on the unforgiving pavement along the boardwalk in the days before the fight, and being on the receiving end of so many brutal leg kicks, I could barely walk to the plane the next day.

Chappie, my manager, trainer, and surrogate father, was worried about me. He insisted on getting the flight atten-

dants to rearrange our seating so that I could stretch out without a seat in front of me. And the whole way back he kept asking how I was, and saying, "Lordy, I shoulda never let you fight that dude."

"What are you talking about?" I asked him. "I knocked him out, didn't I?"

His dark eyes looked solemn, and his shaved mahogany head glistened under the dome lights.

"Yeah, you did," he said. "But sometimes you can win, and still lose."

Yeah, I thought as I shifted into gear and pulled out of the space, seeing Bielmaster's smug expression in my mind's eye. Sometimes you can.

Chapter 2

Rick Walters's office was nicely furnished, the way most suburban law offices are. The carpeting was functional brown, capable of hiding the overt winter dirt until the annual spring cleaning, and the furniture was slightly above what could crassly be called cheap. Even Rick's secretary looked harried and overworked, although I did have to admit, she was a babe. She looked to be in her mid-twenties with dark hair and a bronze-colored complexion. Her smile was dazzling as I told her who I was and that I had an appointment to see Mr. Walters.

Rick came out of his office to greet me, extending his open hand from a rolled-up shirtsleeve.

"Ron, thanks for coming," he said, making me feel extra welcome and a bit uneasy at the same time.

Inside, I checked out the certificates and pictures on his wall. John Marshall Law School, Northern Illinois University, an academy graduation picture of him in uniform shaking hands with the Chicago Police Superintendent, and a final eight-by-ten of him receiving the medal of valor after being wounded in the line of duty. Pictures of his mother and father sat in a gold frame on the front of his desk, which was awash with papers.

He gestured toward the chair in front and leaned over to stretch his back. When he turned and sat down, I automatically looked for the small, star-shaped scar on his left temple left by the bullet that had almost ended his life. The scar was still there, like a small, reddish jewel.

"I guess you want to know what this is all about, huh?" he asked.

"That would be nice."

He grinned and blew out a breath.

"Where to begin?" His eyes jumped toward the ceiling.

I'd been reading people long enough to know that there was more to this one than a simple lawsuit. He looked like I felt when I had a title fight coming up.

"Here's the situation," he said, his expression getting solemn. "Two years ago Dr. Todd M. Gooding was arrested and tried for killing his estranged wife. Her name was Laura. The crime happened up on the North Shore, and the cops and prosecutors did a pretty good job of setting up the case." He frowned. "But they lost. Gooding was acquitted, principally because he had a real good lawyer."

I raised my eyebrows.

"Mason Gilbert," he said.

I considered this and nodded slowly. "Reasonable doubt for unreasonable price."

Rick laughed, then grew solemn again.

"Gilbert was so effective that he won a directed verdict right after the prosecution rested," he said. "Beat them so bad, right out of the gate, that Laura Gooding's family was in shock."

"Yeah, an acquittal on a murder case will do that," I said. "So now they're trying for some financial compensation?"

Rick shook his head.

"It's not like that, Ron. What we're trying for here is more than just money. It's a final try for some measure of justice. Plus, Laura's parents want a shot at gaining custody of the kids. We figure if we can win a huge settlement, have the good doctor found liable, the chances are in our favor.

Gooding was even able to collect on a two-million-dollar life insurance policy as custodial parent."

This was sounding more and more like an uphill battle.

"The case wasn't good enough to win in criminal court?" I said. "What makes you think you can win it now?"

"The standard of proof is different in civil court. We won't be dealing with guilt beyond a reasonable doubt. Just a preponderance of the evidence. Gooding never testified at his criminal trial. This time he'll have to." His mouth stretched into a weak smile. "I think we can win it. And Laura's parents, who are from the South Side here, have faith in me."

"Is Gilbert representing him in the civil trial too?"

Rick nodded, the smile vanishing. "Plus, he's got John Flood backing him up."

John Flood was a private investigator of legendary proportions in Chicago. He'd won so many awards, mostly when he was associated with some case that Mason Gilbert had taken on, that there was talk of making a TV series about him. His most famous case was freeing a guy on death row who was set to be executed for killing a cop. Flood was able to find witnesses who saw the convicted killer some place other than the crime scene, and he walked. It had always bothered me, because I was one of the vocal minority who believed that the guy was, in fact, guilty, and that Flood's investigation wasn't conclusive enough. Still, as far as PIs went, Flood knew how to walk the walk and talk the talk.

Maybe someday I'll have them wanting to make a TV series about me, I thought. "When's the trial?"

Rick inhaled, but paused before he answered.

"Three weeks," he said.

"Huh?"

He licked his lips.

"I know that's kind of tight, Ron . . ." He let the sentence hang for a moment. "But I've had a run of bad luck lately."

"You and me both," I said. "Look, can't you get a continuance or something? Give yourself more time?"

He shook his head.

"I pushed for a quick date," he said. "Figured it would avoid a lot of problems. Gilbert's a master at stalling, and half the time, when he says he's got a full calendar, he means it. The judges all love the guy. It's like he walks on water."

"As long as it's thoroughly frozen, he probably does. What's he weigh, anyway? He's gotta be close to three hundred."

Rick chuckled briefly.

"So why do I get the feeling that there's part of this you're leaving out?" I said. "You're asking me to come into this with only three weeks before the trial. That seems like it's a bit close."

He shifted his gaze to the floor. "You always were good at reading people."

"I'm a detective, remember?"

"Okay, I needed to tell you this, and I intended to . . ."

"Now you're really starting to sound more like a lawyer."

He smiled again, then said, "I had somebody else on board before. Rob Tunney."

"Tunney?"

Rick nodded. "His death sort of upset everything I had planned. Kind of left me high and dry."

"He killed himself, didn't he?"

Rick nodded again. "Two weeks ago. And the worst part

of it is, he must have been keeping most of his notes in his head. Left me next to nothing in the way of case files."

I clucked sympathetically. I'd known Tunney only peripherally. He'd been a retired copper who once had a fondness for the booze. But the last few years he'd supposedly been clean. Still, if he'd been Rick's first choice, what did that say about the faith he had in me?

"Then to top it off, my regular secretary, June, got hit by a car last week," he said. "Broke her hip. I've been using temps to get my stuff done."

"Well, at least they sent you a babe." I jerked my thumb toward the outer office.

"Oh, that's Denise," he said. "My paralegal. She's been great helping out. The temp I've been using is good, but she had to take off early today on some personal business. And we're so far behind in everything . . ."

"Man, if it wasn't for bad luck, you'd have none at all."

"Tell me about it." He compressed his lips and stared at me. "So can I count on your help, buddy? I know it's an uphill battle and long odds."

"My favorite kind," I said, reaching into my briefcase to take out one of my standard contracts.

I'd practiced the line I was going to use on Bielmaster all the way up to the fifth floor where they had him in the cardiac care unit. And it would be respectable enough to keep George out of trouble, too. After all, I already had a job for the moment. Sorry, Lieu, I mentally rehearsed, but I'm involved in a big case right now. One that doesn't have anything to do with George, Chicago PD, Catholic high school girls in trouble, or you. The thought of seeing his nostrils flare in displeasure, as they always seemed to do in my presence, brought a smile to my lips. I rounded the corner, showed my visitor's tag to the nurses' station, and asked where room 527 was.

The nurse, a pretty black lady, pointed to the left down the hallway and said, "Try not to stay longer than five or six minutes, okay?"

"Won't be a problem. I'll be in and out in a flash."

Taking a deep breath, I moved down the slick tiles. The place smelled of illness and antiseptic. Glancing in the open doors as I passed, I saw various people sitting at the foot of hospital beds with television sets mounted on brackets above them. The patients ranged from somnambulant to reasonably alert, and I was glad when I found the right set of numbers. This periodic view of the broken and infirm was tough to take. So was seeing Bielmaster.

He sat propped up on several pillows, his massive frame covered by a folded hospital sheet under a yellow blanket. Tubes looped down from his nose on either side of his face and wires extended from his soft, hairless chest to several sets of monitors displaying the crooked lines of his heartbeat. He slipped on his glasses as I came in and his jaw sagged down slightly. All my preparation for telling him off went out the window when I saw how pathetic he looked, hooked up to all that telemetry and oxygen.

"How you doing, Lieu?" I said, not knowing if I should offer him my hand or not.

I decided what the hell, and extended my palm. He gripped it so feebly that I was sorry I'd made the move in the first place. The man's color looked pasty and just the small movement seemed to exhaust him. My steely resolve to brush him off was evaporating faster than dew on a spring morning.

"Ron, thanks for coming," he managed to say. Even his voice, which had always been harsh and bellicose, sounded thin and reedy. He gestured toward a chair by the bed. "Sit down. Please."

It took me a moment to recover from the shock of him calling me "Ron." It had always been "Shade" before. I shot a quick look at the chair and shook my head. There was no way I was going to conduct this interview sitting so he could look down at me from a position of tactical dominance.

"George said you wanted to see me," I said. Best to cut to the chase, get it over with so I could turn him down and get the hell out of there.

"Yeah." The word sounded muffled, like it'd been hard to say. "Did he tell you about my problem? With Grace. My daughter?"

"A little bit."

His face cracked into a semi-smile, which looked almost ludicrous stretching from under the plastic hoses descending from his nose.

"Grace is a good girl," he said. "Real smart. Wants to be a doctor." He stopped to take a breath, then continued. "Got accepted at Yale. Can you imagine that? My kid going to Yale?"

"Impressive." I was waiting for him to drop the other shoe so I could get it over with.

His gaze lowered, and he paused, his mouth gaping slightly. "There's this guy who's been bothering her. Name's Tim Knop. He served time before and now he's in a halfway house. He's out on parole, and I'm laid up here."

He stopped again, and I noticed that he'd conspicuously avoided eye contact with me. I figured he must have been about ready to ask, and it was hard for him. I stood there in silence for perhaps thirty seconds before I asked, "Look, Lieu, what exactly did you have in mind here?"

His eyes locked with mine. "Shade, you got to protect my little girl from this punk."

Saying the sentence seemed to stress him and he started coughing. I watched the electric blips on the monitors stretch and jump. "I'll pay you. Anything you want."

"Look, maybe it'd be better to have a squad car take a few extra passes around your house till you're up and about."

He shook his head, the skin on his cheeks shaking.

"That ain't gonna cut it," he said. His eyes glistened. "You know how busy we are, and how many times can one squad car swing by per shift? It ain't like I rate twenty-four-hour protection like the mayor, or something."

"Still," I said. "The other coppers will take care of one of their own, won't they?"

"You don't know this kid. It's like he's got some kind of power over her. She's scared to death that he'll be coming for her."

The nurse suddenly appeared in the doorway, frowning.

"Mr. Bielmaster, I thought I told you not to get excited." Moving forward, she looked at me. "Sir, I'm afraid you're going to have to leave."

Bielmaster made what was obviously a laborious swallow and raised his hand. "Just give us another minute. Please."

The nurse's nostrils flared slightly and she shook her head.

"I'm sorry, I can't do that." Her eyebrows rose expectantly at me. "Sir?"

I nodded and began to step toward the door. Bielmaster grunted like he'd been slugged in the gut.

"Shade, I gotta know now. You gonna help me, or what?"

I paused.

"I'm not some muscle-for-hire goon who's going to go beat the hell out of somebody for what they might do, Lieu," I said. "I'm sorry."

"I know that. I just want you to go talk to him," he said. His voice was beginning to sound like a series of croaks edging up the scale of desperation. "He won't bother her once he sees somebody like you watching him. Tell him to back off. And keep an eye on her. She's going to graduate soon, then go off to college. I'll give you anything you want. I'll do anything you want."

"Mr. Bielmaster," the nurse said, inserting herself between us. "You're not doing yourself any good here. You need to calm down." She pointed toward the door and looked at me. "You, leave."

I started to go again and that's when he said it.

"Shade . . . Please."

His words stopped me, and I turned around. This wasn't playing out the way I'd expected. His eyes loomed large and fearful behind the twin lenses.

The nurse's eyes flashed dark and angrily at me.

"I'll tell you what, Lieu," I said, allowing myself a half-grin. "I'll have one of my standard contracts delivered to you here. Then we'll sit down and talk."

I could almost see the relief flooding over him as he lowered his head and murmured a quiet thanks. I wasn't sure if it looked like he was going to cry, or not. All I could think about was getting out of there.

Residual memories from my car's CD player of Linda Ronstadt singing "I Love You for Sentimental Reasons" were floating through my mind as I got out and began walking toward the front entrance of the gym. I saw a familiar lady walking a big black and brown Doberman pinscher heading down the sidewalk with a purpose. The dog's marble-sized brown eyes swept over me with a practiced nonchalance. Deen Kogan had been one of the regulars at Darlene's aerobic classes until recently.

"Hi, Deen," I said as she passed. "Taking Bonnie out for her exercise?"

She smiled. I could have sworn the dog did too. "You bet I am. I'm not about to let a nice day like this go to waste."

"I hear you," I said. "Haven't seen you at the gym lately."

"Yeah, I've been doing Pilates at that new place down at the strip mall. Women's World."

I cautiously scratched Bonnie's huge elliptically shaped head. Her pink tongue lapped up and licked my hand.

"Sorry to hear that," I said. "Come back and we'll fix you up with some karate lessons."

Deen grinned and said, "I'll think it over. Keep your guard up." She proceeded down the block with her faithful pooch, whose stubby tail was rotating with delight.

After setting up not one, but two new jobs, I figured I needed a workout, especially since I'd be working for Bielmaster in one, and taking on Mason Gilbert and the legendary John Flood in the other. As I went inside the gym, Diana Ross and the Supremes were doing a duet of "I'm Gonna Make You Love Me" with the Temptations. I nodded to Brice, the bodybuilder who helped Chappie run the place. He was reading the latest copy of *Muscle & Fitness* magazine, his huge biceps stretching the fabric of his black T-shirt.

"Chappie still here?" I asked.

Brice nodded. "He's working with Marcus."

Marcus was Chappie's newest discovery. He was a big,

rangy kid with quick hands and a good punch. I'd sparred with him several times and thought he had a lot of potential. If he listened to Chappie, he might actually get somewhere in this tough business.

"Hey, Ron," Brice said, putting down the magazine. "You got another title fight coming up, or something?"

"Not that I know of. Why?"

He shrugged. "Just had some guy calling earlier, asking if you still trained here."

"Good," I said, grinning. "Maybe I'll get another shot by public demand, or something."

The gym was set up in three distinct sections: the aerobics room, the weightlifting gym, and the boxing section. The third, my domain, was equipped with every type of punching bag imaginable, as well as a full-sized ring. Chappie had a special light system rigged up alongside the ring so fighters could see how many minutes were left in each round. It was an ideal way to learn to pace yourself. Darlene, Chappie's daughter, was doing the hard sell to a potential customer as I strolled past.

"Oh, this is one of our self-defense instructors," she said, touching me on the arm.

I stopped and eyed the thirtyish blond woman standing there. Nice clothes. She looked like she could afford it. I turned on one of my high-wattage smiles and said, "And any girl as pretty as you should know how to defend herself."

"This is Kris," Darlene said. She was really giving it the hard sell.

"Hi." I switched my gym bag to my left hand and extended my right. "Ron Shade."

"Kris Templer," she said, shaking my hand and smiling back. "Kris with a K."

I smiled too, and continued onward, passing through the next room of grunting, sweating bodybuilders and weightlifters. We'd had an upsurge in bulky types lately, ever since Brice had won some Midwest championship title. Chappie had put a sign in the window advertising it. I was happy for Brice, but couldn't help being a little bit envious that there was no sign advertising "Ron Shade, World Heavyweight Kickboxing Champion training here." That was my own fault. I'd had two good chances to fight for the title, but had to pull out of both at the last minute due to injuries. After the last one, which had gone down to the wire, our local promoter had pretty much written me off as undependable. And who could blame him? So all I could do now was stay in shape and hope that the third time, if it ever got here, would be the charm.

I paused at the doorway and watched Chappie lead Marcus around the ring with the focus mitts. Chappie moved with such a catlike precision that I never got tired of watching him. He'd been a serious middleweight contender in the seventies and eighties, but never lost that fluid grace that made him such a terror in the ring. It had been politics, rather than skill, that had kept him from winning a world title.

"Jab, jab, jab," Chappie was saying, holding the pad up in front. "Right cross, left hook."

The lighting system showed they were in the last minute. I waited and the automatic bell rang about twenty seconds later. Chappie lowered the pads and gave Marcus a small tap on the arm. The much-larger, younger man went over and draped his arms over the ropes, dripping sweat, as Chappie turned to me.

"You come to work out or just stand there?" he said with a grin.

"You guys made me tired just watching," I said.

"Go change. I want you and Marcus to do a little sparring."

I nodded and went back to the locker room. Even though Chappie had offered to let me keep my own locker there like Brice did, I'd declined, preferring to bring my stuff each time. Not only didn't I want to hog one of the few precious lockers, but I had a serious stake in allowing the gym to stay as customer-friendly as possible. I was a silent partner in the place, having loaned Chappie enough to buy it a while back. It made that sign in the window seem even more important.

After changing quickly into my workout gear, a sweat suit and a protective cup, I taped my hands and carried my bag with the remainder of my equipment back to the gym. Chappie and Marcus were engaged in another strenuous round with the focus mitts. I went over to the full-sized mirrored wall and began some shadow boxing. When I felt a bit warmed up, I slipped on my bag gloves and began pounding a rhythm on the speedbag. I always loved doing that. The bell rang and Chappie gave Marcus some low-voiced instruction. It looked like the kid was dropping his right when he threw the left, making him susceptible to a left hook counter. If we sparred tonight, I'd have to look for that.

I went over to the heavy bag and threw a couple of kicks at it. Lately, when I'd been sparring with Marcus, it had been boxing only, but that was because my legs had been so sore. Tonight, they felt good as I slammed the bag. But the lack of running lately had taken its toll on me. I'd gained a few extra pounds and noticed it. I felt slow and sluggish.

Chappie noticed too.

"How the leg feel?" he asked.

"Great," I said. "I'm ready to go."

"Not yet, you ain't. How much you weighing lately?"

"Oh, maybe two-twenty-five."

"Un-huh," he said, letting some derision seep into his tone. "You two-thirty-five if you's a pound. Just concentrate on jumping rope for a few rounds, then do the bags. We'll see about sparring later."

I nodded and went to get my rope before the next round started. I looked up as I heard Chappie yelling at Marcus. "You ain't done till I say you're done."

Marcus tried staring him down, then transferred his gaze to the floor.

"You want to show me something, show me you can listen," Chappie said. He turned back to me. "Maybe you up for a little sparring after all?"

"Sure," I said.

I held out my hands while Chappie slipped on the heavy training gloves and laced them up. Marcus paced around the ring throwing wide, sweeping hooks. His attitude puzzled me. When I'd been his age I'd practically lived in the gym. But, times change, I guess. Chappie slipped in my mouthpiece, and we stepped between the ropes.

We waited for the round clock to start, then Marcus ran forward. He started throwing hard hooks, like he was trying to take me out. I grabbed him, spun, and pushed him against the ropes. When he bounced off I caught him in close and threw some short, hard punches of my own.

"Show me some moves," Chappie said.

Marcus came forward again. He wasn't fighting in his usual boxing style. Instead he was swarming. I was still a tad cold and didn't want to risk getting tagged and knocked silly. But the gym was a macho place, and I couldn't risk whining or stopping. I glanced at the ring timer. We were in the second minute. I continued to throw my jab at him, breaking his rhythm. When he did punch his way in I put up my arms to catch his blows. I noticed that he was still dropping his hands on the way out each time. So the next time I timed it and caught him with a solid left hook. The punch buckled his knees slightly, but angered him sufficiently that he came swarming back in.

"Marcus," Chappie yelled. "Back up and clear your head."

He didn't listen to Chappie. That was his first mistake. He dropped his hands again, and I tagged him with another straight right. If we'd been in a real fight, I was confident that I could have finished him off. But since I didn't believe in gym wars, I danced away. Marcus staggered after me, almost plodding. Finally the round bell sounded. I lowered my hands and he smacked me in the face. It was an arm punch so it wasn't really powerful, but it was a cheap shot and made me mad as hell.

I started to jump in his shit, but Chappie beat me to it, yelling up a storm. I walked off the effect of the blow and was back to normal in about half a minute. Chappie was still chewing him out.

"Sorry, man," Marcus said to me. "Maybe I just worked out too much today already."

"No problem, bro," I said, slapping his glove. He slipped off his headset and I saw that his nose was bleeding profusely. I hadn't realized that I'd hit him that hard. It's especially difficult to really hurt somebody with sixteen-ounce gloves on.

Chappie grabbed the focus pads and told Marcus to take off. I watched him slip out from between the ropes, wiping his nose and heading for the locker room. Chappie shook his head and said, "Don't know what's wrong with that boy. Gonna have to have a talk with him."

"Ah, give him a break," I said. "You were working him pretty hard."

He slapped the pads together, grinned. "And you coulda finished him off after you caught him with that right. In a real fight he ain't gonna get them kind of breaks."

"This wasn't a real fight."

"True," he said, then led me around the ring, working on different punch combinations. The next round he made me work kicks and punches, then a round of just kicks. In regulation kickboxing, the rounds were only two minutes in duration, but Chappie always made me work the standard three-minute boxing rounds.

At the end I was panting like a dog in a car on a hot summer day.

"You been running?" Chappie asked.

I shook my head. "Missed a couple of days."

"Pretty bad for a man who wants to be champ someday," Chappie said.

"If I ever get another shot at it."

A smile cocked his lips, and he patted me on the shoulder. "You gotta have faith, just like you gotta be ready when your chance comes. We'll get there. Just wait. The third time's the charm."

I smiled and nodded. Let's hope so, I thought. Let's hope so.

Chapter 3

The rain began to come down in cold sheets as I ran, watching the sun rise over the crest of Agony Two, the second of the three hills I used to torture myself into shape. Chappie's gentle ribbing last night had had its desired effect on me, but I'd felt the extra weight slowing me down when I'd sparred with Marcus, too. And I was feeling it now. Still, it felt good to be running again, and my sore knee was holding up pretty well. I picked up speed on the downward slope of the hill, zooming by some cars that were stopped in a line for the light. I glanced at my watch and saw that I was about seven minutes behind my regular time. How could just a few extra pounds make so much difference?

Knowing that Rome wasn't built in a day, and also that the excess weight wouldn't magically melt off after one tough run, I decided instead to concentrate on the cases at hand. Bielmaster's seemed simple enough, at least from the onset. Look up this Tim Knop dude and have a little talk with him. Courteous, but intimidating. Then keep an eye on Bielmaster's daughter for a few days during the peak times. Hopefully, the girl would be cooperating by not going to hang out in the park or anything. The weather was still bad enough that she'd probably be home studying anyway. He'd said she was studious. And what else would a Catholic high school girl be doing in late March?

The other case was a bit more problematic. Rick had promised to have copies of the transcripts for me, as well as whatever notes on Rob Tunney's investigation he could find. I didn't like the idea of taking on a heavyweight like

Mason Gilbert on such short notice. In court, just as in the ring, preparation was the key.

A car sped by on the roadway, sending out a spray of cold, muddy water from a puddle and damn near hitting me in the process. I swore at the driver as the car disappeared, trying to memorize the license plate in the gloom of the early morning rain. I could ask George to run it for me, then go pay the guy a visit with a cleaning bill, but I knew that was just a pipe dream. They'd toughened the regulations for running plates nowadays, unlike the old days. Any agency requesting the information left a computer signature for ten days, making it eminently traceable. George got away with helping me more than he should, because of his status as a detective. But the computer trail could conceivably lead to a problem if an officer got caught running a plate for personal use. And I certainly didn't want to put my good buddy in the proverbial trick-bag. On the other hand, I thought, fantasizing a revenge scenario, if I can handle this Bielmaster thing with my usual aplomb, it might put both of us on the privileged persons' list.

George was supposed to get me all of Knop's info this morning, which was aboveboard because the guy was considered a sex offender and had to register with the local PD. Maybe, I thought as I saw the final hill, Miss Agony, looming ahead of me, this Bielmaster thing will be such a cakewalk that I'll be able to devote the majority of my time to getting Rick ready for Mason Gilbert. Hope, hope, hope, I thought as I continued my slow run.

After showering, eating a leisurely breakfast, and feeding my three cats, Georgio, Shasha, and Rags, I jumped in the car and headed for Rick Walters's office. On the way I glanced at my watch and figured George would probably be up and on his way into work as well. I dialed his cell phone number and heard him answer after four rings with his usual gruffness.

"Did I wake Sleeping Beauty, or what?" I asked.

He took a long time clearing his throat and said, "I didn't get to sleep till three-thirty. What the hell time is it anyway?"

"Eight-fifteen. Want to buy me breakfast and give me that Bielmaster stuff?"

"No," he said. "First off, you can buy me lunch for getting you set up with such a plush job. And second, Doug and I are working a case, so I didn't have a chance to get the stuff yet."

"Okay, but if you want me to move on this thing, I'm going to need the info on this kid. Where he lives, works, and all that info."

"Have I ever let you down?" he asked. "Now don't bother me till afternoon."

The connection went dead. I had no doubt that George would have it for me the next time we talked, but it threw me off a bit. I'd already mentally planned my day, and now I had to factor in a delay. It reminded me how much I hate surprises.

I got another surprise when I got to Rick's office. He'd left a message for me that he'd be in court for a few hours, but that wasn't the surprise. Behind the desk, typing at about mach five, was a pretty blondish woman who looked strikingly familiar. She looked up as I entered and canted her head, showing me that the recognition was two-way.

"May I help you, sir?" she asked.

Then it hit me and I smiled.

"Kris with a K," I said. "It's Ron Shade from the gym

last night. I didn't know you worked here."

"Actually, I'm with the legal temp service," she said. "Just filling in till Mr. Walters's regular girl gets better."

"Not that I don't wish her a speedy recovery," I said, "but it is nice to see a familiar face around here. Especially one as pretty as yours."

Kris smiled at the compliment, and I was just about to take the conversation to the next level, like maybe asking her if she was free for dinner, when the little dynamo, Denise, crept up from the side and poked several thickly bound eight-by-eleven stacks of paper against my arm.

"These are the transcripts," she said. "Mr. Walters wanted you to go over them." She had hazel eyes, cat's eyes, and she looked at Kris, then back to me. "If you're finished flirting, that is."

I thought about trying to come up with one of my smart aleck replies, but kept my mouth shut. No sense ridiculing her in front of the temporary help, and I certainly didn't want to come off as a bully in front of Kris with a K. I glanced down at Denise and smiled, grabbing the bound transcript. She held them for a moment and I caught a glint of fierce determination in her eyes. Then she released her hold. I said, "Thanks." It probably would have been a tough fight, but I was sure I coulda taken her.

After getting settled in Rick's conference room with the transcripts, I began reading but quickly found myself needing a cup of coffee. My mind started drifting after about the fifth objection by Mason Gilbert over some sort of procedural error. The judge seemed to sustain him each time, too. Everybody's favorite lawyer since Perry Mason died. Anyway, after about an hour of reading, I'd had enough. I got up, stretched, and opened the door.

Kris looked up from her desk and smiled. She'd been

punching out a staccato rhythm on the keyboard at a rate that made my own pace at the speedbag seem slow.

"You need something, Ron?" I took a moment to assess the smile. She had nice dimples, and a face that could've put her in pictures. The rest of her wasn't bad, either.

It was my turn to smile.

"I could use some coffee, I guess. Is there a machine around here?"

She saved her file on the computer and got up.

"I can make you some. It'll only take me a few minutes."

Denise eyed her with a measure of disdain as she left to fill the glass pot.

"What's the matter, kid?" I asked. "You got something against coffee?"

"No, but I need her to get those briefs done before lunch. If you keep distracting her . . . And please don't call me 'kid.' "

"Hey, what can I say? I have that effect on most good-looking women." I tried one of my killer smiles on her again, but she didn't seem to notice.

"You're done reading the transcripts?" she asked.

"Done reading, yes. With the transcripts, no." I watched her face scrunch up. "Those things are about as interesting as the Nixon diaries."

"They're not supposed to be interesting."

"Well, I've completely lost track of things. It's too hard to get a clear picture of how the prosecution lost." I walked over toward her desk, noticing that it was scrupulously organized, with a picture of her in a cap and gown being hugged by two people I assumed were her parents. They both looked white, while she was dark-complected and Latina-looking. Her eyes followed my gaze then shot back to me.

"Mr. Tunney didn't have any trouble," she said, a note of defiance creeping into her voice.

"Yeah, but look where that got him, and you guys, too," I said, regretting it a second later. I hated being compared to anybody, and her insolence, after what I considered to be a wasted morning, was the icing on top of the cake. Still, she was part of Rick's firm, and he was my client. I took a deep breath and sighed. "Sorry. Look, maybe you or Rick could summarize it for me. We are pressed for time, aren't we?"

Kris came back in with the coffee pot full of water and smiled at each of us. Denise compressed her lips and said she'd ask Rick to go over the case with me again when he got back. Then she turned to Kris, who was pouring the water into the top of the coffeemaker.

"I need those briefs finished as soon as possible," she said.

Kris nodded at Denise, then turned to me. "How do you like it?"

"Black's fine."

Kris smiled again. She did have a beautiful smile. Denise must have read my mind and frowned.

"If you want, I'll get Mr. Tunney's notes and go over those with you," she said.

I nodded, and when she left I looked at Kris.

"Man, that girl's all business, ain't she?" I said.

"They're pretty focused here. I guess they're under a lot of pressure, and they've had some bad breaks lately."

"Not to mention going up against the heavyweight champ, Mason Gilbert," I said. "So what did you think of the gym?"

"It's great. I bought a month's membership last night." She looked me up and down. "I, uh, watched you fighting last night with that African-American guy. It looked pretty brutal. Is it always so rough?"

I shrugged. "That one got a bit more carried away than normal."

She smiled. "I thought you could have finished him in that round, though."

I was just about to say something when little Denise came back in and glared at us. Kris immediately went back to her typing, and I stepped back into the conference room. Denise strode in and slammed the door behind her.

The noise shook off whatever vestiges of lethargy I'd accumulated. I watched Denise go to the long table where I'd been sitting and drop a folder on the desk. She looked up at me.

"Mr. Shade, please don't keep her from doing her work."

"I'll try not to," I said, then, trying for a bit of self-deprecating humor, I added, "But can I help it if I'm irresistible to women?"

Another frown and I knew it was wasted on her. I took the police reports and Tunney's notes, which consisted of a handful of notebook paper covered with scribble and a small appointment book. I prepared for more exciting reading.

Going over someone else's trail has both advantages and disadvantages. It helps to have things all laid out as to whom he talked and when. But on the other hand, it was a given that I'd have to redo all the interviews, so it was almost like starting from scratch. It would be interesting, though, to see if I could spot any inconsistencies in people's statements.

After about twenty minutes I'd finished. Tunney hadn't been much of a note-keeper, but the reports of his investigations were at least readable once I got used to his scrawl. There just weren't very many of them. They consisted of family interviews, alleging that Gooding had been something of a brutal husband, blackening Laura's eyes on several occasions. The interviews with the investigating officers were basically rehashings of the police reports. Laura Gooding had recently filed a petition for an increase in child support, wanting to send their children to a private school. Since Gooding had already been paying a hefty amount in alimony, and had given up the house and Caddie, he balked. Plus, he'd purportedly been upset that she'd begun dating again, and had threatened to try to get custody of the kids, claiming that she was an unfit mother. So that supplied the basic motive. No mystery where to look first when Laura was found lying on the kitchen floor, stabbed six times. Two in the back, one in the side, two in the abdomen, and one more in the chest. That one hit her heart, and was estimated by the ME to have been the final blow. Then he left her on the floor to bleed out. A classic case of overkill . . . It showed more than a little passion. Either somebody was enraged with an axe to grind, or he liked his work. Or maybe a bit of both.

A car fitting the description of Gooding's receptionist's red Firebird, with its distinctive SALLY4TH license plate, had been seen in the area by a neighbor the morning of the murder. His BMW had been in for service, and Gooding couldn't account for his whereabouts when detectives interviewed him. Red Firebirds were pretty popular, as I well knew, so that might be explained as coincidence. Less easily explained were red speckles the coppers had also noticed on the cuffs of his shirt, which they immediately took from him. The speckles later turned out to be Laura Gooding's blood. A button, matching the one missing from the cuff of

Gooding's left shirtsleeve, was also recovered at the crime scene. There wasn't a lot of blood on the shirt, but if he'd been wearing a jacket, that might have taken the brunt of it. Also, I knew from experience that deep stab wounds bleed mostly internally. It's the slashing wounds that open up and spray more. And the ME's report had said these were all deep punctures.

From the sound of things, they had a pretty solid case with the shirt. I checked the transcript section that I hadn't read to see if Mason Gilbert had gotten it tossed on a motion to suppress, but to my surprise he hadn't. Instead, he'd attacked the credibility of the lab work (no surprise), and got the prosecution's expert witness to admit under cross-examination that there was no way of telling when or how long the blood stains had been on the shirt. He also asked if the samples had been tested for the presence of any illegal drugs. Where the Great One was going with that line was anybody's guess, other than the old defense attorney's tactic of attacking the police and the victim when their own client's guilt was obvious. To me the prosecution's case seemed like a slam-dunk.

I heard the door opening and looked up. Rick came in carrying his briefcase and loosening his tie. He set the case on the table and grinned down at me. "Hard at work, I see."

I nodded. "You got any ideas on Mason Gilbert's strategy?"

"Just from what I got reading the transcripts. I have his witness list, too. Plus, the prosecution hit him with a discovery motion." He opened the door and said, "Denise, will you bring me the Gooding file, please?"

"Where'd you find her?" I asked.

"Denise? She's a good kid. Was recommended to me by

a former colleague. Going to law school at night finishing up her degree. She'll make a dynamite lawyer someday."

"Maybe she should consider an alternate career," I said. "Like being a drill sergeant in one of those old French Foreign Legion movies."

He snorted a laugh. "Yeah, she's serious, all right. But that's exactly what I need in an assistant. Especially running a one-man show like I do."

I nodded and tapped the transcript with my index finger.

"Well, I gotta tell you that this doesn't make for exciting reading. Maybe you can bring me up to speed on anything I should know from it."

Rick pulled out a chair and took off his jacket. "Such as?"

"Such as, why the prosecution lost," I said. "From what I've read, their case was solid. Gilbert hammered their witnesses on cross, but it's obvious the guy was guilty as hell."

Rick cocked his head. "You have to remember that a jury, or a judge in this case, has the advantage of seeing and hearing the testimony, rather than just reading it. Inflection, delivery, it all factors in on how much credibility to lend to someone's words." He raised his eyebrows and shrugged self-deprecatingly. "A master lawyer like Mason Gilbert can be very skillful attacking someone's credibility on the stand."

Kris poked her head in the door and smiled.

"Good morning, Mr. Walters." She set a steaming mug of coffee on the table in front of me and then asked Rick if he wanted some. He nodded. As she was leaving, Denise came in and gave her the evil eye.

"Did you finish those briefs yet?" Denise asked.

"Working on them," Kris said.

"I told you I need them ASAP."

Kris nodded and left. When she'd gone, Rick motioned for Denise to close the door, then sighed.

"You really need to take it easy on her," he said.

Denise looked like she'd been hit by a truck. "But we need those briefs and she's been working on them all morning." Her voice had that little singsongy whine that women's voices sometimes get when they're on the edge of almost breaking into tears.

I couldn't resist taking a quick sip of coffee and saying, "Ahhh." She transferred her gaze to me, and if, as they say, looks could kill . . .

"What I mean is," Rick continued, "she's one of the best temps we've gotten since June's been hurt. I don't want to make it so difficult for her that she doesn't want to come back."

I thought I saw the kid's eyes start to glaze over momentarily, so I jumped in. "You know, Rick, it's partly my fault. I did ask her to make me some coffee and that interrupted her typing."

He glanced at me and smiled, refocusing on the file.

"You want to know our strategy?" he asked. "We're going to hit them head-on. I think Gooding's guilty as hell, and intend to prove it. Even though he skated on the criminal charges, this time we'll present everything. We've got to be ready for whatever Mason Gilbert's going to throw at us." He compressed his lips. "We're going to depose his witnesses this coming week. I'd like you to be there for the interviews. You're pretty good at reading people."

"Sure," I said. "In the meantime, I'll have to backtrack over what Tunney did, interviewing the State's Attorneys and coppers."

"Good idea," Rick said.

"I already told Mr. Shade that I'll need to go along on those," Denise said.

Now it was my turn to give the if-looks-could-kill glare.

"That does sound like a good idea," Rick said, grinning. "And call him Ron, for Christ's sake. Everybody else does. Right, buddy?"

The hazel eyes shot toward me, her oval lips in a Mona Lisa smile. I smiled back, then said, "Except for the time when I was in the French Foreign Legion."

George was waiting for me in a booth at a Karson's Restaurant near 111th and Western. He was wearing a sport coat, but no tie. I assumed, from past practice, that he had it rolled up in his pocket. He'd already polished off his cup of coffee and the waitress refilled his and looked questioningly at me.

"Iced tea," I told her.

George grunted and took another sip. If he'd gotten any sleep after I'd called him, it sure didn't show.

"You all right?" I asked.

"Just great," he said, setting the cup down. He reached on the seat beside him and brought up an envelope. "Here." He shoved it across the table.

"And this is?" I undid the clasp on the back and shook out several sheets of paper, one of which had a color mug shot of a sullen-looking youth with short-clipped brown hair, delicate features, and a thick neck. The printing below the picture had KNOP, Timothy C. along with his date of birth, height, and weight.

"I thought you said you didn't have the info?" I asked.

"Called in a marker and had it delivered to my house while I was sleeping." He grinned. "You'd be surprised how quickly things get done when you're doing a favor for a lieutenant. He came through the operation with no problems this morning, by the way."

I read through the rest of the printouts. Since Knop was considered a sex offender, he had to register with his local police department within ten days of his release. He had, giving an address on Troy.

"That's his mother's place," George said. "I got his work address, too."

"So what's the plan on this?"

He raised his eyebrows as he was taking another sip of his coffee. "Hell, you're the one who talked to Bielmaster, not me," he said. "I figured you'd have it all worked out by now."

"Yeah, right. I wasn't even going to take the job, except I actually felt sorry for him when I saw him lying there with all the wires and the oxygen."

He snorted a laugh. "You feeling sorry for him. That's gotta be a first."

"Anyway, I thought maybe we'd take a ride by where this Knop kid works or hangs out and have a little pre-situational talk with him," I said. "You know, kind of lay down the law."

"What's this 'we' crap? You're the one he hired."

I smiled. "I gave him one of our Windy City Knights contracts." Windy City Knights was the name of the security company that George had started with his partner, Doug Percy. They had visions of the company taking off and flying them into early retirements. I was a silent partner of sorts. So far, we'd been struggling along with a few security jobs at some area hotels, taverns, and restaurants, with me filling in a lot of the hours when George had trouble covering them with moonlighting coppers.

"You what?" The cords in his neck stood out in bas-relief.

Now it was my turn to grin.

"Just kidding," I said. "But I do have a new kid at the gym who's interested in doing some work for WCK. He just got out of the army and already has his brown card."

"What's his name?"

"Ken Albrecht."

"Sounds good. I could use him at the hotel tonight maybe. I was gonna ask you."

"Nothing like giving me some notice," I said. "I'll see if I can get ahold of him and show him the ropes real quick."

"Nah." He shook his head. "All you'll do is show him how to talk to the girls. I'll have Doug meet him there."

I shrugged. It was probably better that I hit the gym hard tonight anyway, since Chappie had been complaining about those extra pounds.

The waitress reappeared with my tea and asked if we were ready to order. I got a salad and George asked for an omelet.

"Shouldn't you be watching your cholesterol?" I asked. "Especially after what your favorite boss is going through."

He frowned.

"First of all," he said, picking up his coffee, "I already got a wife to nag me." He took a sip. "Second, I ain't three-fifty pounds of blubber, like Bielmaster is, and third, what's with this pansy-ass salad thing? You been watching reruns of 'Queer Eye for the Straight Guy,' or something?"

"Just trying to drop a few pounds, that's all." I was going to add that he might consider that himself, but thought better of it. He looked like he'd had a rough night.

"Well, all this work I been scaring up for you oughta help in that department," he said, glancing to see the waitress heading our way with the food. "Let's eat fast so we can shoot over to the hospital. Bielmaster called me at home last night and wants me to introduce you to his wife and daughter today."

We met them in the fifth-floor break room of the hospital. Ursula Bielmaster turned out to be a slender, attractive woman who was gracefully entering middle age. She had brown hair pulled back rather severely into a ponytail, a blue sweatshirt and jeans, but somehow, even in the hospital setting, she retained an aura of elegance. She had the look of someone who took care of herself, and I couldn't imagine how the Bielmaster that I'd known and despised for so long had made a catch like her. She looked way too sophisticated. Their daughter, Grace, thankfully took after her mother. She had wavy blond hair and a figure ripening to perfection. Or perhaps it already had ripened. If she was seventeen, she looked twenty-five.

"Ursula," George said, giving her a brief hug, "how is he?"

"He's in recovery," she said. Her words had a slight German-sounding inflection. I saw that her smile was forced, and just below the calm surface the strain was waiting to burst through. Turning to her daughter, she said, "Grace, you remember Detective Grieves."

She and George exchanged nods. He then introduced me, and Ms. Bielmaster and I shook hands and she turned to her daughter. "Why don't you take Detective Grieves down to the break room and buy him a cup of coffee?"

The girl's lips compressed, but she nodded, and she and George walked down the hallway. Ms. Bielmaster watched them for a moment, and turned back to me.

"Mr. Shade, my husband told me about your business arrangement." She licked her lips with a nervous flick of her tongue. "Have you . . . talked to Tim Knop yet?"

I shook my head. "I was planning on doing that this afternoon."

Her eyes stared at me, then shot away. The brief glance was enough for me to see that they were brimming with tears. I reached out tentatively, touching her arm.

"Why don't you sit down?"

Her head shook slightly, but she let me lead her to the stuffed chair by the grimy-looking window.

"I'm sorry to seem so . . . weak," she said. "But this past week has been unbelievable."

"I'll bet."

She took out a tissue and wiped her nose, then stuck it back into her purse. "It's just that this is the worst possible time for Gill to get sick. Grace has been doing so well putting this business behind her. She's been accepted at Yale, you know."

I smiled and nodded. "Your husband told me."

The smile was contagious. "We were really hoping that all this could be avoided. But she seemed to find out before we did that Tim had been released."

That floored me.

"Are you saying that she's already had contact with him?"

Her eyes dropped to the floor, followed by a nod that was almost imperceptible.

So maybe it wasn't a case of a brutal stalker, but rather a couple of young teens in love.

"She has too much at stake," she said, "to lose it all because of a low-life like him. You've got to do something, Mr. Shade."

This case was quickly developing complications that I hadn't counted on. Trying to prevent a couple of hormonally challenged youngsters from seeing each other was going to take more time and man hours than I could conceivably give. I was going to need help, and a lot of it.

I glanced down the hallway to make sure George wasn't bringing the daughter back just yet, then said, "Perhaps you'd better tell me the whole story so I can get a better idea of what it is I'll have to do."

On the drive back to get my car, the light salad lunch was weighing more heavily on my stomach than it should have, due no doubt to the dessert topping of anxiety that the hospital revelation had provided. I was even tempted, as we drove by Jensen's hamburger place, to stop in for a fortifying junk food emergency buildup. I lamented in silence as it disappeared from my passenger side window and continued to mull things over. If Grace Bielmaster wasn't the typical, innocent Catholic high school girl victim that her father had made her out to be, but rather a willing participant actively seeking out this Knop character, it was going to take a helluva lot more than me to keep tabs on her. This was quickly developing into a round-the-clock surveillance case, and there was no way I could do that solo. I told George as much as he dropped me off by my car.

"Well, I'll talk to Ursula about getting a civil no-contact order set up," he said. "Supposedly, he was a model prisoner at St. Charles. Maybe he learned his lesson when he saw that old Sean Penn movie. What's it called? *Bad Boys*?"

"Sean Penn? That was with Will Smith and Martin Lawrence, wasn't it?"

He frowned as we pulled into Karson's parking lot and came to a stop. "Irregardless, pay that little peremptory visit we were talking about to the little prick, and put the fear of Shade into him."

I smirked and opened the door of his unmarked, starting

to slide out. "Yeah, right."

"Hey, do what you do best." He shifted into park. "Remember, we got a lot riding on this case."

The collective "we" meant basically me. While George was trying to please his boss by helping out with a family crisis while the big man was down for the count, I knew the primary reason he was so anxious about it was that he was hoping I'd be able to get my police job back. I wasn't sure what to tell him about that, though. Maybe too much water had passed under the bridge for me to return like nothing had happened.

"Say," he said, "on another note, that Albrecht kid you were telling me about—he sounds like a good Windy City Knights prospect?"

"Yeah, like I said, he's completed the security course and has his brown card."

George grunted an approval. "Okay, get ahold of him and tell him he's hired, pending a background, of course. See if he can meet Doug out at the hotel tonight for training."

"All right." I smiled as I got out of the car. "I'll show him how to talk to all the girls next time I work it."

Back at Rick's office Kris looked up and smiled at me as I entered. The ever-efficient, omnipresent Denise suddenly appeared and handed me a slip of paper with several times written on it in flowing, female cursive.

"And this is?" I asked.

"It's our appointment list for tomorrow," she said. "We're going to meet the police detectives first, then swing back to twenty-sixth and California for the meeting with the State's Attorneys. One of them is now in private practice, and his secretary is going to get back to me as to when we can meet with him."

The hazel eyes glared up at me with their typical look of defiance.

"Good job, kid," I said. "I'll drive. Want me to pick you up here at the office or at your house?"

"I can meet you here. What time?"

I glanced down at the slip of paper. Our first interview was at nine.

"Let's make it around seven," I said. "Maybe quarter to."

"That early?" She seemed a bit stunned.

"Got plans?" I grinned.

"No, I'll be okay." The defiance came back to her eyes.

"I mean, we're going to the North Shore. We'll have to fight the rush hour until we get past the Loop. Plus, we'll have to stop for coffee and donuts on the way."

"I don't eat donuts."

"Me either," I said, "but you don't go up to interview a couple of coppers empty-handed."

"So that stereotype is true?" she asked. "About cops and donuts?"

I was surprised at her attempt at humor. Maybe the ice was starting to thaw between us.

"Everybody doesn't like something," I said, "but nobody doesn't like Krispy Kreme."

A shadow of a smile crossed her lips. "I suppose that's one way of putting it. Not too originally, though."

"Yeah, well, non-originality has its place. I keep forgetting you're not a full-fledged lawyer yet." I turned to Kris, thinking I'd better start to track down Ken Albrecht before it got too late. "Say, I have to make a couple calls."

"You can use *my* phone," Denise said quickly. "She still has a lot of work to do."

Kris rolled her eyes so that only I could see and gave me a lips-only smile.

"Say, Ron," she asked. "You going to be at the gym tonight?"

This girl was interested, I thought. "Wouldn't miss it. You going?"

Kris started to reply when Denise cut in again. "Don't get so tired that you miss our appointments. Remember, we've got to make an early start."

"Yeah," I said. "And don't you forget it's a long drive, so bring plenty to read if you don't want to be a pleasant conversationalist."

The look she gave me told me that in my eagerness to defend Kris, in some obscure way I'd hit Denise harder than I'd intended. Before I could try and say anything to lessen it, she turned and walked away.

Since I was into offending people big time, I figured that I might as well pay that peremptory visit to the Knop kid as George had suggested. On the way, I used up some precious minutes on my cell phone calling the gym to get Ken Albrecht's phone number and then redialing to call him. He sounded like I woke him up, and it bothered me that he'd be sleeping at three in the afternoon, but he explained that he'd just pulled an all-night gig at a White Castle and hadn't gotten home until ten.

"Well, I was going to ask you if you'd be interested in working for Windy City Knights Security," I said. "I told my buddy George Grieves about you."

"That's that Chicago detective?" His voice sounded eager. "Yeah, sure, Mr. Shade. Thanks for recommending me."

"Can you make it tonight? Six to midnight?"

"You just tell me where and when, sir, and I'll be there."

It was refreshing to find someone so enthusiastic to do some work. Especially security work, where the pay was usually bad and the hours worse. I gave him the particulars and told him to meet Doug at the hotel in Lincoln Estates.

"Thanks, Mr. Shade. I really appreciate the opportunity."

"No problem," I said, thinking about telling him to call me Ron. After all, everyone else did.

Chapter 4

The Knop kid had a job as stock boy at a neighborhood liquor store near the big dip where 111th Street inexplicably changed into Monterey Avenue, just beyond Longwood Drive. The street sloped downward in a gentle arc that was flanked on both sides by large, old-style frame houses and brick three-flats, and eventually led to Morgan Park High School and the new 22nd District Police Station. George had told me the kid's uncle owned the liquor store. It was about two or three miles from Knop's mother's house, where he was living, and I wondered if he walked it, took the bus, or had a car. The Bielmasters lived in Mount Greenwood, about three to four miles away. Not a lot of distance to separate potential young lovers.

I regretted not being able to get Grace Bielmaster alone for a few minutes to discuss the situation. I definitely needed to do that to find out what, exactly, I was up against here. That is, if she'd be truthful with me. But one thing I did know, the chances of that were slim to none with her mother hovering around.

Maybe I could go over to Mother Maria and pay her a visit, I thought. Sure, go by, saying I was who? I was way too young to pass for her father, and they might know him at the school. Her father's friend? No, that wouldn't work. Her uncle? Possible. There was almost a generational difference between me and my own half-brother, Tom, who'd served with George in Vietnam, but we were the products of two different marriages. Two different mothers. And the thought of a strange, thirtyish man showing up and just hanging out in front, waiting at an all-girls' Catholic high school would have the nuns reaching for their big metal rulers in a hurry.

I decided to put that on the back burner until I could talk to Ursula Bielmaster about it. Maybe George could convince her to let me talk to Grace alone.

As I came up to Western Avenue, somebody had parked on the street in front of the Beverly Arts Center, forcing me to merge left. Why they didn't make it a no parking zone was anybody's guess, unless they really enjoyed irritating drivers. I waited for the light to change. In any case, if this Albrecht kid worked out, maybe I could use him for stakeout duties. Bielmaster was locked into paying for whatever I deemed necessary, thanks to the contract he'd signed, and I certainly couldn't do round-the-clock surveillance by my lonesome. I continued east.

Farther down the block, a neon sign was glowing and blinking in the deepening late afternoon–early evening twilight. The days were already starting to get noticeably longer, and in another month it would be time to "spring ahead" and get ready for summer. But it was still March, and I could feel the chill when I stepped out of my car and headed for the store.

Longwood Liquors, the pink neon blinked. *Low Prices—High Quality.*

The front window was a mosaic of brightly colored cardboard ads depicting beautiful, well-dressed people holding a variety of alcoholic beverages.

The key to success, I thought. Gorgeous people pushing a feel-good depressant. Perception was reality.

The door jingled with one of those old-fashioned bells as I came in. Behind the counter a heavyset black woman glanced at me and got serious after giving me the once-over.

I'd clipped one of the spare badges I kept for such purposes onto my belt and left my jacket hanging open so that the badge was more or less visible next to my pancake holster and weapon.

"Can I help you, officer?" she asked.

"I'm looking for Tim Knop," I said. "He work here?"

She nodded and picked up a telephone and spoke into it. "Arnie, can you come up front right away, please?"

A middle-aged white guy wearing half-moon glasses and a striped shirt that was folded at the sleeves came out of an office area at the rear of the store. I saw him give me the same once-over as he walked between the racks of bottled liquors and potato chips. I moved my right arm back ever so slightly so that he'd have a better view of my accessories and tried to affect my best, bored cop look. As long as I didn't identify myself as a police officer, and let his imagination make the logical leap, I wasn't breaking any laws. Letting him think I was a copper or a probation officer would guarantee a few uninterrupted minutes alone with his infamous nephew.

"Yes, officer, what can we do for you?" he asked, stopping in front of me and showing me his best attempt at a forced smile.

"Tim Knop," I said. "I need to talk to him. Does he work here?"

The man's eyes widened slightly, then he blinked a couple of times.

"Why, ah, yes, he's my sister's boy," he said, as if using the exact lineage would help distance him from the relationship. "He's not in trouble, is he?"

I shook my head, saying, "Just routine."

Arnie swallowed hard, then cocked his head toward the rear.

"He's working stock out back," he said, nodding to a flimsy set of hanging double doors. "I can take you to him."

"I'll find him."

After I'd walked past him, he said, "He's really a good kid, you know. He's been trying real hard to stay out of trouble."

Don't they always? I thought.

"I'll keep that in mind," I said, and pushed through the double doors.

I found the "good kid" stacking a bunch of cardboard boxes in the stock room. He was wearing a T-shirt and had a fairly decent set of arms on him. Must have pumped a lot of iron in reform school, I thought. But inevitably, as he turned, I saw the pack of cigarettes rolled up in the sleeve on his left shoulder.

"You Tim Knop?"

His head swiveled toward me, his lips pouting in defiance. He had the same curly brown hair from the file folder George had shown me. His face looked more dainty in person, his eyelashes long and his lips full and Cupid-like. But he still looked young. Like he should be playing varsity football somewhere instead of stacking boxes in the back of a liquor store and reporting his places of residence to the PD.

"Yeah," he said, setting the box he'd been holding on top of the stack. "Where's the usual guy?"

I kept my expression neutral.

After a few seconds of silence, he asked, "You're from probation, aren't you?"

I shook my head. "Let's just say, I'm a friend of a friend."

He looked confused, his brow furrowing. "What's that supposed to mean?"

"I'll let you figure it out," I said. "Grace Bielmaster."

"Huh? Grace?" Then his bottom lip drew up tight. "You a cop? He sent you to hassle me, didn't he?"

I leisurely scratched my neck, giving my best impression of an intimidating grin. "I'd prefer to think of it as a little friendly advice."

His mouth opened slightly and he continued to regard me. I noticed his body was tensing like a coiling spring. "Advice?"

I nodded again. "Grace. It'd be best if you stayed away from her."

His face crinkled, twisting into something that resembled a sneer.

"Hey, you can't tell me shit," he said. "And I ain't afraid of you."

"If you aren't, you should be," I said, watching his torso for any hint of aggressive movement. I didn't want to deck the kid, but if he came at me, I'd have no choice.

He balled up his fists and punched a hole into one of the cardboard boxes he'd been stacking.

"Don't even think about it," I said. Something in my voice must have convinced him that discretion was the better part of valor. His tongue darted over his lips, but he stayed where he was.

"So what you saying, man?" he asked, cocking his head back slightly.

"It's simple," I said. "Grace has a whole new life now. She doesn't want to see you. She doesn't want you to call her. If you go over to her house, her school, or get within a thousand yards of her, I'll track you down, and you'll think of your time in stir as Club Med."

His eyes held the look of pure hatred.

"We straight on that?" I asked, holding his gaze. After a

moment more he looked away and nodded.

"Good," I said. "I hope we don't have to have this conversation again." For a bit more emphasis I smiled. It wasn't my nicest smile. As I pushed through the swinging double doors, I saw Uncle Arnie hovering nearby and wondered if he'd been listening in. Not that it mattered. I'm sure the kid would probably tell him, but they couldn't identify me from Adam. Nor would they want to. The kid was behind the eight ball, that was for sure.

As I got back to my car I was reminded of my own situation, so many years before, when I'd walked a mile in almost the same moccasins as Tim Knop. But I'd ended up in the army instead of juvenile jail, mainly because of circumstances and because I'd had George in my corner.

There, but for the grace of God, go I, I thought.

Being intimidating was hard work, and the effort had completely wiped out any nourishing sense of fullness that the light lunch salad had given me. As I swung on to Western Avenue, every fast-food joint along the way called to me with the attraction of a siren's song. After what I deemed a sufficient period of proper rationalization, I pulled into a chicken place and ordered a couple of breasts. The fries came complimentary, and who was I to argue?

As soon as I walked in the back door I had three hungry cats waiting for me. Georgio and Rags, the two males, pranced around with their tails straight up in the air, while Shasha rubbed herself coquettishly against my trouser legs. Georgio must have suddenly caught a whiff of the chicken because he jumped up on the sink and tried to inspect the bag. I gently brushed him back down to the floor but that seemed to perk them up even more.

"Huh-uh," I said, setting the bag on the high counter. "That's *my* chow."

It did little to convince Georgio, who hopped up to smell the bag again in one quick motion. If I had reflexes like that, I'd be unbeatable.

It took some doing, but I finally split a can of cat food among the three of them, and took my own food to the table. I poured myself a glass of cranberry juice, tore open the bag, and started on the chicken. Chappie's crack about me being too heavy had hit home, and I stripped off the skin and tossed out the fries. In my heart I knew he was right, and I still had a workout ahead of me tonight.

The thought of going to the gym to work out the excess stressors that the two headache cases had produced brightened my mood. The thought that Kris had seemed interested in my goings and comings there also sprinkled a bit of anticipatory delight into the mix. She was a pretty girl, and if I kept running into her like I had been . . . Of course, I knew it was bad form to date anybody you work with, but the nature of both our employments at Rick's was temporary at best. So the promise of possibility had me hurrying through the meal.

After disposing of the garbage, placing the glass in the sink with the rest of the dirty dishes for later washing, and checking my mail, I packed my gear, made sure that the timers on my lights were operating, brushed my teeth, headed for the gym.

When I got there I scanned the group of girls doing aerobics and working out. No luck. After a quick sigh, I heard Darlene's voice behind me.

"Looking for somebody, Ron, or just checking out the prospects?"

I turned and grinned.

"Trying to get psyched for your father to put me through another torture session."

Smiling, she said, "Well, your lady did call earlier, asking what time you usually do come by . . ."

"My lady?"

"Kris," she said. "With a K."

"And what did you tell her?"

"Not to come by before nine or ten, if she knew what was good for her. Daddy'd kill her if she distracted you."

I pretended I was going to swat her on the ass, and she scampered away playfully, laughing.

"She'll probably be by later," she said. "Don't worry."

"I'm not," I said, and glanced toward the door leading to the ring.

The workout went pretty well, but that was about the only thing that did. Chappie was working with Marcus again when I got there and told me to jump rope for three rounds to warm up. Since he wasn't watching too closely, I settled into an easy pace until my stomach felt a little more settled. When I sat on the floor to do my stretching routine, I was sweating comfortably.

I started with my legs spread out and bent down, touching my ear to my knee. After about fifteen with each leg I switched to hurdler's stretches. At the end I did the splits, facing each way, and felt totally loosened up.

"Tape up your hands," Chappie called from the ring. "You guys can go a couple. Just boxing."

I wasn't sure that was such a good idea since in the last session we'd had he'd deliberately hit me after the bell. But I figured to give him the benefit of the doubt, and took off my gym shoes and socks. I left my sleeveless sweatshirt on. The footpads slipped onto my sweaty feet easily, and I secured them with a couple of strands of tape. Then I went up to the ring and let Chappie finish taping my hands because it was really hard to put pieces of tape between each finger when your hands were wrapped. After he laced on my helmet, he slipped on the big, sixteen-ounce training gloves.

Marcus nodded to me and slapped gloves as we met in center ring. He began doing his usual bobbing and dancing, but was leaving himself wide open, and there was a funny look to his eyes. I practiced cutting off the ring and caught him on the ropes a couple of times. He covered up as I slammed the body shots home.

"Dammit! Punch yourself outta there, Marcus," Chappie called.

But Marcus just sorta hung there, rocking back and forth.

"Punch your way out, goddamn it," Chappie yelled again.

I drove a couple more body shots to his sides and backed off, not wanting to wear myself out too quickly. Marcus sprang off the ropes and tried to follow me, but his legs weren't moving as fast as he thought they were. I let him think he'd caught me, then sidestepped his looping right and caught him with a left hook.

Stunned, he stumbled slightly then plodded after me. I'd never seen him look so awkward.

"Let your head clear before you go back in," Chappie called out.

I jabbed when I could have hooked and backpedaled, purposely coasting for the next thirty seconds or so till the bell rang. There was no way I wanted to get involved in another damn gym war.

Chappie adjusted my headgear and sprayed some water in my mouth. There was a crease between his eyebrows as he motioned for me to spit in the water bucket and went across the ring to attend to Marcus.

"Use your goddamn head," I heard him say. "Fight smart. What the fuck's wrong with you? You forgetting everything we been working on?"

"What you mean?" Marcus said angrily. "I'm kicking his ass."

Chappie's lecture continued for the rest of the minute break. When the bell rang he stepped out on the apron and continued shouting instructions to both of us, but mostly to Marcus. It seemed lost on deaf ears, though.

The second round was more of the same, with Marcus dancing around, throwing jabs and hooks that were slow and telegraphed. Usually he was panther-quick, but tonight he couldn't seem to move his head out of the way of my punches like he usually did. At first I thought I was having an exceptionally good night, but after the third round it was obvious Marcus was having an exceptionally bad one.

"That's enough," Chappie said, his tone showing his obvious disgust as he stepped into the ring with a towel. "I seen better punches from my grandmama."

Marcus heaved a disgruntled sigh and tore off his headgear. I'd bloodied his nose again. Chappie wiped away the blood and undid his gloves. "Go hit the steam," he said. "I want to work with Ron for a few."

Marcus nodded and ducked through the ropes. Chappie got out the pads and held them up.

"Let's go," he said.

After three rounds of sparring, my arms already felt like lead. Chappie kept urging me on, although I wasn't sure if it was for my benefit, or because he was so pissed at Marcus that he was taking it out on me. We worked on punching combinations, kicking, and punch-kick combinations. By the end of three more rounds of pounding the pads I felt totally exhausted. Sensing that I'd given my all, Chappie lowered them and said, "Take five, then we'll do sit-ups."

I groaned. The abdominal routine that he usually put me through was a killer, especially if he used the medicine ball.

He unlaced my gloves and I headed for the locker room to urinate. There was no way I wanted to take the pounding of the medicine ball to my stomach with even the remnants of a partially full bladder. When I went inside I saw Marcus and another black guy talking. The new guy was a stranger, but he was dressed like a street hustler: leather clothes, baseball cap, cocked to the right, and sunglasses, even though it was dark out and he was inside. They both looked up rather quickly as I entered. I nodded to Marcus and went into the bathroom.

When I came out Marcus was waiting and went right in. He was in his street clothes now, so I figured he'd finished working out. I opened my locker and wiped my face with a towel. The other dude came up to me.

"Hey, man, whatsup?" he said. "We know each other?"

"I don't think so." I held out my hand. "Ron Shade. Pardon the tape."

He shook my hand and laughed. "Dewayne Clifford's the name."

"You must be new here," I said. "You just join?"

"Me? Join?" he said, taking a half-step back and lowering his head so that he looked at me over his sunglasses. "Ain't no basketball hoops here, is there?"

"Not hardly." I grinned at him. "You're a friend of Marcus's then?"

He snapped his head erect and began a slow undulation to some internal rhythm. "You got that right."

I felt uneasy around this guy. The washroom door opened and Marcus came out. He did an exaggerated double-take when he saw me talking to Dewayne.

"Hey, bro, we got to leave," he said. As he slipped on his jacket he made a sniffling sound.

"How's the nose?" I asked him, remembering that I'd bloodied it.

Dewayne started to laugh but Marcus told him to shut up.

"He's friends with the man," he added.

Dewayne stopped laughing and looked at me. I suddenly realized why he'd laughed in the first place. He'd taken my nose comment the wrong way. Or maybe the right way as far as he was concerned.

"You know," I said, "I was wondering why you've been getting so many bloody noses lately."

Marcus zipped up his jacket and started to pick up his gym bag.

"Back off, white boy. What I do ain't none of your business."

"You know what you're messing with?" I asked.

"He told you to back off, honkie," Dewayne chimed in.

"You back off, asshole."

I put my hand on Marcus's arm. He shook it off violently, threw down his bag, and raised his clenched fists.

"Don't you ever touch me again, you white motherfucker!"

I took a step back, ready if he came at me. He stared at me, his lips twisting into a snarl. His sudden rage shocked me.

"Hey, listen, man—" I said.

"You listen, white boy," he cut in. "You ever touch me again I'll kill your ass. Understand?"

"Yeah, I understand. Now you listen. I don't want to see you get into something that's gonna mess you up."

"Trying to watch over us poor, obedient *Neeegroes,* honkie?" Dewayne said.

I pointed at him and said, "You stay out of this, asshole."

"No, you stay outta *my* way, Shade," Marcus said. His face was a twisted snarl. "What I do ain't none of your concern."

"If you end up hurting Chappie," I said, "I'll make it my concern."

"You think you bad?" Marcus said, taking a step forward. "You think just 'cause we spar I can't kick your white ass?"

I stepped back and raised my hands. I'd had enough of the son-of-a-bitch.

"Come on," I said.

Marcus stopped for a second, snorted, then dropped his fists.

"Shit," he said, turning and moving away. "You lucky tonight, man, you hear?" He was using exaggerated gestures and pointing his finger at me as he spoke. "I got better things to do tonight than kick your ass. But don't you ever touch me again, motherfucker, or I *will* beat your ass so motherfuckin' bad . . ."

I stood my ground as he picked up his bag and moved toward the door. He was still talking shit, as they say, but all the while he was moving away. The classic ghetto retreat: backing off by showing bravado. He let the door slam against the wall as he and Dewayne left. I stood there and slowly let my hands drop to my sides, suddenly feeling very, very tired. How could I explain this to Chappie? Or should I even tell him? Diming out Marcus might totally alienate him from the gym, which seemed to be one of the few positive influences in his life. Still, I didn't want to see Chappie get hurt. He genuinely cared for the kid.

Just what I need, I thought, another set of impossible, no-win circumstances. I slammed the locker shut and jammed the lock closed.

As I headed back toward the boxing area I heard someone call my name. I turned and saw Kris, with a K, standing there doing a great job of filling out some designer gym wear, showing off a nice set of curves.

"You made it, huh?" I said.

"So did you, I see." She had on a sleeveless yellow shirt and very short shorts, cut up the sides to display more of her hips. The tights covering her legs had a translucence to them, looking almost like nylons. From the looks of her body, she was no stranger to working out, and there was a sheen of perspiration on her face and neck. Obviously, I'd been so preoccupied after the sparring session that I'd missed her coming in.

"How much longer you staying?" she asked.

"Maybe a half-hour or so. You?"

She raised her eyebrows and wiped one of her wristbands across her forehead. "The same. If I go through another one of Darlene's aerobics classes, I'll be ready for the funny farm."

I was suddenly aware that I must have smelled worse than a platoon of soldiers after a forced desert march and backed up a step.

"Well, I'd better finish up before I cool down too much," I said.

"Say," she said, "I'm new in this neighborhood. Is there any place we can go to afterwards? To replenish our lost fluids?"

"Jensen's across the street. It's a nice place and you can get whatever you want."

"Sounds good," she said. "I'm up for it if you are."

I smiled. "Sounds good to me too."

Chappie didn't seem to mind much when I told him I was knocking off early. Nor did he make any of his usual "women weakenin' legs" comments about me talking to Kris. After all, I wasn't in strict training since there were no fights on the horizon. I told myself that he was preoccupied with trying to get Marcus ready for the upcoming Golden Gloves tournament. But I silently wondered if Chappie might be writing me off since I'd blown my two big chances to win a title.

Naturally, I finished dressing before she did. There's no busier place in the world than the mirror in the ladies' dressing room at the gym. I waited by the front entrance and talked to Brice. He was in strict training himself for a regional bodybuilding contest and looked incredibly ripped. I wondered how much he was spending on the juice, and that brought me back to thoughts of Marcus again. And Chappie.

"Hi," Kris said, coming up behind me. I must have looked startled because she asked if I was all right.

"You blindsided me," I said. "Didn't see you coming."

"You looked deep in thought." She smiled. "I'm ready if you are."

We walked across Western to Jensen's and stowed our gym bags under the table at a booth. Kris moved with me to the counter to get the drinks, and we settled on two bottles of juice. Cranberry for me, apple for her. She began to take out her wallet when I placed my hand on hers.

"This is on me," I said.

She smiled demurely and told me I was a gentleman.

We'd taken a seat by the large window that gave us a

great view of the parking lot and the busy traffic passing through the intersection. The bright lights of the strip mall glowed warmly across the street.

"Felt like it was getting colder out, didn't it?" she said.

"Well, it's still March."

"Yeah, but I'm ready for spring."

"Me too."

"So I take it you know Rick pretty well?" she asked.

I shrugged. "We knew each other back when he was a State's Attorney and I was a cop."

"You were a cop?"

I nodded. That was one topic I didn't want to go into. "So was he, until he became a lawyer. When good cops go bad."

Kris laughed.

"He seems to have a lot of faith in you," she said. "I mean, as soon as the news came out about poor Mr. Tunney, Rick had me look up your number." She took a sip from her bottle. "So how's the follow-up investigation going?"

"I'm off to a booming start."

"Really? So what have you got planned for tomorrow?" She laughed. "Sorry, don't mean to pry, but I was just wondering how much I'm going to have to type in the way of reports."

"I usually type my own reports," I said. "So you don't have to worry."

"Less work for me." She smiled again. "What do you think of Denise?"

"Little Hitler? Or should I say Evita Junior." Kris laughed. I was beginning to like the sound of that a lot. "I shouldn't be too hard on the kid, but, jeese, I wish she'd chill out sometimes. It's going to be a long drive up north tomorrow."

"She going with you?"

"Unfortunately." I raised my eyebrows. "Let's talk about you. How'd you come to be working as a temp?"

She shrugged. "Married too young, worked to put him through school, dental school, and then found out he was screwing his hygienist. Had a messy divorce, got next to nothing, and moved down here from the north suburbs to start over."

"Sounds like you could've used a good lawyer," I said. "You should've taken him to the cleaners."

"It wasn't so much about the money," she said. "It was more about getting out from under. Besides, everybody thinks dentists are loaded, but they're not. He was still paying off his student loans." She took another drink of juice. I interpreted this as a cue to change the subject.

"You used to live up north?"

She nodded, setting the bottle on the table.

"Way up in Palatine. I came down here for a change of venue."

I smiled. "Sounds like you've been picking up quite a bit working at Rick's."

Kris blushed. "I guess I did hear that term mentioned somewhere. The way Denise is browbeating me, I'm bound to pick up something, right?"

"Well, tomorrow you'll have some breathing space. We'll be probably be gone all day on those interviews."

"That'll be nice," she said. "Not that I won't miss you, though."

We talked some more, going into my kickboxing career and her love of sports and animals. When I mentioned I had three cats, she smiled and said she'd like to see them sometime.

That can probably be arranged, I thought.

When we began our walk back to our cars, I noticed it had gotten considerably colder. A bit of moisture hit my face and I noticed tiny flecks whipping through the halo from the streetlight.

"Oh, my God, it's snowing," Kris said. "It was so nice today I thought winter was over."

"Things aren't always what you think they'll be. Like I said, it's still March. Winter probably wants to take one more run at us to show us it ain't through yet."

"I guess so," she said. She stopped by a white Ford Taurus and slid the key in the lock. "This is mine."

I held the door for her as she threw her gym bag inside.

"It was nice talking with you tonight," I said.

"Same here." Her eyes flicked to mine, and she reached up and gave me a brief hug. As she moved away she reached in her pocket and took out a card, pressing it into my hand. "Here's my card. My home number's on the back. Call me sometime."

Despite the weather, my hand felt warm where she touched me. I looked at the card. It was advertising Kris Templer as some kind of temp jack-of-all-trades secretary. I could tell it had been done on a computer because the light snow was already making the ink run slightly. I flipped it over and looked at the number written in looping female cursive. It appeared to be an Oak Lawn exchange. We were almost neighbors.

She said good night and got in the car. I moved to close the door for her, and she reached up and squeezed my hand with gratitude for my chivalry, but also with the hint of a promise of possible things to come.

Chapter 5

The thing about March blizzards in Chicago is that they can be bad, but they normally don't last long. I hoped that would be the case with this one when I got up to do my six o'clock run the next morning. The snow had continued to fall more heavily throughout the night as I'd driven home, and now blanketed the streets with at least several inches. I didn't even want to think about shoveling the walk, much less trying to go my usual five or six miles through the slush. I compromised, doing a quick three-and-a-half-mile jaunt and then a quick shoveling job on the sidewalks. In all probability it would melt by the end of the week anyway. But it was going to make that drive to the North Shore and back pure hell. The first snows and the last snows of the season were always the worst. In the first one people have forgotten how to drive in the stuff, and in the last one, they think they're old pros at it. It would be the Accident 500 on the expressways. There was no way I wanted to risk driving the Firebird today.

I showered and dressed quickly and went out to the garage to make sure the Beater would start. It was an old '79 Pontiac Catalina that I'd borrowed from George's partner back when my Camaro had been stolen. I'd ended up sinking so much money into it for nickel and dime repairs that I decided to keep it, buying it from Doug outright. In the intervening time, so much of it had been replaced and rebuilt, it was almost like a new car. Well, not quite. It still needed some fixing from time to time. Not only was it a mechanic's dream, but the body had enough holes and

Bondo in it to pass for a Baghdad taxi. It turned over like a charm, thanks to the brand-new DieHard battery I'd put in a month or so before. I cracked the garage door to let the fumes out, and let it idle while I went in to feed the cats. The ignition was so worn that the keys slid right out.

I poured a bit of dry food into each of their three dishes, but the crew seemed to sense that I was leaving them for longer than normal and began rubbing against my legs. Since I'd just put on my dress pants, I shooed them away by opening a can of tuna-flavored cat chow and dropping three equal portions in their respective dishes. Rags and Shasha immediately began devouring theirs, but poor Georgio followed me back into the bedroom as I used my brush to clean off any residual cat hair. I'd been channel surfing as I ate and tuned into one of those old BBC Sherlock Holmes episodes. I'd seen this one several times, but still enjoyed watching a master at work. After adjusting my tie, I checked my wallet, IDs, and slipped on my heavy leather jacket. Just as I walked back to the kitchen I heard Georgio cry mournfully. Shasha had finished her canned food, and was stealing his. Gentleman that he was, he merely watched her eat.

"Women, Watson," I heard Jeremy Brett say on TV, "cannot be trusted."

I pointed a finger at Georgio and said, "That'd be a good lesson for you to learn, little buddy."

Both the rides up and back were murder. We entered into a sinuous trail of bumper-to-bumper Sunday drivers, even though it was Wednesday, and limped along from bad to worse as the major expressways intersected and led north. Besides the snow, which I could deal with, and the other drivers, who seemed to fluctuate between ultra-cautious and borderline reckless, I had to put up with Denise's constant driving critiques and safety tips. She'd looked stunned when I'd shown up in the Beater to pick her up, asking, "*That's* your car?"

"My Rolls is in the garage," I said. "Figured this one might be better, considering the weather."

All that got me was a frown.

Little did I know that was the high point. As we merged into the endless, creeping stream, Denise's right foot kept lurching forward, hitting the imaginary brake pedal on the passenger side. I began to worry that she'd eventually punch a hole right through the floorboard.

"How's the brake working over there?" I asked. Another mistake. That spurred her into her "safety zone" lecture on how you should convert the two-second rule to maybe four or five in bad weather when driving on the expressway.

"Where'd you hear that?" I asked.

"Driver's ed," she said, looking at me like I'd just fallen off the turnip truck.

"Well, you want to drive for a while?"

"Me? Drive this? It's like a tank."

"I prefer to call it the new Battlestar Galactica," I said.

Her brow furrowed.

"Battlestar what?"

"Never mind," I said.

To make matters worse, once we got to the fabled "North Shore," we soon found out that the investigation had actually been handled by several detectives from different agencies in the Northern Suburban Major Crimes Task Force. That meant even though the primary dicks had been from Winnetka, where the crime had happened, a lot of the other investigators were at different locations. If we wanted to talk to all of them, it'd mean a lot more running around. We decided on making that determination after talking to the primaries, who turned out to be pretty helpful.

One of them was a female sergeant who'd been in investigations at the time. She was tall, thin, rather pretty, and definitely knew her stuff.

"Why did they try the case at twenty-sixth and Cal?" I asked. Luckily, Denise was keeping mostly quiet during this interview.

"That was our request," the sergeant said. "We wanted to move it out of this area. Figured since Gooding was so well-known around here, and had a lot of friends and patients, the jury pool would be more inclined to see through the bullshit and convict him."

Denise gave a mostly inaudible snort, but thankfully remained silent.

"Did Gooding have any alibi for the time of the murders?" I asked.

She shook her head. "If he did, he never told us. He lawyered up as soon as we brought him in for questioning, and he never testified at his trial."

"I looked over your reports," I said. "You did a good job. The case seemed pretty strong."

"Thanks. We thought so too." She shrugged. "But it's not like it took Sherlock Holmes to figure this one out. Gooding was really the only suspect from the start."

"Are you saying that you built your case that way?" Denise cut in. "That you weren't looking for anybody else but him?"

The sergeant looked surprised, then raised her eyebrows. "In most homicides the offender and victim know each other. Especially in cases involving domestic abuse."

I sighed, then asked, "So what happened? Why do you

think it turned out the way it did?"

"I really couldn't say."

"Come on," I said, trying my most convincing smile. "Give me your best guess."

She shrugged, then smiled back. "The judge was an idiot?"

In the car we discussed the feasibility of tracking down and interviewing all the other detectives.

"Maybe they could tell us about the demeanor of the witnesses when they testified?" Denise said.

I shook my head. "Most likely not. They most certainly would have been isolated under a motion to exclude, so they probably didn't hear the other witnesses."

"Well, something tipped the scales against the prosecution. And we'd better get a handle on what it was so we don't make the same mistake at our trial."

But after talking to two more police detectives, and getting more of the same—they thought the case would be a slam-dunk, and were surprised as hell the way it turned out—even dedicated Denise was ready for the trek back south.

I glanced at my watch. It was close to one. No sense rushing over to 26th Street. They'd all probably be handling their afternoon calls.

"We probably should get something to eat," I said. "Or do you just want to head back? It's been a long day already."

"We still have to go interview the ASAs. And I'm not hungry."

"Well, fine. But I am." I swung the car into the first restaurant I saw, which happened to be a Denny's. Lunch proved to be less than festive, with Denise ordering a salad and me getting a broiled chicken breast, a baked potato, and a large salad.

"You always eat so much?" she asked.

"I'm a growing boy," I offered.

"You'd better be careful or you'll start to pick up weight."

"I've been known to do that occasionally. You been talking to Chappie, by chance?"

"Who's Chappie?"

"Never mind," I said. "If you have to ask . . ."

Amazingly, that shut her up. Midway through the meal I guessed that she was still trying to figure out if Chappie was someone she should have known from the case files. I let her ponder in blessed silence while I tried to contemplate my next move. But my cell phone interrupted that.

"Mr. Shade, it's Ursula Bielmaster," the voice said. She sounded a bit nervous.

"How are you?" I asked. "And how's your husband?"

"He's doing all right. Still in intensive care, of course, but that's to be expected." I heard her sigh. "Did you . . . talk to Timothy Knop?"

"Yeah, I did. Why?"

I heard the sigh again.

"Perhaps it's nothing," she said. "Maybe I'm overreacting, but when I took my daughter to school this morning, I noticed some tracks around our house."

"Tracks? What kind?"

"You know, footprints. They looked like they might be his."

"How do you know that?"

"Well, who else could it be?" Her voice had gone from troubled to plaintive. "I'm sorry. I don't mean to be unpleasant. It's just . . ."

"You're going through a lot." I noticed Denise had quit eating and was now staring at me. "Did George talk to you about obtaining that civil no-contact order?"

"Yes, he mentioned it."

"I think it would be a good idea. Do you have a family attorney?"

"Not really," she said.

"Maybe I know someone who could help out. Would you be available tomorrow morning?"

Denise suddenly looked like she was going to explode. Her eyebrows rose and she compressed her lips, but the overall effect said angry. All that was needed to complete the picture was smoke coming out of her ears.

"I could try to set it up so my attorney friend could meet you at the Daley Center and walk you through it." I glanced at my watch. "Why don't I call you back later on? I'll try to have something set up by then. And I'll come over regardless and take a look around."

"Thank you, Mr. Shade," she said, and hung up.

No sooner did I put my cell phone away than Denise began to tear into me.

"I thought we were your primary client," she said. The emotion was creeping into her voice, too, just like it had in Ursula Bielmaster's. But this was more anger and less despair. "Plus you just got through trying to convince me a little while ago that we should call it a day and try to do the ASA interviews tomorrow morning, didn't you?"

"We could," I said. "I was thinking that maybe Rick could help me out a little with this. Then that would leave us free to do the rest of the interviews." I tried a smile.

She speared a piece of lettuce with a vengeance and said, "We'll just have to see what Mr. Walters has to say about all this."

I left it at that, content to let her have the last word as long as it meant we could pass the rest of the meal in silence.

After suffering through my meal under the baleful eye of Denise, I decided to suck it up and head over to 26th and Cal to see if we could catch a few of those Assistant State's Attorneys. The traffic was heavy through the Loop, as usual, but thinned out miraculously as we neared Cermak. When I sailed past it, Denise flinched.

"I thought you said we were going to—"

"We are," I said. "It's easier if we come in the back way off Thirty-fifth."

She puckered her lips, ready to debate the issue and I held up my hand.

"Look, just relax and leave the driving to me, okay?"

Her mouth opened, but she took in a breath and sat back, crossing her arms over her chest. We rode through the lightly traveled expressway. It was turning into a day of miracles.

The First Judicial District of Cook County was located at 26th Street and California Avenue. It was a classically designed old building, replete with massive stone pillars and beautifully carved bas-relief. But as Chicago grew, the classic architecture gradually became surrounded by the ever-expanding Cook County Jail, which sat adjacent, its high stone walls and concertina wire fences giving a stark contrast to the finely wrought statues. Since we didn't have a court pass, I had to look for a suitable parking space on California Boulevard, which ran parallel to its avenue namesake in front of the buildings. I cruised around the block twice and finally spied someone pulling out. I twisted the wheel of the Beater and spun through the break between the streets, deftly claiming the vacant spot.

When we got out, I patted my pockets for some change to feed the meter. I dropped in a few quarters, which gave us an hour or so.

"If we take longer than this," I said, pointing to the timer, "you'll have to run down and put some more change in this baby, okay?"

"No way," Denise said. "I'm not your gofer."

I shrugged and shot her as wicked a smile as I could muster.

"All right, I'll just bill Rick for the ticket then." I started walking across the park-like island that separated the two streets. I actually wasn't too worried about any meter maids citing me. One of the benefits of driving the Beater was all the FOP stickers that Doug had left on the windshield. It was the best insurance I could have.

I could hear Denise slogging through the snow behind me.

We did manage to track down one of the Assistant State's Attorneys named O'Riley, who wasn't in court. He agreed to give us five minutes while he took a coffee break in their break room. He couldn't really tell us much more than what the police detectives had, other than he'd been just as shocked when the judge acquitted Gooding with a directed verdict.

"I thought we were winning." He was fairly young, with dark hair swept back from his forehead. "I mean, we'd won the prelim, but that was before Judge Conlan and another defense attorney. Then Gooding fired that attorney and hired Mason Gilbert. But even at the regular trial all of our witnesses did pretty good. And I think, despite being up against the Great Gilbert and company, we were holding our own." He shrugged and frowned. "But apparently the judge didn't. Go figure."

"Was it the demeanor of the witnesses?" Denise asked. She leaned forward now, cradling her notebook to her chest like a schoolgirl.

O'Riley canted his head and raised his eyebrows.

"Could be," he said slowly. "Like I said, I thought we'd gotten all the zingers in, the history of domestic violence, the recent spats over the victim dating again and asking for more dough, the blood stains on Gooding's shirt. . . ."

"And the judge ended it right after you rested?" I asked.

He nodded. "Old Judge Foxworth . . . Directed verdict. Surprised the shit out of us, all right. But he had an eye for the ladies, and Gilbert had a real pretty female associate as co-counsel. Plus, you know how pro-defense some of these judges can be. Especially when they've got the Great Gilbert in front of them."

"Everybody's favorite lawyer now that Perry Mason is dead," I said.

I caught a glimpse of a reactive frown from Denise. Guess I'd shattered her idealism by talking bad about lawyers.

"You remember the co-counsel's name?" I asked.

O'Riley bit his lip and glanced skyward. "Mary something, I think. It should be on file. She hardly did anything except sit there and look good. I think she only handled one cross. Julia Horton might remember it, but she's no longer with the office. I think he had an intern with him, too. Mark something or other. I'm terrible with last names."

"We're gonna try to talk to Ms. Horton, too," I said. "Any idea what Gilbert was planning in the way of a defense?"

He shook his head. "Hard to remember . . . We try so many cases."

"Maybe there'd be something in the file?" Denise asked. "Did you do a reciprocal discovery?"

"Yeah, I'm sure they did. It's SOP in all felony cases to file for one." O'Riley glanced at his watch and sighed. "I could probably check the file and see, but I'm all out of time today."

"But we're going to trial on this next week," she said. "Surely you can make some time for us. So *we* might be able to win it this time." The bossy tone and sharp rebuke obviously rubbed O'Riley the wrong way. He compressed his lips and started to get up. I was going to have to get Denise a copy of *How to Win Friends and Influence People* if she was going to keep coming along on these things.

"Maybe we could look through it?" I asked quickly. "That way we wouldn't take up any more of your time? We'd really appreciate it."

O'Riley's eyes shot toward Denise, then moved to me.

"You could go down and have the clerk pull it," he said. "You know the docket number?"

I nodded.

"Okay," he said, standing. "I'll call down to the clerk's office. Ask for Dorita in the records section. She'll fix you up."

When he'd left Denise said to me in the same haughty tone, "Mr. Shade, these files are public record. We don't have to grovel, you know."

"Yeah, I know," I said, "but if we have to file through the Freedom of Information Act it could take us several days. You think Rick wants to wait that long?"

She looked away and shook her head.

"Neither do I," I said. "Now let's see if we can get through the rest of the day without you pissing anybody else off, okay?"

I regretted being so tough with her, but after the tedious driving and mediocre information we'd gotten so far, my patience was at its bitter end. And she wasn't making things any easier. Still, I knew her comments were born out of eagerness and inexperience. I decided to let her review the file first. Maybe that would make her feel more important.

We went down to the clerk's office on the first floor and asked for Dorita. One of the women pointed to a big room with a counter in front of an opening. Behind the opening I could see floor-to-ceiling shelves displaying row after row of tan-colored folders. A heavyset, middle-aged African-American woman was busily fitting more folders into various spaces in the cluttered wall of paper. As we approached she looked at me over a pair of those cut-off reading glasses. Her hair was pulled back into a plain bun and had a few errant strands of gray mingled amongst the black.

"Can I help you?" she asked.

"I hope so," I said, handing over the paper with the docket number written on it. "We need to look at this file."

She didn't take the paper, but rather reached under the counter and came up with a three-by-eleven sheet of paper labeled *Court File Requisition Form*. "Fill this out," she said, and went back to her filing.

I raised my eyebrows, wondering how long it was going to take her to locate this one. After printing the information in large block letters, I pushed it back across the counter top. Presently she came back and glanced down at the form, and then to me.

"You an officer?"

"I'm a private detective." I showed her my ID. "We're the ones Mr. Riley called you about."

She scrutinized the form. On the line of reason, I'd written, "Pending civil case."

"You'll have to look at it right at the counter here," she said. "Ain't supposed to let the files leave my sight, 'lessin it's to a police officer or a State's Attorney."

"Sounds good," I said, before Denise could intercede with her Freedom of Information Act.

She left after looking down at the form, nodding slightly, then was back in a few minutes with the file.

"Wow, that was fast," I said, smiling. "You must be the legendary Dorita I heard so much about."

She snorted a laugh and said, "I still ain't gonna let you take it away from the counter, honey."

Denise sidled up next to me and we turned over each page. Unfortunately, it contained nothing out of the ordinary. Gilbert's discovery motion was in there, but no reciprocal discovery document from the ASA.

"I knew it," Denise said. "They probably didn't even file one."

"Maybe not," I said, reaching for the file. I paged through it, not sure what I was looking for, but hoping I'd know what it was if I found it. I came across a Petition for Substitution of Judges form and pulled it out.

"What's this?" I asked.

She leaned over and looked at it. "An SOJ. All it means is Gilbert asked for a new judge. From Conlan to Foxworth. Standard procedure after the preliminary hearing."

I nodded. "Let me see if I can use my charm to get Dorita here to make a copy of this for us. Maybe Rick will want to go over it." I stood up. "Then we'll head home."

For once I didn't get an argument from her.

Somehow we managed to coast out just ahead of the burgeoning rush-hour traffic jams. By the time we got to the split around 71st Street, where the express lanes end, it was clear sailing all the way to 95th. The state snowplows had done an admirable job of clearing and salting, and the residual snow was lining the edge of the expressway in dirty, grayish brown heaps. Despite the sudden storm, it felt like it was thawing. March—in like a lion, out like a lamb, my mother always used to say. I smiled to myself and out of the corner of my eye caught Denise staring at me, but she didn't say anything.

Back at Rick's office I filled him in on the interviews. We sat in front of his desk while he leaned back in his chair and listened intently.

"So basically, they expected it to be a slam-dunk, and the judge turned out to be an idiot," I said. "I've got a couple of things I'd like to mull over, and then check out."

"Directed verdict, just like we already knew," Denise added.

She always has to get the last word in, I thought. I slyly found my mind wandering to what she'd be like in bed. She was pretty, and had a nice figure, but it probably wouldn't turn out to be an enjoyable experience given her penchant for constant criticism.

I sighed and said, "Look, Rick, I can write up these notes tomorrow and get them to you by Thursday or Friday, okay?"

"You going to type them yourself?" he asked. "How long's that gonna take?"

I shrugged.

"I mean," he continued, "after what happened with old Tunney, I'd prefer to have something solid I could count on as soon as possible." He opened his desk drawer and took out a small, black, pocket-sized tape recorder. "I meant to give this to you earlier, but didn't want you to be tempted to secretly record any conversations at Twenty-sixth

Street." He grinned and held it out toward me.

"And this is for?"

"For you to dictate your notes into," he said. "That way you can just turn the tapes over to Kris each day and she can transcribe them. She's really very good at it, and unless you've got twelve very nimble fingers, she'll be a lot faster than you."

I frowned, but his grin was sort of infectious.

"Okay, but let me ask a favor of you." I figured this would be a good time to broach the subject of getting the civil no-contact order for the Bielmasters. I gave him a brief rundown. "Think you could help her?"

"Sure, no problem," he said. "I'll be downtown in the morning anyway. Have her meet us at the Daley Center at, say, nine o'clock and we can walk one through. Denise can help her."

Out of the corner of my eye I caught her flinch slightly. That made me smile. Sometimes, justice does prevail.

"Sounds like a plan," I said.

Chapter 6

The hint of the thaw was growing stronger in the heavy, moisture-laden air. By tomorrow it would be substantially reduced, and by week's end a novel memory. So there wouldn't be any tracks in fresh snow tonight . . . But I couldn't afford to take anything for granted. At least not until the civil no-contact order was in place. Realistically, it was only a piece of paper, but it would serve as a tool. Something that could give us a bit of leverage. Plus, Knop would be served with the paper and be put on notice. He could be arrested and his probation violated if he was caught hanging around the Bielmasters. Knowing that, along with another one of my little visits, just might be enough to convince him to look to greener pastures. Still, tonight was another matter, and I couldn't afford to drop the ball two times in a row.

I got into my car and pulled out the cell phone as I started it up and waited for the heater to kick on. Denise had declined my offer of a ride home, so I was free until tomorrow. That meant I'd have to take care of business on the Bielmaster case tonight. I looked up Ken Albrecht's number on my phone lexicon and called him. His mother answered and presently he came on the line.

"Mr. Shade, what's up?"

"I thought I told you to call me Ron?"

I heard him laugh. "Okay, Ron."

"You got some time tonight?"

"Sure, I guess so. I was just going to head over to the gym is all."

"I need some help on a surveillance, if you're up for it." I waited half a beat. "It could last into the wee hours."

"Will I get paid?"

"Absolutely."

"Good. I'm in. I'll go to the gym tomorrow." I heard him chuckle. "Heck, I slept most of the day after working the hotel thing last night. Got home about seven, so I'm rested and ready."

I told him I'd pick him up in fifteen and disconnected.

When I pulled up in front of his house, he was out in a flash, jogging toward the car in his desert-camouflaged field jacket. He sort of reminded me of myself ten years ago. We sort of looked something alike, size-wise, although his sandy-colored hair was a tad lighter than mine, and he wore wire-rim glasses.

"This is yours?" he asked. "What happened to the Firebird?"

"It's in my garage. I thought I'd introduce you to the Beater because that's what you'll be driving tonight."

He raised his eyebrows and grinned.

"Hey, after driving Humvees in Iraq, this looks like a Cadillac."

We shot over to the liquor store on Monterey and I showed him where Knop worked, explaining our objectives. Then we headed by Knop's mother's house.

"Our target is staying here with mama," I said. "Once he gets home from work, we'll need to stake out his house and trace any movements."

"Roger that."

The Knop residence was located between Kedzie and Western, near 105th and Troy. It was a neighborhood of solid brick bungalows and an occasional wood-frame house covered with aluminum siding. Solidly middle-class.

Knop's was one of the frames, a grayish-looking house with a big evergreen in the adjacent yard. I drove on past, then turned right and went down the perpendicular street, then turned right again at the mouth of the alley. One thing I love about the city of Chicago is that there's an alley for practically every street.

I counted the houses and as we cruised by the garage Ken pointed to the house and said, "That one, right?"

He'd been counting too. I was beginning to like this kid.

The apron showed some crisscrossing tire tracks, indicating someone had pulled in and out of the garage at some point after the snowfall. That meant it was at least a one-car family. It also meant that Knop apparently had wheels, too. I drove to the adjacent street and turned again.

"I'll show you the victim's house," I said, glancing at my watch. It was close to four-thirty and I assumed that both Bielmasters would be home unless they were at the hospital. "I'll introduce you to them so in case they see you lurking about, they don't take a shot at you."

"It'll just remind me of Baghdad." He grinned. "You were in that Somalia thing, weren't you?"

"Unfortunately."

"Must have been pretty rough."

"It always is when you go in with an unrealistic set of objectives, and the other guys don't have to obey any rules."

We rode the rest of the way in silence, both probably remembering things we'd have rather remained forgotten.

Ursula and Grace were just getting ready to eat, but invited us in anyway. Out of the corner of my eye I saw Ken checking out Grace's ass in her tight blue jeans. I cleared my throat and apologized for the intrusion as I briefed Ursula about meeting us downtown at the Daley Center in the morning to get the no-contact order.

"My lawyer friend and his partner will be down there to help you."

"You think this will help?" Ursula asked.

"It'll be a good tool," I said. "Knop can be arrested if he violates the order."

She nodded and said she'd be there.

"I also wanted to touch bases with you and introduce you to Ken Albrecht. He'll be working with me on this so if you see him around, don't be frightened."

Grace compressed her lips and looked away.

"I'd ask you both to stay," Ursula said, "but I'm afraid I only warmed up enough for the two of us. We're planning on heading over to the hospital in a bit."

After getting their intended schedule, I told them we'd check back later by phone and be outside on surveillance most of the night.

"As always, though," I added, "if you do hear or see anything the least bit suspicious, call nine-one-one. Don't assume that it might be us."

She nodded.

As we walked back to the car Ken glanced back over his shoulder at the house.

"That little gal's a babe, all right," he said. "Can't say I fault the dude's taste."

"Furgetaboutit," I said, doing my best Mafioso accent. "She's too young for you."

We drove back to my place and I fed the cats and checked the mail. The message light was blinking on my phone, and I saw by the caller ID box that it had to be Chappie. He was probably expecting me at the gym tonight, so I had to call him sooner or later. I figured later was the better choice. I changed into some more comfortable working clothes and flipped the Beater's keys to Ken. "It's yours for tonight, buddy. Let's go grab a bite to eat and then we'll start setting up."

Once we got to the fast-food chicken place I realized how hungry I was and ordered accordingly, rationalizing my gluttony with the excuse that I'd be burning the midnight oil and would need the extra fuel. While we waited for our orders, I pulled out the cell phone and called Chappie.

"What time you coming in tonight?" was his first question.

"I can't make it. Got to work."

"Oh. Okay," he said, sounding almost genuine. "You gonna come in tomorrow, though, ain't you?"

"Sure." I was having trouble believing that this was actually Chappie I was talking to. Usually, any time I missed training at the gym was something akin to a class-three felony.

"Saul called me today." His voice still sounded unusually calm. "Wanted to know if you in shape to take a fight on short notice. I told him, hell, yes, Ron Shade's always in shape." I heard his deep chuckle over the phone. "Gonna have to put an extra couple dollars in the collection plate at church for telling a whopper like that."

"What kind of fight? Against who?"

"Don't know yet. He gonna get back to me. All I knows is, it's in Vegas."

"Well, you tell me," I said. "Am I ready, or not?"

"Depends on the stakes, I guess. And who you be fighting." His voice sounded distant. Like maybe he was starting to see me as less of a serious prospect than he used to. "Anyway, I wanted to work with Marcus a bit tonight anyway."

"Okay, well, I'll see you tomorrow, I guess."

"Ain't no guessing about it," he shot back. "You get your ass in here tomorrow for sure. Especially if we might have to fly out to Vegas and fight some dude with no notice. And don't you be skipping them miles in the morning, either."

That was the Chappie I knew and loved.

The counter girl set the bags with our food down just as I ended the call.

A fight, I thought. Probably to replace a tomato can who'd backed out of fighting another tomato can. That's what these short notice things usually were. Filler for some main event at some hotel on the strip. People so drunk and rambunctious that they didn't care who was standing in the ring in front of them getting their brains beat out. I suddenly wasn't so sure I wanted to get involved in something like that, even if it did mean a free trip to Vegas.

I'd given Ken one of our phones with a walkie-talkie mode, and we communicated as we tracked Tim Knop in tandem from the liquor store to his house. When his uncle dropped him off, Knop paused to look around, then headed inside. It's easier doing a surveillance when you have two people, and the tedium of watching both ends of the block began to wear thin very quickly. I told Ken to take a break, and then I'd follow suit. I took a quick drive down the alley and made a mental note of the tire track pattern coming out of the garage, figuring to check it again before I took my break to make sure no one had left the back way. Then I settled in at the end of the block where I had a good view of the front of the house as well as the mouth of the alley. Plus, I was situated between the Knops' and the Bielmasters', so even if Timothy pulled out of the alley at the other end, it stood to reason he'd swing around and go right by me. But nothing was stirring.

I turned on a light jazz station that was mostly instrumentals and kicked back and watched the night settle over the area. The traffic grew more and more sparse, making the tedium more and more apparent. Soon I found myself mulling over the day's interviews with the detectives and State's Attorney O'Riley. They'd all pretty much said the same thing. Gooding did it. He was the only viable suspect, had no alibi to speak of, and had the victim's blood on his shirt. They'd won the probable cause hearing, and seemed confident. A slam-dunk.

So Gooding fires attorney number one, and hires the Great Gilbert. From what I'd read of the transcripts, Mason Gilbert might have had some master plan to pull a rabbit out of a hat, but that's what it would be. His cross-examinations had been designed to discredit and attack, and he was very good at it. But what defense could he have mounted? And why was the reciprocal discovery motion, that O'Riley said was SOP, not in the court file? Plus, I was leaving something out. Perhaps the most important piece. The SOJ. Why would Gilbert file for a change of judges?

From what O'Riley had inferred, the first judge, Conlan, was female, and maybe Gilbert felt she'd be less sympathetic in the case of a man accused of killing his wife. Or maybe there was another reason . . . Maybe Gilbert wanted to get before a judge he knew. Someone he had a better relationship with . . . Someone he knew would be pro-defense . . . He also had a female associate named Mary something . . . Judge Foxworth having an eye for the ladies . . . Sounded like Gilbert knew what buttons to push, all right. I made a mental note to ask George if he knew anything about good old Judge Foxworth.

A flash of movement at the Knops' house caught my eye.

A reflection of light. I got out of the Firebird and jogged up the sidewalk on the opposite side of the street. It looked like someone was going down the back steps. Tim? Definitely masculine, from the walk, but more than that, I couldn't tell. I'd forgotten to ask George if Knop's mother was married or seeing someone. The figure moved down the back walk toward the garage. He was either taking out the garbage or . . . I stood sideways next to a tree, watching, and saw him pause at the side door of the garage. When he went in, I turned and ran back to my car. A risky maneuver, but if he drove off while I was still on foot, there would be no way to tag him. I'd let Ken go on his break at the wrong time.

I got the Firebird started and scanned both ends of the street. Depending on which way he pulled out, I figured I'd have a good chance at seeing him get on the main thoroughfare. I saw light beams shining down the alley facing the opposite direction that I was sitting. That meant I'd have to pull out now and turn around, or risk doing a U-turn and being real obvious. I shifted into drive, checked my mirrors, and pulled out onto the street. I went down a little bit more than half a block, put my turn signal on pretending I was going to turn left, and then shut off my lights and whipped completely around. Down the block, I saw the lights of a car turning ahead of me and pulled on to the street to follow it. It was heading west, the same direction as the Bielmasters' house.

"Ken, where you at?" I called into the phone.

"Just got my lunch. Why?"

"I'm mobile." I gave him my location.

"You want me to run an intercept?"

"Let me see if it's actually him and where he's headed first. But be ready to move."

I stayed far enough back that I could keep up, but not so close that I would be made. Knop or his uncle might have seen my Firebird the other night, even though I'd taken pains to park down the block. But I had to be sure this was him. I flipped down the visor and reached into the back seat and grabbed one of the baseball caps I keep for such occasions. The car slowed for a stoplight ahead, and I closed the gap. It was a dark-colored Dodge Neon. With the bill pulled low, and the visor cutting off any ambient lighting, I figured I'd be pretty much unrecognizable. From the shape of the back of the driver's head, I was pretty certain it was Knop. Then just before the light changed, he turned and I caught his profile, removing any lingering doubts.

"It's him, all right," I said into the phone, giving him the car description and plate number. "Hang tight and get ready."

Knop went west toward Pulaski, still headed in the direction of the Bielmasters'. I dropped back and called Ken to start heading over there. If I could catch him lurking around, it would add more bite to getting that no-contact order set up, and probably go a long way toward violating his probation. I was sure a criminal trespass charge could be arranged. Plus, Knop and I could have a little talk, depending on how cooperative he was when I grabbed him.

But the thoughts of beating the hell out of him troubled me a bit. Ever since my early childhood days, when I was preyed upon by predatory toughs who made my walks to school experiments in terror, I despised bullies. My own pleas to my father resulted in him having my much older brother Tom and his friend George teach me the fundamentals of boxing and self-defense. It was what started me in the martial arts. I hadn't studied my whole life just to beat the crap out of some kid to satisfy Bielmaster.

Knop used his signal and turned right on Kedzie. He was still going in the right direction. I radioed his position to Ken, who gave me a "Roger."

I was going to have to tell him to loosen up a bit. He was still suffering from the military protocols.

I dropped a few cars back and watched the Neon's tail lights proceeding north. He'd turn left at 103rd and be almost at Bielmaster's. Then I'd have Ken set up in front while I went down the block and doubled back through the alley on foot. But instead of going left, the Neon's right turn signal came on. It turned and I slowed down, wondering if he'd make me if I got behind him again.

"Where you at now?" I asked Ken.

"Heading south on Pulaski," his voice said. "Coming up on a Hundred and Third now."

I had little choice but to make the turn and continue following Knop. Ken was too far away to catch up, and if Knop was taking a circuitous route just to shag any possible tails, I'd lose him for sure. As I braked to go right, I saw the Neon slowing in the left lane. Had he seen me? Was he looping around to make a Uie and wave as he went by? I drove past, averting my face as I did so, and watched the Neon turn left into a strip mall parking lot. There was another driveway entrance about 200 feet ahead, and I quickly shot into it in time to see the Neon pulling into a parking spot by a store marked Green Drugs Pharmacy. I parked, cutting off my lights, and sat back to watch. Knop's lanky silhouette shuffled toward the glass doors. What was he buying in that place? Condoms, maybe? So he'd leave no trace evidence . . . I called Ken and told him to get over here.

I waited about twenty more seconds, then glanced around. The strip mall was partially full, but I located another spot that afforded me a decent view of the doors and the Neon, so I quickly moved. That way, if Knop had seen me pull in, and happened to scan the lot, my car wouldn't be in the same place.

"I'm coming up to your location now," Ken's voice said. "Where do you want me?"

"Pull in and I'll direct you to the car. You can pick him up when he leaves."

"Roger that."

At least he hadn't said, "Roger wilco," I thought.

Knop came ambling out carrying a small paper bag after about five minutes and got back into the Neon. As soon as I was sure Ken was on him, I pulled over to the drugstore and went in.

The girl at the counter looked about eighteen and her eyes widened when I flashed my shiny badge.

"That guy that just left," I said, "what did he buy?"

"What guy?"

"White kid, about nineteen, five-ten or so, maybe one-eighty. Brown hair."

Her brow furrowed and she shrugged her shoulders.

"Nobody like that bought nothing here, officer."

I hoped she was going to day classes for her GED.

"He just came outta here carrying a bag." I kept my voice suitably gruff.

She shrugged again, and then I could almost see the metaphorical light bulb go on over her head.

"Maybe he was back in pharmacy," she said, picking up the phone. "Hey, Don, did some white guy buy something back there a couple of minutes ago? The cops are here wanting to know." She nodded, her lips working as if to say, "I told you so," and she pointed toward the back of the store. "Yeah, okay, I'm gonna send him back to talk to you."

"Hey, Ron?" Ken's voice came over the phone.

"Go."

"We're heading east, back towards his place."

"Stay on him," I said.

I walked back through several aisles packed with everything from stationery to greeting cards toward the pharmacy section. The guy behind the counter was an older guy with sparse red hair combed straight back in no effort to hide his high forehead.

"Yes, officer," he said. "What can I do for you?"

Although I hadn't identified myself as a cop, I let the erroneous conclusion ride. It was easier to get information that way sometimes.

"That kid who was in here." I described Knop again quickly. "You remember what he bought?"

"Yeah," the guy said, his mouth puckering into a confused expression. "He picked up a prescription."

"A prescription? For what?"

"Hey." He held up his hands, palms outward, and shook his head. "Privacy laws. Can't divulge that."

I put on my most intimidating frown.

"Just between me and you," I said. "And if I have to drop everything and come back tomorrow with a warrant, I'll remember your face as I take this whole fucking place apart."

I hated to use the profanity, but I figured it would either tip the balance or not. If he was a tough guy, he'd tell me to go scratch my ass. But I was pretty good at sizing people up, and I didn't think he was.

He sighed and pulled up a clipboard with a list of papers on it. "It was a prescription."

"You said that already. What kind of prescription?" I let a hint of menace creep into my voice.

"Cozaar. A hundred milligrams. For a Theresa Knop."

"Theresa?"

He nodded and looked around. "She gets her prescription filled here all the time," he said. "I assumed the young guy was her son."

"What's Cozaar for?"

"High blood pressure."

"He buy anything else?"

The pharmacist shook his head. "Look, officer, like I said, I'm really not supposed to tell you any of this. I could get in real trouble."

"Fugetaboutit," I said, using my Mafioso imitation for the second time that night. "We never had this conversation."

I thanked him and left, saying I must have had the wrong guy anyway. Unless he had a real personal relationship with Knop's mother, he probably wouldn't call her to mention my inquiry. And what could he tell her if he did? That he'd violated his pharmacist code of ethics? As I was walking out Ken came back on the horn.

"Hey, Ron, looks like our buddy's pulling back in his garage."

"Okay," I told him. "Set up down the block and keep an eye out. I'm going to swing by the Bielmasters' and check things out."

"Roger that," he said again.

Dammit, I thought. Either he made us, or it was just a wild goose chase.

As the night drew on, with no activity at either household, other than the lights going out, the boredom of another all-night surveillance became very apparent to me. It had been a while since I'd done this type of drudge duty.

Ken must have been bored, too, because he kept calling me. At about 2:55 his voice over the phone snapped me awake. I sat there looking around, suddenly hyper-alert from the jolt of adrenaline, and swallowed hard.

"How you feeling?" I asked Ken.

"Great," he said. "I got a bunch of sleep today after working last night."

"Think you could stay on the Bielmasters' for another two hours?" I asked. It would be almost five by then and starting to get light out.

"Sure thing, Ron. Why don't you go home and catch some Z's? I'll call you if I get something."

After obtaining his assurance again that he'd call if anything unusual occurred, I pulled the plug and headed for home. I felt stiff from sitting in the cramped confines of the car for so long, and a cold feeling had settled over me. I was home in fifteen minutes and sleeping about five after that, telling myself that tomorrow was, after all, another day.

Chapter 7

The alarm went off a few hours later, leaving me to shuffle through the start of the day in a haze of painful movements draped with a veil of fatigue. When the clock first buzzed at the usual 5:00, I reset it and slept till 6:45. Or tried to, at least. Finally I drifted off only to be awakened what seemed like minutes later, and realized I was already running late. Outside the thaw looked to be continuing, but I knew if I was going to call Ursula Bielmaster to make sure she was meeting us downtown, take a shower, and then get dressed, I'd have to skip my run. Considering the way I felt, like I'd already been in a ten-round fight, that didn't seem to be such a bad idea. I'd have to make up for it with a good workout tonight.

I managed to tie my tie, slip on my sport jacket, down a bagel and drink some warmed-up coffee as I called her.

"I'll be there, Mr. Shade," she said. Then added, "Did you stay out there all night last night?"

"Until about six this morning," I said. "Anything unusual happen?"

"No." She said it almost too quickly. "It just felt good knowing you were keeping watch. I've been under such a strain with all this."

I disconnected after reaffirming the plan and left for Rick's, stopping for a second, and larger, cup of coffee on the way. When I got to his office Kris looked up from her keyboard and showed me a smile.

"Hi. You got some tapes for me to listen to?" she asked.

I snapped my fingers. "I'll give them to you this afternoon, okay?"

She nodded and smiled again, more tentatively this time. "Missed you at the gym last night."

"Yeah, I was busy on another job." I returned the smile. "You going tonight?"

"Sure. What time?"

Just as we were working out the logistics, Denise suddenly crept into my peripheral vision.

"I need to talk to you," she said, walking toward the conference room. From the sway of her hips I could tell that she was pissed. I went in and she closed the door behind me.

"Are you seeing her?" she asked, her face jerking up toward me, her lips drawn tight over white teeth.

Considering how crummy and tired I felt, my first reaction was to tell her to go to hell. But I remembered her almost being in tears before when I'd snapped at her and didn't want to hurt her feelings, even though she was shaping up to be a world-class pain in the ass. She liked to dish it out, but she sure couldn't take it.

"Just a minute," I said, opening the conference room door and staring out. I made a show of covering my left eye with my hand, and then my right, before turning back to Denise. "Yeah, I am. Just fine, I think. Why?"

She puckered her lips. "You know what I mean. Mr. Walters has specific rules about dating the help."

"Well, I'm a contract employee, and I date whomever I please. And all we were talking about was that we both go to the same gym. So quit acting like someone put starch in your underwear, okay?" I took a swig of coffee.

"Well, I won't have it interfering with her work. Or yours." She crossed her arms over her breasts and looked up at me. "Why don't you have the tapes ready? We need them."

"And you'll have them. I'll do my report this afternoon." I made a show of glancing at my watch. "But right now, kid, I suggest we get moving. We have to meet my other client at the Daley Center at nine."

She started to say something more, but I pulled open the door again and stepped out, making sure to smile at Kris as I walked toward Rick's office.

I had to give Denise credit, though. When Ursula finally got to the Daley Center, almost twenty minutes late, the kid volunteered to stay behind and help her get through the process of obtaining the civil no-contact order while Rick and I left for the deposition session in the Great Gilbert's downtown office. Of course Rick had made it clear that's what he wanted, so she had little choice. Still, when I shared a few moments alone speaking to Ursula, I couldn't help but think that there might be a glimmer of hope for Denise. Maybe she would eventually turn into a decent human being after all.

"Now this order will what?" Ursula asked me.

We were standing off to ourselves in the ridiculously crowded lobby, surrounded by people coming and going and huge glass windows all around. Still, there was a strange feeling of intimacy as we talked, our voices hushed to loud whispers.

"Basically, it's a tool to use if Knop comes around your house again," I said. "He can be arrested for violating the order. Once that happens, we can look into getting his probation revoked."

She nodded, looking grim.

"I don't think that's going to stop him."

"Let me worry about that." I reached over and touched her arm lightly. "Like I said, it's a tool."

She sighed, her gaze still on the floor.

"How's Grace holding up?"

With that, she looked up. "She's fine." Her response was almost too quick. Perhaps realizing it, she shook her head. "I mean, I don't worry so much about her when she's at school. They know not to let anyone in."

There go my chances of trying to stop in to see her, I thought. Unless I dress up like a priest.

Out of the corner of my eye I saw Rick look at his watch. Denise started over toward us with a purposeful walk, her usual bull-in-the-china shop approach. She surprised me by addressing Ursula rather than me.

"Are you ready, Mrs. Bielmaster?" she asked, gently laying a hand on Ursula's shoulder. Her eyes flashed toward me and I caught a mean look.

That's my girl, I thought, and smiled back.

Outside, the Loop seemed warmer than it had on the south end. The snow was just about all gone, except for a few small, dirty mounds piled at strategic locations on sidewalks and near curbs. Rick flipped up the collar of his black overcoat. I'd worn a heavy, but stylish, leather mid-length jacket and my short-brimmed hat that made me feel like Frank Sinatra whenever I wore it. I resisted the temptation to burst out with a chorus of "My Way," and pointed toward the nearby Starbucks on Washington Boulevard.

"You drink a lot of coffee, buddy," Rick said, following me into the shop. "I thought you were into physical fitness and all that stuff?"

"I'm also into sleeping, which I hardly did at all last night." I gave the Indian clerk my order and glanced at Rick, who shook his head.

"I don't want to look like I'm nervous during the depositions," he said.

The clerk asked if I needed cream or sugar and I told him no, and paid him as I took a few tentative sips. Hotter than hell, but lifesaving.

"One of the reasons I wanted you there this morning," Rick said, "was to try and read these guys. One's some kind of street artist who can supposedly substantiate Gooding's alibi. The other's an ex-boyfriend of Laura's. They're on Gilbert's witness list, but he's now saying they may not be available for the trial."

"Which means what?"

"They'll be able to read long portions of the deposition testimony into the record for consideration."

"They can do that?"

He nodded. "Civil court's a lot different than criminal court. I take it you haven't had much experience in this arena?"

I took another swig of my coffee. The cool weather had made it almost drinkable.

"Some," I said. "But you're right. I'm mostly used to criminal stuff. Usually I try to avoid lawyers altogether."

He grinned. "Why's that?"

"Because they're assholes," I said, grinning back. "Present company and State's Attorneys excepted, of course."

By the time we'd walked the three long city blocks to Michigan Avenue, Rick had outlined our strategy for the session. I was to sit back and observe the witnesses, noting what I could about their demeanor and looking for inconsistencies in their testimony. "But let me ask all the questions, okay?" He must have repeated that at least three times.

"Don't you trust me?" I grinned and stuffed my empty coffee cup into a wire trash can.

We went through the revolving glass doors of the Garland Building. Ornate gold designs decorated the walls as well as the elevator doors. Gilbert's office was on the eleventh floor. I didn't even ask Rick if he wanted to walk up, and to tell the truth, I didn't feel like it either.

Rick seemed tense as we got out of the elevator. The floors were highly burnished bronze marble, a far cry from the utilitarian carpeting that led to Rick's office. And the gold-leaf lettering on the opaque glass door, spelling out in block letters, MASON J. GILBERT & ASSOCIATES, ATTORNEYS AT LAW. It still didn't prepare me for the inside of the place. There was a small waiting room, manned by a knockout secretary, a gorgeous redhead no less, at a big fancy wooden desk, immaculate except for a phone and a computer monitor. It was one of those super-thin, super-expensive things. Both looked like high maintenance and outta our league.

"May I help you, gentlemen?" she asked.

Rick explained who we were, and that we were here for the deposition. She showed us a semblance of a smile, perfect white teeth as well, and told us Mr. Gilbert would be with us shortly.

I glanced at my watch. The depositions had been scheduled for ten-thirty, and it was almost that now. We'd left the Daley Center early and walked briskly to get here. Not breaking our asses, or anything, but close enough for legal work. And now Gilbert was making us wait. I realized then I wasn't in such a new arena after all.

When you're fighting for the championship, a lot of it involves mental games. Trying to psych your opponent out, so mentally, he'll be off his game plan. Like the champ making the challenger wait there in the ring as long as he can before the fight. Sometimes it works, sometimes it doesn't, but I was sure that's what Gilbert had in mind.

"Do you know how much longer it'll be?" I asked after about five minutes.

The redhead looked up with a surprised expression.

"Just a few more minutes, sir," she said. Her voice was tentative, questioning. Like not too many people would dare question the Great Gilbert's timeliness.

"Can you check?" I said. "We've got a busy day planned, too."

Out of the corner of my eye I saw Rick stiffen as she picked up the phone.

"Ron," he whispered, his voice showing a sense of urgency, "it's okay."

I was about to press her for more, but thought about Rick's comment that he didn't want to seem nervous during the deposition. Didn't want to seem nervous because he was, probably. Going up against the champ. I let it drop, but thought about that old Mark Twain saying that if a jury was composed of twelve people who got together to determine which side had the best lawyer, we'd already come in second. And second was just another way of saying last.

The redhead put down the phone and said that Mr. Gilbert was almost ready. We still had to wait a good five minutes more, and by that time I was more certain than ever that we needed to do something. In a fight, sometimes you have to trade a couple hard shots with your opponent right off the bat to get his respect. If Rick was too tentative to do this, we'd lost before we'd begun. And I didn't like to lose.

The door to the inner offices opened and another hot-looking babe, a brunette this time, welcomed us and introduced herself as Mary. She escorted us to a conference room. The hallway was wide enough to sport the Bears' offensive line, and looked like it was the entryway to a museum of some kind. Framed pictures of Mason Gilbert lined the walls, each one showing him receiving an award or shaking hands with some famous person. There was one of him with the mayor, and the mayor before him, and so on, dating back to one of Mason and Mayor Richard J. Daley himself. On the opposite wall were ones featuring the governors and state politicians of the past twenty-five years. I looked at the one with George Ryan and smirked.

The conference room had a huge, solid-looking table and was lined with leather-bound volumes of the state statutes. Even the chairs looked palatial. I figured we were in for some more waiting, and moved to sit down when the door sprang open and the great one himself entered the room. He looked very dapper in his tailor-made dark blue suit. It was double-breasted, concealing his substantial bulk quite well. At a glance he looked imposing, barrel-chested, and his gray mustache and goatee showed expert barbering as well.

"Rick, how are you?" he said, in a voice that was both resonating and warm. "I'm glad you could come by. Can I get you anything? Coffee, perhaps?"

Rick shook his head and seemed about to introduce me, when Gilbert turned toward the attractive brunette.

"This is Mary Buckley, my associate," he said. "She'll be second chair on this one."

As she moved forward to shake Rick's hand, I noticed a quick movement of her eyes. Something in her body language told me she was nervous. I wondered why and figured to exploit any advantage I could. So when she turned to shake my proffered hand, I smiled and said,

"Mary, huh? Mark mentioned you."

I felt her hand stiffen in mine.

"Mark Shields?" she asked, way too quickly.

I'd touched a nerve all right. And not only with her. The Great Gilbert immediately sized up the situation and interceded with a bellicose, "Rick, who is this person?"

"He's Ron Shade," a voice from the doorway said. I turned and saw a big guy standing there, silhouetted by the hallway lights. He had wavy, reddish brown hair and a big frame. My estimate put him in his mid- to late forties, but he looked in shape. He was taller than me, at least six-four or -five, with a tough look to him. Moving forward, he extended a big hand. "I'm John Flood."

"Pleased to meet you," I said, making no effort to sound sincere.

"Ron here's a private dick," Flood said, half-turning to Gilbert as we continued to shake hands. He had a pretty powerful grip, and I wondered if this was going to degenerate into one of those hand-squeezing contests like John Wayne and Victor McLaglen in *The Quiet Man*. "He used to be on the PD until he got bounced for shooting the wrong person during a SWAT operation gone bad."

"Actually, that's not quite what happened." I grinned broadly. Never let them see you sweat. "I'd be glad to go into it another time, but since we've already been waiting close to half an hour . . ." Flood released my hand, but gazed down at me for a moment more. I was beginning to feel right at home, all right.

"Very well," the Great Gilbert said, as if pronouncing the end to the preliminary festivities. "Rick, have you discussed the offer of the settlement with your clients yet?"

"Yes, I have." Rick raised his eyebrows and shrugged in

something akin to an apology. "I'm afraid they aren't interested at this time."

Gilbert nodded and turned, saying, "Mary, will you show these gentlemen down to conference room C. We'll get things underway."

"Can you give us a moment, Mason?" Rick asked.

"Certainly," the Great Gilbert said, motioning for Flood and Mary to leave the room before him and then closing the door. When we were alone, Rick cocked his head and stared at me.

"What the hell was that all about, Ron?"

"What do you mean?"

"I mean, you were just supposed to observe. You're already antagonizing them here."

"Rick, they're running a game on you. Trying to psyche you out. Intimidate you. I've seen these kind of things all the time in the ring."

"We're not kickboxing here, dammit." His voice cracked as he said it. "I'm in charge. I'm asking the questions, not you. Get it?"

I waited for a moment, then said, "Got it."

"Good." He compressed his lips and I wondered if he was regretting bringing me along.

Maybe when Denise gets here he'll feel better, I thought, but followed him in silence out of the room.

The depositions turned out to be legalized versions of more mind games, and from what I observed, Rick was coming in a poor second. Gilbert and Mary sat on one side of a fine oak table, with Rick and me on the other side. A stenographer, using one of those elongated stenographic machines hooked up to a laptop, sat two chairs away on Gilbert's side, and the witnesses were in between us at the table's end. At least John Flood had crawled back into the woodwork somewhere. The first witness, Harry Norridge, was what they called a "street artist." He looked to be in his late twenties with shoulder-length brown hair and a voice that was more than a few octaves shy of a baritone.

"And so, Mr. Norridge, do you recall where you were on the afternoon in question, October twelfth?" the Great Gilbert asked.

"Yes, sir. I most certainly do." Norridge's voice sounded high-pitched. Like somebody had a grip on his balls. "I was in Grant Park, along Michigan. That's where I do most of my work."

"And did you happen to see a man in the park that day?"

"Yes."

"And you drew a sketch of this man, is that right?" Gilbert glanced over at us. He spoke with expert cadence, as if he and the stenographer had a mental link-up to tell him exactly when to pause for effect.

"I noticed him right off because he had a fascinating facial structure," Norridge was saying. "Very distinctive bones. I like to sketch people like that."

"And then what happened?" Gilbert's voice was clear and perfect, even though the only audience we were playing to was a steno machine.

"I approached him and showed him the drawing," Norridge said. "Asked him if he wanted to buy it." He added with a smile, "It's how I make my living."

"And did he buy it?"

"No." Norridge shrugged slightly. He had very narrow shoulders. "So I gave him one of my business cards with my cell on it. Sometimes people change their minds later and call me up."

I'll bet they do, I thought.

"And did this person call?" Gilbert asked.

"No. I didn't hear from anybody until Mr. Flood called to inquire if I recalled drawing somebody in the park that day. That's when we discovered it was Mr. Gooding."

How convenient, I thought. I wanted to say, in my best sarcastic tone, "What a strange coincidence," but I remembered Rick's admonishment and kept my mouth shut.

Gilbert pulled out a pencil etching encased in an oversized, clear plastic envelope and showed it to Norridge.

"Is this the drawing you did that day, Harry?"

Norridge gave it a cursory glance and nodded.

"An audible reply for the record, please," Gilbert prodded.

"Yes," Norridge said.

"And how do you know this?"

"It's got my signature and the date." He used a dainty finger to point out each.

"Let the record reflect that I'm tendering the aforementioned drawing to opposing counsel for his examination." Gilbert handed it to Rick, who made an interested attempt to examine it and acknowledged orally.

I reached for the drawing and Gilbert blinked, then smiled and nodded. Benevolent of him. It was Gooding, all right, or at least a pretty fair caricature of him sitting on a park bench wearing a sport coat and tie. And the date and signature were indeed there. But it could have been done anytime, I thought. I handed it back across the table. Gilbert asked a few more questions, tying things up, and said, "Nothing further."

It was then Rick's turn. I was expecting that he'd tear into this Norridge dude like a police dog biting through the back end of a burglar's pants, but he hardly asked anything pertinent at all. And when he did, Gilbert would knock him out of his rhythm by jumping in and saying that he wanted an objection noted for the record. It was even spooking the stenographer. Rick finally got Norridge to admit that he could do drawings from photographs, and these could be done at any time. He left it at that.

Next came some lounge lizard named Paul LeMatte. He looked to be in his late thirties with dark hair swept back from his forehead and a stud earring in his left ear. He walked in with a swagger and sized up Mary and the stenographer with looks that told me he thought he was God's gift to women. Before he sat, I noticed that his pants were so tight he must have used a shoe horn to slip his wallet in. The gist of his testimony was that he and Laura Gooding had been high school sweethearts.

"She was Laurie Pearson back then. When I knew her," he added with a knowing grin. I could tell he meant in the biblical sense.

"So tell me, Mr. LeMatte," the Great Gilbert asked, raising one eyebrow and pausing for a second to glance at Rick, "did Laura Gooding, nee Pearson, ever have a proclivity for using illicit drugs?"

"Objection, for the record, please," Rick said. "Hearsay."

LeMatte looked confused, and Gilbert said, "Objection is noted. Now go ahead and answer the question, Mr. LeMatte."

LeMatte shrugged and smiled. "If you're asking if she liked to get high, yeah. We used to party together."

"Objection. Relevance," Rick said.

I was beginning to be proud of him. But Gilbert just kept having the objections noted and went right on leading LeMatte through all the sordid details of Laura's drug usage in high school.

"And did you ever know her to use cocaine?" Gilbert

asked, after getting LeMatte to state that he'd seen Laura Gooding socially a few times after her divorce.

"Yeah," LeMatte said, shrugging.

"And did you use it with her?"

"I did, but actually I was just pretending to." He shrugged again. "You know how it is. It puts them in the mood."

"Indeed I do not," Gilbert said, followed by, "Nothing further."

Rick seemed stymied. He asked a few questions about where and when these dates took place. LeMatte was unable to give exact locations, but did describe the inside of Laura Gooding's residence with alacrity.

After Rick had gotten about as much as he could, he quit and the lizard left. I watched his butt jiggle in the tight pants as he walked by and thought how much I would have liked to knock the shit out of him just on general principles. Maybe a second little interview, one without the Great Gilbert and a stenographer, would be in order.

Gilbert told the stenographer that was all and waited until she'd gathered her stuff and left. Then he leaned forward on the table, his bulk supported by forearms in the tailored sleeves of his suit, and spoke in a tone that was both forceful and gentle.

"Rick, I purposely questioned Mr. LeMatte in this format to give you a preview of where this could go if we do proceed to trial." He paused and canted his head, staring at Rick with earnest-looking eyes. "Neither my client nor I have any desire to besmirch the reputation of the late Laura Gooding. However, I do intend to offer up all the pertinent facts, and it may reopen old wounds for the remainder of her family."

"Sometimes the truth hurts, Mr. Walters," Mary Buckley said. It was the first thing I'd heard her say all afternoon. I saw a glimmer of something in her eyes again, and when she caught me staring at her, she looked away. What was it? Nervousness? Guilt?

"Reconsider on the settlement offer," Gilbert said, in the same serene voice. "It's best for all concerned."

"I'll talk to my clients again, Mason," Rick said, standing and shaking the big man's hand. "But it looks like we'll be going to trial."

I stood up too, and shook Gilbert's hand, resisting the temptation to slap it, ring-style. But when I turned to offer my hand to Ms. Buckley she was already on her way out the door.

When we got to the waiting room, Denise was sitting there writing some notes on a legal pad. She looked up as we came in, smiled, and stood up. Something in Rick's expression must have told her how it went because she immediately gathered her stuff up and fell into step with us as we exited the door.

We all stayed silent walking to the elevators. When the car came and we stepped inside, Denise finally asked us:

"So how'd it go?"

Rick sighed before he answered. "I guess I never realized until today how totally outclassed I am going up against that guy."

"Bullshit," I said. "That's just what he wants you to think. The guy's all smoke and mirrors. He's got nothing."

Rick snorted and shook his head. "Yeah, right."

"What's he got?" I said, my voice rising a bit. "It was a classic case of having no case, so you come up with a horseshit alibi and attack the victim. It's what assholes like Gilbert do. Why else would him and that Flood asshole have brought up that stuff about me getting bounced from the PD?"

"Ron—" Rick started to say more, but I cut in.

"It's just like a fight. He's trying to do a psych job on you. A lot of times one fighter will psych his opponent out, especially if he's got a big reputation."

"He has that," Rick said.

"He's a shitbird," I said.

"Ron, look." Rick's tone was laced with anger. "This isn't one of your kickboxing matches, okay? It's a whole different arena. Just let me handle things."

Denise had almost interposed herself between us, giving me a fierce glare, as she put a hand almost protectively on Rick's shoulder. He seemed to stiffen suddenly at her touch, and she removed it, but the look in her eyes remained, telling me all I needed to know. This wasn't about getting her law degree, gaining experience as a paralegal, or even about winning this case. She was jonesing . . . for Rick.

"Believe me," I said, "I can tell when a guy's bluffing. I've been up against the best. This guy's beatable. He wouldn't have pulled this little stunt today if he wasn't. And did you see the way that Mary chick reacted when I mentioned that name? She's a chink in his armor."

"Stay away from her, understand?" Rick said. "The absolute last thing I need is for you to approach one of Gilbert's associates, especially a *female* associate."

Denise's eyes flared with more intensity. For a second I thought she was going to take a swing at me. The elevator slowed to an abrupt stop and the doors opened. It seemed to signal the end of our privacy, and with that, our conversation. We stepped out and Rick asked Denise what else they had on their calendar.

"There's that Keller DUI in Bridgeview tomorrow

morning, and the Peterson adoption," she said.

"Okay, since we're down here we might as well do some work on that. You bring the laptop?"

She held up her shoulder bag and nodded.

Rick turned to me.

"Ron, why don't we call it a day. We can touch bases tomorrow afternoon about one, okay?"

"Sure." I looked at Denise. "I'd like to finish up those interviews in the morning if you're up to it."

"We can do that."

"Did you get a copy of that no-contact order for me?"

She reached in her bag and handed me a thick envelope.

"Mrs. Bielmaster has one, and there's another copy in here for the local police department."

"Fine, thanks," I said. "See you tomorrow morning."

As I strolled back to the parking garage I thought about the Gilbert fiasco. From the looks of it, Rick was about ready to fold before the fight had even started. If it was one thing Chappie had taught me, it was never to give up, especially when things looked bad. Trying to bowl somebody over with bluster usually indicated a fundamental weakness somewhere. To me, that meant Gilbert knew Gooding was guilty, and had gotten off in the criminal trial. Hopefully, the civil trial would show what happened, and he'd lose. No chance of jail time now, but having to pay two and a half million bucks would buy a lot of misery for him. And after today, I wanted to see that.

In boxing, orthodox fighters are taught to work everything off the left jab, setting up the more powerful right cross. But sometimes you can catch your opponent off guard by throwing a sneaky lead right, which is considered anathema. The mention of the name to that Mary Buckley had been a sneaky right, and it had gotten a surprising response. I needed to press that advantage and find out what I could. I made a mental note to follow up on that lead. Rick wouldn't have to know.

I got to the parking garage and patted my pockets for the ticket. The attendants, a guy and a girl, were sitting several windows down, chatting and laughing. A big sign said to use the automated teller machine. I inserted the ticket, was told how much to pay by a flashing display, and stuck the bills into the slot. The machine gave me my change and the display thanked me for my patronage. The raucous laughter continued from the adjacent windows. At least somebody was having fun while they were working.

Chapter 8

On the way back south, I stopped at an Office Max and made a copy of the no-contact order. Then I called Ken Albrecht.

"You up for some more surveillance work tonight?"

"Sure, Ron. But I don't know how late I can stay." He sounded apologetic. "I have to work my other security job tomorrow morning."

"No problem. I just need you to fill in for me a while tonight. I'll relieve you at midnight, okay?" I absolutely had to get a workout in tonight or Chappie would kill me. Besides, he'd sounded funny on the phone when I'd talked to him yesterday. I wanted to see what was up.

"When do you need me?" Ken asked.

"I'll swing by now," I said. "I'm in the neighborhood."

I was at his house in ten minutes, and in another five we were heading over to 111th Street.

"You drink?" I asked.

He gave me a sideways look and grinned.

"Sure, don't everybody?"

I didn't want to ruin his idealism by telling him that I didn't. Instead, I asked him what he liked.

He shrugged. "Beer, I guess."

"Good." I took out my wallet and handed him a twenty. "I'll drop you off down the block, and when you see me come out of this liquor store, go in and buy a six-pack. Keep your eyes open for a young white kid. I'm pretty sure he'll be talking to an older guy behind the counter."

Ken nodded, all serious.

"He's Tim Knop, our target," I said. "I want you to get a look at him up close, but don't want him to know what you look like for now."

"Roger that."

"You forgot to say 'wilco,' " I said, smiling.

The door jingled when I went in, and Uncle was behind the counter doing something with the cash register. He looked up, all smiles, and asked what he could help me with.

"Where's Tim at?" I said, keeping my voice imbued with as much intimidation as I could muster.

He looked at me more closely, a faint recognition dawning in his eyes, his mouth hanging open for a moment, then his lower lip tightened up in a puckering movement.

"I remember you," he said. "And I know you're not from probation. So why don't you leave him alone, for Christ's sake?"

"I got some papers to serve him with." I patted my jacket pocket.

"Papers? What kind of papers?"

I stared at him for a second, then said, "Where's he at?"

"I don't have to tell you." His voice rose an octave, like a small kid faking bravado as he whistled past the graveyard. "This is borderline harassment. I'll call the Office of Professional Standards."

"Good, you do that. Now, where the fuck is he?" It was the second time in two days I'd used the "F" word for effect. But I was playing a role, and it looked like I was batting a thousand.

His lips trembled for a moment, then his throat worked as he swallowed.

"He's in the back." He looked down. "Same place as last time."

I nodded a mock thanks, and strode toward the double doors that led to the stockroom. Knop was there all right, but he'd obviously been listening. Instead of stacking boxes, he was standing in the middle of the floor, arms akimbo.

"My attorney told me to ask for your badge number," he said.

I smirked.

"He did, did he?" I held up the no-contact order. "Here's a little something you can show him instead." I held it out toward him, and when he made no move to accept it, I laid the paper on a nearby stack of bottles. "It's a no-contact order preventing you from approaching, contacting, or harassing the Bielmasters, or going near their property. You'll be officially notified by mail tomorrow or the next day, but I wanted to bring by another copy so there's no misunderstanding."

His frown looked as sour as his uncle's had. Maybe it ran in the family.

"I ain't been harassing nobody," he said.

"Yeah, right. I happen to know that you were hanging around there night before last."

"That's bullshit."

I smiled.

"Look, kid, let me spell it out for you," I said slowly. "Go by their house, call them up, go by the school, contact Grace in any way, and I'll have you back in stir so fast your fucking head'll be spinning." I figured the use of profanity one more time would add the necessary element of intimidation. "And this time it won't be no namby-pamby juvenile detention facility. You're over seventeen now, brother, which means you get violated, you be doing penitentiary time."

His lips moved, but no sound came out. For a moment I

thought he might rush me and I'd have to deck him. The prospect of doing so brought a delicious, but guilty, feeling of anticipation to my mind. He was obviously no match for me physically, but the prospect of finally being able to confront one of my abstract problems in a physical manner that I was confident of, filled me with relish. Still, he was a kid, and I also knew that if I did flatten him, I'd probably regret it later.

"If you're feeling froggie," I said, winking at him, "leap. But keep in mind it'll be a quicker way back to the big house. Once you get out of the hospital, that is."

He blinked, and for a second I thought I saw his eyes well up, and the tension seemed to dissipate from his body, like the air going out of a balloon.

"Look, just leave Grace alone, got it?"

He wiped at his face as he partially turned away.

"You got it all wrong about Grace and me, mister. All wrong. I never meant to hurt her . . . Never forced her to do nothing . . ."

"Un-huh," I said, and patted the no-contact order several times, staring at him all the while. He'd been officially served in person, and would be again by mail, so tonight, if he was out lurking, he'd be in cuffs tomorrow. I slowly turned and went back out the doors. The uncle was standing where I'd left him, behind the counter. He had the look of a defeated man. I waved to him as I walked past.

I went out to my car, got in, and waited. After about ten minutes I saw Ken leaving the store carrying a six-pack of beer under his arm. He walked slowly, nonchalantly, down the street. Just a young guy home from work and ready to enjoy a few beers in front of the tube. When he got close I started the Firebird and pulled around the corner out of sight, just in case. As soon as I stopped he got in.

"I hope you like Bud," he said, holding up the connected cans.

I shook my head. "It's yours. You see our target?"

"Yeah," he said, turning to put the beer on the back seat. "That's Tim Knop, huh? Doesn't look like much."

"Right now he looks like a thorn in my side. You eat dinner yet?"

"Not really."

"I'll drop you off at my house and you can take the Beater. Go get something to eat and then set up on Knop's place. He should be leaving the store any time now."

"You gonna be at Bielmaster's?"

"For a while. But I absolutely have to get to the gym tonight."

He nodded, then started to say something, but stopped.

"Yeah, I know," I said. "I'll be back to relieve you by eleven or so."

Ken grinned. "You think all this work for Windy City Knights will get me in good with Detective Grieves? I really was hoping to get on the PD soon."

"Sure it will," I said. "You'll be as good as in with his recommendation." Great advice, I thought, coming from the guy who was fired from the force.

It was close to six by the time I dropped Ken off, shot home to feed the cats, and grabbed my gym bag. I checked my messages and found three from Chappie telling me to make sure I called him as soon as I got in, and to make sure I made it by tonight for a workout. His tone in the last message had a note of urgency in it, so I dialed the gym and got Brice.

"Is Chappie there?" I asked him.

"Yeah, but he's in the ring working with Marcus," Brice

said. "Hold on and I'll go tell him it's you. He's been saying that if you called, to get him right away."

"No, don't bother him." I knew how seriously Chappie took his training sessions, whether it was with me, Marcus, or Raul, and I certainly didn't want to interrupt the process. "Just tell him I'll be there shortly."

I called Ursula Bielmaster next and asked if I could stop by to talk to her and Grace. She said they were just finishing supper and to come ahead. After making sure my light-timers were all set, I was walking out the door a few minutes later. On the drive over I contemplated what I wanted to say to them, and how I could go about it. I still had to get Grace alone to ask her a few things before I could really pin down exactly what I was up against. But it was a delicate situation and I had to be discreet. Another idea flashed in my mind as I turned down their street and pulled up several doors from their house. The neighborhood looked quiet and peaceful in the fading winter darkness. The days were already getting noticeably longer, and pretty soon it would be time to spring ahead on the clocks as daylight savings time began. I switched to the talk mode on the cell phone and called Ken, asking if he was there.

"Roger that," he said.

"Any activity?"

"Negative. I watched the target enter his house ten minutes ago. I'm set up so I can see if he leaves by car, too."

"Good. Stay ready. I'm going to call you again in about ten minutes and ask you again if you're in position. Just say that you are."

"Roger that," he said.

I smirked at his military protocol and resisted the temptation to say, "Shade out."

I walked down half a block to Bielmaster's and rang the

bell. An enclosed porch separated the steps from the actual front entrance. I waited while the curtain moved back on the interior door and a female silhouette appeared against the backlit living room. It was Ursula. I waved and called out who I was.

She came through the porch and let me in, smiling. Grace Bielmaster greeted me shyly as I was ushered inside and sat on the couch. She was wearing a brown sweater and tight jeans, and had a paperback book in her hands. I couldn't quite see the title. A framed family photo graced the mantel across from me. Ursula, Grace, and Papa in his dress uniform. He had a big grin on his face. Something I certainly wasn't accustomed to seeing.

"I just stopped by to tell you that I personally served him with the no-contact order this evening," I said. "If he comes around here at all, he violates the judge's order and can be arrested."

Ursula smiled and heaved a sigh. "Thank you, but do you really think that it will keep him away?"

"It's another tool," I said. I started to say something else, then paused and did an exaggerated yawn.

"You look tired, Mr. Shade," Ursula said.

"Yeah, long night last night." I smiled as benignly as I could. "We were outside watching the place."

She smiled a silent thank-you. I smiled back.

"Say, you wouldn't have any coffee by chance, would you?"

"Certainly. I'll get you some. How do you like it?"

"Cream, no sugar, please."

Ursula nodded and got up, leaving Grace and me alone for the moment. Her gaze followed her mother, then went to me. From there, she adjusted herself in the chair and opened her book. It was a paperback version of *Suddenly, Last Summer.*

"We need to talk," I said.

She looked down at the carpet. "I know."

I glanced toward the kitchen. Mrs. Bielmaster moved past the door with the glass coffee pot, filling a cup. It looked like she was gonna nuke it.

"When would be a good time?" I asked.

She sighed and bit her lip.

"Here," I said. "My card. My cell phone number's on it. Could you call me sometime tonight or tomorrow?"

"We're going over to the hospital tonight. And I have drama practice tomorrow."

I glanced at the book. "Tennessee Williams in a Catholic girls' school?"

She almost smiled as she shook her head. "No, I'm just reading this on my own. We're doing Shakespeare. *A Midsummer Night's Dream.*"

I heard the bell of the microwave ring. "You said just cream, right, Mr. Shade?"

"That'd be fine." I turned to Grace and lowered my voice. "I've heard your parents' version of this, I've heard Tim Knop's version. Now I need to hear from you. Call me."

She nodded as her mother came back in the room with a steaming cup of coffee. I thanked her and took a sip. It was just this side of awful, but it had served its purpose. Now for the rest of Plan B.

"Like I said, Knop's been served with the order, so if he comes sneaking around here, myself and my partner will drag him into the station and sign complaints." I picked up the phone, making sure the mode button was still on talk. "Ken, you still in position?"

"Roger, boss," Ken's voice said.

"Anything stirring?"

"Nothing. All's quiet."

This time I beat him to it. "Roger, keep me posted. Shade out."

I could barely suppress a grin as I took another drink of the coffee and then stood.

"We'll be out there all night again, watching his every move. Don't worry about a thing. If he comes here, we'll be on him."

"We feel so much better knowing that, don't we, Grace?" Ursula turned to her daughter, who shrugged a quick smile.

On the way to the gym I mulled over what Grace was likely to tell me if and when she did call tomorrow. Considering that women, even young women, seldom become pregnant after one brief encounter, except in books, movies, and the plays of Tennessee Williams, Tim Knop's version was probably a little bit closer to the truth than what Bielmaster had originally described to me. That left me with three versions . . . Four, if you counted the actual truth. But even if she didn't call, my secondary plan might shed some light on the situation anyway. I'd let Ken sit on Knop's house until eleven. If, when I relieved him, the target was still chilling at home, I'd give it a few hours and then head back myself. If the Bielmaster women thought we were out there all night, and if the news of this surveillance somehow got tipped to the target, that, in itself, would be elucidating. And the dividend would be, Knop might think we were out there watching, too, even if we weren't. It was something just this side of a mind game. A psych-out. Sort of like having a big, bad reputation. Like the Great Gilbert making something out of nothing.

I wished I could have made Rick see that.

When I got to the gym I nodded to Brice, who said that Chappie was still in the boxing section. I figured I'd just head over to the locker room and change to save time, but as I started across the room I heard a feminine voice call my name. I turned to see Kris approaching, looking like a *Sports Illustrated* swimsuit model in spandex. This outfit definitely was designed to accent her best features. And there were plenty of them to accent, too.

"Hi," she said, stopping next to me. She looked slightly flushed, but not real sweaty. "I was wondering if you were going to show. Missed you at the office."

"Yeah, Rick and I parted company downtown earlier."

She rolled her eyes. "Don't I know that."

I looked at her questioningly and she smiled. It was a very nice smile. She had great teeth. Perfectly aligned. Her parents had probably spent a fortune on good orthodontics.

"Denise practically went ballistic when she found out that you didn't leave me those tapes," she said. "I didn't know whether to try to cover, or just tell the truth."

"Oh shit, I forgot about them." I shrugged. "There's always tomorrow."

"Is that a Ron Shade proverb?"

"Actually, it's an old Spanish saying. But I like it." I grinned. "I really will have them tomorrow. After I finish here, I've got a surveillance planned, so I'll have plenty of time to talk into a tape recorder. Want me to include any jokes?"

"A surveillance? On the Gooding case?"

I was just about to tell her it was unrelated when Chappie called out to me. I saw him motioning me toward the office with an urgency I couldn't ignore.

"I'll tag up with you later," I said. "My trainer wants a word with me."

Kris smiled and nodded. I half-turned to avoid two girls walking and chatting as I was moving toward the office, and caught a glimpse of her watching me.

Chappie motioned me to sit down in the chair next to his desk. He always referred to it as his "serious speaking chair," and it was usually reserved for business of one kind or another.

"Got that call from Saul today," he said. "That Vegas fight's on, if you're interested."

"Sure, why not? Maybe it'll get us noticed. I could use another shot at the title."

He nodded, his face serious.

"Who's it against?"

He shook his head. "Not sure. Saul told me they asked about you. How good you was, was you in shape, could you take a fight on short notice . . ."

"I hope he talked about me in glowing terms."

Chappie smiled. "You got that right. He bragged you up. Great fighter. Professional. Always in shape. Never backs out." He chuckled. "He gonna have to go see his rabbi Saturday to make up for all that lying."

"Thanks a lot." I studied him. Something was wrong. He was holding back. "So what's the problem?"

He licked his lips and looked down. "It's international rules. Fight's gonna allow them damn leg kicks."

I shrugged. "That'll just mean I'll have to knock the dude out quicker."

"Or dance," he said. "How your leg been feeling?"

"My leg's fine. I can do this, no sweat. How's the money?"

"Still waiting on all the details. Like I said, they just

asking at this point. Nothing for sure yet." He sighed and shook his head. "You know, I still ain't been feeling right about letting you fight that last one with them leg kicks."

"Hey, as long as I know it's coming. The good thing is, there won't be any minimum kick rule either, and that's always a plus."

"So it's a go then? You feel ready?"

"Ready, willing, and hopefully able."

"Good." He stood. "I'll take you through the rough one tonight, then we'll spend the rest of the week going light. This is Thursday, so we got about eight days. Once I find out more about who you be fighting, we'll figure a fight plan."

"Sounds good," I said, standing. He was still seated and staring at me. "What?"

"Who's that girl I saw you talking to?"

Oh great, I thought. Here comes the women-weaken-legs speech again.

"Just a friend," I said. "We're working at the same place right now."

"You know the rules."

"How could I forget them? You remind me every week or so."

He grinned and told me to get dressed and meet him in the ring in five.

The workout went pretty well, as ball-busters do. I went through my usual warm-up and stretching routine and did one round on each of the bags. That made three. Marcus was working the speedbag next to me and at the buzzer break he looked at me.

"You tell Chappie about the other night?" he asked.

I shook my head.

He stared at me sullenly, then said, "Thanks."

"Thank me by staying away from that shit. And that Dewayne Clifford guy, too."

He turned without speaking and began the rhythmic pounding again, even before the minute break period was over. I watched him work. He was an impressive kid headed down the wrong road. I wondered if there was anything I could do. The buzzer sounded and I began my next session on the bag. When I finished I was starting to sweat. All warmed up, I turned and saw my buddy Raul Sanchez slipping into the ring with Chappie. He motioned me over, and I nodded to Marcus and left.

Working with Raul, who's lighter and faster than I am, was always exhausting. He had the edge on speed, but didn't hit as hard. We were both wearing helmets and sixteen-ounce gloves, which reduced the punching power. After two rounds I started to find my rhythm and my second wind. I caught him against the ropes and punished his body. When I delivered the last blow I heard him grunt and backed off a tad, letting him off the hook. Chappie gave me hell between rounds.

"You train that way, you gonna fight that way in the ring for real," he said, his finger inches from my face. "Now don't be messing around like that again. You get your man in trouble, you finish him, understand?"

I nodded and adjusted the helmet slightly with my gloves. When I turned my head I saw that we had an audience of one. Kris was watching from the doorway.

Intent on looking impressive, I was Mr. Quick for the next three minutes. Chappie yelled for Raul to start hitting me hard with the leg kicks. He looked at me and I nodded. The first one bounced off my left thigh. We were wearing foot protectors, so the force was diminished slightly, but it still hurt. In the real fight we'd both be barefoot. If my opponent's legs were conditioned to receive and deliver punishment, I'd be in for a long night. On the other hand, since I was taking the fight on short notice, maybe it was better not to look too impressive. All I had to do was win.

I paid the price for my ruminations a split second later when Raul came across with a hard right that stung me. Instinctively, I lashed out with a left hook and caught him on the button. He went down like an unraveling clothesline. He lay on his back and I walked to the other side of the ring. A neutral corner, waiting for the imaginary ten count. I saw the flash of a grin as Chappie knelt, checking on him, taking out the mouthpiece with one hand and giving me a thumbs-up with the other, indicating that Raul was okay and that the hook had been picture-perfect.

Yeah, I felt ready. Whoever, or whatever, was waiting in Vegas, I thought, bring 'em on.

After we made sure Raul was all right, and I'd gotten my debrief/critique from Chappie, I headed for the showers. It was close to nine, and I had just enough time to clean up, run home to grab my weapon and surveillance stuff, including the miniature tape recorder, and get something to eat before relieving Ken. Kris was sitting on the bench along the wall of the aerobics room and got up when I started across.

"Hey, Ron."

I paused. She'd obviously showered and changed into her street clothes, a nice navy sweater and some snug blue jeans. She'd redone her makeup, too.

"Quite a performance, big guy," she said.

"Aww shucks, ma'am," I said, feigning a cowboy accent. " 'Tweren't nothing."

"Is your friend going to be okay? I jumped when you hit him. It looked like his feet left the floor."

"He's fine. But that's why we stopped. I hit him a little harder than I intended. It was instinctive, and that's what you get when you drop your guard."

"I'll have to remember not to do that around you," she said, showing me those perfect teeth again. "So, we have time for another juice date?"

I smiled back.

"Nothing would please me more, but unfortunately I have that surveillance. I have to go relieve my partner."

"Yeah, so is this a Gooding thing?" Her lips jerked into a quick Mona Lisa smile that disappeared. "I mean, am I going to hear about it on tape tomorrow?"

"Wait and see," I said. "But I'll definitely have them for you in the morning."

"Good. That'll keep Denise happy."

"Hey, don't let her get to you. I figured out why she's so hyper."

"Because she's not getting any?" she said with a sly smile.

I was almost taken aback by her remark, but I liked forward, no-nonsense women as well as the next guy.

"I think she's got a case of the jones for Rick," I said.

"Does she?"

I was a bit surprised again, this time because she was familiar with the street term, which I had figured on having to explain. This was one interesting lady, all right. I was beginning to realize that there was a lot more to her than I originally thought. And, Chappie's warning aside, I hoped to get the opportunity to learn more about her at some point in the very near future.

Just not tonight, I thought.

"Say," I said, turning to head for the men's locker room. "It seems like we're always having conversations when one of us is sweaty. I'd better hit the shower."

"Okay, but hey." She held out a piece of paper with some writing on it. "Here's my numbers. Home and cell. Call me sometime."

I gripped the paper between my forefinger and thumb and said that I would, resisting the temptation to ask if this was in case I'd lost her card from before. I smiled instead, thinking that things were definitely looking up.

Chapter 9

When the alarm went off at 6:15, I silently cursed myself for deciding to get up and run. I could have cursed out loud, since it wouldn't have bothered the cats, all three of whom just looked at me sleepily before lowering their heads to go back to sleep. But I knew, as I pulled on my sweatpants, socks, and double sweatshirts, that the run was a necessity if I had a fight in eight days. That decided, I slipped on my stocking cap, laced up my running shoes, and grabbed my cold weather mittens. Before I closed the back door I re-checked the keys in my left glove. I always kept my right hand free so that I could deliver a solid punch if I had to. In troubled times I also had a small derringer that I could keep in the mitten as well. But today I figured my straight right would suffice.

It was just beginning to get light as I made it out onto the street, and started running under the nascent sky and streetlights. The temperature had continued to rise, and most of the fallen snow was now reduced to standing puddles or piles of slush. That, along with the days getting warmer and noticeably longer, made me feel strangely optimistic. Maybe we'd have an early spring.

As I rounded the first corner and headed down for the long stretch, I did what I usually do whenever I had a long run and a lot on my mind. The first thing I thought about was the upcoming fight and I took some small solace in not knowing who my opponent was. It was one way to avoid a case of the nerves. In my previous two big title shots, the training had been almost as much mental as physical.

Leading up to both of them, I kept seeing my prospective opponents, Anthony Berger and Elijah Day, dancing just ahead of me on every morning run, or looking around a corner at the gym when I was struggling to get in shape. This time no one lurked ahead except an unknown figure: Mr. XXX. The triple X guy was nebulous and less threatening, but on the other hand, not knowing who I would be facing made it impossible to envision the delivery of a countering straight right over my opponent's lazy left jab, or feeling the arcing impact of a perfectly delivered left hook. I'd felt that last night at the gym when I'd caught Raul.

I switched to the roadway as the sidewalk ended near the second set of railroad tracks. A car honked as it went by, swerving way farther than it had to, and sending a spray of cold slush over my legs and feet. Since I had my mittens on and couldn't give him the finger, I put my left hand on the inner aspect of my right elbow and lifted my right arm in the second most recognizable symbol of flashing someone the bird. The driver slowed, and for a moment I fantasized him stopping to make something of it and me getting a little bit of extra sparring in. But the car sped up and disappeared, the red taillights glowing ever fainter as the early morning continued to lighten.

Back to the tasks at hand, I thought. The Bielmaster case. I'd stayed on the surveillance until just past midnight. The ruse that I'd tried, calling Ken in front of Grace and making sure I told them how we'd be out there all night again, made me more convinced than ever that Grace was tipping Knop to our presence. This, in turn, brought up a couple more questions: Had she been a willing participant, rather than a victim? And did her father use his clout to get Knop sent away for a few years on a statutory charge? It would have been mean-spirited and vindictive, and sounded exactly like the "Lt. Bilemaster" that I'd come to know and not love. Grace was probably carrying around more than her share of guilt over the whole affair. It might explain her reticence to talk to me. She'd seemed distant in a nervous, almost ashamed sort of way when we'd met. But after all, she was still pretty young, and I knew from experience that when faced with a rough situation at a tender age, you don't always make the right decisions. I filed that one under "further investigation needed," and toyed with the idea of letting Ken take over the surveillance duties while I concentrated on training for this fight. Mr. Triple X surfaced in my thoughts again.

I tried to tell myself that all I had to do was win. Looking impressive might not even be necessary. If I looked too good, the champion's people might figure I was too dangerous and not want to give me a shot at the title. On the other hand, not looking good might make them think I wouldn't be a good draw.

Mind games. They'd snuck up on me anyway. Just like they were sneaking up on Rick. I had to figure a way to make him see that. At least we had worthy opponents in the Great Gilbert and John Flood. Too worthy in Rick's eyes. They were using their reps to psych him out, to get him to feel defeated before they even started. Gilbert's ploy yesterday had been coupled with a settlement offer. Why would they do that if they had a strong case? The answer was, they knew they didn't, so they tried to dazzle us with bullshit. Smoke and mirrors, just like I said. Why else would Flood have tried to embarrass or discredit me in front of everybody by bringing up the SWAT foul-up and my less-than-glorious exit from the police department?

They messed with the wrong guy, I told myself, and threw a double jab, right cross, left hook combination as I was running. In my mind's eye, I saw Gilbert knocked on his fat ass.

That whole session yesterday had been nothing but bullshit, and I made a mental note to have George run checks on Gilbert's two surprise witnesses. I could have done it myself, but the service I used was slow and somewhat less than thorough, whereas George could do it on the sly on the police computer in a matter of seconds. He owed me for getting me into this Bielmaster mess anyway.

I turned a corner and headed for the third hill of my four-mile run. The wind shifted and suddenly I felt a cold chill where the slush had soaked through my sweatpants and shoes. A good reminder that sometimes things have a way of sneaking back to come bite you in the ass.

When I walked into Rick's office at 9:05, I was carrying a paper bag with two coffees, extra sugar packets, and three little creamers. Kris looked up at me and smiled.

"I come bearing gifts," I said, holding the bag up, "and tapes."

"Oh good," she said.

"I finished them while I was on my surveillance last night, and I did manage to put in a joke or two from time to time." I took out my coffee, and then set hers on the desk. "I didn't know how you liked it, so I got you extra cream and sugar in the bag."

"Thank you. You're so sweet."

Before we could say anything else, Denise was on us like a circling hawk, asking if I'd brought in the recordings for Kris to type.

"Yes, ma'am," I said, trying for cordial humor.

"Well, why aren't you working on them then?" she said,

directing her stare at Kris. Then to me: "Mr. Walters is waiting in his office."

I watched her butt as she walked away. Perky under the plaid dress she was wearing. I wondered if she ever loosened up enough to have any fun.

Kris shrugged and winked at me as I left. Inside his office Rick had a bunch of papers spread out in front of him on his desk. He looked up and nodded as I came in.

"Just going over some of my notes on the depositions from yesterday," he said.

"Yeah," I said. "I wanted to talk to you about them. I'm going to run a records check on those two knuckleheads."

He shook his head. "I don't know . . ."

"What's not to know? Gilbert obviously was trying to intimidate us. He doesn't have a case and he knows it. Ask him who he thinks killed Laura Gooding."

"I intend to," Rick said. "In court. When I get Gooding on the stand. In the meantime, I don't want it to seem like we're trying to intimidate his witnesses."

"Intimidate? Hell, I ain't even got started yet."

"Ron," he said, his voice full of warning, "let's tone it down a notch, okay? He was just extending an offer. Trying to be courteous. Letting me know that if we proceed to trial, it could get ugly."

"It's already ugly."

"Ron, it's what lawyers do." He stared up at me with something akin to condescension.

"Shit. Can't you see that you're falling for his mind game?" I was getting angry now. The morning's run had done little to relieve the sense of frustration I'd been feeling since yesterday's depositions, but maybe it had buoyed my confidence that I could persuade Rick to see the light as well.

"It's just like a fight," I said. "Your opponent wants you to think he's this big, invincible, tough superman . . ."

"Look, will you stop with the damn kickboxing metaphors? I understand your point, but this is a different arena here. My arena." He paused and took a breath, still staring up at me with anger in his eyes. "Now just stop with all your theorizing and start doing what I'm paying you to do."

I started to say something, but thought better of it. No sense getting him any more pissed off than he already was.

"I mean," he continued, looking down at the sea of papers on his desk, "all I need you to do is follow up on the things Tunney already investigated, make sure we can locate our witnesses, and check out any last-minute things I need you to, all right?"

I nodded. Peripherally, I saw Denise standing off to my right, giving me the evil-eye stare.

"Good." He picked up some papers, but I could tell it was just to have something to do. To look busy rather than look at my reproachful expression. "Now, what have you got planned for today?"

I took a breath. "Well, I guess I'll follow up on that last State's Attorney interview. The one who's in private practice."

"Good. Take Denise along. I've got a few other cases in court, then I'll swing back here and read your reports. You bring in that tape?"

"I might be able to move faster on this alone," I said. "Why don't you keep Denise here working with you? You two could go to lunch and unwind, or something."

I saw her stiffen at my suggestion, her eyes widening in anger.

Rick sighed. "Look, Ron, I'm sorry if I came down on you kind of hard. I know you're only trying to help." He shot me a weak smile. "But let's try to work together as a team, okay? This is the biggest case of my career so far, and I think I've got it pretty well thought out."

"As long as you have a fight plan, sticking to it is half the battle," I said. "At least that's what Chappie says."

But what I didn't say was that Chappie always adds, "As long as it's the *right* fight plan."

As we were driving back up to the North Shore, I was in such a foul mood that I reached into the back seat of the Firebird and took out my CD case. I noticed Denise watching me, still with the residual evil eye, so I decided to try and bridge the gap a little.

"What are you in the mood for?" I set the case on her lap. "I've got Sinatra, Elvis, Linda Ronstadt . . ."

"Whatever," she said.

"No, you choose. Got Gloria Estefan in there, too."

"What's that supposed to mean?"

Oh great, I thought. Looks like I touched a nerve with that one.

"Well, you're Latina, aren't you?"

"Is that supposed to mean Hispanic?" Her tone was snippy. Condescending.

"What is your last name anyway? I remember Rick introducing us, but I got a terrible memory for names."

"A good trait for a detective."

"Yeah," I said, feeling a twinge of anger myself now. "Too bad there isn't a copy of Dale Carnegie's book in there."

"Who?"

"He wrote *How to Win Friends and Influence People.*" I gently took back the case, removed *Sinatra Reprise: The Very Good Years*, and shoved the disc in. The Chairman of the

Board. It was time for us guys to take a stand. He began singing "The Last Dance."

I should be so lucky, I thought.

We rode on in silence, listening. If she liked or disliked the music, she never let on. By the time number twenty, "Theme from *New York, New York*," came on, we were almost there.

Julia Horton turned out to be nothing like I expected. She was kind of heavyset, in a big-boned sort of way, and had one of those dainty faces. But she had a mouth like a sailor. Plus, she smoked. The hazy air was really making me uncomfortable as we sat in her private office on the fifth floor of a suburban office building. She seemed to notice Denise and me wincing, and blew a stream of smoke away from us.

"Sorry," she said, "but every time I try to quit these fucking things, I gain a ton of weight." She gave a mock grimace and held her hands out to her sides. "And as you can see, I can't afford that."

I smiled noncommittally, thinking that losing the pounds would beat trying to get a lung transplant.

"Getting back to the Gooding case," I said, trying hard to take shallow breaths.

"Yeah, really fucked up," she said. "We thought we had it won. Thought it was a slam-dunk. That judge was a real asshole. Good old Foxworth." She took another drag and smiled as she let the smoke seep out of her mouth with her words. For a moment, it looked almost sexy. Like Lauren Bacall in *To Have and Have Not*. *"You know how to whistle, don't you, Harry? You just put your lips together and blow."* But Lauren Bacall was too thin for this comparison. . . . Maybe Jane Russell saying the line?

"Why do you think the judge went with a directed verdict?"

She tilted her head a little and smiled. Definitely Jane Russell-ish.

Unfortunately she blew out more smoke as I pondered the image in black and white. She suddenly emitted a cough.

"You okay?" I asked.

She nodded, finishing her hacking. "Guess I really do need to quit." She took one more drag and stubbed out the butt.

Praise the Lord, I thought.

"Him and Gilbert go way back," she said, shaking her head. "He always had an eye for the ladies, too. Maybe that's why Gilbert had Mary Buckley as his second chair. She's hot. Not that he let her do much at the trial except sit there, smile at old Foxworth, and look pretty."

"I take it she's a bimbo?" I asked.

Having gotten her coughing fit under control, Horton again reached for her cigarettes. She shook her head as she fished one out.

"No, she's a sharp cookie," she said, sticking the cigarette between her lips, but not lighting it. "She used to work for our office. Went head-to-head with Gilbert on a couple of occasions. Won one, lost one. He was impressed enough to hire her."

I raised my eyebrows. "Who better than a former prosecutor to have in your corner?"

Horton smirked and flicked her Bic. At least she blew the smoke away from me again.

"Good thing they haven't enforced the no-smoking policy in private offices," she said. "I don't have a fire escape." She grinned and so did I. "What else can I tell you? I thought we'd win hands down. Should've won, too, but we didn't."

"Any idea why?"

She smiled again.

"You gotta be kidding, right?" I saw a flash of something in her eyes as she canted her head. "I already told you Foxworth was a joke. I'd come in, in the morning while we were at trial, and hear him and Gilbert swapping jokes in judge's chambers."

"You're not saying he unfairly influenced the judge, are you?" Denise asked. From the mixture of horror and outrage in her tone, I figured her idealism was going down for the third time.

Horton shook her head as she brought the cigarette to her lips again.

"I'm glad you guys are going after Gooding civilly," she said. "How much you asking for?"

"Two million," I said.

She nodded an approval. "The prick can certainly afford it. Nail the bastard."

"He's claiming to be almost broke," Denise said.

"Don't you believe it," Horton shot back. "Mason Gilbert doesn't come cheap."

"We're looking at all his assets," Denise said. She started doing a muffled little cough, and I wondered if the smoke was bothering her as much as it was me.

"O'Riley said to ask you about Mark Shields," I said, watching Horton's reaction carefully. All I saw was confusion.

"Who?"

I pretended to look down at my notes. "Mark Shields. Supposed to have been an intern, or something, with the Great Gilbert."

"The Great Gilbert," she said with a laugh. "I like that. The prick." She took another hefty drag as she contemplated. I was beginning to wonder if this interview was worth the price my lungs were paying. "Oh, okay. Now I remember. He was an intern, all right. Mary introduced us once during a recess. Nice kid. Don't know what happened to him."

"Know anything more about him?" I asked.

She shook her head, then said with a sly smile, "Well, he was good-looking."

"Anything else you can think of that might help us?"

Horton looked thoughtful for a moment, took another long drag on her square, and blew a stream toward the ceiling.

"Not really." She smiled wistfully. "Just nail the bastard. He did it. No doubt. He should be sitting in a cell somewhere worrying about when he's going to get the needle and banging his head against the walls."

She was definitely a girl after my own heart, but I'd eaten enough secondhand smoke for one day.

"Sounds like you should've stayed a State's Attorney." I stood up. Denise did the same, but Horton just got a faraway look in her eyes.

"Yeah, sometimes I think so, too," she said.

Back in the car I suddenly had an idea. I looked at Denise and asked, "What law school do you go to?"

"Why?"

"Do you always answer a question with a question?"

"I'm studying to be a lawyer, aren't I?" And for the first time I thought I saw a hint of a smile on her lips. Maybe the weather wasn't the only thing thawing. "John Marshall."

"Good place to start," I said and began heading for Plymouth Court.

"Wait a minute. We're not going there, are we?"

"If it's one thing I've learned in this business, it's to trust your gut. I've got a feeling that we need to trace down this Mark Shields guy."

"But we may be wasting time," Denise said. The whine in her voice was back. So much for warmer weather and thawings.

"I don't think so. The mention of his name affected that Mary Buckley chick. It's something we need to follow up on."

"But I've got work to do. Back at the office."

With Rick, I thought with a grin. "Just think how proud your boss will be if we come up with something. Plus, we need to check out all the angles. I'm sure Rick would agree. Want me to call him?"

"No," she said, as if doing so would disturb the Pope at afternoon vespers.

"Okay then. I'll walk you through some of the basic techniques for investigation."

"I'm studying to be a lawyer, not a PI."

"And it's something every good lawyer should know how to do—investigate a case from the ground up. Find the truth." I could see from her expression that I wasn't getting anywhere. "Besides, you won't always have me around to wet-nurse you."

"Yeah, right." She crossed her arms over her breasts and went into her customary little pout.

But to her credit, once we got to the law school, she directed me to the library and began helping right away. Except for my Beretta setting off the security metal detector, and having to show my identification and PI license to a host of nervous security guards, we found the yearbooks with no problem. But that was where the trail ended.

"See?" Denise said. "No Mark Shields listed. Can we go now?"

She'd been almost this side of helpful during the search, but whether that was because she genuinely wanted to assist me, or that she just wanted to get back to Rick's sooner, I harbored little doubt.

"We can," I said, glancing at my watch. Ten-thirty. It was still early. I did a quick scan until I found the section I was looking for. The phone books. I went over to them and pulled down a thick volume of the Yellow Pages.

"Now what are you doing?" Denise asked.

"Looking up law schools."

"And may I ask why?"

I ran my finger down the page until I found the alphabetical listing.

"Copying machine close?" I asked.

She pointed to one across the way.

I closed the book, keeping my index finger in the spot I'd found, and fished in my pants pocket for spare change.

"Does this thing take dollars?" I asked.

She rolled her eyes, reached in her purse, and took out a small change purse.

"Here." She handed me a couple of quarters with a heaved, theatric sigh.

"Thanks," I said, opening the cover and placing the page facedown on the glass. I held up the quarter. "I'm good for it."

She rolled her eyes. "And we're doing this for . . . ?"

"To save time. Beats writing out all the addresses of places we're going to check."

"You don't mean this morning, do you?"

I grinned and nodded, dropping the quarter into the slot. The machine came to life and the light rotated, spilling out under the closed flap where it couldn't cover the bulk of the book.

"And how long are we going to spend on this wild goose chase?" she asked, crossing her arms again.

"As long as it takes," I said, remembering an old Airborne expression.

After zooming by Kent Law School, due to its proximity, we then got on LSD and went north to Sheridan Road, which, in turn, led us to Northwestern, the library, and ultimately pay dirt. The third time was the charm. I felt Denise standing close, looking over my arm, as I tapped the yearbook with my finger.

"Julia Horton was right," she said. "He is cute."

"Control your hormones. We've got work to do."

I bummed another quarter from Denise and copied the page with Mark Shields's photo and brief bio on it. There wasn't much, other than he'd made *Law Review* his final semester. Next, in the hallway, I called the secretary's office at the law school section on my cell phone. She proved to be about as helpful as the copy machine had been.

"I'm sorry, sir, any information about our students is confidential," she said.

"But it's important I get in touch with him. There might be a job involved."

"Our placement center can help you then," she said. "Should I transfer you, or do you want to call back?"

"Just give me the number, please," I said, figuring I'd have a better shot if I called directly, avoiding the stigma of being shuffled around, transferred from one uncaring bureaucratic flunky to the next.

The placement center woman was nicer, but equally unhelpful. "I can take your information and have someone follow up on it, sir, but I can't give you any direct contact information. I'm sorry," she added. At least her voice was less gruff than the secretary's had been. I left her my cell phone number and my answering service number.

"Have you tried the alumni association?" she asked before we disconnected.

I hadn't, but I did, to similar avail. Shields had graduated, and seemingly severed all ties to his alumni. I exhaled slowly and looked around, spotting a row of pay phones set against the wall about a hundred feet away. "You got your cell phone with you?"

She nodded.

"Come on," I said to Denise and headed toward the bank of phones. "We can operate from over here. You have any more change?"

She dug out her change purse again and handed it to me.

"Call Rick and see if he can give you the bar association number. If Shields made *Law Review*, did an internship with the Great Gilbert, and graduated, he's most likely practicing law somewhere."

She started dialing, frowning. As she put the phone to her ear and spoke, I could hear that she'd called information.

"I'm not going to bother Mr. Walters with something so trivial," she said, pressing one. I kind of half-listened to her conversation while I had one of my own, trying to reach George, first on his cell, then at work, and finally at home. Ellen, his wife, said he was at work. I redialed and this time was lucky enough to get his partner, Doug Percy.

"Sorry, Ron, Georgie's at the grand jury," Doug's voice said. "They been slower than molasses in January lately.

Was waiting for him so we could go to lunch, but I may have to sneak out soon by myself."

"Who's running the show with Bielmaster out?"

"Lieutenant Case," he said. "Good guy to work for. Everybody's happy and productive for a change." He paused a moment, then asked, "Anything I can help you with?"

Even though Doug was George's partner, and I was sure he knew that George did special favors for me from time to time, off-the-record favors, I didn't want to mention them to Doug.

"Just tell him to call me on my cell, would you?"

"Ten-four," Doug said. "Say, how's that new kid working out? What's his name? Ken?"

"Great," I said. "I've been using him on the Bielmaster case doing surveillance."

I heard Doug's deep resonant chuckle over the phone.

"That's good. He seemed like a sharp kid, and Georgie's been on pins and needles over that thing ever since you started. You'd think he had just as much riding on it as you do."

After the concluding amenities, I disconnected, but pondered what Doug had said: ". . . just as much riding on it as you do." Almost, I thought. And none of the pressure.

Denise hadn't had any success with the bar association either. So much for the easy way, I thought. There was nothing left for us to do but head back to the south end. Unless . . .

Emptying Denise's change purse on the chrome shelf of the pay phone, I sorted out the quarters, dimes, and nickels. She had enough for about three calls, if they were local. I took out my wallet and extracted the last three singles I had and handed them to her.

"Be a doll and go back to that change machine in the library, will you?"

I expected her to complain about being a gofer, but she surprised me, taking the bills without comment. When she came back, she set several rows of quarters on the shelf.

"I had a couple, too," she said. "Figured we might need the extras."

"Very good," I said, smiling. I pulled out the phone book that was on the shelf perpendicular to the wall. It was attached by a chain through the binding to prevent people from stealing it. Cumbersome, but we were at a law school. I flipped it open and looked up Shields in the directory. The listed names spanned several columns. I checked for Mark first, and then went back to the beginning.

"We'll try these two Marks here first," I said. "Then go through and try the others. Bypass any with just initials for now. Those are probably single women."

Denise frowned. "I figured those would be the ones you'd try first."

"Not when I'm working."

"And what am I supposed to say?"

"Listen and learn." I dropped the quarters into the slot and called the first Mark Shields. After three rings a woman answered. I asked to speak with Mark and she told me he wasn't at home.

"May I take a message?" she asked.

"Yeah," I said. "My name's Terry Kovacs. Mark and I went to law school together at Northwestern and I was hoping to—"

"You must have the wrong person," she interrupted. "My husband's a plumber. He ain't never been to law school."

I apologized profusely and hung up. Turning to Denise, I said, "Get the picture?"

She rolled her eyes and sighed. "I suppose. Where did

you get the name Terry Kovacs?"

"From the yearbook. You can use Veronica Heath. That's another one. See if you can get somebody who is or knows the right Mark Shields."

"Why can't I just use my cell phone?"

"Because we don't want a Chicago area code popping up on someone's caller ID. Get it?"

Again without comment, she plucked a couple of quarters from the shelf and ran her finger up the list of Shieldses from the bottom. "I'll work from this end. It'll be simpler."

"Sounds good."

We went through the coin supply fairly quickly, and I had to send Denise back to the library to break some larger bills and change them. Finally, after about fifteen wrong numbers, we hit pay dirt.

"What did you say your name was?"

"Terry Kovacs." I felt a surge of adrenaline shoot through me. Like I'd finally felt a tug on a fishing line.

"Mark's my brother's kid."

I circled the number I'd just called and pointed to the phone. Denise stopped dialing and wrote it down.

"Yeah, I think he mentioned you. You got his number?"

"It's unlisted, and he don't like anybody giving it out. How do you spell Kovacs?"

"Just like it sounds," I said, then repeated the letters. "I'm actually from out of town. We're calling from the school, trying to get the old group of us who made *Law Review* together for a party. I'd really appreciate if I could get ahold of Mark."

"Yeah, well, like I told you, he don't want me to give it out."

"Well, can you call him and tell him to call me?" I read the number off the centered telephone. "Or you can give him my buddy Ron's cell number." I rattled off the number.

"I'll see what I can do," the person said, and hung up.

"That him?" Denise's eyes looked almost hopeful.

"Maybe an uncle." The pay phone rang suddenly, and I picked it up. "Hello?"

No answer, then a click.

"Who was that?" Denise asked.

I shrugged. "Somebody calling back to verify the number maybe."

Her brow furrowed. "But why?"

That was the million-dollar question, I thought. Why refuse to give out any information on someone, and then call back to verify a phone number? What could make someone that paranoid?

On the way back to Rick's, Denise surprised me by asking if I would play that Sinatra CD again.

"He had a certain style, didn't he?" she said. "I never appreciated him before."

Too busy listening to the lightweight crap of today, I thought. George and my brother Tom had instilled an appreciation of the music of their generation when I was growing up. I thought about George and dug out my cell phone, pressing the directory for his cell. I got his voice mail again and glanced at my watch. It was close to 1:30.

Nothing's going easy today, I thought.

About twenty minutes later we were pulling up to Rick's office building. Kris was wearing the headset to listen to my tapes, and typing very rapidly. She smiled at me as we came in, but never seemed to miss a beat. Behind the desk in his private office Rick looked haggard.

"I just remembered something else," he said.

"And from the looks of you, it ain't good," I said.

He shot me another weak smile. "Among your many talents, are you by any chance a process server?"

"Does a bear go caca in the woods?"

That got a hint of a smile out of him, but his whole posture looked stooped and bent. Like he was bearing some tremendous weight.

"Gilbert called me again this morning," he said. "Wanted to know if I'd discussed the settlement offer with my clients."

"Good," I said. "That means he's running scared."

"Yeah, right." Rick snorted and shook his head. "I'm not so sure I'm making the right decision here, Ron. I should be thinking what's best for Laura's family."

"Like I told you, he's trying to intimidate you. He's trying to bluff you with his rep."

"Just like kickboxing, right?"

Though the sarcasm wasn't heavy in his tone, it was still apparent. And it still stung.

"Poor old Tunney had all the records of who was served on my witness list. I'll have to contact each one of them and make sure they got the subpoenas and checks."

"Sounds like a long process. You need a hand?"

He sighed and smiled again. "I think Denise, Kris and me can handle it. We'll be burning the midnight oil a bit, though. And I'll need you to serve anybody who either hasn't been served or wasn't located, tomorrow, okay? You mind working on a Saturday? You might be able to catch a lot of them home."

"Sounds good." I glanced at my watch again. Two-ten. Almost time for school to let out. "You don't need me for anything more today, right?"

He shook his head, still battling defeat, and losing.

I said a few more things to try and bolster his confidence and left. On the way out Kris looked up, hit the pause on the tape player, and slipped off her headphones.

"Whew, I need a break," she said.

"My jokes getting to you?"

She laughed. "Those are about the only things I look forward to around here." Her eyes moved quickly around the office. We were alone. "So, you're not going to the gym tonight, are you?"

"Got to. I've got a fight coming up." I looked down at her and smiled. "How about you?"

"Well, I haven't got any kickboxing matches in my immediate future, but it is Friday night . . ." Before she could finish, the door opened and Rick stuck his head out. I could see Denise's glare behind him.

"Ron, you still here?" He flashed me a lips-only smile and said, "Kris, I'm probably going to need you to hang over a bit later than usual tonight, okay?"

"No problem, Mr. Walters," she said, and winked at me.

George's call set my cell phone ringing as I was starting up the Firebird. When I answered it, he seemed almost jovial.

"You up for a late lunch?" he asked. "I'm starving. Been in court all fucking day."

"Does that mean you're buying?"

I heard him sigh. "Sure. Why not. Where you at?"

I told him and he became upbeat again. "Hell, I'm just getting off the Ryan now. I'll be at Karson's in ten."

I told him I'd meet him there and headed east on 95th Street, and swung south at Central to avoid the bottleneck at Cicero. Taking a combination of side streets and thoroughfares, I managed to beat him by a few minutes. Inside,

I took our usual booth by the window, making sure George would be able to sit facing the door, and glanced outside. The snow was pretty much relegated to piles of white, speckled with filth. Puddles of water seeped from every one of them, and in the rare places where there was no concrete, the ground looked dark and muddy. Almost like nature was finally getting around to revealing that the ground was wet, soft, and nasty. Pretty soon it would be springtime, my favorite time of year.

George came in whistling and with a sly grin on his face. He slipped off his overcoat and hat, tossed them into the seat beside him, and sat down with a contented sigh.

"You seem in a good mood," I said.

"I am," he said. "Had a prelim this morning, then waited around all damn day for the grand jury. Finally got to testify at one-thirty."

"You get a true bill?"

He smirked. "Does a bear shit in the woods?"

I smiled back. "You know, you ought to consider coming up with a less offensive line. I know I have."

"Yeah, right." He reached for a menu. "What you got a taste for? I'm starving."

The waitress came over with two coffee cups and took our order. We spent the usual amount of time on the regular social amenities, like family and current plans. He seemed particularly interested that I had another fight coming up so soon.

"And this one's in Vegas?" he asked, taking another sip from his cup. "You gonna need any security?"

"I might. Still have some things to work out before it's a go."

"Yeah, well, I could use a trip west." He leaned back and stretched. "Man, in a way, it's a good thing the brassholes are getting so sensitive about our overtime. Gives me a green light to go home since I been on the clock since eight this morning. And since I'm off call at five, I should have a nice start on a weekend off."

"Didn't they do a news segment about you city workers milking it when you were supposed to be working?"

"Hey, the wheels of justice turn slowly." He grinned as the waitress set a big plate of spaghetti and meatballs in front of him, and two broiled chicken breasts for me.

"So tell me about the case," he said, swirling his fork in the pasta. He stuck a big glob into his mouth.

"Which one?" I asked, although I had a pretty good idea.

His mouth twisted into a scowl and when he'd finished chewing enough that he could open it, he said, "Whatda you think?" He chewed some more. "The one that I keep getting phone calls about." He shook his head and buried his fork into the spaghetti again. "Christ, Bielmaster is calling me twice a day, leaving messages."

"Why doesn't he just call me?"

George held the next forkful close to his mouth, but hesitated, grinning. "Maybe he don't want to talk to you. Or maybe, he wants to hear the straight scoop from someone he knows won't bulljive him."

I ate some chicken. I figured the high protein meal would be light enough to get me through the rest of the day and still give me room for a snack before my evening workout. Luckily, Chappie had said the hard training sessions were pretty much over with until fight night.

"So?" He shoved the pasta into his mouth, then speared a meatball.

I brought him up to speed on the surveillances, the no-contact order, and my conversations with Knop. He nodded in approval.

"Couldn't have handled it better myself," he said.

"There's another small complication."

"Oh?"

I took a deep breath. "I think this is more of a case of *Romeo and Juliet* than *Cape Fear*."

"Huh?"

"*Romeo and Juliet*. It was a play by Shakespeare. These two young—"

"Shit, I know that. What was the other one?"

"*Cape Fear*. It's an old Robert Mitchum movie. He's an ex-con stalking Gregory Peck's young daughter. They did a remake of it back in the nineties with Robert De Niro."

He scrunched up his face, took a slug of coffee, and ate another meatball.

"So what you're saying is Bielmaster's kid is jonesing for this Knop idiot?"

"Sure looks that way. I ran a little test, purposely letting her and her mom know we'd be doing the surveillances. Knop's been about as active as a choirboy during Lent."

George ran his tongue over his teeth, causing his lips to bulge.

"Great. Does the old man know?"

I shrugged. "I'm beginning to think he was less than honest with us in the beginning, hoping, just like you said, that I'd go kick the shit out of Knop and scare him off."

"Well, did you?"

I shook my head. "Like I said, I talked to him. Twice, trying to put a little scare into him. But that's all." I drank some of my own coffee. "I'm beginning to wonder, if Grace Bielmaster was a willing participant, rather than a real victim, if Knop deserved to do all that juvie time. Like maybe Bielmaster used his clout to get the kid sent away real good."

George was finishing the last of his meatballs.

"So what if he did?" he said. "I don't blame him. Kid knocks up your teenage daughter, you ain't gonna invite him over for tea."

"Yeah, but—"

"But, nothing. He didn't do nothing more than any parent would do." He was using his fork to emphasize his gestures. "You ain't got any kids, so you don't know, but lemme tell ya—"

Just as he was about to finish, his cell phone rang. He paused in mid-gesture, looked down at his belt, and answered it.

"Grieves," he said. His expression got serious. "When?" I saw his eyes dart toward the street. "Shit. I'm on my way."

He snapped the phone shut.

"What's up?"

"Homicide," he said, wiping his mouth and glancing at his watch. "Gotta meet Doug out there now. You mind taking care of this? I gotta get all back up to the Second District."

"Sure, no problem," I said, grinning. "I'll just put it on my expense account. Charge Bielmaster for it."

George grinned back. "That'll make my day."

"Hey, I need you to check on somebody for me, okay?"

He stopped and glared down at me.

"Who?"

I handed him a sheet of paper with the names of the two witnesses we'd heard the depositions from in Gilbert's office as well as Mark Shields.

His brow furrowed.

"What's this?"

"The other case I'm working," I said. "The one with

Rick Walters. See what you can find out on the first two, and the last one is a witness I'm trying to find. I wrote down his uncle's address there."

He crumpled the paper as he shoved it into his coat pocket.

"What the fuck am I, information central?"

"No," I said, "you're the guy who promised to buy and stuck me with the check."

He was slipping on his coat now, his head moving up and down, with a cocky little bounce.

"Oh yeah, we're the homicide capital of the country, and I'm the guy who's got to go out and try to solve them, and all you think of me as is a shortcut for your own cases."

"Well," I said, grinning, "I sort of think of them as *our* cases, buddy."

"Yeah, right. You know, these checks leave computer identifiers for ten days now. I sure hope the boss don't come and ask me why I ran any of these guys."

He punctuated his frown by shoving his hat on his head and heading out the door. I watched him moving briskly toward his unmarked and knew that if he got around to checking on the three guys I'd asked for, it wouldn't be in the foreseeable future.

I'd parked down the block and walked slowly, watching as the cars and buses lined up in front of the school. An audible bell rang and suddenly the doors opened and a sea of young girls, all dressed in nice navy skirts and flats, began flooding outward. I scanned the crowd for Grace, realizing that it was like looking for a four-leaf clover on a summer day. I'd already circled the block several times making sure Knop wasn't prowling about. Nor did I see any sign of Ursula Bielmaster. I needed to catch Grace alone to have that heart-to-heart talk about things. And just as suddenly as the flood of young females had sprung out the doors, I spotted her walking with two friends, her head turned in conversation with one of them, laughing and smiling, her books cradled against her chest.

"Grace," I called, and watched the lovely young face turn, still holding the remnants of the smile. It faded as she saw me. Perhaps she'd been expecting another owner of a masculine voice.

She began walking toward me, and I became cognizant of a beeping automobile horn behind me. I glanced over my shoulder and saw Ursula Bielmaster pulling into a vacating parking spot in a Buick Le Sabre. Grace was almost alongside me now and I fell into step beside her. We only had about twenty feet to her mother's car.

"I was hoping you'd call me," I said. "We need to talk."

"I can't right now," she said, nodding ever so slightly at the Le Sabre.

"I understand. But please. Get in touch with me."

She whispered an "Okay," and kept walking. I took a few steps ahead and opened the car door for her. Ursula seemed impressed to see me.

"The ever-present Mr. Shade," she said. "It's comforting to see you here. Especially on a day when I'm a few minutes late."

"We're trying to stay on top of this for you," I said. Grace wouldn't look at me as she buckled the seat belt. "Any problems last night?"

"No, we both slept like babies. Thank you so much."

I nodded a smile. "My partners and I have been splitting up the surveillance pretty well. Say, can I take you two for a cup of coffee? We can discuss things a bit."

Ursula looked at her watch. "I'm afraid not. We have an

appointment at three-fifteen, and then we want to go over to the hospital."

"I have drama tonight, Mom," Grace said, almost inaudibly.

"Another time then," I said. "We'll be out there on surveillance again tonight, but remember, don't hesitate to call if you need something."

"We won't, Mr. Shade. Goodbye."

I watched the Le Sabre pull on to the street and make its way off, feeling another chance to get a grip on this case slip through my fingers like smoke.

The hospital corridor was full of food trays stacked one on top of the other. I wound my way through them, determined to get to Bielmaster's room and press him for some answers. If, in fact, he'd known about Grace's complicity all along, if that was the case, then we needed a new set of ground rules. The nurse was a few rooms away from me as I entered.

"Please don't stay long, sir," she called after me. "It's dinner time."

I silently wondered if that was anything like feeding time at the zoo. Bielmaster sat upright in his bed, the special mattress angled up at about forty-five degrees, and his forearms rested on his removable tray. His color looked pasty, and the dollop of flesh under his chin rested on the high collar of the hospital gown. Several wires extended out of the short sleeve, and went to a set of monitors behind him, each showing a different picture. One, which was obviously his heartbeat, showed an uneven pattern of moving peaks and valleys. He looked up when I came in, and I saw him give a little start.

"Shade. What? Is Grace okay?"

"Yeah, Lieu, she is," I said, trying to calm him. "I just came to give you an update."

He let out a few breaths through his mouth, like he was beginning to pant from exertion. I didn't know if I should call for the nurse, or what. His mouth stayed open and he pointed to a pillow in the chair beside him.

I didn't know if he meant for me to sit, then he snapped his fingers and pointed again, this time with more urgency, his mouth still hanging open.

"You want this?" I asked, picking up the pillow.

He nodded emphatically and I gave it to him.

He immediately held it to his chest with both hands and kept his mouth wide open. I watched, fascinated in a morbid sort of way, as he emitted a very slight sound.

He swallowed with difficulty, then released the pillow.

"Had to cough," he said weakly.

I raised my eyebrows, suddenly realizing that on the other side of the thin hospital gown, the poor guy's chest had been cracked open and stapled back together.

"What's happening?" He still hadn't recovered his full faculty for speech.

The nurse came in, speaking cheerfully, before I could say anything, and set a bowl of gruel on the tray in front of him.

"And here's your apple juice," she said, setting a small plastic cup down next to it with a straw sticking up. "Can I get you anything else?"

"Not right now, thanks," he said. His voice sounded a tad stronger, but still a shadow of its former brassy self. His eyes moved to me, exaggerated and huge behind the thick glasses.

"Like I said, Lieu, just wanted to give you an update." I told him about getting the no-contact order, the surveillances, and the conversations with Knop. It was almost word-for-word what I'd said to George a half an hour earlier. Now for the touchy part, I thought.

But before I could begin to broach the subject of exactly what had happened before between his daughter and Tim Knop, I saw a solitary tear wind its way down Bielmaster's left cheek. He quickly reached up and wiped it away.

"Shade." His voice became tremulous again, and he extended his open hand out toward me. "I can't tell you how much it means to me, you doing this." Another tear began to worm its way down his cheek. "I won't forget. I swear to you."

I shook his hand, and once again felt the chance to solidly take command of this case evaporating in front of me.

Both cases, actually. In Rick's I was handcuffed by his unwarranted respect for the Great Gilbert, and we were beaten before we even started. And this one, where I was hobbled by being handcuffed to Bielmaster's hospital bed. Knop knew I was tailing him, and if he ever decided to sprint, I'd never catch him.

Chapter 10

I took the necessary steps to contact Ken and bring him up to speed on our modified surveillance plan. I also discussed the possibility of him working completely solo while I was out of town. He seemed brimming with eager confidence. He only had one important question.

"So, does that mean I'll be able to drive the Firebird when you're gone?"

"Sure thing," I said. "But you'll be responsible for all your own tickets."

I picked him up from his house and we drove over to mine to get the Beater. I saw him eyeing the Firebird as he took the set of keys for the other car.

"Next week," I said.

After feeding the cats, who acted glad to see me for a change, I fixed myself a quick broiled chicken breast and baked potato, then packed up my gear. It was getting close to five and I figured an early workout was in order.

When I walked into the gym about twenty minutes later, Chappie looked up and grinned. He was on the phone and pointed to the chair next to his desk. I dumped my bag on the floor and plopped down, feeling the air go out of the cushion under me. Listening to one side of the conversation, I gathered it was about the upcoming fight.

"Okay, Saul," Chappie said. "See what you can find out and get back to me."

I figured he must be talking to Saul Bloom, the local guy who did all our promotions and set up our fight cards. He was a pretty straight shooter who knew his stuff. Chappie hung up, looked at me, and shook his head.

"Something's up with this fight," he said. "Don't know just what yet, but I got Saul working on it."

"I thought he set it up?"

"Un-un. Some Vegas dude contacted him. He don't know no more than me right now. Just that it's set for next Saturday night."

"The loneliest night of the week."

"It can be. That's why I'm going with you." He grinned. "Got Vic Roddy lined up, too, as cutman."

"He's good."

"Gonna see if I can get Raul to go along to help me work the corner. If not him, maybe we take Alley."

Alley was a young Russian kid who was training under Chappie. He'd just turned pro, but had had a substantial amateur career.

"Either one's fine with me," I said.

Chappie grunted and looked at his watch.

"They two hours behind us in Vegas," he said. "Saul gonna make some calls and get back to me. Plus, I gotta call my travel agent."

"How many days we spending out there?"

"Shit, I figure at least a week."

"A week? I can't afford that. I still have a couple of cases I'm working here, you know."

He shrugged and raised his eyebrows. "Lots of stuff to see and do there. Plus, the air's a little thinner. You should go out there to get used to it before the fight or you'll be sucking wind come them late rounds."

I shook my head. "Can't do it. Friday's about as early as I can manage it. Is there a weigh-in?"

He sighed. "Still waiting on all that, but since you heavy-weight, you don't got to worry none about dropping any pounds. I just wished we knowed more."

"Me too," I said, getting up. "Might as well get started."

He got up as well. "Sounds good. You go through light workouts from here on out, leastwise till we figure out a fight plan once we know who we fighting."

I wanted to say, "What do you mean, 'we'?" but thought better of it. Chappie was as much a part of every fight I'd been in as if he'd been right there in the ring with me. I couldn't count how many times I'd heard his voice, somehow filtering in over the roar of the crowd, giving me instructions, telling me how to get out of trouble. There was no one better, and with him in my corner I felt a surge of confidence.

I changed to my regular sweats and went through my warm-up stretching and skipping rope routines. Then I pounded out several rounds on each of the bags. I was feeling pretty good when Chappie came in, slapping the focus mitts together.

"Ready for some real work?" he asked.

We got into the ring and he reset the timers. We went through the basic drills, jab, jab, right cross, left hook as we danced around the ring. He told me to mix in some kicks. Then he got the longer pads and we worked on leg kicks.

"You think you be ready for these?" he asked during a round break.

"I'll just have to knock him out early, like you said."

He grinned. "You looking good, my man."

"You taught me well."

"What you got is a whole lotta quick." He fitted his hands into the focus mitts again. "And you can't teach quick."

We were set to go again, when Brice's head appeared at the door.

"Chappie, phone," he called out.

"Who is it? Take a message. We training." Chappie's voice held an undercurrent of anger. He hated to be interrupted during a session, and Brice knew it.

"But it's Saul," Brice said. "He told me to tell you it was urgent."

Chappie raised his eyebrows.

"Maybe I better take this one," he said. "You do some shadow boxing. I'll be back."

I danced around the ring throwing combinations at Mr. Triple X and slipping imaginary punches. When the bell sounded signaling the end of the round, I glanced toward the door to see if Chappie had come back yet. He hadn't, so I moved slowly around the ring alone in the square jungle, wondering who I'd be facing for real in a week in a strange place. I took comfort in the fact that Chappie would be there with me. And Vic, too. Raul worked as a mechanic during the day, and trained at night. Alley had a night job as a janitor and trained during the day. Whichever one of them came along, I'd feel fortunate.

I was sweating profusely and felt about done for the night. I stared up at the rows of three vertical lights, red, yellow, and green, on the side of the ring posts. Chappie had them installed with special timers, so that each one glowed for one minute. That way you learned to pace yourself for the three-minute rounds. Kickboxing rounds were only two minutes, but I always figured training with the standard three-minute boxing rounds gave me an extra edge when it came to stamina.

"Hi," I heard someone say, and turned to see Kris standing there, smiling. She was still dressed in her office clothes and holding her purse. "Just got off. Mr. Walters kept me there typing up all those subpoenas he wants you to serve tomorrow. I saw your car as I drove by and figured I'd stop and see if you wanted to go get a drink or something when you're done."

She was wearing a navy skirt and her legs looked shapely and chic in her nylons.

"That's the best invitation I've had all day." I was trying to think of something witty to say when Chappie came hurrying into the room. He had a big grin on his face, and looked at Kris, and then to me.

"Ah, miss, would you excuse us for a second?" he said. Kris looked at him and nodded. She started to walk away, then turned.

"Why don't you just call me then?" she said. "I need to change clothes and freshen up a bit."

"Okay, give me about an hour," I said.

"Better make it two," Chappie said. "We gotta talk."

"Talk?" I said, grinning. "I thought I was here to work out."

He watched as Kris stepped through the doorway separating the boxing section from the rest of the gym. When we were alone again he gave me a stern look.

"You remember the rules, right?"

"How could I forget them?" I asked, hoping I wasn't in for another lecture about women weakening legs before a fight and the tale of the unscrupulous promoter who'd set Chappie up with a hooker before one of his big fights. "You remind me at least twice a week."

"Well, I got good reason to," he said. "I just got off the phone with Saul." His voice was a low whisper, like we were sharing a secret that he didn't want anyone else to know yet. A trace of a smile graced his lips. "That fight next Saturday . . . It's for the heavyweight championship of the world."

* * * * *

It was a combination of ebullience and escalating nerves as I proceeded over to Kris's place after showering and sitting in Chappie's office trying to find out exactly who my opponent would be. Despite several calls in to Saul, Chappie could find out very little, which was troubling. Apparently, the scheduled opponent had gotten injured during a sparring session, and they looked at a list of possible alternates and found me. My fight the preceding month had gotten some notice, although I didn't think I'd looked that sharp. But maybe that was why they'd decided on me. Pick someone beatable . . . Someone hungry, and willing to take the fight on short notice. Ultra-short notice, the way it was playing out. But it was for the championship I'd chased for so long . . . For all the marbles this time. Who cared if I didn't have a lot of time to prepare . . . If I didn't know who I was fighting . . . The brass ring was suddenly coming into view, and there was no way I was going to miss a chance to grab it.

"All he know is that it's some Russian dude," Chappie had said, after hanging up the phone. "Won the belt in Europe, fighting under them international rules. This his first fight in the U.S."

"Good," I said. "Maybe the glitz will affect him."

Chappie shook his head and grinned. "I can't believe we getting this chance, outta the blue like this. Too good to be true." He snapped his fingers. "Gotta get ahold of Alley. If this dude's Russian, I want someone with us who speaks the language. Get us some intel."

"Raul's gonna be disappointed."

"Shit, we gonna take him, too. Raul can be your sparring partner, and Alley can hang out getting us a line on this chump."

"Maybe we should send him out ahead of us," I said. "Remember, I've still got plenty of loose ends to tie up here before we go."

"Say what?" He frowned and looked at me, leaning forward. "Ron, how bad you want this, baby?"

I looked back into his eyes and took a deep breath before I answered.

"Bad," I said. "Real bad."

He nodded. "Then we can't afford no one-day-before-the-fight trip. We gots to go out there a couple days in advance."

I remembered the intensity in his face as I now struggled to put the fight out of my mind.

The buzzer for Apartment 3A had a hand-printed card in the slot above it: K. TEMPLER. I pressed it and heard Kris's voice asking who it was.

"It's Ron Shade."

The door buzzed about three seconds later. I pushed it open and trotted up the three flights of stairs. She was peeking out the partially open door as I arrived at the third-floor landing.

"My," she said, showing me an alluring smile. "You bounded up here like a man with a purpose."

"I do have a purpose. I'm taking a pretty lady for a late dinner, right?"

"Actually," she said, stepping back and opening the door wider, "you took so long to call back that I started cooking something. I figured you weren't going to call or anything, and I was famished from sitting in that office all day. So, you hungry?"

"Yeah, sure am."

"Great, because there's nothing more depressing for a girl than eating a dinner on Friday night alone."

She'd changed out of the navy blue skirt and white silk blouse that I'd seen her in earlier. Now she wore a form-fitting pair of black slacks and dark sweatshirt. It had the Northwestern University logo on it.

"You went to Northwestern?" I asked.

She smiled again. "No, my ex did. But I like the shirt."

It looked pretty new, but I didn't comment on that. Maybe the break-up was more recent than I'd figured. My mind was still going 240 with thoughts of a championship belt within grabbing distance.

"I was just there today," I said.

"Really? How come?" She reached for my jacket.

I shrugged. "Trying to trace down a witness." A smell of something spicy wafted over to me as I was taking it off.

"Find him?" she asked, putting the jacket in a closet and closing the door. It suddenly struck me that the gesture sort of presupposed that I'd be staying a while. I reassessed the line of her hips in the tight slacks and wondered how this one was going to play out tonight.

"What makes you think it was a 'him'?" I asked.

She shrugged. "I just assumed, I guess. Wondered what was in store for me on your tapes tomorrow, is all." She looked me up and down. "You want a drink before dinner?"

"Some water would be nice."

"Water?" Her eyebrows rose in unison.

"Yeah. I don't drink, plus remember, I've got a very important fight coming up in less than a week."

"That's right."

She beckoned me into the kitchen and took out some bottled water from the refrigerator. The apartment was small, but tidy. No pictures adorned the walls, and the furniture looked kind of worn. Like it had come furnished, but not with the best. Several cardboard boxes sat stacked in a corner. When she saw me looking at them, she made a quick dismissive gesture.

"Don't look at that stuff," she said. "I'm still in a state of moving in here."

I grinned. "Your housekeeping puts mine to shame. What are you cooking? Smells great."

"That's the sauce. I like to let it simmer. I'll need to put the pasta on in a few minutes." She bit her lower lip slightly and worked her tongue over her teeth. "I'm afraid I made it the other day. It's just a warm-up. Is that okay?"

"It's fine. My meals usually consist of broiled chicken breasts, salads, and steaks."

"That sounds interesting. So tell me about your day." She went to the stove and checked a pot on the stove. Then she tore open a bag of spiral-shaped macaroni and poured it in. "Who were you looking for at Northwestern?"

"Ah, just tracing down a long shot," I said. "You'll hear all about it on the tapes, whenever I get a chance to do them. How about you? Get all those subpoenas done?"

"Oh, God," she said. "Talk about a hostile work environment . . . I had Denise standing over me asking every few seconds, 'You got those done yet? You got those done yet?' " She'd done a pretty fair imitation of Denise's intense tone. "I could have used a trip to the gym tonight."

"Speaking of the gym," I said, letting the sentence hang for a few seconds. I told her about the upcoming fight, and the circuitous routes that had taken me so close before. She sat down across from me and seemed to listen with rapt interest. The timer went off and she jumped up and drained the macaroni, then set out the dishes, asking if I wanted some wine to go with the meal. I declined, holding up the water.

"Well, I'm going to have some," she said, taking a dark

bottle out and setting it on the center of the table along with two long-stemmed glasses. She pushed one in front of me and smiled. "In case you change your mind."

Even warmed up, the sauce was pretty good. Kris seemed disappointed that I ate light, but I reminded her that I was in training. This brought an exaggerated frown, and a coyly asked question as to whether I liked her or not.

"What's not to like?" I said. "You're a beautiful, vibrant, intelligent woman."

"You really think so?" She poured herself another glass and then filled my glass too. I let it sit, watching her eyes looking at me over the rim of her tilted flute. "It's been a long time since someone said something that nice to me."

"It shouldn't be," I said. "You should have someone who appreciates you."

Her stare was intense for a moment, and I wondered what she was thinking. Standing, she retrieved both our glasses and moved around the table.

"Why don't we go in the living room?"

It was only a few feet from the kitchen. A sofa, one chair, and a television with a cable box. No VCR or DVD players in sight. An end table held the room's only lamp, although a ceiling-to-floor column of light fixtures adorned the opposite wall, but those were probably more furnishings. The whole place had a temporary feel to it. A superficiality, leaving scarce clues to the personality of the occupant. I wondered how long she'd been there, and figured that the break-up she'd mentioned before had really left her devastated. In more ways than one. The drapes were open and looked out on a cement balcony and a quiet street scene beyond. More apartment buildings, cars, and twinkling streetlights.

"Nice view," I said, walking over to check on my car. I'd

set the alarm, so I wasn't real nervous about it, but an occasional check never hurt anything.

She used the remote to turn on the TV, but left the lights off.

"Wait till it gets a little darker," she said. "Then it looks almost pretty. Plus, you can see into the apartments across the street." She giggled and drank some more wine. "You'd be surprised at what people do, leaving their drapes wide open with their lights on."

"My, aren't you the curious neighbor."

She patted the sofa beside her and I walked back and sat. Our legs were touching.

"So, you're not going to drink your wine?" she asked. Her words were starting to slur a bit, and her gestures were ever-so-slightly exaggerated. "I mean, I'll feel bad if you don't."

I shook my head and smiled. "Sorry. I can't."

"Hmm." She finished off the rest of her drink and then reached for my untouched glass. "So let me ask you this . . . If only one of us gets drunk, doesn't that constitute an unfair seduction?" Her free hand came to rest on my thigh. "Hmmm?"

The last thing I'd intended was to get her inebriated and into the sack. I thought about what to say to kind of back out of the situation without hurting her feelings and still leave the door open for a future date.

"Maybe we need to slow down here a little bit," I said.

"Why? Don't you find me attractive, Ron?" It was said in a mocking way, but I caught an undercurrent of raw emotion in the tone.

"Of course I do."

"Theeeennn," she said, drawing out the word, "let's quit wasting so much of each other's time." She leaned forward and kissed me on the lips. It was a light kiss. A gentle brushing of flesh. When she drew back, our eyes locked and her stare was sheer intensity. Her mouth came forward again, her lips opening, her tongue darting. I felt her press against me, and suddenly I sensed we were both tipping over the precipice of that familiar, yet dangerous, slippery slope.

It was close to two in the morning when I slipped out of Kris's bed to pad to the washroom and grab my cell phone. I listened to the soft snuffling of her breathing for a few minutes and reflected on the accelerated path our relationship had taken. I really hadn't planned it this way and had no idea we'd end up in bed when I'd trotted up those stairs like a man on a mission. It had been a very pleasant interlude, born perhaps from her need to feel some sort of reciprocal masculine attention . . . An affirmation of her attractiveness, her femininity, so to speak, after what she'd described as a less-than-happy marriage. The lonely lady, used to sitting at home and innocently spying on her neighbors, starting to find her way back to a social life by taking small steps. Still, the wine had offset me. It made me feel disingenuous to a small degree. As if I'd noticed her vulnerability, and let the liquor weaken the last of her resolve. But she'd turned into a tiger in bed, being decisive and initially dominant, and making love with a driving intensity. Yet, as I stood in the doorway of her bedroom, I recalled a strange detachment that I'd seen flash in her eyes after we'd finished and she didn't seem to notice my gaze. This was a girl who was on a quest. Perhaps to find something. Perhaps to find herself. I felt privileged that she'd invited me along.

After stepping into the living room, I dialed the number for Ken's cell phone. He answered on the third ring.

"Yeah, it's Ron. Anything happening?"

"No, sir," he said. "All quiet at both places. The Bielmasters' lights have been out since midnight. No movement at all at Knop's, either."

"All right, might as well call it a night," I told him. It looked like my give-them-notice-we're-out-there plan was working.

Chapter 11

The rain hit me hard on the face as I started my morning run. It was way too warm for any more snow, but the drizzle still felt cold. The morning had stayed dark and gray, refusing to lighten up with the promise of sunshine. But the rain would probably get rid of the residual piles of the dirty snow. I'd left Kris a note thanking her for a wonderful evening, promising that I'd call later, and made one of my Lone Ranger exits shortly after talking to Ken on the phone. Then I managed to grab a few hours of solid sleep before getting up at a late 7:45. Unusually late for me, but I'd promised Rick I'd meet him at his office at 9:30 to pick up those subpoenas he wanted me to serve. Plus, with the new stakes in the fight, I could little afford to miss a run. The rain slowed me more than I liked, making me more cautious than normal at corners and intersections, but I still managed to make the five miles in under forty minutes.

My cell phone rang when I was drying off from my shower. It was Rick.

"Hey, Ron, I wanted to remind you about those subpoenas this morning."

"Be there in thirty, buddy," I said.

On the way over I reflected that I'd driven practically the same way only a few hours before. Kris's apartment was in Oak Lawn, just like Rick's office. Convenient for her. Maybe this temp job would turn into something more if Rick saw how capable she was. And if he won this Gooding case, of course. I had the feeling that if he could overcome his self-doubt about going up against the Great Gilbert, he'd cream the guy. My thoughts returned to my own case of self-doubting, now that I knew I was going into the fight of my life in seven days. But I still didn't even know my opponent's name. Nor his face. Mr. Triple X was a vague shadow in front of me. A Russian . . . That could mean just about anything. But if he was the champ, one thing for sure was that it probably wouldn't mean easy.

The parking lot for Rick's building was practically empty. He shared it with several other professional people, among whom were a dentist and a pediatrician. So I wasn't too surprised to see a few other cars there this early in the morning. One of them was a black Crown Vic with tinted windows. It seemed out of place for the clientele. Inside things got even more out of joint when I saw John Flood standing in the outer office talking to Rick. He turned as I came in and the right side of his mouth twisted up into a hint of a smirk.

"Morning, Shade," he said. He had his arms on his hips, drawing back his jacket. I noticed a snub-nose .38 in a clip-on holster, butt-first on his left side. Cross-draw. The weapon was chrome, and had a couple of thick, flat rubber bands around the handle. An old-time CPD trick to assure a quick, solid grip when drawing fast.

"Big John Flood," I said. "What are you doing out south this way?"

"I had some business with your employer. Maybe he'll trust you enough to tell you about it." He shook hands with Rick and said something about Mason being anxious to hear from him, then moved past me, making sure to brush against my arm, as he went toward the door. I stared after him, thinking that one of these days I'd like to take him off at the knees.

"What did that asshole want?" I asked.

Rick looked stunned at what I'd called Flood. Then he recovered. "He was just dropping off a letter from Mason Gilbert. He wanted it hand-delivered today because of the weekend."

"You gonna open it?"

Rick flipped the envelope against his hand a few times and said, "Yeah, I am, but let me give you those subpoenas first."

I didn't know if he was waiting to open it out of some misplaced deference to the Great Gilbert, or because good old John Boy had hit the nail on the head: Rick had some reservations about me. I'm sure he was going to be overjoyed when he heard Chappie wanted me to leave for Vegas in a couple of days.

We went into his inner office and he reached on to his desk and gave me a stack of subpoenas.

I stared at the envelope Flood had given him. He slowly picked up his letter opener and slit the flap. I watched his brow furrow a bit as he read.

"So what's it say?" I asked.

"Gilbert is advising me that he has a minor scheduling conflict. Wants to know if I'll agree to a by-agreement continuance."

"By-agreement? You going to agree?"

He shrugged. "Don't know. I guess I could always use some more time to prepare, but I fought so hard to finally get this on the calendar. Every time I'd try for a trial date, he'd say he wouldn't be available. I mean, I know the guy's firm has a lot of cases, but . . ."

"Plus, you worked so hard on these." I flipped the sheaf of envelopes. "This guy's running another game on you. Why can't you see that?"

"Ron, I told you before, I'm in charge of this case, okay?"

"Then take charge of it and quit letting this guy get to you. He hasn't got a case, and he knows it. You can beat him. Believe me."

He smiled slightly and nodded. But it was a tentative smile.

"So you want me to deliver these, or what?" I asked.

He took a deep breath, looked me square in the eye, and said, "Let's go for it."

I arranged the subpoenas in order of locations and began my trek. It was busywork rather than investigative, but it gave me a chance to think. Most of the witnesses were up in the North Shore and Naperville area. One kid, a witness who had seen Gooding driving his receptionist's red Pontiac Firebird around the area of the murder, was now in DeKalb at college, or so his parents told me when I stopped by their house. I figured I'd have to save that one for a nice Sunday drive. All things considered, I made very good progress by the time Kris called me at about 11:30.

"Hi," I said, remembering I'd left my cell phone number on the note. "I was thinking about calling you."

"Really?" Her voice sounded like it rose an octave. "I was hoping you would. I was wondering if you'd like to come over for lunch, or something."

The "or something" sounded interesting.

"I'm way up north on my quest for justice, serving those subpoenas you so dutifully typed out yesterday." I paused, considering the ramifications of seeing her tonight. As long as I got an afternoon workout in, and Chappie didn't find out . . . "I was thinking maybe we could do dinner and a movie tonight. If you're free, that is."

"Let me check my schedule," she said with a hint of allure in her voice. Then added a second later, "Okay, I'm free." Her laugh sounded almost musical over the phone.

"So how does sevenish sound? I've got to get a workout in after I finish these."

"It sounds great, but . . ."

"But?"

"Don't use up all your energy at the gym."

I told her I wouldn't and disconnected. Chappie wouldn't be happy if he knew I was seeing someone socially right before a fight, but I'd never totally bought into his old theory that "getting some leg" was inimical to a fighter's performance in the ring. Maybe the day before or of the fight, it would be. I remembered the story about Muhammad Ali having five girls in bed right before he got his jaw broken by Ken Norton. But my big night was still a week away, and with both of us working, and me going out to Vegas as well as shadowing Knop in my spare time, chances are this would be my final interlude with Kris until I came back. I still hadn't told Rick that I'd be leaving, and wondered what his reaction would be. I'd have to make sure we didn't have any loose ends hanging before I left, whenever that might be.

Which reminded me that I needed to see if I could line up Ken on a semipermanent basis for the next week to take over the Bielmaster case. My gut told me that the "Big Brother is watching you" routine had stymied Knop, at least temporarily. Maybe Monday I'd pay another visit to the liquor store, let him see me in the Firebird. That way he'd associate me with the car, and every time he saw a red Firebird the pucker factor would automatically assert itself in the back of his shorts. We'd still have the Beater as our unidentified surveillance vehicle. Our USV. There, I'd coined a new acronym. Something I'd always wanted to do. Plus, we only had to keep this charade going until

Bielmaster got out of the hospital. After that, it would be his problem to deal with. I'd be out of the equation, or at least until he pulled the strings to get me reinstated on the PD like he'd promised George. But was I sure that was what I really wanted?

I saw the exit coming up for Naperville and hit my turn signal.

My FOP lawyer had represented me through the dismissal hearing, and the court case. That had taken forever, and the court upheld the firing. The lawyers had then started an appeal process, but the case now seemed caught up in an infinite loop of continuance after continuance of court dates that would never come. If Bielmaster could break the logjam, pull in some markers, and get me reinstated with full bennies and back pay, I'd be sitting pretty no matter what I ultimately decided to do.

It made making sure I'd covered all the bases for that case before I left for Vegas all the more important.

I felt distracted and preoccupied, even though I was sitting across from a beautiful woman in a nice restaurant later that evening. Kris looked at me from over the rim of her wine glass.

"So, is the dinner disturbing you, or are you thinking about something else?" she asked me, setting the glass down.

I smiled. "Just got a lot on my mind is all. Sorry."

She reached across and squeezed my hand.

"Want to talk about it?"

"There's not much to talk about," I said, and actually, that was the truth. After a reasonably successful trip delivering the lion's share of those damn subpoenas, I'd shot over to the gym for a late afternoon session with

Chappie. After showing me the contract they'd faxed, and marveling over the large amount of money offered, he took me through ten rounds of punching and kicking with the pads. Then Raul came in and we went a couple with the headsets and sixteen-ouncers. During the workout, Chappie had filled me in on who Mr. Triple X was.

"His name's something like Sergei Seleznyov. Supposed to be about six-four and weighs plenty more than you." He grinned and slapped the focus mitts together. "That good. Give you the edge in speed. Like I said, you either quick, or you're not. We figure out a good fight plan and whup his Russian ass good."

Let's just hope he ain't big and quick, I thought. I didn't want to say anything negative in front of Chappie, lest I risk another of his positive thinking lectures. And when he told me to go home and get some rest tonight, I assured him that I hoped to be in bed early . . . Which was actually not very far from the truth either.

I looked across the table at Kris and the waitress came, refilled our coffee, and asked if we wanted dessert.

"None for me," I said, resisting the urge to use a line from an old Clint Eastwood movie, "That's already been taken care of."

Kris ordered some vanilla ice cream with chocolate sauce. When I smiled at her choice she stuck her tongue out at me.

"Why not?" she said. "I'm entitled, aren't I?"

"Certainly," I said.

She smiled and leaned toward me.

"Tell me what's bothering you, Ron. Is it the Gooding case?"

"The Gooding case? Not hardly." I sighed. "Well, maybe a little bit."

"Why?"

"Rick, mostly. He seems like he's letting this Gilbert idiot intimidate him."

"Well, Gilbert does have an awesome reputation as a lawyer, doesn't he?"

I frowned. "What does it matter how big he is if he's rotten on the inside? Rick could mop up the floor with him if he'd only get past the guy's rep. It's just like kickboxing."

"The bigger they are?"

I raised my eyebrows, suddenly hoping that was true.

"So what is your feeling about the Gooding case?" she asked. "I mean, I've listened to your tapes—great jokes, by the way—and I've got a feeling that you think he did it."

"Oh, he did it, all right. No question about it."

"But the criminal case?"

"The criminal case doesn't mean anything other than the Great Gilbert got him off when he shouldn't have. The system failed. Let a killer go free. Happens all the time. More often than people realize. That's why I'm hoping he gets his head handed to him on this wrongful death suit. Sort of a second chance for justice. A final judgment, so to speak."

"Why do you think he got acquitted criminally?"

I shrugged. "From what I hear, Gilbert was tight with the judge." I made a mental note to ask George if he had any skinny on the Great Gilbert or old Judge Foxworth. "A judge who's pro-defense isn't concerned with doing what's right in the interest of truth and justice. He's more interested in his own agenda."

"Wow, that sounds pretty harsh for someone who works within the system," she said.

"But that's just it," I said, grinning. "I don't. I'm not opposed to stepping out of bounds on a few plays if it's what needs to be done." The waitress came back with Kris's ice cream and handed me the black folder with the bill. I popped it open and took a look.

"So, are you saying you don't always follow the letter of the law?" She picked up her spoon. "Can't that get you in trouble? I mean, what would Rick say about that?"

"Rick needs to learn two fundamental lessons."

She paused, smiling. "Going to keep me in suspense?"

"Not at all," I said, shaking my head. I held up a finger, ticking off the first one. "Gilbert is a piece of crap, and two, sometimes, when you're dealing with a piece of crap, you just gotta throw the rule book in the toilet."

As it turned out, I didn't need to worry about Chappie finding out anyway. When I was heading back to Kris's apartment, my cell phone rang with an intrusiveness that interrupted the pleasantries of our conversation. We'd been holding hands as I drove, her left in my right. I looked at her and said, "Sorry, but I have to answer this," thinking that it might be Ken with a problem on the Bielmaster surveillance, but silently hoping that it wasn't.

After I'd said, "Ron Shade," I heard George's familiar snorting laugh.

"You answer your cell like that?" he asked. Then did a mocking imitation of my name.

"For a guy charged with the awesome responsibility of transforming Chicago from the homicide capital of the country, you seem pretty flippant."

"Hey, we're doing our part," he said. "Look, I need a big favor. You busy tonight?"

"Yeah, I am."

I heard him sigh. "Look, Ron, the regular guy we had scheduled to cover the bar at the hotel tonight called off, so Doug was gonna cover it, but we just picked up that suspect on that homicide. He's ready to talk, and we're waiting on the State's Attorney now."

"And?"

"And I need you to help me out, buddy." His voice had suddenly taken a much friendlier incarnation.

"George, I can't," I said, glancing over at Kris. "I'm taking a very nice young lady home from a pleasant dinner date."

"Aww, shit, I shoulda known you'd be out getting laid." I heard him sigh. "Ron, this is really important. Our contract with the hotel is coming up again, and if they don't renew because we couldn't cover things . . ."

"Yeah, I know." I glanced at my watch. It was 8:40. "The soonest I could be out there would be nine-thirty."

"That'd be super. I'm counting on you now."

He hung up and the line went silent before I could ask him if he'd run those informational checks on the names I'd given him. I clucked in disappointment as I pulled into Kris's apartment building complex.

Turning toward her, I touched her hand and said, "I'm really sorry. It's work and I can't stay."

She smiled and her fingers brushed my face.

"It's okay. I understand," she said. Then, after looking down, added, "What time do you get off?"

"Not till four," I said. "We have to close up the bar and a few other things."

"Oh. That's kinda late."

I reached for my door handle. "I'll walk you upstairs," I said.

* * * * *

I was at the hotel about forty minutes later listening to my friend, Kathy Daniels, sing her usual version of "I Love You for Sentimental Reasons." When she saw me, she immediately smiled and motioned me over without missing a beat on the piano. I stood there listening to her voice as it seemed to effortlessly glide up the scale, hitting just the right notes to send shivers down my spine.

When she'd finished, and the applause had subsided, she asked why she hadn't seen me there lately.

"Working a couple of consuming cases," I said. "I've been listening to your CD, though."

"You'd better," she said. "Now, what do you want to hear?"

She sang everything so well, it was hard to decide.

"How about that jazzed-up version of 'As Time Goes By' that you used to sing for me when I was feeling blue?"

"You got it. But you're not feeling blue tonight, are you?"

"Only for missed opportunities," I said.

I went to the bar and the bartender gave me my usual club soda with a lime twist. I shoved a dollar into his tip glass and leaned back, letting Kathy's fine voice sort of wash over me, thinking about how I did feel. Strangely enough, I hadn't felt that bad about George's call. In fact, I'd sensed a strange sort of relief. Like I was given an out that I secretly had been hoping for. It had nothing to do with Chappie's admonition, or keeping my date with Kris from him. It was something else. Something different. Like Kris and I were suddenly moving way too fast for things to feel comfortable. To feel right. She was very pretty, and a real tiger in bed, but I wondered if that was part of it. She'd claimed to be on the mend. I equated that with meaning on the rebound. It was too easy to make the wrong decisions when you were in that emotional state. Yet she hadn't seemed fragile at all. More predatory than vulnerable.

So maybe this wasn't such a bad break after all tonight, I thought, just as Kathy was finishing up the song.

The bar was extremely dead for a Saturday, and I told the manager I was going in by the pool to take a break. The recreational area was adjacent to the upstairs bar, so I'd be available in a hurry if any trouble broke out. Plus, I had a radio for the front desk to call me if they needed me. I unlocked the door, turned on the lights, and pulled up a chair. I still had my pocket tape recorder with me, so I took the time to dictate my mental notes and observations on the Gooding case. That way I could just drop it off bright and early Monday morning, and not have Denise badgering me about it. I purposely omitted my request to George to run criminal history checks on the Great Gilbert's witnesses, and my hope that he could find an address for the mysterious Mark Shields. But I did mention that I was in the process of doing these checks myself. I also noted how the mention of Shields's name had sent Mary Buckley into a mini-tizzy. It could all turn out to be nothing. A case of unrequited love, for all I knew, but it was worth checking out. As George always said about investigating homicides, nothing is unimportant until you've positively determined it is.

My radio squawked and the girl at the front desk told me there was someone on the phone for me. I told her to put it to the pool extension and picked it up.

"Just checking to see if you showed up," George's voice said.

"Hey, I ain't no city worker. When I'm supposed to be on the clock, I really am."

I heard his deep chuckle.

"Things must be going good on the homicide front, huh?" I asked.

"It's a beautiful thing," he said. "The fucker's in there crying for the camera, telling us how sorry he is that he shot the wrong person on his drive-by. Too bad they already had the Oscars."

"Say, since you're just sitting around there with your thumb up your ass, did you have time to run those checks for me?"

"Jesus, Ron, you know I'm trying to clear a homicide, don't you?" His tone had grown suddenly angry, and I could tell he was probably near exhaustion. "And no, I ain't. I been busy, dammit."

"Fine," I said, as evenly as I could. I didn't want to piss him off. My reply seemed to have the opposite effect. I heard him sigh.

"I'll, ah, try to get to that sometime later. Okay?"

"Sure. Thanks," I said. "Say, let me ask you something else. You know anything about Big John Flood? He ex-CPD?"

"That piece of shit? I doubt it. If he ever was on the job, he forgot his roots. It was him and fucking Mason Gilbert that got that asshole DeWayne McKafray off after he killed that copper in Two."

"What about Judge Samuel Foxworth? You know anything about him?"

"Foxworth? At Twenty-sixth Street? He's an asshole. What else is there to say?"

I shrugged, even though I knew he couldn't see it. "He tight with Gilbert?"

I heard George snort. "The whole fucking judicial system's tight with that prick. They line up at regular intervals to ceremoniously kiss his fat ass."

I chuckled. "That anything like kissing the Pope's ring?"

"For them, yeah. Speaking of which," he said, "come to think of it, I do remember a good story about old foxy Foxworth. It was back in the old days, when they still brought all the hookers to Eleventh and State for night court. There was this back elevator that we shared with the lawyers and judges so we could bring prisoners up to the rooms. After the bond hearings, we used to use it so we didn't have to wait. Well, one time, I'm trying to get up to the top floor to deliver a special report, so I used my special key for this elevator, and I'm waiting and waiting. I kept pushing the damn button, but it was still taking forever. So finally, after leaning on the thing for about ten minutes, I finally hear it starting to come down to me. And then, when the doors pop open, I look over in the corner I catch a glimpse of this judge, his black robe hiked up over his shoulders, putting his equipment back in his pants, and this hooker getting up off her knees."

I chuckled. "A little pretrial agreement?"

"Probably more like paying for services rendered in trade," he said. "Anyway, the asshole just glares at me, finishes zipping up his pants, and just shoves the hooker out the doors in front of him, without so much as a word to me."

"Probably didn't like to be interrupted when he was supervising someone serving out their sentence." I waited and then asked the obvious. "So it was our buddy, I take it?"

"That piece of shit, Foxworth," George said. "When the elevator dinged open, it was all I could do not to use that old Jimmy Stewart line, 'Another angel got her wings,' but I kept my mouth shut."

"Good line," I said.

"The guy they got in charge down there now, Paul Beavers, would never put up with that bullshit. He's good. He's real good." I heard someone call to him in the background. "Why, what's Flood and Foxworth got to do with anything?"

"That case I'm working for Rick Walters. Flood's working with Gilbert and they're the opposing counsel."

"Jesus, good luck," he said. I heard the voice calling his name again. "I gotta go. You on top of that Bielmaster thing?"

"Got it covered, boss."

"Good," he said. "Keep it that way," and he hung up.

Besides staying up until the wee hours closing down the bars and making sure all the exterior doors in the hotel and adjoining office complex were locked, the night was uneventful. At the end of my shift, however, I was ready for bed. I made it home in record time, thinking the whole way about my next move, but too tired to get any new ideas. In the end, I compromised, undressed, and set the alarm for a solid 9:30. Since it was close to 5:00 already, and the sun would be coming up shortly, I adjusted the clock's alarm back to 11:00, and settled under the covers. I must have been asleep as soon as my head hit the pillow.

The alarm woke me from one of those disturbing anxiety dreams in which I found myself wandering around a large school, suddenly aware that I had a test in a class that morning, and hadn't studied for it. I think it was algebra, or something. The exact location of the room escaped me, and I knew I was running late. Then I further realized that I hadn't been to the class all semester. The bell on the wall above my head began ringing, and as I tried to focus on it in the dream, my viewpoint sort of telescoped and the school bell merged with the insistent alarm clock. I had all three cats curled in different positions pinning my legs and arms with the covers. Georgio, the closest one to my face, looked up with sleepy disapproval at my twisting to reach the alarm button. He rotated his head in a smooth motion and immediately went back to sleep. I, however, made the supreme effort and actually swung my legs out from under and set my feet on the cold floor.

It was 11:02. Score one for the miracles of modern clocks.

I stumbled to the kitchen, poured some coffee into a mug, and set it in the microwave while I collected my running clothes. Although I felt like hitting the sack for about five more hours, I knew I'd have to get the run in now, before my inevitable afternoon workout with Chappie.

Thank God we're in the light work phase, I thought as I went downstairs and plucked my smelly sweat clothes from the makeshift clothesline. They were ripe, all right, but scavenging for a clean set would be a luxury I couldn't afford. I made a mental note to toss them in the washer afterwards, though, and figured I'd just have to keep going fast enough that no one would try to join me.

After slurping a few bitter sips of the microwaved brew, I laced up my shoes and took off on a fairly quick jaunt.

The run must have been what I needed to chase out the cobwebs, because by the time I finished, my head was clear and I'd decided on a new course of action concerning Gooding: Big Rich.

Rich Stafford was a reporter friend of mine who worked for the *Chicago Metro News*, one of the three major papers in the city. It wasn't nearly as prestigious as the *Tribune*, nor as likeable as the *Sun-Times*, but Big Rich was a first-rate reporter and a resource that I'd used more than one time to find out about the untraceable. The only problem was I didn't have his home number, and he'd always shunned cell phones, so I'd have to wait till tomorrow. But considering that it was a given that I was going to spend the day with Chappie anyway, this didn't seem like such a setback. I made a mental note to give him a call and filed it with all the rest of the clutter.

A message from Chappie was waiting for me when I came in to check my answering machine.

"Where you at?" the tape of his angry voice asked. "Don't you be slacking off on me, now. We got us a championship to win, remember?"

It ended with an admonishment to call him immediately, which I did. The conversation was a continuation of the taped interrogation.

"So where was you?"

"I was running," I said. "I had a late one last night."

"With who?"

"With about three hundred guests at the hotel. I got stuck working that gig."

"Oh," he grunted, probably mulling over chewing me out, but secretly pleased I hadn't been out on a date. "Well, grab yourself something light to eat and meet me at the gym by one-thirty. I been trying to get ahold of Alley and Raul all damn day."

After he hung up I drank some orange juice, took a quick shower, and then made one of my protein drinks in the blender. Then I packed my bag and headed for the gym.

The workout went okay until Alley finally showed up. Chappie had been taking me through a few rounds with the focus pads. Raul hadn't been sparring since I'd laid him out the other night, and I worried that he might have been hurt worse than we originally thought. But when I asked

Chappie what he'd heard, he dismissed the question with a shake of his head.

"No sense worrying 'bout that," he said. "Raul know what he's doing. He a fighter."

I threw a double-jab, right cross, left hook combination at the pads.

"I know, but I can still be concerned, can't I?" I said.

He was about to answer when we heard the front buzzer ringing.

"That got to be Alley," Chappie said, backing away from me and slipping through the ropes. He jumped down the ring steps with a grace that made me marvel. "Shadow box the rest of the round out. I be back."

I did my usual series of combinations, trying my best to visualize a big, lumbering Russkie stumbling around in front of me. But without knowing who or what my upcoming opponent looked like, I found the task formidable. I stopped and rested my arms on the ropes until the bell rang.

Chappie frowned when he saw me resting as he came back in with Alley, but he didn't say anything. Alley was grinning from ear to ear, as usual.

"Hey, Ron," he said, with his thickly accented English. "You fight for championship, huh? Is great news."

"We'll see how great it is once he gets in there," Chappie said. Always trying to push me to train harder. But once we got into the ring, I knew I'd thank him. He had Alley change into his gym shoes and work the pads, shouting directions for both of us as we danced through three more rounds. When the bell finally rang I was drenched and feeling like I'd been trying to pull a freight train.

"Take five while I make a call," Chappie said. "Somebody's supposed to be getting me some tapes of the chump we fighting."

"I thought we were done?" I called after him.

"Not till we do sit-ups," he said over his shoulder.

That meant at least fifteen to twenty more grueling minutes. I blew out a breath and turned to cuff Alley on the shoulder.

"So you coming with me to Vegas?"

"Me?" His grin was so wide it almost looked affected. "Ya, I go. Help training."

"The guy I'm fighting is Russian," I said. "You ever hear of him?"

His lips drew together. "Who?"

I searched my memory for the name that Chappie had told me. "Seleznyov, or something."

"Seleznyov?" He changed the inflection of the name when he pronounced it. "Sergei?"

"Yeah, I think so." His expression suddenly seemed paler. "Why? You know him?"

Alley's eyes opened wider. "Russian National Boxing Champion. Super-heavyweight. Very big. Very strong. Fast. Good boxer."

His stunning description suddenly made me wish that I had six months, rather than six days, to prepare. I swallowed, not wanting to ask the question, but knowing I had to.

"So," I said, "who's better? Him or me?"

Alley's jaw dropped like a yo-yo, and he tried to recover with a quick smile. But his eyes told me all I needed to know.

Chapter 12

A white three-quarter moon had hung suspended against a light blue sky when I'd done my roadwork at 6:15 the next morning. I reflected on my previous night's conversation with Kris about why I couldn't come over, explaining about the upcoming fight. "Well, if you need to relax a little, maybe I could help," she'd said. When I went on to explain that I had a case of the growing nerves, and that I needed some space, she'd been surprisingly understanding.

"Okay, Ron, but if you change your mind, call me," she'd said, and ended with, "I'll be looking forward to seeing you in the morning then."

But instead of going directly to Rick's, I took off for the North Shore early to serve the rest of Rick's subpoenas. Ken had left me a voice message at 5:29, saying that it was starting to get light, and nothing was stirring on the Bielmaster or Knop fronts. He'd done solo surveillance the past two nights without as much as a peep or a whimper out of Knop. Maybe our scare campaign was working. I figured to up the ante a tad with a conspicuous trip past the liquor store to let him see the Firebird sometime today. Let him think there was always somebody watching him.

I was done with the subpoenas by 10:40 and decided to take a quick detour downtown and see if I could tag up with Big Rich. Unfortunately, I'd somehow forgotten that no trip to the Loop is ever quick unless you park on the outskirts and take a ride with a suicidal Third World taxi driver. I circled the block about sixteen times trying to find a metered parking place to open up. Since I had the Firebird, which was devoid of the rows of FOP stickers that adorned the Beater, I didn't want to risk the convenient alleyway, fireplug, or bus stop. Of course, if I got a parking ticket, I could always have charged it to client expenses, but I hated to stick Rick with an unnecessary tab. I rounded the corner again and saw a space by a fireplug.

Screw it, I thought, pulling the Firebird up to parallel park. If I get a ticket, I'll charge Bielmaster.

The Metro Building was a block away from its big brothers, the *Chicago Tribune* and *Sun-Times*. The bas-relief soldier was still fighting the Indian on the cornerstone as I walked by the Michigan Avenue Bridge. The weather was continuing to warm up, and I took it as a sure sign that spring was almost here when I saw a garbage scow chugging up the Chicago River. Pretty soon they'd dye it bright green for St. Patrick's Day. But I'd probably be in Vegas when that happened.

Inside, I was given the once-over by a security guard who asked what my business was. I told him I was there to see Rich Stafford and gave him my name. He consulted his directory, and picked up the phone. After a brief conversation he hung up and handed me a visitor's tag and a sign-in sheet.

"He says you know the way," the guard said.

"We'll see about that in Vegas," I said, happy that I'd been able to fire off my first smart-ass esoteric comment of the day to someone who had absolutely no idea what I was talking about.

Big Rich's office was on the sixth floor, but I resisted my temptation to take the stairs in favor of the quicker elevator. Besides, Chappie's "light workout" of yesterday had turned into something more akin to a gut-cruncher. Plus, I'd already done my morning run. It was time to even out and conserve energy. To maintain my conditioning, not strive for new muscle soreness. I was in about as good a shape as I could hope to be taking a fight on short notice. Thankfully, I hadn't let myself slip, like some fighters do, so I was always in pretty decent condition. But, would that be enough to beat Sergei Seleznyov, the giant of Mother Russia? I wondered silently as the doors opened on the sixth floor.

Big Rich was seated behind his usual highly organized desk, his bulky frame totally obscuring his chair, talking to some guy. Rich wore a short-sleeve shirt with the collar open, his tie lolling off to the side in a relaxed knot. When I walked in he shoved his thick glasses farther up on his nose and grinned, his teeth looking small under his overlapping mustache.

"Hey, Ron, long time no see." He stood up with the concerted effort it takes when you weigh around 300 pounds, and extended his big hand.

We shook, and he introduced me to the other guy. "This is Len Jellema, a good buddy of mine."

I shook hands with Jellema. He was a big guy who looked like he could handle himself. His grin was friendly and easy under a big mustache.

"Glad to meet you," I said, and then to Rich, "Can we talk?"

"Sure," he said. "Len, we'll tag up later for that coffee and conversation, okay?"

"Sure thing," Jellema said. "Nice meeting you, Ron."

I said, "Likewise," and waited until he'd left. "Who's he? Your editor?"

Big Rich shook his head. "Actually, he's a retired college professor."

"College professor?"

"Yeah, but he writes, too." He grinned. "And I'm

thinking about writing a book."

"Great. You're going to give me a walk-on part, I hope."

"Of course," Big Rich said as he sat down in his big padded chair. It squeaked in protest under the weight of his bulk. He reached for his pack of cigarettes, shook one out, and stuck it in his mouth.

"Hey, I'm training for a fight," I said.

"You're always training for a fight," he said, bringing his lighter up, but not flicking it. Instead, he used it as a pointer. "Okay, you got thirty seconds to pique my interest."

"What do you know about the Gooding murder case?"

"The Gooding case?" He raised his eyebrows and considered this. The cigarette moved up and down as he worked his mouth into a thoughtful frown, then he swiveled in his chair around to his computer and pulled open his drawer. He sorted through a bunch of disks and inserted one into the slot. The cursor flashed across the screen and he clicked on several files. Articles jumped into view, and his head canted to the side as he read, clicked, and read some more. He still hadn't lit up the cigarette.

He recited the facts of the case, the dates of the trial, and the acquittal. "Justice, Chicago-style, triumphs again, thanks to a directed verdict from old Judge Samuel A. Foxworth." He took the cigarette out of his mouth and stuck it behind his right ear. "Okay, consider me piqued. What's this about?"

I gave him a rundown of my current involvement in the civil action. After listening carefully, he squinted and pursed his lips, looking like a bespectacled fish wondering what life was like on the other side of the bowl.

"There's a story in this," I said, prodding him. "You

could write a book about it. I even got a title for you. *A Journey for Justice.*"

He frowned. "Wasn't that Johnny Cochran's title?"

I shrugged. "Okay. How about *A Final Judgment*, then?"

"How about I go back to my real stories and concentrate on trying to win a Pulitzer?" He plucked the cigarette from its perch and grinned again. "Although . . ."

I raised my eyebrows. "Yeah?"

"I could possibly do something on this, if you win. How's the case look?"

"Mason Gilbert is the defense attorney."

Instead of showing shock and awe, Big Rich merely nodded.

"It figures. And also goes a long way toward explaining the directed verdict in the criminal case."

"It does?" I said, feigning ignorance. It never hurts, when dealing with a good-natured egotist, to let him think he's telling you something you don't already know.

"Gilbert and Foxworth go way back," he said. "Foxy Foxworth, he liked to call himself. Solid machine judge, always kept a low profile, made some horseshit decisions from time to time. I think he retired last year, though. Word was, they were looking at him real close, and he got tipped that another Greylord was in the works."

"Grey what?"

Big Rich did a double-take. "You're kidding, right?"

I shook my head. "Humor me."

"Operation Greylord? Gambat? Ring any bells?"

"Not really," I said.

"Come on, it was big news back in the eighties and nineties."

"When?"

He sighed. "Operation Greylord. A federal probe into judicial misconduct in good old 'Crook County.' Happened in about 'eighty-four, I think. I can't believe you never heard of it."

" 'Eighty-four? I was in grammar school, for Christ's sake."

"Gambat then. That was more of the same, only later. Nineteen-ninety, or thereabouts."

"High school."

"Well, shit, the trials lasted till at least 'ninety-two or 'three."

"I was in the army. Out of the country, being all I could be, in a little place called Mogadishu, Somalia. We were lucky to get copies of the *Stars and Stripes* once a month."

He gave me a crooked smile and leaned forward, gesturing with the still-unlit cigarette as he said, "All right. I'll get a little history lesson as well as what I have on the Gooding case together for you. Want to stop by later, or should I just e-mail it to you?"

"E-mail," I said. "I had to park by a fireplug just to get here this morning."

"All right," he said, handing me one of his cards. "Call me if there are any problems. And, of course, I'm going to expect an exclusive if you beat the Great Gilbert."

"You got it." I looked at his card. "When did you get a cell phone?"

He grinned again. "You got to keep up with the competition, or you'll get left behind, my boy."

I thought about that as I rode the elevator back down, hoping that the Firebird had missed the sharp eyes of the ubiquitous meter maids, and wondering if I'd be as successful dodging those heavy punches Saturday night.

On the way back south, I made an unsuccessful attempt

to contact George about those criminal history checks. He was still sleeping, and Ellen said that he'd told her not to wake him up before noon.

"I'm sorry, Ron, but him and Doug have been working around the clock on this latest homicide," she said.

"No problem. Ask him to give me a call when he wakes up. Otherwise I'll call back."

I went back to dictating my most recent efforts on the Gooding case into the tape recorder. If Big Rich was right about the judicial corruption angle, it would explain why the state had lost what they'd thought to be a slam-dunk case before. It would also be difficult, if not impossible, to prove. Still, if the Great Gilbert had played it fast and loose, it had to be because even he knew that the case was unwinnable. If I could make Rick see the light before I left for Vegas, I'd feel like both of us had a fighting chance to win.

I took the exit at 111th Street and cut back west on Monterey. It was close to 11:30 and I figured it was time to put Plan B into effect with a little more Intimidation 101. I passed the liquor store and pulled over to the curb on the other side of the street so I could watch the entrance in my sideview mirror. It was clear in front of the place, and nobody went in or came out for several minutes. I silently hoped that it wasn't closed, thinking I should have gotten a better idea of the hours.

No time like the present, I thought, and did a looping U-turn when the traffic cleared. I edged along so the side of my car would be visible through the diagonal wires that laced the glass on the door. There were so many posters on the windows advertising great-tasting beer, wine, and assorted other booze that they'd have to look through a gap to see anything. I wanted them to know the color and style but not much else. This was going to have to be a quick in-and-out trip, designed to disturb. To mess with their minds a bit. Less, in this case, was more.

The jingle sounded familiar when I went inside. Another angel got his wings. Or was I playing the devil this trip? Knop's uncle was behind the counter with the heavyset black clerk working on inserting the register tape. They both looked up with a smile, but the man's faded when recognition kicked in.

I nodded a hello.

Uncle's mouth bunched up before he spoke.

"What do you want?" he asked. His voice made a stab at bravado, but it fell far short. Plus his body tensed slightly, but enough to tell me that he was more than just a little afraid.

"Tim here?" I asked, using my most matter-of-fact tone as I reached for a package of sugarless peppermint gum and tossed it on the counter.

The black woman snapped the plastic holder down and finished threading the tape.

"This be all, mister?" she asked, scanning the gum. In the movies the tough guy would have just pocketed it and glared, but that would probably come back to haunt me somehow. I didn't need them phoning in a complaint report to the 22nd District. Plus, I'd left it vague enough that they probably still thought I was a cop.

I stared at Uncle, who still hadn't answered. He tried to meet my stare, but couldn't and looked away.

"Where's Tim?" I asked again.

"He's in back. Working on stock." His voice cracked slightly. "We got inventory coming up."

I held out a buck to the woman, who was seemingly oblivious to my concerted effort to look tough. Knop should have had this gal run interference for him.

She passed me my change and I picked up the gum.

"You want a bag?" she asked, her voice ripe with antagonism.

I shook my head and peeled back the wrapper on the gum, extracting a piece of gum and conspicuously letting the wrappers fall on the floor. The woman's dark eyes followed their descent, and I suddenly felt a twinge of guilt because I knew who was going to have to pick them up. But still, I had to play the role.

"I won't disturb him," I said. "Just tell him he's been doing a real good job of doing what we talked about. He knows what it is." I folded the gum in half and put it in my mouth, chewing it a couple of times as I turned and walked back toward the door and gripped the handle. "Tell him I'll still be out there watching, too."

I walked with slow deliberation around the Firebird, on to the street, and paused, for effect again, to look back into the store over the roof. I could see Uncle back a ways, peering out through the reinforced door.

Mission accomplished, I thought, as I twisted the key, checked the mirrors, and peeled away from the curb.

Back at Rick's it was obviously getting close to lunch time. Kris was gathering up her purse when I walked in. She shot me a quick, but beautiful smile.

"Hi. Didn't expect to see you this morning," she said.

I glanced at my watch. Five after twelve.

"Got time for lunch?" I asked.

I saw her eyes shoot to the left, then back.

"I have to run a few errands during my lunch hour," she said. "Probably just grab some fast food to eat in the car."

"Okay." I held up the mini-tape. "Got this done this morning."

"Great. I'll get to it right after lunch." She took the tape and stuck it in her purse. When I raised my eyebrows she made a quick look around and said in a hushed tone, "So I don't lose it. Denise has a habit of going through my desk rearranging things when I'm not here."

Rick stepped out from his inner office with Denise at his side. It was a toss-up which one looked more down. I told Kris to have a nice lunch and walked over to Rick.

"What's up, buddy?" I asked. "You look like you just found out the well was poisoned."

He started to say something, then sighed and ushered me in his office. Denise stayed outside. "You serve the rest of those summons?"

"Sure did. Got most of the coppers this morning. They weren't too pleased at the prospect of being grilled by the Great Gilbert again, but most of them are glad you're going after Gooding, though. That guy's about as popular as an Arab at a bar mitzvah."

Rick smiled. "Actually, Mason called this morning. Wanted to know if I'd discussed the revised settlement offer with my clients."

"That's interesting. If I didn't think you knew better, I'd say he was running scared."

Rick snorted. "Hardly. He reiterated that Gooding wants to spare his kids the trauma of another trial. Doesn't want to subject them to the pain of the incident all over again."

"That's touching," I said. "Maybe he should've thought about that before he whacked their mother."

"That's only part of it," Rick shot back. "I also heard that Gilbert is employing Dunton and Associates."

The way he said it, with finality and emphasis, made me

think that it was supposed to mean something big. I waited a few seconds and then said, "And they are?"

He looked stunned for a moment. "They do jury profiling. They're top of the line in the field. You know, what type of juror is most likely to vote which way in a given circumstance." He leaned back in his chair, his forehead showing the beginnings of some permanent creases, and cupped his hands over his temples. "Just what I needed to hear with the trial date and jury selection coming up next week."

"Wait a minute. Gilbert told you this?"

Rick shook his head. "No, Kris did. She has a girlfriend, who knows one of the secretaries at Gilbert's law firm. She happened to tell Kris because she heard she was working here."

I considered this, but didn't like it.

"First of all, you're worrying way too much about this. That's what? Third-hand information? Second, I been doing some digging and have a possible new slant on things."

"What's that?" He dropped his hands and leaned forward.

I suddenly wondered how much to tell him. If I did mention the specter of judicial corruption in the first case, would he be buoyed up, or dismiss it as unreliable? After all, what evidence did I have? But I decided to go for it.

"We know Gilbert and the judge were tight in the criminal case, right?"

Rick nodded.

"Well, I asked a reporter friend of mine about old Judge Foxworth, and he told me hizzoner was as crooked as a dog's hind leg." I gauged his reaction. It seemed to stun him. "So if that was the case, it makes sense now that

Gilbert is playing these mind games with you, trying to get you to go for the settlement. He knows his client is guilty. He knows he's gonna lose."

Rick looked down and shook his head.

"Ron, even if what you're saying is true . . ." His head wobbled some more. "I'm not sure . . . We can't go making some kind of wild allegations against a respected criminal courts judge. It could blow up in our faces, big time."

"Well, let me see what else I can find out," I said, not wanting to give his doubts a chance to kick in. "Like I said, I'm still running down a few loose ends."

Rick looked up and nodded.

"What else you need me to do?" I asked.

He considered this for a moment, opened his desk drawer, and set a large manila envelope on the calendar pad. It had TUNNEY scrawled in black marker across the front.

"This is poor Rob's notebook," he said, taking out a small folder. "I've been matching up his reports, what there were of them, with this." He flipped through it, rapidly at first, then slowing and going page by page. "Looks like we've just about covered everything except here." He held the open page out toward me. *See SF* was written on February 11. Two days before his suicide.

"I figured he was trying to track down Sally Forest," Rick said. "Though for the life of me, I can't figure out why. We have her deposition and it was pretty basic. Mason hardly objected at all, and agreed to stipulate that Gooding had been driving her car that day."

I looked quizzical. "Sally who?"

"Forest. Gooding's receptionist. He was driving her car when those kids spotted him in Laura's neighborhood, remember?"

"Oh, okay," I said. "You want me to follow up on it?"

He nodded. "Did you get those tapes to Kris to type?"

"Yeah," I said. "But basically they say what I just told you."

"Fine." He sat up and picked up his pen, looking suddenly like he was ready to do some real work. "I've got a ton of things to go over before the trial starts. I need to reread all those transcripts again, and figure out my questions." He got a faraway look in his eyes and smiled. "You know, for the longest time, it seemed like this trial would never get here. Always some continuance or delay. And now that it's so close . . ."

"Nerves," I said. "I'm feeling them, too."

"You are?"

"Yeah," I said. "But for a different reason." I figured that it was as good a time as any, so I told him about the fight in Vegas.

Chapter 13

When I called George back it was 12:45 and Ellen said he still hadn't gotten up. She told me to hang on and I heard her voice calling to him. He came on the line about a minute later sounding like a hoarse frog.

"Grieves," he said.

"Shade," I answered.

I heard a burst of air that I interpreted as a laugh.

"Sorry, brother," he said. "Doug and I were up most of the damn night trying to get that homicide nailed down. With this damn forty-eight-hour rule in effect, not to mention that videotaping bullshit, it makes for a lot of crunch time. Christ, you gotta be Steven fucking Spielberg nowadays to get a goddamn homicide cleared."

"The wheels of justice turn slowly," I said. "But whatever happened to the old slogan, 'We'll solve any crime on overtime'?"

"It got worked to death."

I laughed, and then asked the question: "Say, you have time to run those criminal history checks for me yet?"

"Huh? Oh, yeah."

"So?"

"Trying to think," he said. I could almost picture him on the other end of the line, standing there in his underwear, unshaven, rubbing his big hand over his face. "I think they both came back with rap sheets, but I can't remember for what."

"Can you find out? It's important."

"Christ, everything's important to you." Fatigue and irritation had crept back into his voice. I figured I'd better not push it. As it turned out, I didn't have to. "Look, I left the printouts at work. I'm going in in a little while, so I'll get back to you."

"Thanks, brother," I said. "Uhh, do you remember if you found an address on that Shields kid?"

"You really like to push it, don't you?" His tone was still gruff, but I sensed a playfulness about it this time. "Didn't get to that one. You got a DOB, or anything?"

"No."

"Then it's gonna take me some time, which up until this morning, I didn't have a whole lot of."

"Well, I really need it," I said, trying my best to convey sincerity.

"And people in hell need ice water. I'll call you later."

He hung up and I was left with the empty connection and a whole lot of nothing else.

Sally Forest had gotten married and moved shortly after the original Gooding trial, and was now Sally Panekis. Her old landlady gave me her forwarding address and phone number in exchange for a twenty, which I recorded as "expenses, no receipt" in my notebook under Rick's name. She had lived in a three-flat in Evanston, but was now in a swank-looking Georgian home in Wilmette. By the time I traced her down, it was pushing three in the afternoon. I took a minute to review her deposition, which stated unceremoniously that she had loaned Dr. Gooding her red Firebird that morning because his car was in the shop. At least I couldn't argue with her choice of vehicles. Since it was a Wednesday, the office had been closed, and Gooding dropped her off at her fitness center where she spent the day.

Pretty damaging testimony since it put Gooding in the same type of car that was seen around Laura's neighborhood. The times matched up, too. But the only cross-examination from Gilbert was to elicit that Gooding had returned the car later that afternoon, and he'd appeared normal when she saw him. Like Gilbert didn't want to prolong her appearance any longer than necessary. Reading between the lines, I figured that using her car wasn't the only thing Gooding was doing. No mention of that was in any of the official police reports, but that didn't mean anything. Something to check into, I thought, and wondered if Tunney had been pursing the same angle. He'd been around the block enough times to know the score.

This house was a real step up from the lone apartment in the three-flat. From the looks of it, there were at least three levels, and probably a plush basement, too. My basement had a cement floor and heavy rafters as a ceiling. This one probably had a bathroom just as big. It was a grayish brick structure with a gabled roof, and plenty of nicely crafted windows. Sally Forest had obviously married into money, or something. I dialed the number as I walked up the front sidewalk and rang the bell. She answered with a breathless, "Hello," as I made it to the front door.

"I'm trying to get ahold of Sally Forest," I said.

"That's . . . my maiden name. Why?"

"Ms. Panekis, I'm Ron Shade, an investigator working for Walters and Associates." Rick really didn't have any "Associates" after his name, but it sounded impressive, and since I was in the land of the rich and fatuous, I figured I needed all the help I could get. "I believe my associate Mr. Tunney already spoke to you last month, but I need to go over some things."

"I got no idea what you're talking about." Her voice was

a mixture of confusion and irritation.

"It's about the Gooding case."

"The Gooding case? Todd?"

"Right. Say, we really need to talk about this face to face."

"Well, I'm sorry. I was on my way out."

"It won't take long," I said, trying to imbue some charm and persistence into my tone. "Plus, I'm on your front porch right now. Could you come to the door?"

"You're what?" Her voice went up an octave or so. I heard some heavy breaths and could tell she was walking. Sure enough, the lacey drapes next to the door parted slightly and I waved. The figure on the other side of the glass jumped back.

"You have to leave right now. I don't want to talk to you." She disconnected. I hit the redial button and heard the phone ring twice before it instantly cut off again. Undaunted, I leaned on the doorbell buzzer for a solid ten seconds or so. The drapes parted slightly and she yelled through the glass that she would call the police if I didn't leave.

"Fine," I said. "When they get here I'll just have them witness that I'm serving you with a subpoena then. They'll have to help me serve it because it's an order of the court." They didn't, but I was banking that she wouldn't know that.

"A what?" she asked.

"A subpoena for a court appearance. I have one right here if I need it." Again, it was a little white lie, but what the hell. I was on a roll.

"What's that mean?"

"It means I really just want to talk to you for a few minutes, then I'll go away and you'll probably never see me again." I waited for that to sink in, then asked, "May I come inside?"

The solid wooden inside door opened, but a pane of solid storm-door glass separated us. Sally Panekis, nee Forest, was a good-looking blond dressed in a print silk blouse and dark tailored jeans. It wasn't hard to picture Gooding eying her in nurse's white, with a crisp, candy-striper-type hat on, drawing people into his office. She looked about twenty-eight.

I smiled. It was one of my high-wattage smiles. Her eyes narrowed.

"Let me see some identification," she said.

I held up my PI card along with the shiny police badge, and one of Rick's cards. She gave them a cursory glance, and then brought her eyes back up to mine. She had the bluest eyes I'd ever seen.

"What do you want?" she asked again. Not a rocket scientist, this gal.

"I have some questions about your deposition. It was the same thing Mr. Tunney talked to you about, probably. Shouldn't take long."

"Who is 'Mr. Tunney'? I never heard of him."

I raised an eyebrow, strictly for effect.

"An associate of mine. Older gentleman."

I watched her brow furrow. Either she had a real short memory, or Tunney hadn't gotten this far after all. She looked at her watch nervously, then back to me, the tip of her tongue darting out to coat her lips. "Look, my husband's gonna be home any minute, and I can't afford to have him see you here. Can you come back tomorrow?"

I shook my head and reached inside my upper jacket pocket and took out an envelope. It actually contained a receipt for an old veterinarian bill that I'd forgotten about, but it looked semi-official.

"I'm afraid I'll have to go with the subpoena, then."

She checked the watch again and looked at me. This time I could see pleading in those blue eyes.

"There's a Starbucks over in the strip mall," she said. "I'll meet you over there, okay?"

I nodded. Of course, there was a chance that she wouldn't show up at all, but I sensed that her concern for not having to explain whatever she thought this was to hubby would override any sense of guile on her part. I put the envelope back into my inside pocket and said, "I'll follow you."

The Starbucks was a typical Starbucks. You seen one, you seen 'em all, the saying goes. I bought a regular coffee for her and blackberry sage tea for myself, and we sat in at a table near the back.

"I'd appreciate it if we can make this quick," she said, holding her cup with both hands.

"Sure," I said, taking out my notebook. "You're sure you don't remember talking to Mr. Tunney?"

She shook her head. "No one's talked to me about Todd since the trial." Her brow furrowed again. "Hey, wait a minute, he was found innocent before. I thought you couldn't be tried twice for the same thing."

I smiled.

"Actually," I said with the slow deliberation of someone who knows he has the overwhelming assurance of being absolutely right, "you're partially correct. He can't be tried criminally for the same offense. This is a civil action."

That seemed to dazzle her enough for me to begin going over the basics of her deposition. She replied with the same pat answers, but I noticed she kept wiping her hands on her pants. I flipped the notebook closed and smiled my most knowing smile at her. Her eyes met mine for only a moment before flashing away.

"So," I said with a measure of finality. "Why don't you tell me the rest of it?"

"What rest of it?"

I sighed and patted my pocket.

"What you didn't tell the police or the lawyers in your deposition," I said. "What really happened that day Gooding borrowed your car." She stared at me, blinking rapidly. "And don't think I don't already know."

The blue eyes dropped downward.

"Look, mister, I've got a whole new life now. A great husband, a great house, a nice neighborhood . . . We're talking about maybe having a baby next year."

The ideals of North Shore bliss, I thought. But I said, "Then you'd better cooperate with me now so I can try to keep you out of it."

Her perfect teeth closed over her lower lip. For a moment I wondered if she was going to suddenly get up and leave, telling me to go pound sand, but when she looked up again, I knew I had her.

"You can keep me out of it?" she asked.

"I'll do my best," I lied. But it was a reassuring-sounding lie.

She took a deep breath and began. Gooding had been borrowing her car routinely for the previous three weeks, always on a Wednesday, to drive up to spy on his ex-wife. Since it was Sally's aerobics day, he'd just drop her off and pick her up when she'd finished.

"But that day he didn't show up at the regular time," she said. "I kept trying his cell phone, but all I got was his voice mail. I was about ready to go nuts when he called me." She glanced around before continuing. "He sounded real, I don't know, tense. Todd got that way when something went wrong. When he needed you to do something just right."

"What did he say?"

"Just that I should take a taxi home, and he'd drop the car off later." She frowned. "I asked him what was wrong, worried he'd been in an accident or something, but he just snapped at me. It seemed like such a little thing to get so mad over . . ."

"And did he drop the car off?"

She nodded. "Yeah, I guess so. He never showed up for dinner or anything, like he used to on Wednesdays, but the next morning I looked out and saw his car was gone and mine was back."

"What about the keys?"

"He had his own set," she said, looking down again. "It wasn't until I heard what had happened to his ex that I figured it out."

"So you knew?"

She nodded again. A solitary tear wound its way down her cheek. "Yeah. I found a remote—one of those garage door opener things—clipped to my visor. When I asked him about it later in the week, after the cops had come to talk to him, he turned all white and ran out of the office. When I went home that night, the garage thingie was gone."

"Were you and he seeing each other?"

She heaved a sigh. "Yeah, yeah, we were. I was young and foolish, and was screwing the boss. He was always bringing me nice presents, you know, nice stuff. But after that garage door thing, I got scared. I mean, what if he woulda come after me?"

"Why didn't you tell the cops?"

"They never asked me," she said defensively. "Plus, I

couldn't make myself believe he really did it. I mean, after all, we used to . . ."

"Yeah," I said.

Rick was ecstatic when I told him what I'd found out, even though he had to stay late to wait for me to get back from the North Shore. I'd called the office on my cell phone, saying I had important information and needed him to stay put till I got there. Kris had seemed interested, too, but when I got there Rick told me that he'd already sent her home for the day. Denise, however, faithful as a lap dog, was waiting with him in the chair against the wall of the office.

"This is fabulous, Ron, just fabulous," he said, sitting behind his desk with his hands steepled in front of one of the widest grins I'd seen lately. "Not only does it go to a pattern of behavior, but it shoots his alibi all to hell, too. And you said she's agreed to testify?"

"I finally convinced her that it was best to do the right thing."

"Is that what old Rob talked to her about?"

I shrugged. "She said she never talked to Tunney."

He made one of those "hmmph" sounds. "Maybe he was more out of it than I realized." Then, cocking his head toward me, he asked, "So what do you make of it?"

I was about to say that it was too early to tell, and that a good investigator never makes assumptions until he's gotten all the evidence. I wondered if Tunney knew that, or if he'd passed some final mental buoy on the way round the point of no return. But I knew Rick's confidence had been eroded lately.

"It means," I said, "that Gooding, and hence the Great Gilbert, have both, to quote an old army term, stepped on their dicks."

Rick huffed an embarrassed-sounding laugh and turned red. I remembered that Denise was in earshot and rolled my eyes. Like she hadn't heard that kind of language before.

I followed up, still trying to bolster his confidence.

"I told you you had him. This puts another nail in Gooding's coffin."

"You know, you may be right," he said, leaning back and putting his hands behind his head.

No "maybes" about it, I thought.

"And the best part," Rick said, "is that she's already on our standing witness list. I was figuring on just using her deposition to save time, too. No wonder Gilbert was so light on the cross and stipulated to her deposition so easily."

"And what does that tell you?" I asked.

He looked at me with a quizzical expression.

"That the Great Gilbert knows the real story," I said. "He was just hoping you wouldn't find out in time. Just like he knew Gooding was guilty in the first trial. Like I told you, he's an asshole."

"Well now," Rick said, sitting forward and resting his forearms on the desktop. "Technically, as a defense attorney, he wasn't required to turn over any information or evidence to the prosecution, even if it points to his client's guilt. It's part of the checks and balances of our legal system."

Denise leaned forward, too, beaming at the ethics-in-law lecture. He was starting to sound just as platitudinous as one of those phony TV lawyers on a David E. Kelley show.

"Yeah," I said, "well, so much for the pursuit of justice, I guess."

Rick said he'd make some provision to have Sally

Panekis served by his regular process server Wednesday, since I'd be going out of town. He wished me luck on the fight, too. That left me Tuesday to set everything up on the Bielmaster matter, tie up any loose ends for Rick, and pack. I also had to make arrangements for the cats being fed, their pans cleaned, and the mail taken in. I called George and caught him up and awake for a change.

"I need a favor," I said.

"Knowing you, that probably means you need a couple of them."

"You must be physic."

I heard him snort.

"That's psychic, and no, I ain't. You're just easier to read than a fucking book." His voice went from a low rumble to a heavy sigh. "Look, I'm on my way to the hardware store. Meet me at Karson's in about forty minutes for a quick cup and tell me about it."

The forty minutes ended up giving me just enough time to shoot home, feed the cats, who were all lined up waiting as I walked in the door, and pack my gym bag. I also did a quick check of my E-mails, and found Big Rich's under the heading of "Educate yourself, youngster." I downloaded the attachment and printed it out.

When I sat across from George at our usual booth I couldn't help but notice the bags under his eyes seemed to have gotten worse. When I asked if he was all right, he snorted and said, "Nah, every time I try to get some sleep, you call me."

"Sorry," I said, wondering how to broach the subject of the criminal history checks, the Bielmaster/Knop affair, and feeding the cats for a couple days.

"Ah, hell," he said. "It wouldn't have made any difference anyway. Right after that, the damn upstairs toilet went on the blink. Ellen was screaming 'cause it was overflowing on the floor. I jumped outta bed and grabbed my piece, thinking somebody'd broke in."

"How bad is it?"

He shrugged. "It just needed to be plunged a little, is all. But she broke the damn flusher monkeying around with it." He pointed to a bag from Home Depot.

"Ah, Mr. Fixit." I grinned. "I'll call you the next time mine breaks."

"Yeah, right." He took a swig of his coffee and held up his hand. "Don't even ask. I got the scoop on what you needed. Doug was in finishing the reports and dropped it off on the way back. Just keep it between me and you about this, okay? With these damn computer trailers they got on everything now, it shows up for something like ten days on any plates or people we run. If the brassholes find out I been doing you an informal favor here . . ." He let the sentence trail off and spread some perforated computer printouts on the table.

"Okay, this Paul LeMatte dude has a little bit of a sheet. Who is he again?"

"Supposedly one of Laura Gooding's ex-boyfriends. The Great Gilbert's using him to trash her reputation. Make her seem like a slut and a drug user."

"Figures," George said, his grin reflecting the cynicism of his next words. "Three DUIs, six larcenies, four burglaries, and ten PCSs. The guy's a shithead."

I glanced at the summarized listing. "Only three convictions?"

He nodded and flipped the page. "It gets better."

I scanned the new sheet, this one for street artist Harry Norridge, the guy who drew the caricature of Gooding on the day of the murder. Or, as the lawyers would say, allegedly drew it. His real name was Harold E. Pennington III. He was originally from the North Shore, but he liked to hang around downtown. His arrests were mostly small-scale stuff, from shoplifting to disorderly conduct. He did have three arrests for PCS, though.

"Vice busted him a couple of times for soliciting in the washrooms in Grant Park," George said. I looked at him.

"He gay?"

"What do you think?" His big finger tapped the paper. "Now check this out, Mr. Hotshot Detective. See the pattern? Take a look at Norridge's last arrest. It was two years ago in District One for possession of a controlled substance." George then flipped the page back to LeMatte's sheet. "Now lookie here. Another PCS arrest last year for this piece of shit, once again by CPD."

"Interesting," I said.

"Yeah, hypes of a feather . . . And guess who represented them both times?"

I raised an eyebrow. "Not the Great Mason Gilbert?"

He nodded. "Small world, ain't it?"

I looked at the dates again. Norridge's arrest had been before the Gooding case, LeMatte's after the acquittal. I wondered if LeMatte had been on Gilbert's original witness list for the criminal trial.

"I'll bet he got 'em both off, too," I said.

"Right again. You want to try for 'Double Jeopardy' this time and take a guess who the judge was?"

"Judge Foxworth? On both cases?"

He smirked. "Well, that was kind of a half-assed response, but at least you phrased it as a question."

"Okay, *Alex*. Now let me ask you something. You ever hear of Operation Greylord?"

"Greylord? Sure. It was that sting that netted a bunch of judges and lawyers, and"—he raised his eyebrows and looked down at the table—"a couple of coppers, too, unfortunately."

"So you think Foxworth could be dirty?"

He shrugged again. "Yeah, well, who knows? Suspecting a judge is dirty is one thing, but it takes a lot more proof than finding a few horseshit decisions he's made over the years."

"Well, can we look into it?"

"Yeah, right. Why don't we waltz right down to Twenty-sixth Street and tell the head judge that we think one of his boys is a crook." He rolled his eyes and took a swig of coffee. "Those judges are insulated, Ron. You can't even fucking sue 'em, for Christ's sake."

He had a point, but still, knowing how Gilbert probably won the Gooding case, and being prepared not to let that happen again, made this one all the more winnable.

"So what's going on with the Bielmaster thing?" he asked.

I brought him up to speed on the latest tactics and told him I needed to make sure Ken would be able to handle the surveillance alone while I was in Vegas.

"Vegas?" he asked, crinkling his brow. "So it's on for sure?"

"Yep. Saturday night," I said, smiling. "And, it's for the championship."

His face lit up like a Scotch pine at Christmastime.

"Hey, that's great, Ron. Who you fighting? Elijah Day again?"

"I wish. It's some Russian dude I never heard of. At least with Day, I knew what to expect."

"Shit, you'll murder the bum." He punched me lightly

on the arm just as my cell phone rang. I looked at the screen and saw it was Kris's number.

"Hi," I said, pressing the button.

"Hi, yourself," she said. "What you doing?"

I gave her a brief rundown and said I was heading to the gym.

"Yeah, he's got a fight to win, so quit bothering him," George yelled out from across the table.

"Who's that?" she asked.

"Oh, just some big, dumb homeless guy that I felt sorry for," I said. "Say, why don't you come to the gym and I'll buy you a drink or something afterwards?"

"Sounds good," she said, and told me she'd see me there.

George was staring at me with a knowing smirk as I set my phone down.

"So what's this one's name?" he asked.

"Kris. She works out at Chappie's gym."

"Man, it's just like I always say," he said. "If you're not working out, or getting laid, you're bugging me to do some kind of favor for you. Just remember, you owe me big time, buddy."

"How could I ever forget? You remind me about ten times a week." I picked up the criminal history sheets and folded them into my pocket. "Thanks for these, but did you get anything on that Mark Shields guy?"

"Jesus H. Christ on a bicycle," he said, taking out his cell phone. "You never give up, do ya?" He started dialing. "Lemme check with my buddy in records. He was supposed to run that down and get back to me."

I was wondering when the right time would be to ask him to take care of the cats as he grunted into the phone, talking to his on-duty friend.

"Is that so?" he said. "All right, keep me posted, on the QT."

I looked over at him expectantly but he shook his head.

"Not much to go on without more pertinent information," he said. "But he's working on it. I'll have to get back to you."

"I appreciate it."

"Anyway," he said, picking up his coffee cup and shooting me a wry grin before he drank. "Sounds like you got enough to chew on as it is with . . . what's her name? Kris."

"With a K," I said, nodding.

Three hours later Kris and I sat in a booth in Fox's pub sharing a glass of wine for her and a large cranberry juice for me. The workout had been uncharacteristically mild, but I knew Chappie didn't want to take the chance that I might be injured this close to the fight date. Kris was waiting for me in the parking lot when I came out, after hearing my explanation that Chappie would freak if he saw us leaving together. We'd forfeited any late evening meal for a chance to just sit and talk.

"So when are you leaving?" she asked.

"Probably Wednesday," I said. "Chappie's making the arrangements, and he wants us there a few days ahead of time to get used to the climate."

She took a sip of her wine, looking at me over the rim of the glass.

"So does that mean stopping by tonight is within the realm of possibilities, or out of the question?"

I grinned.

"I'd really like to, but I need to conserve my strength."

"How about if I do all the work?" She shot me a Mona Lisa smile.

I took my time considering the possibilities, but shook my head. "I'm sorry. I can't."

"Too bad," she said, showing me that alluring smile again. "Will I at least get to hear your voice? Any tapes for me to listen to and type?"

"I'll probably drop one off before I go. I guess I should do an official report for Rick, even though he already knows what I found out today."

"And what was that?"

"Gooding was having an affair with his receptionist. He borrowed her car on the day of the murder and was seen driving it. The Great Gilbert was stipulating to a few of the facts in her deposition, but with what she told me today, Rick's going to have to subpoena her."

"Wow. Why?"

I was about to answer when the waitress came by and asked if we needed any refills. We both declined.

"If I tell you now," I said, "then you won't have any surprises when you listen to the tapes."

"That's right, I won't." She finished off the rest of her wine and reached over, touching my hand. "Are you sure you won't come over tonight?"

"Regrettably, I am."

"Fine." She withdrew her fingers. "And when will you be getting back?"

"Probably Sunday night."

"Good, that'll give me something to look forward to." Her smile was so nice that I didn't even want to mention that I'd probably be so sore that the only thing I'd want to hold would be an icepack or a hot water bottle.

Chapter 14

I sat back and listened to the pilot's admonition that all cell phones and laptops had to remain off during the flight, and felt the slight tightening in my gut as I heard the big turbines revving up. Not that I was afraid of flying. I'd done enough of it on everything from DC-10s to Black Hawk helicopters in the Army. No, this time it was a case of the creeping nerves of not knowing exactly what I'd be facing in Las Vegas. And the sense that there was urgent, unfinished business that I'd be leaving unattended at home. The plane began speeding forward; I waited for the lift-off and glanced over to watch the ground getting smaller and smaller as we ascended. I'd taken the aisle seat, giving Alley the window seat with Chappie in the middle. Across the aisle, Raul and Vic Roddy sat grinning. This was a free trip to Vegas for them and the beginning of a great test for me. I hoped I'd be up to the task.

My final Chicago run had been cold and blustery that Wednesday, at five in the morning, but I was somehow heartened when I noticed it was already getting light out. Going from the darkness to the light . . . metaphorical, but it reminded me that spring was just around the corner. The days would be getting longer, and maybe somehow time would be extended for me. But even though we'd be gaining two hours on the flight west, I still felt like time was slipping through my fingers like a rope made out of smoke.

I'd made certain that Ken had the Bielmaster surveillance covered, using my Firebird in combination with the Beater. Plus, I'd asked George to make a call to the Commander in the 22nd District to alert him of Ken's presence and to also keep making those ride-bys. George still hadn't gotten back to me with anything on Mark Shields, and my not being around to gently prod him would no doubt shift that favor to the back burner. But then again, that was the beauty of cell phones with their free long-distance rates. I'd have to give him a call. And Kris had asked me to call her about the fight from Vegas, too. It was kind of nice knowing I had someone special waiting for me back home, win, lose, or draw.

Let's see, I thought, if I get up to run at five, Vegas time, it'll be seven in Chicago. Certainly doable.

And then there was Rick's case. I'd dropped off the tape detailing my latest findings regarding Sally Panekis, more out of a sense of professionalism and completeness than anything else. After all, I'd already told Rick about it, and he was feeling pretty good. I felt less guilty about leaving while he was riding the crest of the wave, so I figured that turning in the report would give a certain tangibility to my contribution. Not like the way old Rob Tunney had left him high and dry. Of course, I fully intended on coming back, whereas Tunney's trip out of the picture had been a one-way ticket.

I thought about Tunney as we leveled off and the flight attendants began walking down the aisle hawking earphones for the movie. Chappie held up a twenty and looked at me. I shook my head, lowered the tray on the back of the seat in front of me, and took out my pen and notebook.

"I think I'll just record my thoughts," I said.

"Just make sure they all about winning," Chappie said, and handed a set of earphones to Alley before slipping on his own set. I went back to my notebook scribblings.

TUNNEY, I wrote, then thought again about what Rick

had told me two days ago.

"I figured he was trying to track down Sally Forest," Rick had said, holding out the notebook with the *See SF*. Written on February 11. Two days before he took his own life.

I wondered what demons Tunney had been harboring to drive him to such an act. Had there been any signs? Any way to prevent it? But why wasn't he able to do something as simple as tracking down Sally Forest? He'd been a copper for almost thirty years and probably still had contacts in the PD . . . Finding out she had moved, married, and changed her name to Panekis would have been duck soup for him. But she said he never talked to her. Had something happened that day to really send him over the edge? I made a mental note to ask George what he knew about Tunney's death. Just so I could eliminate any loose ends in my own mind. The plane suddenly hit some turbulence and the FASTEN SEAT BELTS sign came on.

After all, loose ends can trip you up.

The airport in Vegas was all glitz. Shiny, stainless steel arches over rows of slot machines. Everywhere you turned bright lights advertised big jackpots. It took us about thirty minutes to claim our luggage, after which we went outside. The hot dry air hit me like a blast from a sauna bath, and it dawned on me that although we'd left Chicago at 10:20, it was only around noon here. Alley seemed fascinated with the tall palm trees that graced the lush center area that separated the opposite lanes of the street.

"What you call these trees?" he asked.

"Palm trees," Chappie said, holding up his outstretched hand. "And just remember that everybody around here has an open one, ready to put in your pocket."

We spent the next ten minutes explaining to Alley what Chappie had meant and grabbing a shuttle bus to the MGM Grand Hotel. The bus driver made a few deft turns and got us on a main drag that wound out of the desert and toward the substantial city skyline. Huge towers seemed to spring out of nowhere against a backdrop of distant mountains. When we got on the strip and passed the famous sign welcoming us to "Fabulous Las Vegas, Nevada," the glitzy façade seemed to extend as far as the eye could see.

"We got us an interview with some ESPN guys at two," Chappie said, looking at his watch. "I gotta make some calls. Get us set up in one of the boxing gyms for workouts, too." He seemed kind of nervous when he looked at me. "How you feeling, Ron?"

"Great," I lied. Actually, the nerves were starting to gnaw at me, and I wondered if I'd be going home a champ, or a chump.

The fountains in front of the hotel danced in time to Elvis's voice singing "Viva Las Vegas," shooting sprays up at least seventy feet in the air. We'd done our pre-fight interview, our workout, and eaten a light dinner at one of the buffets. I kept glancing at my watch trying to adjust to the new time zone and lull myself into the belief that I had more of it than I actually did. I silently wished I'd had more time to prepare for what in all probability would be the fight of my life, and I hated the thought that I might have come all the way to Vegas to lose.

With Vic and Raul hitting the tables in the casino with a vengeance, Chappie, Alley, and I went walking on Las Vegas Boulevard, trying to melt in with the constant throngs of people. We'd stopped in front of the Bellagio to watch the water show, tired of dodging the constant handouts from the ubiquitous lines of Hispanics who offered escort service handouts every hundred feet or so.

Alley, eager to please, had accumulated quite a collection of them and finally asked me what they were.

"Advertisements for hookers," I said.

"Huh?"

I pointed to the picture on the cover and rubbed my index finger and thumb together. "Girls for money."

"Oh," he said, showing a mixture of awe and understanding.

"Toss those in the trash," Chappie said. "We got no time for any of that shit till after the fight."

I smiled at him. Same old Chappie. One of the ESPN broadcasters, an older guy who had covered boxing in the seventies, had recognized Chappie during our interview.

"Say, aren't you Chappie Oliver?" the guy had asked.

Chappie nodded.

"You fought Marvin Hagler, right?"

Chappie nodded again, with a slight smile.

"I covered that fight," the broadcaster said. "It was one of the greatest I've ever seen. I thought it was even money going into the seventh."

"Well, Marvin, he was the better man that night," Chappie said with a wistful look in his eyes.

Now, as the fountains continued their dance, I studied Chappie's profile. The flashing lights made glossy patterns on his shiny mahogany skin and shaved head. Darlene had told me about the Hagler fight once. It had been his well-deserved chance at the championship, but two weeks before fight night, his son, James, had been killed in a gang shooting. It had been a drive-by. James had been fifteen, and a fine amateur fighter set to enter the Junior Golden Gloves. A good boy, Darlene had said, and his death seemed to kill part of Chappie, too. He broke training to deal with the tragedy, and paid for it in the ring, fading halfway through, and getting a terrible beating from the champ. Even though he continued to fight for years afterward, he'd left something in the ring that night, and never was able to bridge that infinitesimal distance that separates the very good from the great. He retired, never having gotten another crack at the championship belt that he'd so coveted.

Recalling the look on his face at the news interview that afternoon, I realized that I wasn't just fighting for me in this one.

"What you thinking about, Ron?" he asked me, turning to look at me. His gaze was piercing and the lights continued to play over his dark face.

"I was just reminding myself how lucky I am to have you in my corner," I said.

He smiled.

"We gonna win this one. I feel it."

I hoped he was right.

Another full day passed without me seeing my opponent. We'd sent Alley out on a recon mission to scope out the other camp. He'd returned to the room looking nervous and shaken. This bothered me a bit, since he'd been very relaxed on our morning run.

"Sergei look good," he said, flashing a quick grin that looked about as honest as the kid caught with his hand in the cookie jar. "Good shape. Really good shape."

Silently, I wished he hadn't told me that. He must have realized he'd slipped up even before Chappie yelled at him.

"Don't even tell me you talked to him." Chappie's eyes narrowed. "I told you just to check things out, not get all sociable."

"Sorry, but Sergei see me. He know me from Russian boxing team. We talk."

"Shit," Chappie said.

"Hey, it's okay," I said. Turning to Alley, I asked, "What did he say? He ready for this one?"

Alley's mouth kind of pulled down at the corners and it looked like he was searching for the right words. Finally, he took a deep breath and said, "He ready. He say you gonna lose, Ron."

"Shit," Chappie said. "He gonna be eating them words. The motherfucker."

"Hey, it's okay," I said. "I didn't come out here expecting a cakewalk, right?"

Chappie spent the next ten minutes telling me how bad we were going to kick "that big Russian's ass," as we packed our gear to head to the gym. I knew it would be a light workout, and I was actually looking forward to it. The morning run had done a lot to ease my anxiety. We'd gotten up at six and marched through the almost deserted casino, occasionally spying blurry-eyed losers who still sat in front of the brightly lit machines, pumping in coin after coin. It was the only time I'd seen the main street empty, and the run had been sort of relaxing in the still-cool desert air. Now, however, the heat was back, and despite everything that people said about it being a "dry heat," it still felt plenty hot to me.

On the cab ride to the gym, I began to long for a glimpse of this Sergei guy, so I could size him up. Maybe try to concoct some strategy. We'd struck out on getting any tapes of his previous fights. All I knew was that he was supposed to be big and tough. The international rules bothered me also. That meant leg kicks were in. But there wouldn't be a minimum number of required kicks, so maybe I could just stay away from him until he got tired.

My cell phone snapped me out of my reverie. Chappie gave me a dirty look when I answered it.

"How's the training going out there?" George's voice asked me.

"Great," I said. "Wish you were here."

"That makes two of us." I heard him sigh. "Temps dropped down to the forties with a cold rain."

I had a sudden flash of cool weather and rain-slicked streets and began to feel kind of homesick.

"Anyway," he continued, "I finally got a line on that Mark Shields guy you asked me about. He used to live on the South Side, near to where you said his uncle lived. Thirty-ninth and Claremont."

"Used to live?"

"Yeah," he said. "But as of last year, his driver's license shows surrendered to a foreign state. Arizona, to be exact. You want it?"

"Yeah, definitely," I said, reaching into my pocket for a pen. I had no paper so I had to borrow a tablet sheet from the cabbie.

"Hope he don't charge us extra for that," Chappie muttered, angry that I was doing detective work on the way to training.

I ignored him and wrote down the address that George read off to me, 301 West Jefferson, Phoenix, Arizona.

"A long way from Chi-town," he said.

"Yeah, it is."

But, I thought, not too far from Las Vegas.

Chappie could barely contain his anger when I told him I had to make one quick call before we started the workout.

"Sure, go ahead, do that," he said, walking out of the

locker room. "All I'm trying to do is get you ready for the championship, is all."

I grinned, wondering which one of us wanted it more, and dialed the number for Rick's office, glancing at the cell phone clock. It was still set on Chicago time and showed 4:36 p.m. I hoped that he'd still be there, but all I got was an answering machine. I left a brief message asking him to call me tomorrow regarding a possible important development and terminated the call. I didn't have his home number in my phone lexicon, and doubted that his number would be listed. Besides, Chappie was right about having a fight to get ready for. I clipped the phone to my belt and shoved my pants into the locker.

Time to face the music, I thought.

The last few workouts before a fight were usually designed to just keep me sharp. By that time in the training cycle, all the hard sparring and cardiovascular exercises should have already put me in the best shape possible. This time I'd taken the fight on such short notice that Chappie was a little more worried that I wasn't at my best. I knew I was in as good a condition as I was going to get and hoped it would be enough. But conditioning wasn't the real problem at this point. Nerves were. The closer the fight got, the more my doubts and insecurities gnawed at me. It was like having something eating at my gut from the inside.

It was a gamble doing sparring two days before the fight as well, risking a cut or injury before the actual match, but we decided to chance it. After all, we were in Vegas, and Chappie lined up a really tall sparring partner for me.

This guy, a black guy named Shadrock Smith, must have been six-six and had a lean build. Chappie smeared my face up good with Vaseline to deflect the blows, and laced the protective helmet on, as well as the sixteen-ounce gloves.

"I want you to practice getting inside, under his jab, and do the shoeshine on him," he told me.

The "shoeshine" meant delivering a combination of rapid body blows. It was particularly effective against a taller opponent, if you could get past his longer reach. The name came from the hand action, which old-timer boxing experts likened to the snapping of a shoeshine rag.

"Alley, get over here," Chappie yelled.

Alley, who had been working one of the bags, trotted over, a big smile on his face.

"Da, Chappie," he said.

"Don't 'da' me. Tell me about this Sergei guy. How's he fight? He left- or right-handed?"

Alley thought for a moment and assumed an orthodox stance.

"That good," Chappie said. "Means we don't have to worry none about dealing with some lefty."

"He got good left, too," Alley said, swinging out a hook. "Knock out many Cuban with left. With right, too."

Oh great, I thought. Knockout power in either hand. This was shaping up to be a real fun match-up.

Chappie frowned.

"Wish I could go look at this dude . . . See him sparring, or something. Wonder how good he is with his feet?"

"He look pretty good," Alley said.

"Ain't you full of good news," Chappie said, frowning again.

"But Ron look better," Alley added, smiling. The kid was completely without guile, and that somehow made me feel a little better.

Shadrock turned out to be a pretty skilled boxer with a pretty decent jab. He was catching me regularly the first round, until toward the end of the three minutes I caught my rhythm and began to slip it. Then I'd duck under and punish his rib cage, just like Chappie had instructed. After three rounds, he winced and went down on one knee.

"I'm gonna need some padding, bro," he said. "I only do this part-time."

"That's good," Chappie said, stepping forward with a pair of focus mitts. "Take five and go find some then. We got some more work to do."

We went over punching and kicking drills for the next three rounds. When the bell rang, Chappie looked around the gym but Shadrock was nowhere to be seen.

"Looks like that motherfucker took off," he said with a satisfied-looking smirk. "Just as well, we done what we needed to do anyway."

He took me through a light punching drill for one more round, then we did sit-ups and he told me to hit the steam. Even though we were in the desert, the cloudy heat felt good. I sat with a towel around me and inhaled, feeling the hot air in my nose and throat. I'd had little difficulty slipping Shadrock's jab, which, by boxing standards, had been pretty formidable. Now if I could bring that same technique to the ring on Saturday . . .

The door to the steam room opened and Alley stood in the opening, partially obscured by the cloudy air.

"Ron, phone," he said.

Phone? I wondered what the hell he was talking about, as I got to my feet and stepped out into the instant coolness of the locker room. Alley pointed to my locker, from which I heard the distinctive ringing of my cell phone. I unfastened the key from my towel and moved to the locker, getting it open just as the ringing stopped. The number had a Chicago area code, and although I didn't recognize it, I hit the recontact button. Rick answered almost immediately.

"Hey, what's up?" I asked.

"Ron? I just tried to call you. I checked the office voice mail and got your message."

"Yeah, I got a line on that Mark Shields guy." I was sweating so profusely I was leaving quite a puddle on the floor. I sat on one of the benches and leaned forward so the towel would absorb more sweat. Alley went to the basket and grabbed a fresh towel for me.

"Who?" Rick asked.

"Mark Shields. He was an intern with Gilbert during the Gooding trial. Just the mention of his name seemed to make the great one's co-counsel nervous. Remember? Mary something."

"An intern?" I heard him sigh on the other end. "Nothing he could say would help us. It would all be considered privileged."

He sounded deflated.

"It won't hurt to ask, will it? He's out this way in Phoenix."

"Phoenix? I thought you were in Las Vegas?"

"I am. But I figured if it was okay with you, I'd rent a car Monday, after the fight, and drive out to see him." When he didn't reply, I added, "I wanted to check with you first, so you didn't see the rental on the expense sheet and think I was running a game on you." When he still didn't reply, I asked, "What's wrong?"

"Oh, nothing," he said, but I could tell he wasn't being truthful. "Just some complications, that's all."

"Complications?"

"Yeah. We're gonna have to drop the whole plan to call Sally Panekis."

"What? Why? She told me she was willing to do the right thing and testify for us."

"My process server tried to deliver that subpoena to her today. Couldn't find her."

"Huh? I gave you her new address, didn't I?"

"Yeah, but she's no longer there. Her husband said she's away visiting her sick mother."

"Where's 'away'?"

"He wouldn't say."

"Well, shit, did your guy lean on him a little?"

"No, he didn't." His voice held a petulant tone, but softened slightly when he added, "The poor guy looked like he'd been in some sort of accident. I guess his face was swelled up like a catcher's mitt. He just wouldn't stand there and talk."

I wiped my face with the clean towel.

"Anyway, I came back into the office to try and figure a new strategy."

"As long as you don't give up. Remember what Winston Churchill said."

"And what was that?"

"Never, never, never quit," I said.

I heard him chuckle. "Okay, buddy. I won't."

We chatted for a few more minutes and then hung up, with me thinking that I'd have to remember those words myself come Saturday.

Chapter 15

I got my first real glimpse of Sergei Seleznyov Friday morning at the weigh-in. It was just a formality, really, since we were both heavyweights and had no maximum weight we had to come in under. I walked out of the changing room and into the events center that they were transforming into the auditorium-sized room where the fight would be held. Several news cameramen were filming the proceedings, including the ESPN guy who'd taped our respective interviews the day before. The one older boxing broadcaster smiled at us when we came in, but his partner was holding a microphone in front of this huge guy standing off to the side of the scale. Our eyes met and locked for a second and I knew in an instant it was him. Not like it wasn't a no-brainer. Who else would be standing around in his underwear wearing a silk fighting robe at a pre-fight press conference weigh-in? His eyes were dark and flat-looking, and his face showed hardly any expression at all. Impervious, untroubled, totally confident. After a moment he looked away when the broadcaster asked a question. As the challenger, it was proper protocol for me to get weighed first.

I wasn't quite prepared for him to be so tall and broad. Even under the light robe he wore, his shoulders and chest looked enormous. He had a long face, with a big jaw and a nose that told me he was used to getting hit with little effect. I felt like Sylvester Stallone staring up at Dolph Lundgren in that old *Rocky* movie. I moved in closer and Seleznyov towered over me by at least four or five inches. That was bad enough, but after a question about his physical conditioning for the fight, his expression twisted into a scowl, and he shirked off his robe, revealing a chiseled build with no perceivable fat at all. His hands looked like blocks of granite suspended by steel cables, his legs tree trunks.

"Sergei is disappointed, naturally," his trainer was saying to the interviewer in heavily accented English, "that his original opponent, Trey Gillian, had to cancel due to an injury." The guy was short and stocky, with a face that reminded me of a caricature of a pig. "But he has seen Ron Shade fight and expects to have a good match." He looked directly at me and added, "And a victory, of course."

I was already starting to feel a shiver of apprehension when I felt Chappie's fingers rubbing the back of my neck.

"This is better than I hoped for," he whispered into my ear as he guided me to the scale. "He muscle-bound. Gonna tire real bad in them late rounds. All we gotta do is rope-a-dope him."

"Rope-a-dope" meant letting him fire away at me until he'd punched himself out, then coming back strong. It was effective against certain types of opponents, mostly those who had a looping punching style. If this guy was a good boxer, he might already know that.

I tried to look confident and nodded toward the big Russian, slipping off my own robe.

I was in pretty good shape, though not as cut-up as I usually was. Still, I was no slouch myself in the muscle department. As I stepped on the scale, I averted my main gaze away from him, but out of the corner of my eye caught him staring. Maybe he was as impressed with me as I was with him. I wouldn't know until we stepped into the ring.

The official set the big weight at 230, and the indicator hit the bottom of the metallic rectangle. He raised his eyebrows and set it back to 225. The indicator was still at the bottom, so he kept adjusting it backward until he stopped at 215. The indicator needle went back up, striking the top portion of the metal. He used the smaller weights to finalize my reading at 218.

He called out the number and told me to step off. When Seleznyov stepped on, the indicator shot to the top with a metallic click. The official started to adjust the weights, but the Russian reached over and pushed the big weight on the scale to 250. The needle was still hitting the top of the metal rectangle. The official nodded appreciatively and used the smaller scale weights to bring it up six pounds. The needle hovered at the line mark, and Seleznyov raised his massive arms above his head as the official called out, "Two hundred fifty-six and three-quarters."

Yeah, I thought. What's thirty-eight pounds between the best of enemies?

We grabbed a leisurely lunch at one of the buffets and then began a slow walk down the strip. It was mostly just to forestall the case of the nerves that had started at the weigh-in. He wasn't Mr. Triple X anymore, and he looked plenty tough. As we moved down the crowded sidewalks, I remembered the pre-fight physical, and the doctor whistling in amazement as he wrapped the blood pressure cuff around Seleznyov's right arm. I silently reflected that I was in for the fight of my life.

We stopped in the middle of an extended pedestrian bridge that allowed us to walk over Las Vegas Boulevard from the MGM to New York, New York. Chappie and Alley looked up at the fake skyline and I glanced at my watch. Two-thirty Vegas time, so it was 4:30 back home. I took out my cell phone.

Chappie seemed to sense my anxiety, as he always did,

and asked, "You ain't planning on taking that thing into the ring, is you?"

I grinned.

"Only if I could phone in an order for brass knuckles halfway through."

He shook his head. "Ain't gonna need none. He big, sure, but he look slow, too. I was watching his moves. Bet you anything, he throws them long, looping punches that you can see coming a mile away." He raised his hands and began moving his head, throwing a couple of snapping jabs, then a right. "We gonna stick and move, stick and move. Keep making him miss. Slip that jab and get inside, do the shoeshine. That gonna take it out of him. Then by round five, he gonna begin to tire, and his behind gonna be ours." He threw a couple more punches, ducked and slipped an imaginary opponent, then threw an uppercut. "You kill the body, the head will die, and he got way too much body to protect. By eight or nine, the ref gonna be counting that boy out."

"Maybe I should have you fight the dude," I said with a grin.

He grinned back. "Sheeeit, we don't want to kill his ass, do we?"

We decided to ride the roller coaster at New York, New York, but as we walked along the ersatz streets and shops, I told them to go along without me and sat at one of the little tables outside Little Italy. I took out the cell phone again and dialed George's work number. Amazingly, he answered on the second ring.

"I thought you always waited for it to ring three times so people would think you're an overworked city employee?"

"Hell, that's what I am," he said. "How's the training going out there?"

"It's all over but the fight now. Went for my final run

this morning. Did the weigh-in and medical a little while ago."

"So you feel ready?"

"As ready as I'll ever be, I guess." I suddenly wanted to change the subject. "Say, I need a favor."

"Don't you always?" His tone was light. "And what is it this time?"

"Can you get with Ken and make sure he's got that Bielmaster thing covered? And see if he can feed the cats for two extra days. I'm not coming back Sunday night like I thought I was."

"No? Gonna try to get lucky?"

"I'm gonna drive out to Phoenix to interview that Mark Shields guy."

"Huh? As I remember you're usually pretty sore after a fight. Or is this one gonna be a cakewalk?"

"Hardly. I got to meet my opponent today."

"And?"

"Remember Ivan Drago in *Rocky IV*?"

"Yeah, but Rocky knocked the crap outta him, didn't he?"

I chuckled. "I think he paid off the scriptwriters."

"Ah, you'll murder the bum, Ron. What kinda odds they got? Put five hundred down for me on you to win by knockout."

"Yeah, right," I said. "And I suppose you'll wire me the money?"

"I'm good for it," he said, and hung up.

I glanced at my watch again. It was close to three. I did some more mental arithmetic and figured that Kris had had enough time to get home from work. I dialed her home number and got her machine. I left a quick message saying that I was thinking about her and that I'd try her cell. This time I caught her sounding a bit breathless.

"I just was heading to the gym," she said. "Figured that

maybe somebody there could tell me how you were, since you haven't let me know." I couldn't tell if her tone sounded hurt or facetious. This was turning into a long-distance, high-maintenance relationship. Something was gnawing at me. But, she was on the rebound from a bad marriage and I had to keep reminding myself that she was still fragile.

"Sorry, we've been training nonstop since I got here."

"So you find out who you'll be fighting?"

"Yeah," I said. I gave her a quick description of Super Sergei.

"Well, I know for a fact that you're in pretty good shape yourself," she said. The lightness was back in her tone. I almost hated what I had to say next.

"I have to stay out here a couple days longer than expected," I said. "I won't be home Sunday."

"Oh no? Planning on celebrating?"

"This is pure business. I've got a lead I've got to follow up on the Gooding case."

"Oh? That sounds interesting. What is it?"

Just as I was about to tell her about Mark Shields and my trip to Phoenix, I heard the ominous chirping sound that meant my battery was low.

"Are you there?" she asked.

"Barely. My battery's going out. I could be gone any second. You gonna tell me you miss me?"

"I miss you. Now what were you saying about the Gooding case?"

"You'll have to listen to the tapes when I get back," I said.

"Ron, come on, don't tease me."

"I'm checking on a guy named Mark Shields in Phoenix," I said, but the phone chirped a final time, and I was suddenly cognizant that I was talking to dead air.

Chappie and Alley came ambling back, spinning tales of

amazement about the neat ride on top of the building. I told them I'd get it on the flip-side, and we continued our walk. At Paris, Paris we took the elevator ride up the replica Eiffel Tower and got a bird's-eye view of the rest of the strip. Alley said he wanted to go see the pirate ship, and we headed farther north, stopping for a gondola ride at the Venetian, and appreciating the fine-looking ceiling art mimicking the Sistine Chapel. Alley told us he'd seen the real work on one of his trips in Europe with the Russian boxing team. Across the street, after watching the cast prepping for their nightly pirate battle, which was still hours away, we decided to go back to the Mirage to grab an early supper at the buffet.

We got there in time to see one of the unimpressive daytime eruptions of the volcano, which had thrilled us the night before. This time I saw a gas jet sticking out of one of the artificial rocks in the water, and it reaffirmed the superficiality of the whole scene for me.

Anything can seem more than it is, I thought, if you read enough into it. I realized something, standing there, with a sudden clarity that can only come from watching a phony volcano sputter and erupt with water that would seem colored with lighting when darkness fell. In my own way, I was being just as much of a defeatist as Rick was, thinking that this Sergei guy looked unbeatable. He was probably feeling the nerves just like I was, and if he wasn't, he shoulda been.

Inside, we walked down the long hallway and looked at the slumbering white tigers inside their sterile-looking glass cage. They had lions at the MGM in a similar set-up, but this one was more barren. A group of Oriental tourists tapped on the wall, yelling in a foreign language at the tigers, and holding up a camcorder. I saw a yellow eye on one of the beasts open at the sound, rotate slightly, then close again. So much for taking the beast out of the jungle.

Chapter 16

I woke up again at 5:00 a.m. Saturday morning, even though I knew I didn't have to go for a run. The fight was about sixteen hours away, and I hardly felt rested at all. Sleep had proved elusive in Vegas, although I wasn't sure if it was due to the time change, or if it was really true that the casinos pumped a lot of oxygen into the ventilation systems of the hotels to make people less tired so they'd spend more time losing money in the casinos.

I rolled over on my back and stared up at the ceiling in the darkened room. Chappie would want me to sleep more and rest the whole day up until fight time, but I felt too restless. It wasn't just the nervousness about the fight creeping up on me, either. Something else kept gnawing at me. Something I couldn't put my finger on. A feeling of imbalance, of something not quite right. What it was, I didn't know, but it lurked somewhere in the murky shadows of my mind, like the tiny scratching of a captive animal, wanting to claw its way out.

For the hell of it, I started going over the two cases in my mind. Bielmaster and Gooding. I needed to get hold of George again. Ken too. Get an update. Make sure he would be able to feed the cats Sunday and Monday for me. Then there was the matter of Mark Shields. I didn't know exactly what he'd have to say, or if he'd even talk to me at all, but it was worth a shot. Maybe I could gain an edge somehow. If nothing else, I was curious why his name had had that effect on the Great Gilbert's pretty young co-counsel, Mary What's-her-name.

But I'd promised Chappie I wouldn't make any more phone calls until after the fight. In an effort to be slick, he'd palmed the recharging unit from my room when we'd chatted last night. I let him think I didn't see because his case of the nerves was getting bad, too. I hoped it wasn't because deep down he didn't think I had a chance to win.

A wave of fatigue crept over me, and I rolled over and pulled up the blanket, intent on trying to grab a few more hours' rest, knowing I was going to need it in about fifteen hours.

The metal table felt cold under my legs as Chappie knelt in front of me wrapping my feet. I'd elected to go with the foot wraps even though I'd been informed my opponent was going barefoot. I was used to fighting with the foot protectors on and figured it would give me a minute bit of comfort feeling something around my feet. My hands were already wrapped and initialed. Vic Roddy stood in back of me rubbing my neck slightly, an unlit cigar hanging from his pendulous lips. His fingers felt strong and I knew between him and Chappie, I'd have around seventy years of cumulative ring experience in my corner tonight.

One of the guys from the Russian's camp was there also, along with an official whose job it was to watch and make sure no one did anything illegal during the wrapping process. We'd sent Alley to watch Sergei's preparations.

"And make sure you chat with him in Russian, too, telling him how Ron is the greatest fighter you ever seen," Chappie had told him.

Alley grinned and nodded, but if he understood, I had no idea.

"How come you wrap foot?" the Russian watcher asked, pointing. "Sergei no wrap his."

"Sergei gonna be wrapping his head once we get through with him," Chappie said. "Now shut the fuck up."

The Russian scowled at the insult and said, "You gonna lose," as he walked toward the door.

Chappie stood and glared at the man. "Go ahead, say something else." The guy looked at Chappie, swallowed hard, and quickly slipped out.

"We shoulda signed *you* up for a preliminary bout," I said.

He chuckled and grabbed the focus pads, slapping them together.

"Shit, you gonna give 'em all they can handle. Come on, let's get you warmed up. Don't want you to make that walk to the ring cold."

The walk to the ring has often been described as the loneliest walk in the world, and I knew from experience it was. Everything, all the fears, all the doubts, all the pressures converged as I headed out of my locker room and down the back hallway. The walls were big white cinderblocks and it smelled of some kind of disinfectant. I'd worked the pads until a sheen of perspiration had coated my body, then Chappie and Vic had slipped my black silk robe over my shoulders and a towel over my head. To enter the ring without properly warming up, or dry, was a clear-cut invitation to a flash knockdown.

Up ahead I saw the hallway funnel toward a doorway, where two uniformed hotel security guys stood. As we got closer, one opened the metal door and pulled it toward us. The aisle between the stands looked black and littered with paper cups, programs, and torn candy wrappings. Beyond it I saw the lights and the ring.

"Good luck," one of the guards said as I walked by.

People began reaching down, yelling, their voices all merging into the cacophony of an indistinct roar. I kept my focus straight ahead, trying not to think about anything but getting to the ring. My stomach felt a tad queasy, but I knew from experience it would fade as soon as that first bell rang.

Three steps up and on to the ring apron, then between the ropes. It was here. It was finally here. Chappie and Raul stepped in the ring with me. Alley and Vic waited down in what would be the blue corner. Our corner. Two men, each with a camcorder trailing cables, moved around with us, focusing on me, then Chappie, then back to me. I moved around the ring, throwing a few punches, kicking my legs slightly to keep them loose, and bouncing against the ropes. They felt tight, which meant less room to lean back should Sergei catch me there. The canvas felt heavy under my feet, too. It was a "puncher's canvas," that was for sure. Lots of grip.

Although the ring was full of people—announcers, the ref, officials—Sergei had yet to make his appearance. As the champ, it was his right to enter last, and I hoped that he wasn't going to try to delay things by making me wait. It was a mind game that a lot of fighters used. Then I saw him moving down the same aisle I'd used. His robe was white and satiny-looking, with green trim. It billowed out as he took purposeful strides toward the ring. His face looked shiny with Vaseline and sweat.

I told myself he had to be as nervous as I was.

He showed amazing flexibility for such a big man when he easily snaked through the ropes, and I felt a sudden jolt of nervousness. He lumbered over to me and nodded slightly. I nodded back, continuing to move around, keeping loose and ready, vaguely cognizant of the announcer's voice as he made the introductions.

"In the blue corner, weighing in at two hundred eighteen pounds, fighting out of Chicago, Illinois . . ." the man's voice echoed, and I was suddenly taken with the immensity of the place. The crowd looked dark, except for the rows closest to the ring. Several round-card girls in skimpy bikinis stood below, eying us.

"And in the red corner, weighing in at two hundred fifty-six pounds, and fighting out of Moscow, Russia, the International Heavyweight Kickboxing Champion of the World, the Russian Tank, Sergei Seeeleeezzzneenooofff."

He raised his arms and a corresponding roar erupted from the stands. A lot louder than the polite cheering that had followed my name. Guess I knew who the crowd favorite was.

The ref called us to the center of the ring. Chappie slipped my robe off my shoulders as Sergei's cornerman did the same for him. Seconds later, we were face to face.

"I gave you boys the instructions in your dressing rooms," the ref said. He was a fifty-something white guy with streaks of gray in his hair and a bow tie. He'd already begun to leak under the arms through his light blue shirt. The lights above us were hot. Sergei stared directly into my eyes. I stared back momentarily, then looked away. He grinned.

Good, I thought. Let him think I'm scared. It'll make him overconfident.

But I was only kidding myself. Overconfident or not, this guy looked like a T-72 tank in front of me.

"I expect you to break when I say 'break,' understood?"

We both nodded.

"Okay, touch 'em up and let's have a good, clean fight."

I held my gloves up and he slapped them with his. I felt

the shock go up my arm. Was he really that powerful, or was it just another show of bravado? I'd soon find out.

We moved back to the corners and Raul winked and slipped through the ropes. Alley gave me a thumbs-up. Chappie stood in front of me and took my face in his hands. His eyes looked as serious as I'd ever seen them.

"You can do this, Ron. I knows you can. Just follow our fight plan and dance till he get tired."

I smiled and he slipped my mouthpiece in and smeared some more Vaseline over my eyebrows and forehead. I turned, bouncing on my toes. The referee stood in the center holding his arm up, and beyond him, Sergei looked like a gleaming white tower. His trunks were the same white as his robe, trimmed in green. Mine were dark. Good guys wear black, I told myself as I heard the bell ring.

I watched him move forward, hands held high in a boxer's stance, his body gliding with a grace that surprised me. I'd expected him to lumber in a straight-up European style, from what Chappie'd said, then suddenly worried that he'd just told me that to keep me from worrying.

His jab shot out and caught the left side of my face, jarring me from any reveries. It was a hard jab, almost like a regular punch, and it woke me up. I danced back without firing off one of my own and felt the sting subside. Sergei moved forward again, cutting off the ring. I threw a jab of my own, coming up just a bit short and got popped again. This time I saw him start to set himself for a right cross to follow, but I backed away. The bell rang after what seemed like an endless feeling-out period of us exchanging leg kicks. Back in my corner Chappie held an icepack against my chest and gave me a quick pep talk.

"You looking good. Gots to start slippin' that jab of his, and keep moving to the right. Stay away from his big right hand." He rubbed the bag over my legs, and the cool wetness felt good. "That boy gonna get tired. Mark my words. He gonna be gettin' tired real soon. Real soon."

When the bell rang for the second, I was feeling loose and ready.

Dancing, I swung to his left, away from one of his powerful rights. A lead right. Didn't he have any respect for me? I needed to start scoring, but every time I looked for an opening, his long jabbing left darted out and either caught me or pushed me away.

"Slip! Slip!" I heard Chappie's voice over the din, suddenly coming in clearly just like a radio channel. I remembered our work at the gym and moved my head just enough to let the next jab slip by, then moved in and delivered a one-two combination to his body.

He whirled when I was inside, his huge arm encircling my back, and when his immense weight pressed against me, I suddenly saw the canvas rising up. I landed hard, with him on top. The ref called, "Break" and pulled him off me, then helped me up. My chest stung as I tried to catch my breath. The ref said, "None of that, now," and wiped off Sergei's gloves. He came over to me, grabbed my gloves, and wiped them on his shirt, saying, "Let's keep it clean."

I nodded and drew in another deep breath. As I moved forward I caught a glimpse of his leg rising up and smacking me on the right thigh. It stung, but I punched back, missing.

We circled in the center, each throwing a kick. I was content to go for his legs, as was he, but it was like bouncing off two tree trunks. He was used to leg kicks and I wasn't.

Just as I started to find the range with my jab, the bell rang and we turned and moved back to the corners.

Chappie and Raul were inside the ropes, setting down the stool for me to sit on and holding an icebag against the back of my neck.

"Endswell," Chappie said, holding out his hand. Vic's arm snaked through the ropes and handed it to him.

"You got to start slipping that jab," Chappie said. He held the cold, flat metal of the endswell against my cheek and left eye. "Just like we did the other night, remember? Stick and move, stick and move."

"You'll get him, champ," Raul said.

The whistle sounded and Chappie smeared more Vaseline over my face before departing, and said, "Work that body." I stood just as the bell rang and knew they'd taken the stool out through the ropes.

Sergei's expression looked almost like a leer as he moved across the ring. Taking me down to the canvas with his superior weight had been a cheap shot, and I knew I had to get his respect this round. I flicked out a jab and felt it connect, then bounced back, smacking his left thigh with another kick.

He came right back, swinging a left hook that whistled by me.

"If that one had connected it woulda been over," I heard one of the announcers say.

I worked some more front kicks to his legs, pummeling them inside and out. He retaliated with a snapping right kick of his own that caught me on the left thigh. It felt like I'd been cracked with a two-by-four. And it slowed me as he darted close.

His left fist slammed against my right ear, sending everything into an echoing, distorted-sounding blur. As I danced away he caught me on the shoulder with a right, knocking me backward, then his leg flashed upward on a collision course with my head. I got my gloves up just in time, but the jarring impact sent me reeling.

I felt the canvas under my forearms, and looked up, everything still in slow motion with distorted sound.

"Thrrreeee . . ." the ref counted, leaning over and swinging his arm in front of me.

"Fooouurrr . . ."

I took a breath and got to my knees.

"Fiiiivvvveee . . ."

My head felt clear. I heard Chappie yelling, "That was a slip. Wasn't no knockdown."

The ref stopped counting at eight and moved in, taking my gloves.

"You all right? Wanna go on?"

I nodded and he wiped my gloves on his shirt and stepped back, waving us together.

Sergei's grin looked malevolent as he came at me, his right cocking backward slightly.

I danced away; even though I could feel myself coming back, I wanted to be absolutely sure. When he got in range I popped him with a quick jab, doubling it up, and then bounced a right off his head. It didn't seem to slow him at all, and I danced away again.

The bell rang.

The icepack felt good against my neck and Chappie shot a stream of water over my face. His voice began to come into focus.

". . . wasn't no fucking knockdown. That motherfucking ref's blind, but that's okay. Just keep doing what you doing. He getting tired. Real tired. Just keep doing what you been doing. Stay away from him and work the legs and body. He gonna be getting real tired real soon."

I heard the whistle meaning seconds out and took a

couple more deep breaths. Chappie stuck my mouthpiece back in and helped lift me to my feet.

The bell rang. We both moved to the center of the ring and traded jabs. I used my left leg to hit him a couple front kicks to the body. After the third one he swung forward and kicked my right hamstring, sending me down. My ass hit the canvas hard, and I frowned.

"Come on, come on, get up," the ref said.

These were international rules, and foot-sweeps were legal. I got to my feet and waited while the ref wiped my gloves on his shirt. Sergei was looming a few feet away and came right at me. I popped him with a left jab, but he fired off a quick right that caught me on the temple. For a second, the black lights eclipsed my vision, then I felt myself moving instinctively to the left. He stepped toward me and threw another kick, which caught me in the gut. I bent slightly and he followed up with a one-two set of punches. The second punch, a hooking right, clipped my head and I felt myself going down again. This time I was on hands and knees, watching the ref motioning him to a neutral corner. Then he came back in front of me and swung his arm, picking up the count. But I had plenty of time. Everything seemed to be moving in slow motion.

"Fooouurrr."

Sergei was across the ring, resting his arms on the ropes and flashing me that leering grin.

"Fiiivvvveeee."

I shifted my gaze to my left. Where was Chappie?

"Siiiiixxxx."

I looked right, starting to panic. Then I saw Chappie's face, dark and intent; he was yelling something and motioning with his hands. I knew he wanted me to get up.

"Seeeevvvveeenn," the ref was saying.

I took another quick breath and readied my legs.

"Eeeeiiiight."

I stood and breathed deeply again. The ref told me to step to him and I did.

"You all right? You want to go on?"

I nodded and he grabbed my gloves and wiped them. I saw Sergei lumbering forward, and I knew he was going to come at me with everything he had.

I forced my legs to move, dancing in a circle away from him. He'd proven adept at cutting off the ring, and made his move to try and trap me in a corner. But the movement bought me a few more seconds, and I could already feel my senses coming back. I zigged left and then moved right, but he was ready for me, suddenly seeming to step right in front of me and started throwing leather. I got my arms up just in time and the first two blows bounced off my forearms and shoulders. He drew back to deliver another left but I reached out, grabbing him like an unlikely lover, tying him up so he couldn't punch. He grunted and I held on, waiting for the ref to come break us.

When the ref's arms snaked between us I let go, but Sergei tossed a quick right that clipped me on the jaw.

"Hey, no hitting on the break," the ref cautioned.

Sergei nodded and raised his hands. The foul made me mad as hell, and I wanted to stand and trade with him. Then I heard Chappie's voice in my brain: "Stick and move, stick and move," and I started dancing again.

He moved straight at me, throwing a long, lazy jab that I managed to step under and tattooed his body with four hard shots. He looped his arm around my neck and held me, until the ref came to break us again. I felt his chest heaving against me with each of his breaths.

We squared off in the center just as the bell rang. I

moved back to my corner to the welcome sight of the stool and Chappie with the water bottle. Raul sprayed me with water as I sat down, and someone put an icepack against the back of my neck, reviving me. Slowly, everything came into focus.

"You still fighting behind him," Chappie was saying. "Don't let him catch you again, but if he do, tie him up just like you been doing."

I saw the round-card girl sashay past me wearing a tiny bikini, her breasts looking like the twin moons of Jupiter.

The whistle sounded and Chappie said, "We need this next round, bro. Otherwise we gonna be too far behind."

I nodded and stood up. My legs were starting to feel heavy. Like I'd run ten miles already.

"What round is this?"

"Five coming up," Chappie said. "Do that shoeshine."

Great, I thought. In eight minutes of fighting I'd been knocked down twice.

I spent this round firing kick after kick to his body and legs. He tried several times to mount an offense, but I was getting better at slipping inside and delivering a fast combo to his gut. He began to work more kicks to my legs, catching me in the inside left thigh. After the third one, I'd slowed up enough for him to catch me along the ropes again. I covered up and felt him slam home shots to my sides then move up to my head. I tried to reach out to tie him up, but we were both so slippery with sweat that he managed to shake me off and start punching again. A hard right thudded off my temple, but there was no way I was going down again. Instead, I pushed to my right and spun him on the ropes, shooting in a quick left right to his face and watching him recoil in surprise and pain. I backpedaled out to the center of the ring. This wouldn't be won by me trading punches with him along the ropes. I needed to keep moving. I risked a display of bravado and waved him to come to me. He bounced off the ropes and came forward, straight at me.

Angles, give him angles, I thought, and stepped right, delivering a solid kick to his left thigh. I could see several red welts on the skin. At least I was connecting.

I shot a jab at his face as he was turning toward me, doubled it, and sent a right cross zinging in. It snapped his head to the side, but he shook it off and began swinging in looping arcs. I stepped inside and did the shoeshine again. He shoved me away, and I stumbled to regain my footing when his foot flashed up and hit me south of the border. I had my protective cup on, but the impact still made me wince with pain. I kept moving away, waiting for the ref to say something, but Sergei kept coming right on. I tried to dance, but my legs were slow, so when he got close I grabbed him again, and held on until the sick feeling in my gut started to subside.

"Break it clean," the ref said, and stepped between us. I was ready this time in case he tried to hit on the break again, but he didn't. His breathing was coming in whooshing grunts. The ref stood in front of him and said, "Keep those kicks up."

Thank God for small favors, I thought, and raised my hands.

The bell rang.

When I plopped down on the stool this time Chappie knelt down and began rubbing my legs with ice cubes. I took in some water from Raul and spit it out. My breathing was starting to get back to normal.

"That was good, Ron, real good. We getting there. We getting there. Two more rounds and he's ours."

If I have two more rounds in me, I thought.

I flashed back to the gym, and my last sparring sessions there with Marcus and Raul. We'd routinely gone ten or twelve rounds, and I hardly ever felt this tired. And those were three-minute rounds, I remembered. These were only two each.

"What round we at?" I asked.

"Six." Chappie leaned close. "You hear him breathing in there? That mean he getting tired. He ain't got nothing left. Look how he hanging his arms. Keep that body working and then, when his hands come down again, go upstairs."

The sixth round was a repetition of the fifth. I did notice Sergei's hands starting to droop, and this gave me more of an incentive. I fired a roundhouse kick up at his head but he blocked it and tried to sweep me again. This time I was able to pull away.

His jab was getting lazier and lazier, and the straight right had seemed to lose a lot of its sting. Once, when he came across with a solid punch over my jab, it snapped my head around, but the black lights stayed away this time. I suddenly felt a wave of confidence and moved forward, intent on delivering a solid combination to his big face before the round ended. I feinted with a front kick, and, as he bent slightly, I shot out a quick double jab, then drew it back and fired off a hook. His head sprayed a shower of sweat with the impact and he lurched forward. I worked the body again, and heard him grunt with each punch. But he clubbed me with two fast punches and then shoved me away. As he stood there I brought a side kick up and hit solid abs. It felt like I was kicking a wall, and when I brought my foot down he seemed to bridge the distance and shoot out a straight right that was so quick I didn't know it had hit me until I felt the impact. He tried to follow up with a left hook, but I was able to dance away again. When I blinked I felt the blood running around my left eye and down the side of my face.

I'd been cut. How bad? I wondered.

The sight of my blood seemed to energize him, and he moved forward, firing off a deft combination of left jab, left jab, right cross. I managed to slip the right. Before I could counter, the ref came up and told us to break. I backed away from him, not wanting to get hit, and luckily he missed with a looping right hand.

"I said break, goddamn it," the ref yelled. He stared at Sergei for a second, then turned and grabbed my arm, leading me to the corner of the ring. "Doc," he called. "Can you take a look at this?"

A pretty red-haired lady with glasses stepped up on the ring apron and held her splayed fingers toward my face. She was wearing latex gloves, and they came away red.

"How do you feel?" she asked. "Want to go on?"

"Absolutely," I said.

She nodded and the ref motioned us back and yelled, "Time on."

We started toward each other, me wiping my eye with my glove, and knowing he was going to try and work the cut. But he was starting to huff and puff a little, and he was carrying his hands low, just like Chappie had said. We squared off, exchanged a few punches and kicks, and the round ended.

Vic Roddy was inside the ropes as I got back to my corner, and as soon as I sat down he was squeezing the cut shut. Three Q-tips stuck out of his lips, and he plucked one and moved it up to the cut.

Chappie was off to the side now, holding the icebag to my neck, and wiping another on my chest and legs.

"Ron, them hands are coming down now. He ready to go. The man's tired, real tired. It's time, bro. It's time."

"How bad is it?" I asked.

Vic grunted noncommittally. I guessed that meant not to worry. But there was no way I wanted to see this one stopped on a cut. The whistle sounded and Vic plucked the second Q-tip from his lips. He acted like he had all the time in the world.

"You can do it, Ron. You can do it. Time to put him to sleep," Chappie said.

The bell rang and I rose up to my feet, oblivious to any pain from the cut or the blows I'd taken.

"What round?" I asked.

"Seven," Chappie said.

"Lucky seven," I heard Alley yell.

Lucky seven, I thought. It's time.

I moved out to the center, feeling strangely light on my feet. As Sergei got within range I fired off a quick kick to his left calf. Then another. He stepped back and began to circle to his right. I moved in and tattooed his face with three quick jabs and danced to my right. He was trying to cut off the ring again, moving on a diagonal, and stepped directly in front of me, so I feigned a left and snuck in a lead right that caught his nose and snapped his head back. He snorted out a reddish spray and threw a counter left hook. It caught me on the forehead and I felt myself starting to bleed again. Instead of moving away, I fired back a quick left of my own, catching him along the jawline.

He ripped in another left-right and I did the same. We stood toe-to-toe and I felt jarred by the next series. But I wasn't even close to going down. Some of his power seemed to have faded. I went downstairs with the shoeshine, then brought a left hook up to his jaw.

He lurched backward and spun to the side, trying to catch himself by bending at the waist, but his gloves brushed the canvas. I was about to smash a right to his exposed side when the ref was in between us, motioning me to a neutral corner. At first I thought he was going to have the doctor look at my cut again, but then I realized he was giving Sergei an eight-count. I watched the big man standing there, his mouth wide open, sucking air, his long arms dangling in front of him, and I knew I had him. If I could only get in close with the right combination . . .

The ref motioned me forward and Sergei brought his hands up high. I threw a quickie kick to his left thigh, bounced my foot off the canvas, and shot it back up in a side kick. The blow landed just up under his rib cage and I heard him grunt. For a second he seemed stunned, then his mouth twisted slightly and he moved forward, cocking back his big right hand. But mine was already shooting up in an arcing uppercut. It connected on the side of his jaw and his head bobbled. He took two stumbling steps, like a drunk on his way to the pavement, and landed face first on the canvas.

The ref was pushing me away, pointing to the neutral corner again, tolling off the count. I watched his arm swing with each number.

Four, five, six . . . Sergei's head jerked and he moved up on his forearms and elbows.

Seven, eight . . .

Oh, please, God, don't let him get up, I thought.

Nine . . . The ref waved his arms and shook his head.

I felt like collapsing on the canvas, but instead, I raised my arms as I saw Chappie, Raul, and Alley scrambling between the ropes and running across the ring toward me.

International Heavyweight Kickboxing Champion of the World, I thought.

Chapter 17

My ringside celebration as champion was short-lived. After having been presented with the belt, and doing the customary post-fight interview, I was escorted through the aisle while the raucous crowd continued to yell and throw paper beer cups around. I stripped off my soaked trunks and took my time in the shower washing off the sweat and blood. When I'd finished, Chappie told me they had an ambulance waiting to take me to the hospital for stitches and the customary CAT scan.

The pretty blond physician shined a light in my eyes and told me to follow the movement. A redhead and a blond both looking into my eyes in the same night, and me feeling like I got run over by a truck.

"Any double or blurred vision?" she asked.

"Only when I laugh," I said.

"Excuse me?"

"He making a joke, doc," Chappie said.

"Yeah, I consider myself kind of a funny guy," I added.

She smiled. "I'll bet you are. I'll take that as a no."

"How about we go out to dinner after you stitch me up?" I asked, trying to give her one of my high-wattage smiles. "I'm the champ, you know."

She raised her eyebrows and gave me one of those looks that I knew I should take as a no.

"Let's see how you feel after we get done," she said, scribbling something on her clipboard and moving between the break in the floor-to-ceiling curtains. "I expect you'll be here a while. We're kind of backed up."

"We'll make it breakfast then," I called after her. The slight movement brought flashes of pain throughout every part of my body that moved.

"You got energy for that?" Chappie asked.

"Hardly."

Gonna be sore in the morning, I thought, and lay back against the pillow and closed my eyes.

"Chappie, where's my belt?" I asked.

"Right here," he said, standing and pressing the stiff leather against my arm. "You done good tonight, Ron. You the champ. You fought your heart out and you won. I'm proud of you."

The totality of everything, all that we'd been through in these whirlwind past days, suddenly came rushing down on me, and I didn't know what to say.

"I couldn't have made it without you," I said. I heard my voice croak.

He patted my arm and smiled.

"Where's Alley and Raul?" I asked.

"They went back to the hotel. Probably be playing the tables with all that new money you made for 'em."

I suddenly remembered I was supposed to have him put $500 down on the fight for George.

"Shit, I forgot to make a bet for a buddy of mine."

"No sweat, we gots plenty," he said. "We Vegas-rich now."

"What do you mean?"

"Odds were seven to one against you," he said. "Alley put down five hundred, Raul two grand, and me, I put down ten. I'll split it with you."

Ten grand, at seven to one . . . "Seventy thousand dollars? Like hell. You won it."

"Yeah, and you earned it."

* * * * *

The doctor's prophecy turned out to be correct, and by the time I got released from the ER it was almost six in the morning. I had been stitched, scanned, poked, and given a shot, and the pain of having had a very large man beat on me for almost fifteen minutes was starting to take its toll. The cab dropped us off in front of the hotel and we began the long trek through the smoky casino toward the elevators. I'd told Chappie that I had to stay in Vegas longer than originally planned, and he'd insisted on staying there with me.

"You don't need to do that, you know," I told him as we walked through the double sets of doors.

"Gots to keep you out of trouble," he said. "Plus, I can look up an old buddy of mine moved out here from Chicago. Percy Spurlock Parker."

"He a fighter?"

Chappie shook his head. "Writes mystery stories. Maybe he can do one about you sometime."

"The only mystery I'm interested in is where the bed is." We finally got to the mirrored hallway where the elevators were, to go to our floor. "I'm gonna put the Do Not Disturb sign on the door and sleep until tomorrow."

"Okay, I'll run Alley and Raul to the airport and check on our Phoenix flight," he said. "We gonna need to rent a car once we get there?"

"Probably."

"I'll check into that, too."

"You keep this up and I'll have to start introducing you as my PI associate."

"Sheeeit." He grinned. " 'Fore you ever do that, I'll get myself a real job."

When I got to the room I realized I needed to soak in a

hot tub. I called room service and asked for more clean towels as soon as possible. Before I headed for the tub, I went over to the table by the balcony and pulled back the drapes. Through the glass doors I had a view of another section of the hotel, and in the distance, some purplish mountains. Vegas looked almost peaceful again, and I remembered that those early morning runs, when the strip had been deserted, had been my favorite parts of the day. I hadn't been able to use my cell phone in the hospital, and had some calls to make. It was 6:50 so that meant it was almost nine back home. I hit the selector for George first to tell him I won.

"See, I told you. I knew you would." His voice sounded ebullient. "This is great. Outstanding."

"Yeah, it's been a long road."

"Not that," he said, sounding playful. "I was talking about five yards at seven to one. What's that? Thirty-five hundred?" He paused. "You did put the bet down for me, didn't ya?"

"After all you've done for me lately? You think I'd forget?"

Reminding him to touch bases with Ken again, and making sure he was covering the Bielmaster surveillance, I told him I'd see him Wednesday and called Kris's number. To my chagrin, all I got was her answering machine. I left her a quickie message saying that I'd won, I was thinking about her, and that I had to do a follow-up interview out this way and would be back Tuesday. I thought about leaving a teaser saying that we could perhaps get together for dinner, but decided against it. This fight seemed to have taken more out of me than I'd figured. It felt like every damn inch of me hurt. When I ended the call I found myself wondering where she was.

Maybe she went to church, I thought.

But I didn't have to wonder long. My cell phone rang and I saw her number on the caller ID screen.

"Hi," she said. "I was in the shower."

"Wish I could've been there," I said.

"Mmmm, me too." Her tone sounded almost perfunctory. "So, you won your fight, huh?"

"Yeah. Want to hear about it?"

"I'd rather hear about when you'll be back."

"Tuesday," I said, a bit disappointed that she hadn't shown more interest in what was my shining moment.

"So why are you staying out there again?"

I tried to rotate my neck and felt a twinge of pain.

"Well," I cleared my throat. "I found out one of our possible witnesses has relocated to Arizona. Figured I might as well interview him while I'm out this way."

"Really. Hmmm. Who is it?"

"A guy named Mark Shields. Did Rick have you type up a subpoena for him?"

"It doesn't ring a bell," she said. "Is it an important interview?"

"Very," I said. "Why else would I pass up a chance to come back now and have you tend to my wounds?"

We chatted for a few more minutes and the door to my room abruptly opened, accompanied by a knocking. A Hispanic woman entered and smiled. "Housekeeping," she said.

"Well, babe, I gotta go. The maid's here and after she finishes I gotta date with the mattress."

"Okay," she said, sounding hesitant. Could it be jealousy? "Call me when you get back."

I promised I would and hung up. I slowly got to my feet and saw the maid watching me warily. I suddenly realized how I must look. A bruised and swollen face with wrap-around sunglasses on top of a body that was moving like the Frankenstein monster.

"Soy luchador," I said. *"Boxadoro."*

Her eyebrows rose. *"Un boxedor? Esta bueno?"*

I tried a casual shrug and immediately regretted it.

"Mucho trabajo," I said, remembering a phrase that Raul always used. *"Poco dinero."* Lots of work, too little money.

The next morning we were at McCarran International Airport bright and early. The security screeners looked at me cautiously when I removed my sunglasses and put them in the inspection basket. The area beneath my eyes had darkened which, along with the swelling and the dark stitch work, made me look like a refugee from an old 1950s horror flick. When it came time to raise my arms for the body scan and pat-down, I felt like every muscle I'd ever used was wired to an electric stun-gun.

"Oh yeah," Chappie said, "I didn't need to stay. You in real good shape to go chasing after some detective bullshit in a strange place."

The security guard looked from me to him and back to me again.

"My associate has a penchant for irony," I said, stepping over to a chair to put on my shoes.

The actual flight from Vegas to Phoenix was mercifully brief. It seemed like we'd just taken off and ascended to our apex, when we started to descend. I'd taken the window seat and watched as the arid desert became bigger and bigger. Lots of sagebrush and cactus, distant mountains, a ribbon of highway, and hopefully in Phoenix the answer to a large portion of what was missing in the Gooding caper. Why had Mark Shields's family been so evasive when I'd called about him? And why had the Great Gilbert's lady lawyer gotten suddenly pale when I'd mentioned the name "Mark"? Hopefully I was within a few hours of finding out.

Below us, streets and houses started to appear. Against a backdrop of distant brown mountains, the buildings and structures grew more densely packed, and the airplane began to bank as the pilot's voice announced that we were beginning our approach to Phoenix.

"It's a balmy ninety-five degrees, with clear skies," he said over the intercom.

I turned to Chappie.

"I hope that rental car you got us has good air-conditioning."

He grinned. "Me too."

The car turned out to be a big, cream-colored Lincoln Continental with power windows and a cooling system that would have worked on an Abrams tank. Chappie insisted on driving, and I slid very gingerly into the passenger seat.

"Good choice," I said. "Plenty of leg room, which I need right about now." My legs hurt so bad I felt like seeing what the going rate for wheelchairs was.

"Shoulda got us a Cadillac," he said. "The Champ oughta ride in style. Now where to?"

"Well," I stretched out as I reclined back in my seat. "It's a hundred and six miles to Chicago, we got a full tank of gas, half a pack of cigarettes, it's dark, and we're wearing sunglasses."

"Dark? What the fuck you talking about?"

I raised my glasses from my swollen eyes.

"*The Blues Brothers*. You know, when Elwood picks up Jake outside of prison?"

He frowned. "What's that? Some white boy movie?"

"It's a classic."

"Sheeeit." He started the car. "Now the original *Shaft* with Richard Roundtree—*that's* a classic."

I lowered the glasses. "Maybe it would have been better to just take another taxi. Now we're gonna have to stop and ask for directions, and I'm too tired and sore to get out of the car."

"So I gotta do it?" he asked, frowning.

"Hey, you're the one that was just talking about *Shaft*, ain't ya?" I said, dropping my voice in my best imitation of Isaac Hayes. "Can you dig it?"

The lady at the car rental place had been nice enough to run a quick Mapquest for us to 301 West Jefferson, and I read off the directions as Chappie drove the big Lincoln through the crowded city streets. Phoenix had an impressive array of buildings, mostly in tan or pastels, or else all steel and glass. I began to wonder if this Shields guy lived in some swank downtown apartment, or something. It took us three turns around the block before we finally realized that 301 was the huge building right in front of us. The one with the big sign stating it was the Maricopa County Administration Building. Chappie pulled to a stop in front of it and looked at me.

"This it?"

"Looks like," I said.

His brow furrowed. "This a county building."

I adjusted my aching body in the seat and nodded. It hurt.

"What's up with this?" he asked.

"I wish I knew," I said, reaching for my cell phone and checking Phoenix information for a Mark Shields, only to be informed that his number was nonpublished. I wondered if I could have George recheck that address he'd given me. I tried his cell phone and got his voice mail. I tried his house and got his answering machine. I was about to try his work number when a motorcycle cop pulled alongside us and tapped on the driver's side window.

Chappie glanced at me, then lowered the window.

"You can't park here," the cop said. "Fire zone."

"Hey, brother," I said. "I used to be on the job in Chicago."

He nodded, obviously as impressed as I used to be when somebody laid that line on me. Undeterred, I forged on.

"We're looking for a buddy of ours from Chi-town. Moved out here and gave us this address. Go figure, huh?"

"What's his name?" the cop asked.

"Shields," I said. "Mark Shields. We went to law school together at Northwestern." I figured a little white lie was in order to sweeten the pot.

"The County Prosecutor?" the cop asked.

"Yeah," I said. "He musta known it'd be better for us to tag up at his office since we had an early flight."

He nodded, his skepticism fading somewhat.

"He's usually up in room two-oh-six," the cop said. His body moved and I could tell he'd shifted back into first. As he sat back and let the clutch out, he said, "Parking's over there. Have a nice day."

"Sheeeit," Chappie said. "That's the nicest the police ever been to me."

"Maybe he thought you were Shaft," I said.

We tried the County Prosecutor's main office first and the prim and proper looking secretary, after eying us suspiciously, said that Mr. Shields was in court.

I nodded and said, "Oh that's right. He did tell us to check room two-oh-six, didn't he, Mr. Shaft?"

Chappie smirked, and then said, "Right on."

I thanked her very copiously and we edged out the door. It suddenly dawned on me how we must have looked. Both in dark pants, T-shirts, and dark sport coats, wearing sunglasses, and me walking with a limp. They probably thought the new Men in Black had arrived. We made our way down the hallway and over to the escalators.

"You gonna keep wearing your sunglasses inside?" I asked Chappie.

"Yeah," he said, then smiled. "What's that they used to say? It's a black thing."

"Well, it's a black and blue thing for me."

We got to the top of the metal stairs and saw a sign with an arrow indicating rooms 200–210 were straight ahead. Room 206 was four doors down on the right. It looked empty except for a few deputies and the standard courtroom personnel. The judge was off the bench and everybody looked relaxed.

"Let me do the talking," I whispered as we pulled open the glass door.

"Ain't that what I been doing?"

A young man sat at a long table in front of an empty jury box. He was busily going through files and scribbling on a yellow legal pad. His suit was light gray and inexpensive enough to tell me that he had to be a public servant. When he looked up I saw the yearbook picture of Mark Shields, plus a couple years' maturity, staring back at me in the flesh.

"Mr. Shields, I'm Ron Shade." I held out one of my cards. "I wonder if we could take a few minutes of your time."

He set his pen down and looked at the card, then back to me, then at Chappie.

"And this is?"

"My associate, Mr. Oliver."

"You got a card, too, Mr. Oliver?"

Chappie shook his head.

"I usually use his," he said.

Shields raised his eyebrows, still giving us careful consideration.

"What exactly can I do for you?"

"We need to talk," I said.

"About what?"

"About Todd Gooding. Mason Gilbert."

His head jerked back fractionally, but I caught the reaction. He slipped my card into his pocket and motioned us toward an open doorway, beyond which lay a conference room with a long table, chairs, and a couple of phones. Once we got inside, he closed the door behind us.

"What's this about?" he asked.

"I'm working for an attorney back in Chicago. We've got a wrongful death suit going against Gooding and we're almost ready to go to trial. I'm trying to tie up all the loose ends." I paused and reached up, taking off my sunglasses. "I know how I hate it when somebody talks to me and I can't see their eyes."

"Jesus, what happened to you?"

"I was in a fight in Vegas," I said.

"I'll say."

"You should see the other guy," I said. "Now, about the Gooding/Gilbert connection?"

He considered this, then asked, "This attorney got a number I can verify what you just told me?"

"Sure." I reached for my cell phone and got Rick's office number out of the lexicon. I wrote it down on one of the many court forms that had been strategically stacked on a shelf near the end of the table.

He looked at it, and I said, "It's in Oak Lawn, Illinois, if you want to verify it. His secretary is named Kris, with a K, and his paralegal is Denise."

Shields blinked twice as he stared back at me, licked his lips, and said, "Have a seat. I'll be back." He then turned and left, letting the door pneumatically close behind him. I lowered myself into a chair and motioned for Chappie to do the same.

He glanced around and I could tell that he was a little bit nervous.

"What's the matter?"

He shook his head. "Don't like this."

"What?"

"When the man leave you alone in a room, and leaves out like he got business, no good usually come of it."

"Shaft can handle it," I said, putting my sunglasses back on, and quickly adding, "Can you dig it?"

After about ten minutes I was beginning to wonder if Chappie was right, when the phone began to ring. We were the only ones in the conference room, but I still didn't know if I should answer it. The door popped open and a deputy grabbed the ringing phone. He identified himself and the room number, then listened.

"You Shade?" he asked, looking at me.

I nodded.

"Mr. Shields says he's waiting for you in his office. You know where it's at?"

I told him I did, and rose ponderously from the chair. The walk back downstairs took us another five and the same secretary was just as wary when we went back into her waiting room.

"Mr. Shields says he'll see you," she said, pointing at

me, then looking at Chappie, "and you can wait over there."

He glanced at me and I nodded.

I pushed through a swinging wooden gate that was about three feet high and stepped past the barrier that separated the office section from the massive waiting room. She escorted me to a hallway and then indicated a series of offices, telling me it was the third one on the left. Inside, Shields sat behind a big, gunmetal-gray desk. Behind him was a window that looked like it would have to be opened with a crowbar, a bookcase with lots of finely bound volumes labeled as legal sections by raised gold letters. His desk area was clean and orderly. Obviously the sign of a disciplined mind.

"Sit down, Shade." He indicated the chair in front of the desk.

I lowered myself once more, going very slowly down until my sore ass hit the seat. It was a wooden chair, and I knew I was going to have to make this interview pretty quick or be sorry later.

"How'd you find me?" he asked.

"It wasn't easy."

"Come on. I ain't in the mood." His words had an echo of Bridgeport in them.

I thought about saying, "Neither am I," but decided I could draw a few more flies with honey than with vinegar.

"I used to be a cop." I took off my sunglasses again. "I still have sources in the department. If it's any consolation, it probably wouldn't have been possible if I hadn't stretched the rules a bit."

"So what do ya want with me?"

I smiled. "Do you know how gratifying it is to come all this way west and hear a South Side accent coming from a man who's obviously doing so well?"

"Cut the shit."

"A man after my own heart," I said. "Like I told you, I'm investigating the Gooding case for a wrongful death suit. Your name came up, and I wanted to hear what you remember about it."

He shook his head. "Don't have anything to say."

I shrugged. It was time to try a bluff. "What would you say if I told you I had a subpoena in my pocket?"

"It won't do you any good. I was attached to Gilbert's defense team. Anything I know would be privileged. Even if I agreed to testify, which I won't, Gooding would have to waive his right to attorney-client privilege." He steepled his fingers and stared at me. "You think Mason Gilbert's gonna let him do that?"

"What about off the record?"

"There isn't any 'off the record' with that case." He dropped his hands and leaned forward. "I'm sorry. Now if you're done—"

"I'm not," I said. "I need to know why every time your name's mentioned, Gilbert's pretty little co-counsel, Mary Buckley, turns white as a sheet. And why your family gave me the runaround when I tried to look you up the first time. And why you're using a county building as the address on your driver's license."

He smirked.

"So that's how you found me." He leaned back in his chair and put his hands behind his head. "That's my right, as a county prosecutor, to use this address. I make a lot of enemies."

"I'll bet you made a few back in Illinois, too." I was running out of time and getting nowhere. It felt like I was out in the deep end of the pool and couldn't feel my feet touch the bottom. "Shall I tell you what I think? It's obvious that Gooding killed his wife. It was calculated and premeditated. He got caught, and his first attorney was a dickhead who handled mostly civil stuff, so Gooding went straight to Mason Gilbert, who's a white Johnny Cochran. Only there was no race card to play in this one. The Great Gilbert took one look at things, realized the case was a sure loser, so he filed an SOJ, used his connections in the clerk's office to get a certain judge, one that he had something on or knew he could pay off, and lo and behold got a directed verdict." I paused to gauge Shields's reaction. He slowly took his hands away from his head and moved forward, laying his forearms on the desktop. His mouth was still a set line.

"So then," I continued, "you enter the picture, fresh out of law school and still all idealistic and thinking that the system works. Then all of a sudden you realize Gooding's a shitbird, and guilty as hell, and maybe you figure out what the Great Gilbert's got in mind. So you turn tail and run as far away from Chicago as you can. How am I doing so far?"

He almost seemed ready to say something, but his lips drew tighter.

"Come on, Shields, at least tell me if I'm right or wrong."

I watched the color rise into his cheeks and he brought his hand up to his face, then ran it through his hair. His mouth opened slightly, but no sound came out for a good ten seconds, after which he sighed heavily.

"Mr. Shade . . ." He stood up. "I'm sorry that you had to come all the way out here for nothing."

Chapter 18

The plane ride back to Chicago was long and tedious. We'd spent our last night in Vegas uneventfully. Chappie had gone to visit his buddy Percy, and I soaked in a hot tub again. I was beginning to feel like an uncanned prune, since the massive bruises on my legs and sides were turning a nice purple. After an optimistically early breakfast, we conned a limo driver into driving us to the airport for ten bucks, and got there in plenty of time for our supposed 12:30 flight. I made a quick call to Kris, hoping to catch her before she left for lunch.

"Hi," she said. "When will you be home?"

"Hopefully by five or so," I said.

"Great." She hesitated, then asked, "So are you coming over tonight? I'd like to hear all about your trip."

I considered this. My body still ached. All I really wanted to do was stretch out in my own bed and sleep. Plus, I felt I'd been letting my other cases slide and I just didn't feel up to entertaining her romantically until I felt better. But to tell her that was another matter. Would she understand? I decided on what my mom used to call a little white lie.

"I really can't tonight," I said. "I have to touch base on one of my other cases. Probably due to pull surveillance duty tonight." I hoped that this "little white lie" wouldn't come back to bite me on the ass.

I heard her sigh. "Well, okay, I understand. How'd it go in Phoenix? Gonna need me to type up any interesting notes?"

"I'd better talk to Rick privately about that one," I said. "We need to discuss strategy, but I'll suggest that he put Mark Shields on his witness list."

"Wow," she said. "That sounds important. Is it?"

"I gotta keep some mystery about me, don't I?" I said, realizing my cell phone battery was getting low again and wanting to tag up George before it went out. "I'll call you later, okay?"

I tried to call him and reached a series of voice mails, answering machines, and "he ain't here." Chappie and I grabbed a quick lunch at the Burger King inside the terminal and moved down to the gate.

That's when the delays started. First, the flight was late arriving from Chicago, then it was announced that there would be another delay while a minor mechanical problem was resolved. That sent everybody into a nervous tizzy until it was explained that one of the tires needed to be changed. The collective sigh of relief was punctuated by a gut-punch follow-up: The new tire was being flown here from O'Hare, ETA three hours and forty minutes.

I prayed for a tail wind.

My phone rang and, luckily, it was George.

"You been trying to get ahold of me?" he asked.

"Yeah, working on a case?"

I heard him snort. "Working on staying out of trouble. I got my tit in the wringer because of you, buddy."

"Huh? What are you talking about?"

"Seems that Soundex and driver's license check on that Shields guy you wanted me to do attracted somebody's attention."

I was perplexed. "How?"

"That's the sixty-four-thousand-dollar question. IAD interviewed my buddy in records about it." He paused and I heard him sigh heavily. "Remember those identifying tracers I was telling you about? Every time you run somebody?"

"Yeah."

"Well, somehow they traced the check back to his terminal."

"Jesus, I'm sorry. You gonna be okay?"

I heard him laugh. "I can handle it. So far, he ain't given me up, claiming that he don't have no idea who ran the guy. Maybe somebody used his terminal when he was taking a piss or something."

I grimaced, regretting having asked him something that could be potential trouble. I apologized again.

"Hey, like I told ya, I can handle it," he said. "Now, when you getting back here to pay me that money I won?"

"Our flight's delayed. May be quite a while. I need you to get hold of Ken for me to feed the cats and cover the Bielmaster surveillance tonight."

"What am I, your fucking secretary?"

"No, look, my cell phone's about to run out of juice. I need the favor."

"Yeah, when don't you?"

"Tell Ken I'll make it up to him. Tell him to go ahead and take the Firebird tonight."

"He's been doing that anyway."

"And tell him to feed the cats," I repeated. "Unless you want to."

"Un-uh. I'll let him do the honors. Call me when you get in, and don't forget my money."

He hung up just as the low-battery chirping began.

I found an unused outlet and dug my charger out of my carry-on luggage. Then Chappie and I settled back to wait for the changing of the tire.

When I woke up about two hours later I realized I'd somehow slumped down in the less than comfortable chair with my feet on my suitcase and my head leaning over on Chappie's shoulder.

"Since we in Vegas, I don't care," he said, grinning. "But if we'd been in San Francisco I woulda belted you awake so people wouldn't be wondering who be the husband and who be the wife."

"Sorry," I said. "How long have I been out?"

"Long enough. Figured you needed the rest." He stood up. "They finally getting ready to board."

I glanced at my watch. It was almost 2:00. And with a four-hour flight, and a forty-minute bus ride from the airport, I estimated we could actually be home by seven. Then I realized I'd forgotten to factor in the time change. More like nine at night. A lonely time to be at the World's Busiest Airport. My excuse to Kris was turning out to be more prophetic than I'd originally imagined. I unplugged my phone, with the freshly charged battery, and debated whether or not to call her now. I decided to wait. Better to be sure of when we'd be landing, than to give her another excuse why I couldn't come over tonight.

We got on the plane and I took my usual aisle seat. I hoped that the dude who'd changed the tire had remembered to tighten the lug nuts. We taxied out a little ways from the gate and began the waiting game some more.

I found a copy of *USA Today* folded up in the seat-flap in front of me and started to read it. One of the front-page stories was about the suicide of a Washington journalist. Friends and colleagues were quoted as expressing total shock, but many recalled, after the fact, that he'd been systematically cleaning out his normally cluttered office and giving things away recently. A telltale sign, often missed.

That started me thinking of Big Rich, and how I had to give him a call and update when I got back. Of course, what did I have to tell him? But something else began to gnaw at me.

Suicide . . . Rob Tunney had committed suicide. Tunney, whose lifetime in police work had translated to a shoddy, incomplete investigation for Rick. A bad way to go out. Had that been one of the signs? His missed interview with Sally Forest, his sketchy, incomplete case notes . . . Not like the man at all, supposedly. George had known him better than me. Always said he was a good cop. Too good to jump out of a high window of his downtown office. And why hadn't he followed through on interviewing Sally Forest if he'd set the day aside to do that? *See SF* in the notebook Rick had shown me.

Sally Forest, now Sally Panekis. And what about her? She'd seemed sincere about now realizing that Gooding was a scumbag and doing the right thing and coming to testify. Suddenly she goes to parts unknown to visit her sick mother. Rather than staying with her hubby, who'd been in some sort of accident. "A face like a catcher's mask," Rick had said. . . . Then she disappears.

And Mark Shields, leaving absolutely no trail when leaving Chicago to follow Horace Greeley's advice. Unlisted phone, untraceable address, protective family. Plus a sudden IAD investigation right after I happened to talk to him. I was beginning to wonder if these were mighty strange coincidences. Maybe . . . But I was beginning to worry that if I kept flipping over the lily pads, there might be a big old crocodile waiting under one of them.

And if someone had been leaning on a few people, what about Tunney? Maybe I needed to call George back and ask him a few questions about the old guy's suicide. After all, I'd never heard of a copper who'd offed himself and not used his gun. I folded the newspaper and stuck it back in the flap as the big engines began to rev up, and the lights and buildings of the strip became smaller and smaller as we lifted off into an uncertain sky.

The flight attendants came by offering earphones and we bought two and settled back to watch the movie. I hoped it would take my mind off the strange uneasiness I was feeling. After all, it should have been a momentous occasion. I was coming back from Las Vegas the heavyweight champion . . . Something I'd coveted for several years. Now I finally had it, and even had the belt in my luggage to prove it. I tried to lose myself in the movie, a romantic comedy, but midway through I found my mind wandering and glanced over at Chappie. He'd fallen asleep, the earphones still looped in his ears. I smiled, but deep down a feeling twisted in my gut, and I couldn't shake it. Like something bad was stalking me, lurking around one of the dark corners I'd passed in the last few days and somehow I'd missed it.

Things started to unravel shortly after we touched down in Chicago. While we were waiting for our luggage, I turned on my cell phone and saw that I had three missed calls. Two from George and one from Kris. George's had a 9-1-1 after it. I dialed his cell first. He answered on the second ring.

"Ron, where you at?"

"Just landed at O'Hare. Waiting on our luggage now. Why? Afraid I'll run off with your thirty-five hundred from Vegas?"

I heard him sigh and knew something was seriously wrong.

"No." His voice was heavy. "It's Ken. He's been shot."

"What? When?"

"Earlier tonight. In front of Bielmaster's. In your Firebird. The ETs are going over it now."

"What happened?"

"Looks like somebody drove or walked up alongside the car and fired three rounds through the window. Hit him in the head, the left shoulder and neck."

"Oh, sweet Jesus. How bad is he?"

He sighed again, hesitant. Always a precursor to bad news.

"I don't know. He's in surgery now at Christ Hospital."

"I'm gonna head over there." With a frantic sense of desperation I looked at the slowly rotating luggage carousel, hoping in vain to see our suitcases. "Where you at?"

"Actually, I'm on my way to the hospital now, too, but for a slightly different reason." He gave it a momentary beat, then said, "There's more. Grace Bielmaster's missing."

"Missing?"

"Yeah. I'm waiting for Ursula now so we can go over and break the news to the El Tee."

"Is Knop involved in this?"

"Looks like. Knop's gone, too. Took his mother's car, and he broke into his uncle's store. Stole a bunch of cash, and a gun from the office."

"So he's the one that shot Ken." I said it as a statement rather than a question.

"At this point that's the assumption we're going on. I put the car into LEADS and got a pick-up order out on him. Armed and dangerous."

I told him I'd see him at the hospital and disconnected, thinking that if I hadn't taken that worthless side trip to Arizona, that might have been me lying in the hospital fighting for my life.

As soon as I hung up Chappie knew that something was wrong.

"What's up?" he asked.

I told him.

He nodded solemnly and said, "Go on, catch you a cab. I'll get the bags and take the shuttle bus home."

I called Kris on the way. Her voice sounded stressed, like she'd been crying or upset or something.

"Ron, are you all right?" she asked.

"I'm fine, but a friend of mine was shot. I'm on the way to the hospital now."

"Oh, my God. I heard about it on the news. At first they said the car belonged to a Chicago-area private detective, and when they showed it on the screen, I thought it was you."

"No," I said. "Our flight got delayed. It was a young guy who worked for me."

"This is terrible, so terrible." She paused, then said, "Can you come over? We need to talk."

"I can't right now, babe. I have to get to the ER."

"Tomorrow then? I really need to see you."

"I'll call you," I said. The cab was nearing the shuttle bus parking area where I'd left the Beater. "I gotta go now."

"Call me tomorrow," she said. "Don't forget."

I told her I wouldn't and hung up, reaching for my wallet to pay the cabbie.

Emergency rooms at night are always filled with an assortment of weirdos, and the one at Christ Hospital was no exception. I told the security guard that a friend of mine had been shot, and he directed me to a chair to wait. Several sets of people sat huddled together in the black vinyl chairs, blankly staring at some late night talk show. I paced back and forth, wanting to know what was going on behind those frosted glass doors, but no one came out to talk to me. I was just about to approach the guard again when the doors opened and George popped his head out and nodded to me. His expression looked grim as I walked over to him.

"Man, am I glad to see you," I said.

"Figured you might be down here by now."

"Any word?" We started walking down a wide corridor.

He shook his head. "Still in surgery. Looks like there were at least four shots fired. Three hits. Maybe we can recover the one for a ballistics match-up."

We came to another waiting room, this one more like a regular room with some chairs and a sofa set on chrome legs. A man and a woman sat on the sofa holding hands and looking haggard as hell. The woman's face was tear-streaked.

"Kenny's parents," George said. We walked in and he introduced me.

Awkwardness overtook me immediately and all I could think of saying was he was a tough kid.

His mother smiled slightly, as another tear wound its way down her cheek.

"Going through all that in Iraq," she said, her voice sounding like it was about to crack, "and then coming home safe and having this happen."

I didn't know what to say. I opened my mouth, but just bowed my head. George grabbed me by the shoulder and moved me out the door.

"Let's get some coffee," he said. "You folks need anything?"

They both declined.

In the hallway I took a deep breath and asked if they had

any leads on Knop yet.

"Nothing." George's face looked grim. "But the more we find out, the better he looks for it. We'll get him."

"Not if I find him first."

"Hey, stay out of it," he said, slowing down. "And I should add that Bielmaster is none too pleased with you, by the way."

"Huh?"

"Me and Ursula just told him about Grace. We thought they were gonna have to open him up again just to get his heart slowed down. We finally had to call the nurse to give him a sedative."

"He can't possibly blame us for this."

"Not *us*. You. He was cursing your name up and down."

"Great," I said. "Just what I wanted to be. Back to number one on his hit parade. Plus, a real nice kid takes a bullet that was probably meant for me, and the idiot I've been trying to please is using me as a scapegoat. He know his daughter was most likely communicating with Knop?"

George shook his head. "I thought you were gonna tell him."

I frowned. "Yeah, well, I intended to, but the timing wasn't quite right."

"Is it ever?" he asked, and pointed to another room on the left. Inside were several vending machines. Ursula Bielmaster stood there drinking from a small paper cup.

"Mr. Shade." She recoiled slightly. "What happened to your face?"

I suddenly remembered that I'd forgotten to wear my sunglasses, and although most of the swelling had gone, I still had the darkened patches under each eye.

"Nothing," I said. "How are you holding up?"

She shrugged and flashed what passed for a weak smile.

"And the young man who was shot?" she asked. "How's he?"

George held his hand out and waggled it. "Still touch and go."

"Mrs. Bielmaster," I said. "I'm sorry this happened this way. Any word from Grace?"

"None." She took another sip. "At first, when I heard the popping sounds, I thought it was a car backfiring, or something. Then I heard the horn blowing. I went to the window and couldn't see anything, but called nine-one-one anyway."

"A good thing, too," George said. "The quick response made the difference. The uniforms found him and called for an ambulance right away."

"And then, after they'd arrived," she said, "I went up to check on Grace . . . That's when I realized she was gone."

"Any signs of forced entry?" I asked.

George shook his head.

"Mrs. Bielmaster, is there any chance that Grace might have gone willingly with Knop?"

Her mouth sagged open, bracketed by deep lines on either side. When she started to speak, her voice sounded strained.

"I . . . I don't know," she said. "It's all so . . . like a bad dream. Like we're living a nightmare."

George reached out and patted her arm.

"It's time I took you home," he said, glaring at me. "Just let me have a few words with Mr. Shade here."

He kept his hand on my arm as he walked me out of the room and down the hall, out of earshot.

"Look, let it rest, okay?" He pointed a big finger at my face. "I already told you the old man's mad as hell at you. We'll get Knop. I had a citywide put out on him. And we're running this as a probable kidnapping, so we got a wiretap in his mother's phone. He'll call her eventually. Hopefully, sooner, not later."

"I want in on this one," I said.

He shook his head.

"Why?"

"Because, Ron, you're still a civilian." His voice was terse, like he was reprimanding his kid. "The main thing now is we have to get Grace back safe, and we got a helluva lot more resources to do that than you do."

The only thing he didn't say was, *And you've messed it up enough already.* But he didn't have to. His tone said it all.

Chapter 19

When I'd left the hospital at around 1:00 a.m., Ken had still been in surgery. The next morning, after a fitful four hours of sleep, I awoke at six and immediately called. The emergency room nurse wouldn't give me any information, so I got dressed and drove over there. A triage nurse told me that they'd fashioned a makeshift bed for Ken's parents and that they finally seemed to be getting some rest.

"I can understand not wanting to disturb them," I said, "but can you at least give me an update on how he's doing?"

She smiled and nodded. "Let me go take a look, okay?"

I took a seat in one of the same black vinyl chairs that I'd seen last night and waited. After about fifteen minutes she came back.

"He's out of surgery, but not out of danger," she said. "The bullets did a lot of damage, but he was lucky in some ways. The trajectory of the one that hit his head seemed to angle upward, like maybe it was partially deflected or something. Minimal brain damage, but there was still an internal hematoma, so they had to do surgery there to relieve the pressure. The one in his back was a through-and-through. Lots of internal bleeding, which is what they were trying to stem. It's the one that went through his neck that's the problem. They had to do a trach."

I grimaced. The thought of him breathing through a slit in his throat . . .

"Can I see him?"

She bit her lip slightly, then motioned for me to follow,

pressing a code into the keypad next to the frosted glass doors and then leading me down a long hallway. The ceramic tiles on the wall were tan, as was the floor. Periodically, doors with clear glass windows in them broke the evenness of the wall's surface. People lurked behind the windows, busily doing various tasks and totally oblivious to us. Finally, we came to an area designated ICU, and protected by a closed double-door that said Absolutely No Admittance Without Escort.

The nurse turned to me.

"No more than a couple of minutes, okay?"

I nodded.

She pressed more numbers on the keypad and the double-doors opened. No one looked up at our presence. Several men and women, all in hospital scrubs, sat behind a half-counter busily writing on clipboards, and an impressive selection of television monitors, some showing a series of pulsating lines, sat on a shelf behind them.

Ken was in one of the rooms off the adjacent hallway. His head was canted left against the thick pillows, his eyes closed, and the expression on his face distorted by the array of tubes taped to his mouth and a bunch more coming out of his neck where the slit was. I could hear the rise and fall of his breathing, which sounded raggedy at best. Several IV lines sprouted from his bare arms, the clear lines connected to the hanging bags suspended from extended metallic hooks over the bed. Above his head a color monitor displayed what I assumed was his heartbeat in red against a blue background. It looked regular, like waves lapping against the shoreline.

"He's going to be critical for the next twenty-four hours or so," the nurse said. "Now, you really aren't supposed to be in here unless you're family."

She touched my shoulder gently and I started to turn, but stopped long enough to whisper a silent oath to him.

I'll get the son-of-a-bitch that did this to you, brother. I swear I will.

After grabbing a breakfast at a restaurant, I nursed their bottomless cup of coffee until I figured it was safe to assume that Rick would be arriving at his office. I drove there and waited until I saw him pull up.

"Ron. Jeese, what happened to you?"

"I was in a fight, remember?"

"Oh, yeah, did you win?"

Ordinarily, I would have responded with some smart-ass comeback, but having just seen Ken put a damper on any good spirits I might have had.

"We need to talk," I said. "I found Mark Shields."

Rick motioned me to the office, reaching into his pants pocket for his keys as we walked across the parking lot.

"Well, the trial starts tomorrow," he said. "We'll have to do jury picks and then get down to brass tacks Thursday and Friday. I don't suppose you found out anything that's going to alter the course of our strategy, did you?"

We were alone inside the dark office, and after turning on the lights we went to his office. I sat in front of his desk and gave him a rundown on my Arizona interlude. When I was finished he frowned and shook his head.

"Just like I thought, then." He averted his eyes. "A wild goose chase."

"Not really," I said. "Think about it. Shields went to a lot of trouble to conceal his moves. The only reason I was able to trace him was through my special contacts in the PD. Even though he wouldn't tell me anything, he made no effort to deny my own theory about the Gilbert/Gooding thing. If we put him on the witness list, it's bound to throw the Great One off his game, even if Shields never testifies."

"Ron, we can't go and accuse the opposing counsel of paying off a judge on a criminal murder case." He shook his head. "It just isn't done."

"But it will let him and his pal Gooding know that we know what they did." I leaned forward, feeling the anger at his timidity welling up inside me. Or was it anger over Ken being shot? I wasn't sure, but I knew I had to do something to convince him he had a chance at winning or he'd be defeated before the damn trial started. "This guy Gilbert's a real piece of work. You gotta quit thinking of him as some paragon of the law. He's a street fighter . . . as dirty as they come. You can't be afraid to drop one south of the border to let him know you're just as tough."

He smiled slightly. "More kickboxing metaphors?"

"Hey, it worked for me, didn't it?"

"Yeah," he said, but the word was barely audible. He looked down at his desk and took a deep breath. "So you're saying I should go get a subpoena certified for Shields and fax it to the County Prosecutor's office in Arizona?"

"That's what I'm saying."

"Okay. I'll get it done today. As soon as Kris comes in, she can type it, and I'll send Denise down to the clerk's office."

I was about to give him some more encouragement when my cell phone rang. I fumbled for it, hoping it wasn't bad news about Ken coming to me. But the number was unfamiliar, with a 219 area code. Indiana.

"Shade here," I said.

The voice on the other end was tentative . . . no more than a breathless whisper.

"Mr. Shade, it's Grace Bielmaster. I'm in trouble and I need some help."

I could feel my heart speed up.

"Where are you?"

"We're someplace in Indiana." She paused, then added, "At a motel somewhere."

"Are you all right?"

"Yeah, I guess so. I—" Her words faltered. "He went out to get us something to eat. I've only got a few minutes here. He took my cell phone and wouldn't let me call anybody. He got mad and broke the phone in the room, too. The maid let me next door, but I've only got a minute and he'll be back. I'm not sure what I should do."

"Grace, have you called your mom yet?" It was an effort to keep my voice calm.

"No."

"Has he hurt you at all?"

"No, he hasn't, well, last night he did slap me when I told him I wanted to call my mom, but he didn't really mean it."

Great, I thought. She was already falling into the role of the reluctant victim, making excuses for the idiot she was in love with.

"What's the name of the motel? Where is it?"

"I'm not sure." I could hear her fumbling with some papers. "Oh, wait, here's some phone book. The Sleepy Hollow. Mr. Shade, can you come and get me?"

"I'll be there as fast as I can. You need to call the police, though. They're looking for you."

"No." Her reply was so quick that I was afraid she was going to hang up. "No, no cops. I don't want Timmy getting hurt. Besides, he didn't really abduct me or anything. We ran away together. I went with him willingly."

"I know," I said. "How long before he gets back?"

"Oh no, he's pulling in now," she said, the alarm pervading every word. Then she hung up. I waited as the screen on my cell phone asked me if I wanted to save the number. I pressed yes, then immediately dialed Indiana information.

It took me another call to get an Indiana name and address to punch in the phone number from which Grace had called. The computerized voice spit out the information in mechanical fashion, and I listened to it twice, writing it down to make sure I had it: The Sleepy Hollow Motel, 380 N. Jackson, Bremen, Indiana. Rick did a quick Mapquest for me on his computer, as he listened to the brief summary of the Bielmaster caper. When I got to the part about Ken being shot, he said, "Jesus, Ron, be careful."

I told him I would and turned to leave. It looked to be about a two-hour drive. On the way out I bumped into Kris, who was just arriving.

"Ron," she said, reaching up to embrace me. Her welcome was more emotional than I was expecting, but I gave her a brief hug. "I'm so glad you're okay. How's your friend?"

"Still in a bad way." I tried a quick smile. "Look, I have to leave now. Got something important that can't wait."

Her lower lip drew down at the corners and she gripped my arm.

"I need to talk to you," she said.

"I know," I said. "I'll call you later."

"Don't forget." She gave my arm another squeeze. "Please, don't forget."

On the way to my car I debated calling George. I knew he'd be super-pissed if I didn't, but I also knew he'd send the local constabularies rushing over there. Knop was definitely armed. It could end up with Grace getting hurt, or worse. The last thing I wanted Bielmaster to hear about was his daughter in the middle of a barricaded suspect situation. They could take off again, too, and if she thought I'd tipped the cops, the chances of her calling me again would be slim to none. Plus, deep down inside my gut I felt the burning knowledge that I'd made a mistake . . . A miscalculation . . . I'd obviously underestimated Knop. Badly. And the results had been tragic. I couldn't set them right very easily, but I wanted to be the one to bring Knop in. And maybe, just maybe, he wouldn't want to come along easily.

Chapter 20

I circled the Sleepy Hollow Motel twice to get, as they say, the lay of the place. An ironic choice of words, since the joint was sandwiched between a set of railroad tracks and a bunch of tall trees on the main highway that led into the town. It was far enough away from the small city to make me wonder if it was an unincorporated county area. Certainly a good location for a cheap, "no-tell-motel" sort of place, and a good one for a couple of teenage runaways to hole up. Teenagers . . . I reminded myself of the unpleasant memories of Ken lying on that hospital bed with tubes sticking out of him. I couldn't afford to waltz in there this time, thinking I was dealing with a mixed-up kid. The cost of underestimating this adversary had been too high.

The motel was divided into two sections. The first one, built in an L-shape adjacent to the office, had a two-story section on one side and a row of joined, single flats on the other. They were red brick, which appeared sturdy enough until I looked at the roof and eaves. The wood beams needed a coat of paint badly. Some kind of extended one-story building, apparently a bar or restaurant, divided the first portion from the second, which appeared to be another two-story section probably added on at the same time as the one in front. The doors to the rooms opened to the sidewalk on the first floor and a five-foot cement slab of a balcony on the second. It had an almost dainty black metal banister running along between some massive white pillars. Maybe the architect had seen *Gone With the Wind* on cable before he designed it. But after a closer look I decided that he'd probably seen it in a theater. Either way, he would have to have been a little bit drunk at the time.

A dark-colored Dodge Neon, Knop's mother's car, was backed into a parking space in the second section. The front plate had been removed. Smart move. Indiana cars didn't have any front plates, and backing it in would probably insure that no roving police cars would run the rear plate since it wasn't easily visible. That meant that he knew the cops would be looking for him.

I pulled down the highway and stopped on the shoulder, beyond the railroad tracks. I needed to know which room they were in, but with the two stories, it was hard to tell. I figured that they were probably staying out of sight in the room, so parking on the far side at the bar seemed to be the best approach. Before I shifted into gear, I rechecked my Beretta and slipped the pair of handcuffs I'd gotten out of my equipment bag onto my belt on the left side. I put the long, flat handcuff key into my back pocket so I could reach it with my left hand. That would leave my gun hand free.

Shifting into gear I shot past the motel and did a quick turn into the lot, cruising slowly up to the opposite side of the lot where Knop's car was. A sign in the window of the restaurant advertised that it was open. I got out and stretched. My body still felt stiff and far from back to normal. I walked with slow deliberation toward the juncture of the restaurant and the solid row of one-story flats. A roofed-over section provided a darkened passageway between the two sections and I flattened against the wall and surveyed the place. There were about ten rooms on top of each other, running the length of the section. The Neon was at the far end, but that could mean one of the far rooms, or close access to the metallic stairway. The smart thing to do would be to disable the car, just in case they slipped by me. But I didn't want to go walking down there presenting a good target, either. Suddenly the wall I was leaning against started to vibrate slightly and I heard something. A woman singing. "Celito Lindo." A Spanish song. I moved up to the corner and peeked around. No one around in the parking lot. This section was made of dark cedar wood and had some dirty-looking windows. I casually moved around the corner and saw the laundry sign on the open door. The woman was singing as she leaned against a washing machine that was obviously in its spin cycle. She looked middle-aged and Hispanic. Mexican, probably, judging from the style of her clothes and high cheekbones.

"Buenas tardes," I said, smiling as I entered the room.

She stopped singing and her dark eyes flashed with alarm so I reached in my pocket and took out my all-purpose police badge. The dark eyes widened and I said, *"Soy policia. Habla ingles?"*

"Yes," she said, eying me with suspicion. I was wearing my usual black pants and navy jacket, which hung just low enough to hide the pancake holster for my Beretta on my belt.

I pointed to the Neon. "The boy and girl driving that car. You know which room they're in?"

She nodded. "Two-fourteen. On top near the end."

I looked down the expanse of rooms.

"You clean that one yet?"

"Si."

"And you let the girl use the phone in the next room?"

She nodded again.

"They in there now?"

She shrugged. "I tink so."

"All right," I said. "Here's what I need you to do. Take some towels up to the room and knock on the door. Tell them it's housekeeping. Then move away and I'll do the rest."

Her lips drew together, and she moved to a stack of folded white towels.

"Give me your master key," I said.

She paused, unhooked a ring of keys from her belt and sorted through them, handing me the bunch of them with one held straight up. As I took it, I thought again about Ken, and realized I didn't want her put in harm's way.

"Senora," I said, *"poco pelegroso,* so move away *muy rapido* after you knock, *comprende?"*

"Si." She took the towels and we moved toward the stairway. I followed behind her, our shoes making chunking sounds on the rickety metal stairs. The sound ceased when we got on the concrete slab. I could tell by the woman's walk she was a bit nervous. I took out my Beretta and held it in my right hand down by my leg. With my left, I reached out and grabbed a handful of towels from her.

"After you speak, keep walking," I whispered.

We got to room 214 and she raised her right hand, rapping her knuckles on the solid wood.

"Who is it?" I heard a male voice call.

"Housekeeping," she said, then quickly looked at me.

I gave her shoulder a gentle push and held the towels high, blocking the door's peephole. If Grace answered the door it would complicate things. I'd have to shove her out of the way and hope that Knop wasn't standing there holding the gun. But knowing what I did about Knop, and taking into consideration what Grace had said about his controlling actions, I figured he'd be the one who came to the door. Whether or not he'd be empty-handed, I could only hope.

It cracked open, the chain-lock stretching taut in the

open crack between the door and the jamb. I caught a glimpse of a masculine arm and threw my weight against the door as hard as I could. The chain-lock gave with a piercing snap and the door smashed back against Knop. I bulled my way in and saw him tumbling backward awkwardly, his arms waving for balance. His hands were empty. Grace sat on the bed, fully clothed, but with her hands over her mouth, her eyes wide with terror. The gun sat on the nightstand next to the bed. A big, mean-looking blue steel revolver with a six-inch barrel.

Knop managed to catch himself and remain upright, glancing at the pistol. I lashed out with a snapping front kick to the back of his left thigh. He recoiled in pain, but threw a clumsy right lead at my head. My left jab snaked out and caught him in the mouth. His lip split open. Stepping forward, I delivered a hook to his gut. He bent over and I grabbed his arm, twisting him face-first down onto the dirty-looking purple carpeting. I could feel the air whoosh out of him as I straddled his back, wrenching his left arm behind his back and pinning it in an upright position. I reached to my belt for the handcuffs, ratcheting one cuff around the upturned wrist. His right arm flailed and I pressed the barrel of the Beretta close to his face, letting the cool metal crease his cheek.

"Put your right arm behind your back, you little jerk," I said.

"No, please, Mr. Shade," Grace cried. "Don't hurt him!"

"You told him where we were?" Knop managed to say, his face twisting in her direction. "You stupid bitch."

"Shut up," I said, "and give me one good reason why I shouldn't just blow your head off."

"Go ahead, do it." His face rotated back toward me, the

words sputtering from the bloody flow from his mouth. "I knew it was either gonna be you or that other big guy doing me, anyway."

Other guy? I wondered if he was talking about Ken.

"Is that why you shot him, asshole?" I pushed his face to the carpet.

"Mr. Shade, please, no," Grace said. "I went with him. He didn't kidnap me, or anything. Please, don't hurt him. Don't hurt him."

I glanced at her and saw she was in tears. Sighing, I shoved the Beretta into my pancake holster and reached for Knop's right arm. He was reluctant to let me cuff him so I exerted some pressure on his left wrist until he complied. With the second cuff in place, and his arms secured behind his back, I stood up, but kept my foot on his hips. With two fingers, I picked up the revolver by the checkered wooden grips and moved it away from Grace.

"Are you all right, kid?" I asked her.

She nodded.

I took out my cell phone and handed it to her.

"Here," I said. "Call your mother."

After touching bases with George and then the local gendarmes, I turned Knop, the gun, and his mother's car over to the locals. George had told me that he had to collect the primary detective assigned to Ken's shooting, and then they would be en route.

"You can do that?" I asked playfully. The relief of having handled the situation successfully was flooding through me. "Pick your cases like that?"

"Hey, when it's involving the kid of a CPD lieutenant, nobody's gonna be complaining," he said. And to my surprise, he added, "Good job, Ron."

Ursula Bielmaster requested that I drive Grace back home as soon as possible, and I loaded her suitcase into the trunk of the Beater and headed back east. The drive was mostly all expressway so it went pretty quickly. I did take the time to grill her a bit about exactly what she remembered about last night.

"Timmy called me about seven." She looked down at the floorboards. "You see, we'd been talking to each other a lot since he got back."

"I kind of figured that."

Out of the corner of my eye I caught her glancing at me. She compressed her lips, then went on.

"He seemed real scared. Real nervous. I mean, we were talking about maybe seeing each other again. He never forced me before. It was something my dad thought, and . . ."

She sighed.

"So he called and said we had to leave that night if we were ever gonna be together. Said my dad had somebody that was gonna kill him."

"Why would he think that? Was he talking about me?"

"I don't know. Did you go see him at work?"

"I stopped in there a couple times. I never threatened his life, though."

"He said this big guy did." She turned to look at me. "I mean, Timmy was pretty strong and not scared of things, but this time he was really shaken up. Told me the guy punched him and stuck a gun in his face."

I shook my head. "That wasn't me." It didn't sound like Ken, either.

"I didn't think it was," she said, looking at me for a moment, then turning her head away. I could see she was crying.

"Anyway," I said, "so when you left, did he say anything

about shooting my friend? Like he thought it was me or the guy who threatened him?"

"No, I already told you he couldn't have done that." Her hand wiped away the tears. "We were going to sneak out and leave after my mom went to bed. I heard the sirens in front and knew something was going on. I thought maybe Timmy got caught, or something, so I called him. He was home waiting. I took my suitcase and went out the back door and he picked me up on the next block about ten minutes later."

Was this the truth, I wondered, or just her way of trying to cover for her boyfriend?

"What am I gonna do, Mr. Shade? I don't even want to go home anymore." The tears were starting to flow again, like an unstoppable faucet. "I don't know if I can face my dad. What am I gonna say?"

I considered this. I wasn't so sure what I was going to say to him myself. Finally, I said, "I'll talk to your dad. Don't worry about it."

"You will?" Her voice was halting.

"Yeah."

"I don't even want to go back to school either. If he thinks I'm going to Yale now, he's crazy."

"That would be a mistake."

She cried some more. "Now you sound like him."

That one kind of stung me. I searched my mind, trying to figure out what to say to a mixed-up seventeen-year-old who thought the whole world was against her. Then it came to me.

"You know, back when I was your age," I said, "I was in kind of a similar situation."

I called the Bielmasters on my cell phone when I was

about a block from the house. Luckily, Ursula answered and I told her it would be better if she escorted Grace right into the house and had a girl-to-girl talk with her. I also asked if her husband was there.

"Yes," she said. "He came home this morning."

"Good. Tell him I need to talk to him."

I pulled up and gave them time to notice us in front. I told Grace to stay in the car until her mother came out for her and went around to the trunk to get her suitcase. By the time I had it open, both Bielmasters were standing on their front porch. The old man's gaze, over the tops of his glasses, reminded me of a hawk. Ursula came to the car, and I opened the passenger door. Grace got out and hugged her mother. A single tear wound down Ursula's left cheek as she mouthed, "Thank you," to me. I nodded and let them go up the walk. The old man started bellowing at his daughter as soon as she got to the steps.

"Grace, do you know how much embarrassment you've caused?"

"Hey, Lieu," I said, moving up to the steps and setting the suitcase on the top section.

His glare turned back to me, the ends of his mouth twisting downward like he'd just eaten something sour.

"And what you got to say for yourself, Shade? You really fucked this one up, didn't ya?"

I reminded myself that he'd just gotten out of the hospital from a triple bypass.

"Why don't you do everybody a favor and calm down a bit?" I said. "She's been through a lot."

Ursula, her arm still around her daughter's back, quickly ushered her inside the house. Bielmaster glanced after them, then turned back to me.

"Hey." His finger jutted out toward my face. Since he

was standing on the top steps, he towered over me. "You don't tell me how to raise my own child."

"Then listen to me as a friend and colleague. Let things cool down before you—"

"You? A friend?" He scrunched up his nose. "You're shit, Shade. I hired you to do a job, and look how you fucked it all up. Letting my daughter get abducted by that little asshole . . . You were supposed to be guarding her, for Christ's sake."

I reminded myself again that he'd just been released from the hospital.

"That's not exactly what happened," I said.

"The hell it isn't. I'm gonna see that son-of-a-bitch put behind bars for life for this one."

"Look, let things calm down before you go rushing off half-cocked."

"Half-cocked? You son-of-a-bitch."

"You'll need to settle down and talk to your daughter." This was going nowhere. I turned to go. "Just don't try to do it today."

"If you think I'm paying you for this shit, you're crazy," he called after me. "You're fired, too."

That stopped me. I turned back to him.

"You know, a good friend of mine was shot in front of your place watching your family." I could feel my anger burning. I wanted to grab him and slap the shit out of him. "Plus, you signed a contract for our services."

"That ain't my problem. If he'd been doing his fucking job—hell, if *you'd* been doing *your* fucking job, none of this woulda happened at all. Like I said, I ain't paying you shit. You don't deserve it after this."

I reminded myself for the last time about his release from the hospital.

"Okay, I'll consider our agreement terminated as of right now," I said, grinning up at him. "I'll send you a bill by the end of the week."

"And it'll go right in the trash."

"Fine. I have a real good collection agency that will be more than happy to garnish your paycheck."

He started to reach down for the suitcase and grimaced in pain.

"And if you think," he said, straightening up, "I'm gonna do anything to help you get back on the job, you're nuts."

I smiled. The smart thing to do would be to just walk away. I knew that. But when have I ever done the smart thing?

"You can keep the police department," I said. "And one other thing. I was wondering if that heart surgery was going to change you at all."

He stood there on the porch, his lower lip and chin jutting out in defiance.

"But you're still an asshole," I said, and walked slowly back to my car.

Chapter 21

Between the two long drives, the interlude with Knop, and round two with the Bielmasters, I was feeling pretty beat. I also realized I hadn't eaten since my quick breakfast that morning. I checked my watch. Four-twenty-three. I pulled into the first fast-food joint I saw and grabbed a couple of burgers, some fries, and a coffee. I'd worry about the fat content and the cholesterol later. I dialed Rick's office to see if he'd gotten that subpoena faxed but only got his answering machine. Tomorrow was the beginning of the trial. Hopefully, I'd given him enough of an ego building that he knew he could win. It was all a matter of following the fight plan, I thought, and smiled to myself, thinking about the belt. The championship, the Bielmaster case being over with, Rick's pretrial investigation wrapped up . . . Everything seemed to be moving toward closure, and I knew I should be glad. But instead of relief, I had a burning in my gut. Something was still gnawing away in there.

My cell phone knocked me out of my reverie.

"Shade," I said as I answered it.

"Yeah, Ron, it's George." His voice sounded weary and far away.

"Where you at?"

"Still in Indiana. We're trying to wrap things up here, but we hit a few snags." He cleared his throat. "You didn't mess this piece at all, did you?"

"No, I turned it over to the cops. Why?"

I heard him sigh.

"It hasn't been fired," he said. "All the rounds are still

live, too. So unless Knop had more ammo, and a bottle of Hoppe's, this probably ain't the gun that shot Ken."

I thought about my return-trip conversation with Grace.

"Yeah, the Bielmaster girl said that he didn't do it. Told me they left after they heard the sirens."

"Yeah, that's what this kid's saying, too."

"Hey, has Bielmaster got any friends on the PD?"

He snorted. "Yeah, maybe one or two."

"No, seriously."

"Seriously? Christ, Ron, the man's a CPD lieutenant. Of course he's got friends. Lots of them. Why you asking?"

I told what him what Knop had said about a "big guy" threatening him. "According to Grace, that's why they felt compelled to take off." I heard nothing but silence on the other end of the connection. "Can you ask him?"

"Ask him what? If he sent somebody to strong-arm the punk that was banging his daughter? He's my boss, for Christ's sake, and I wanna keep my job for a little longer. You ask him. You gotta be his fair-haired boy now after getting the girl back, right?"

I chuckled. "Not really."

"He ain't still pissed?"

"More than just pissed," I said. "He fired me."

"That asshole."

"I already called him that."

"Huh? Not to his face, I hope."

"Yeah, when he was on his front porch."

"Shit."

"Well, anyway," I said, "I been thinking about this whole shooting situation. You think the big guy Knop was so scared of could have been Ken?"

"Ken? I thought he was just doing surveillance? Why would he try to strong-arm Knop?"

I'd asked myself the same question.

"Don't know," I said. "But he's the only big guy I could think of."

"I'm running something else down." His voice was serious again. "You remember how I told you my buddy got his tit in the wringer because of them SOS computer trails that show up?"

"Yeah."

"There was one on your Firebird," he said. "From the Cook County Sheriff's Police computer."

"So . . . maybe Ken was driving my car and some county cop ran the plate?"

"Don't know. We're checking now. Running it to ground. The nice thing about this technology is that it tells us not only who, but when it was run. And this one was run two hours before Ken was shot."

This wasn't making a lot of sense.

"Speaking of Ken," I said, "how's he doing?"

"Still in a coma. We're using that in our interview, that it's still only an attempted homicide, to try and get Knop to crack. But . . ."

"But?"

"I'm beginning to think"—George's voice sounded flat, dispirited—"that maybe it wasn't him."

"I got another question for you. You know anything about Rob Tunney's death?"

"Just that it was supposed to be a suicide. Why?"

"A couple things been bothering me."

"I hope you're not gonna try and tell me that you think a closed suicide case should be reopened."

"Think about it. Ever hear of a copper doing himself any other way than using his piece?"

"Ahhh, I don't know. If that's all you got it's pretty thin."

Something else suddenly flashed through my mind.

"Hey, you got your book of on-call judges?"

"Yeah," he said.

"Look up Foxworth for me."

"You ain't thinking about asking me to call him, are ya?"

I laughed out loud.

"Just tell me what his first name is."

I heard him sigh, but I could tell he was paging through the booklet. "Okay, let's see . . . Foxworth, Samuel A. That what you wanted to know?"

I thought about the last entry in Tunney's journal. *See SF.* Rick and I had assumed it meant Sally Forest, but what if he'd meant Samuel Foxworth?

"I'll get back to you on that," I said, and hung up.

I was sure I had Rick's home phone number somewhere, but just couldn't find it. In the meantime, I remembered that I had to call Kris. She answered after three rings.

"Hi," I said. "I'm in the neighborhood. Mind if I come by?"

"Ron, oh . . . This isn't a good time to come by." Her tone sounded strange. Evasive, with a hint of nervousness. "Tell you what. I'll meet you someplace. I need to talk to you."

"All right. Name it."

After a few seconds of silence, she said, "There's a Starbucks on Cicero, by Ninety-fifth Street. I'll be there in ten minutes."

Something was up, I thought as I hung up. This wasn't feeling right at all.

I had to crank up the heater a bit on the way. The temp was dropping, and it was getting almost downright cold again. Kris was waiting for me, nursing a bottle of water at a table when I got there. I went to the counter and ordered a regular coffee and pointed to hers in a questioning manner. She shook her head. I took my time putting a dash of cream in the coffee, variety being the spice of life, and headed over to sit opposite her.

"Oh my God, your face," she said, looking at me as I took off my sunglasses.

"Yeah, well, you shoulda seen the other guy." I grinned and winked, but it didn't seem to affect her. I noticed she'd kept her dark leather jacket on, like she wasn't expecting to stay long.

"How's your friend?" she asked. "Any word?"

I shrugged. "About the same. Still in a coma."

She reached out and touched my hand. Her fingers felt tentative.

"I'm sorry," she said.

"Yeah, I've been going over it again and again in my mind. Something ain't right, but I just can't figure out what it is."

I noticed that she looked away, then down when I'd said that. Something wasn't quite right here either.

"You all right?" I asked. "Looks like something's bothering you."

Her lips compressed. "Ron, I need to tell you something."

The way she ended the sentence told me she had more to say, but wasn't saying it. I nodded encouragingly.

"But before I do," she said, "I need you to know that . . ."

Her voice faded. Whatever this was, it wasn't coming out easily, and I had a strong hunch I wasn't going to like it when it did.

She took a deep breath. "That I never meant for anyone to get hurt. Not your friend, certainly not you. It's just, sometimes you get in so deep, you don't realize what's happening until it's too late."

I felt a sudden revulsion in my stomach. Like I'd been punched in the gut. "What are you saying?"

Another deep breath. Her fingers brushed mine.

"You're a special guy. I never meant for . . . this to turn out this way." She looked a step away from breaking into tears.

"You've said that before."

"I know," she said, composing herself. "My name's not really Templer. It's Rand. Kris Rand. I work for an investigative firm in San Francisco."

I nodded, watching her carefully. It was all starting to come together for me.

"My firm has very close ties to Mason Gilbert's." Her eyes searched my face. "We've done work for him in the past. My boss told me that I had to come to Chicago to go undercover. I would be working for Gilbert."

"But you'd report to John Flood," I said. It was like looking through the binoculars and adjusting the focus. Suddenly everything goes from a soft blur to crystal clarity in a second.

"Yes," she said, looking down again. "Gilbert pulled some strings to get the temp firm to hire me, and with my doctored résumé, I was a shoo-in to get the job at Mr. Walters's."

"How did Gilbert know there'd be a vacancy?"

Her mouth opened, as if to speak, but she swallowed hard again.

"Let me guess," I said, remembering how Rick had told me his regular secretary had been the victim of a hit-and-run. "Flood arranged that too."

She looked down and nodded. "I didn't know about that until I was already in."

"And you've been feeding him information on the case. Telling him all my moves," I said. "Up to, and including, my tracking down Mark Shields."

"That seemed to really freak them out. They kept pressing me for more information. They asked me when you'd be back, but I never dreamed that they'd go after you like that."

"So you told them about my other case?"

"Just what you'd told me in conversation." Her hand reached out for mine, but I pulled away. "Ron, you've got to believe me. I never wanted anything to happen to you. I thought you were coming back earlier, like you'd said, then, after I heard on the news that someone had been shot in your car, I knew."

"Kinda slow on the uptake, weren't ya?" I said. "Did you get paid overtime for going to bed with me?"

Her eyes filled up with tears.

"I deserve that, but please, believe me when I tell you that wasn't part of it. I really—"

"Yeah, right," I said, cutting her off and standing. "Let's go."

"Go? Where?"

"To see Rick," I said. "You're gonna tell him your little story so he's prepared to ask for a mistrial tomorrow, and then we're going to see a buddy of mine named George so he can clear up the shooting. It was Flood, wasn't it?"

She shook her head.

"I had nothing to do with that."

I felt such rage, it was all I could do to keep from slapping her. But I don't hit women, so I grabbed her arm and ushered her toward the door.

"Come on," I said. "We'll take my car."

I was so focused on maintaining control as we did the

two-step across the lot, that I didn't pay any attention to the beat-up green van idling in the lane, other than to glance to make sure it was stopped. Something about the driver struck a chord of familiarity in my brain, but I half-walked, half-pushed her in between the Beater and the car next to it. Suddenly the van pulled up behind us, blocking us in and obscuring the view of the Starbucks window. It had a solid, windowless rear section. I was fumbling with my car keys, when I heard the side door on the van slide open, followed by an ominous metallic chucking sound. I glanced over to see John Flood pointing a sawed-off shotgun right at us.

"Get in, Shade, or I'll blow you apart right there." His voice was a snarl.

I thought about trying to run, but Kris was in front of me, and we were sandwiched in between two cars. Even if I forced my way over her, he'd cut me in two before I could take a step. Then another familiar face hopped out of the passenger side of the van and went around the front of the Beater, effectively cutting off even that remote avenue of escape. This one I recognized. Paul LeMatte, the scumbag ex-boyfriend.

"Come on," he growled. "Get in now. Keep your hands where I can see 'em."

I moved toward the open door, debating whether I could reach for the shortened barrel and try to disarm him. As if reading my thoughts, Flood moved back in a crouching walk, farther into the recesses of the vehicle. LeMatte was pushing Kris right behind me.

"John, what are you doing?" she asked, her voice edging toward panic. "I don't want to be a part of this. Let me go. Please."

"Shut up," he said.

LeMatte pushed her up into the van right after me.

"On your knees, Shade," Flood said, still holding the shotgun. Keeping his finger on the trigger, he released his grip on the pump section and reached into his pocket, taking out two pairs of chrome handcuffs. He tossed them on the floor next to LeMatte, who got in and slid the door closed behind him.

"Cuff 'em," Flood said. "Behind their backs, then get his gun." He grinned. "I know pretty-boy Shade always packs."

I was hoping LeMatte, despite his substantial arrest record, wouldn't know much about handcuffing techniques, so I put my arms behind me, keeping my palms together to give myself as much movement advantage as possible. I felt him ratchet the cuffs over my wrists, then he did the same to Kris, pulling her arms back with a quick, forceful movement. She gasped in pain.

LeMatte laughed and pushed her down to the floor. I felt his hands roughly searching me moments later. He pulled back my jacket and unsnapped my Beretta. He took out my car keys, too, but other than that, despite the many times he'd been arrested, his search was almost superficial.

"Nice piece," he said, shoving it in his belt. He went to Kris and took his time touching and squeezing every part of her body, copping cheap feels.

"All right, that's enough," Flood said. He lowered the shotgun and stepped in front of us, pointing to the long bed of the van. "Lay down over there. Both of you."

We struggled to move across the hard metal floor on our knees and curled down on our sides. I heard a snapping sound, and when I looked up I saw a big canvas tarp descending over us. It stirred up a film of dust in the air that set both Kris and me coughing under the dark covering. It smelled of mildew and dirt.

"All right," I heard Flood say. "Paul, you drive the van. Obey all the speed limits and don't get stopped by no cops. Harry, you take the broad's car. I'll be in Shade's. Any questions come up, use the walkie-talkie mode on the phones. Got it?"

"John, I don't think I wanna get involved in something like this," a rather high-pitched, effeminate voice said.

It was Harry Norridge, the "street artist," Gilbert's other "miracle witness."

"Shut the fuck up," Flood said. "You already are involved. Just do it."

Chapter 22

I was lying on my left side on the metal floor of the van, the arm under me going to sleep fast, and my right shoulder feeling the strain of the restricted angle. The cuffs hadn't been double-locked, either, and when I tried to move I felt another notch ratchet tighter. Pretty soon they'd totally cut off my circulation and I wouldn't even be able to move. LeMatte stopped abruptly, sending me rolling forward, then back. I heard Kris groan in pain.

LeMatte's cell phone chirped and a gruff voice garbled through. Flood's.

"Where you at?"

"Coming up on the country club," LeMatte said.

"Good. I'm a block or so behind you. Keep going."

That meant we had to be going west. No country clubs the other direction. East would only bring us back into the city. West . . . That probably meant some remote location . . . A forest preserve, maybe?

I heard LeMatte singing along to a song on the radio. His voice wasn't any better than his search of me had been. Maybe I'd be able to have them put that on his tombstone, if I was lucky. I struggled to work the fingers of my right hand into my back pocket. It was where I'd left the handcuff key when I'd taken down Knop earlier. Since I'd turned him over to the Indiana coppers, they'd uncuffed him themselves and given me back my cuffs. I'd stashed them in the glove box of the Beater and forgotten to put the handcuff key back onto my key ring. Thank God for forgetfulness. It was one of those Safariland keys that was perhaps an inch-and-a-half long with a flattened section for easy turning. My fingers brushed against it. I arched my back and dug deeper. Finally I managed to secure it in a delicate grasp and slowly extract my hand.

The cuff ratcheted tighter and I grunted and bumped up against Kris's back. Next to me I felt, more than heard, her sobbing. She knew the game was up as well as I did. She'd served her purpose, and now they wanted to take care of any loose ends. I wondered if LeMatte and his buddy Harry Norridge knew what was eventually in store for them.

Keeping my back arched to take the pressure off my left arm as much as I could, I worked the flattened area of the key between my fingers. I felt clumsy and inefficient. From the way he'd secured my hands, leaving them palms together, I knew that LeMatte didn't have any formal training in handcuffing techniques. I prayed that he'd also been stupid enough to leave the keyhole facing toward my back. If he didn't, my chances for successfully unlocking them, even with the key, were slim to none. And slim had left town.

Holding the key between my fingers, I pressed it over the surface of the cuff, hoping it would find its way into the hole. It was like playing golf in total darkness. I had a momentary rush of panic when I couldn't find the hole, thinking it must be on the other side.

Deep breaths, I told myself. You can do this.

I tried again, this time feeling each side of the cuff with the pads of my forefinger and thumb. My forefinger encountered a small, nipple-like bump, but my thumb felt the hollowed-out edge of the rim of the keyhole.

I had a chance if I could unlock it before time ran out. Or before my hands stopped working due to impaired circulation.

I estimated that we'd been driving for at least ten or fifteen minutes. The phone chirped again.

"Where you at now?"

"Coming up on Route Forty-five," LeMatte said.

"Keep going. The next stop sign is a Hundred and Fourth Avenue. Slow up and wait for us there."

I had about a mile. Fingering the key again, I tried to press it into the hole several times, but I just couldn't get the angle right. I was coming up from below, and the fit had to be straight on.

The key slid from my grasp. Fear gripped me again as I had a sudden flash that LeMatte heard it, but the stupid son-of-a-bitch kept right on singing. He must have thought he was Sinatra reincarnated or something. I rolled more on my back and searched by feel for the key. All I felt was the metal ridges of the floorboards. I took two rapid breaths and tried again. A mile . . . If we were going around fifty that would only take a little over a minute. I heard LeMatte speak into the phone.

"Flood, I'm at a Hundred and Fourth. Whadda ya want me to do now?"

His voice sounded a bit nervous. Good, that further pushed the odds in my favor. If I could get loose. I resumed my now-frantic search of the floor.

"We're pulling up right behind you now," I heard Flood's voice say.

"Okay."

"You and Harry hang back here for a couple of minutes," Flood said. "I'm going up the road about a quarter of a mile. There's a turn-off there that'll take us up into the woods. When I call you, come on down and then go past me up the hill."

"Ain't them entrances blocked by chains?" LeMatte

asked. His words spilled out rapidly.

"I'm gonna cut the fucking lock and lower the chain, asshole." Flood was obviously calling the shots, but it sounded like he wasn't real happy with his helper.

My fingers walked outward in expanding circles. I tried to figure the exact spot my hands were when the key had slipped from my fingers. Adjusting my position a bit more, I brushed my hands over the floor again and felt something. The key.

Carefully, I tried to pick it up. Couldn't quite do it.

"Paul, you there?" The voice was different. Higher-pitched. Squeaky. It had to be little Harry.

"Yeah," LeMatte said.

"He call you yet?"

"No."

It sounded like Harry wasn't the picture of confidence either.

I tried to wedge the key in the lock again, but heard Flood's voice tell them to come on down. The van jerked forward, rolling me back and forth again. The key all but slipped from between my fingers again. I felt for the keyhole. The van slowed, then turned right, coming to a stop.

"Keep going up the hill by the pavilion," I heard Flood say, not over the phone this time. He must have been right by the driver's window. "Then get 'em outta there. I'll be up as soon as I reset this chain."

"How we gonna get out?" LeMatte asked.

"I have my own lock, you moron."

Not the sharpest knife in the drawer, I thought. It was getting down the wire. I had maybe thirty seconds to get free. Putting everything I had into it, I tried again.

Fit the key into the hole, I thought, over and over . . .

I felt it slide in. Pushing it as hard as I could, I twisted the key counterclockwise. The pressure from the cuff went slack and I blew out a slow breath.

The van was traveling up a hill or grade now. I held onto the key and looped my left arm out from under me. Transferring the key to my left hand, my free hand, I felt for the other keyhole. Even though I couldn't see because of the tarp, it was much easier with my arms in front of me. I unlocked that cuff and slipped them into my belt. We were rolling to a stop now. I reached forward, pressing my body close to Kris.

"Don't talk," I whispered. I felt for her arms, then moved my hands downward to her cuffs. I tried to fit the key into the hole on the left one just as the van began to slow to a stop. The key slipped away, but not out of my grasp. I heard the door open, then slam shut. I searched for the right one.

LeMatte was whistling as he moved around to the back of the truck. I heard the clunk of the handle and LeMatte said, "Shit." The jingle of keys. He'd forgotten to unlock it. That bought me a few precious seconds. Once again, slipping the hollow key into the hole, I twisted and felt the cuff release just as the door opened.

"Rise and shine," LeMatte said.

I grabbed two handfuls of the rough tarp and sprung upward, throwing it out and over him. He uttered a sharp, inarticulate grunt, but by that time I was wrapping the tarp tighter and delivering as many punches to it as I could. I felt my knuckles skim and tear open. Giving the covered LeMatte as hard a shove as I could muster, I grabbed Kris's hand, one of the cuffs dangling from her wrist, and pulled her out of the van.

"Come on," I yelled, trying to figure which way to run.

It was dark, but the immediate area was clear of any

trees or shrubbery for about thirty yards. I pulled her along, trying to make the treeline, which loomed like a distant safe house. Something sounding like an angry hornet whizzed by my left ear just before I heard the explosion behind me. LeMatte had gotten free. Another bullet zoomed by us as I zigzagged, pulling Kris along with me. The ground slopedc downward, which gave us a small reprieve. We crashed into the massive thicket as what seemed like a thousand small, hostile branches assaulted us. I continued pushing through and then took both of us to the ground. Up on the hill, I heard a commotion of voices.

"What the fuck happened?" Flood yelled.

"I don't know. The fuckers escaped somehow."

"Pull those cars up here and shine the lights down on the trees there," Flood said. "Ain't nowhere to move without tipping us off where they are. Get them flashlights too."

The moon was just a sliver in the sky, but I still saw Flood's silhouetted form standing on the high ground, holding the sawed-off. I dug my fingers into the ground, searching for mud. The earth was dry and powdery. I spat on my fingers and rubbed them into the dirt again, then smeared what I could muster on my face. I turned to Kris, who was breathing faster than a sprinter after a 200-yard dash. I moved to smear her face also, but she balked.

"Don't move," I whispered. "We have to stay still. It's our only chance. Movement will give us away."

"They're going to kill us, aren't they?"

"Not if I can help it," I said, my voice still hushed. "Here, smear this mud over your face. It'll make you harder to see."

I was thankful we both had on dark clothes. It was getting colder by the minute, and I realized that our frosty breaths could give us away once they got the lights on the area.

The first car, Kris's, pulled up onto the hill and then down toward us, the high beams flicking on. It was aimed off to the left. The van came next. I pushed Kris farther down the slope and off to the right. Moving slowly, we managed to travel back about six more feet.

The Beater crested the hill and I suddenly felt a ripple of anger. How dare they use my trusted vehicle? It was like Black Bart stealing Silver from the Lone Ranger. The Beater's high beams switched on as well, and I saw the two henchmen join Big John Flood on the top of the hill.

"You go off that way," Flood said, pointing Harry to the left. "You go to the right." He tapped Harry on the shoulder. "If you see them, light 'em up with your flashlights, and I'll do the rest."

Send your expendable native bearers out to beat the bushes for the tiger, while the great white hunter sits and waits with the rifle, I thought. Brutal, but effective.

They meant to kill us. No doubt. I was facing three armed thugs, at least one of whom, Flood, seemed highly competent. And me with no weapons, no light or compass, and saddled with a hysterical female. My best chance of survival would be to leave her and head deeper into the woods myself. That's probably what she would have done to me, if the positions were reversed, I thought. But despite her deceit, I couldn't just leave her out here to die alone.

It sure looked bleak, though. I took as deep a breath as I dared, and readied myself. Sergei had looked big and overwhelming too, I remembered, but Chappie told me to follow our fight plan. And these three jerks were no champions.

I felt around again, moving over a set of thick, exposed

roots sticking out of the ground. We'd been torn by errant branches and bramble bushes. Sticker burrs covered my clothes and Kris's. Her hair was full of them, too. Maybe they would slow down our adversaries just enough . . . If I could get the drop on one of them, recover a weapon, then we'd have a chance.

"Shit," one of them shouted. It was LeMatte stumbling over a bush. "There are stickers everywhere."

"Shut up," Flood said, sweeping the area with his flashlight. "You're giving away your positions."

Noise discipline. Flood knew his shit, but his two helpers were just city boys in the woods. And I'd been an Airborne Ranger.

Chappie's advice. Stick to your fight plan. But what was it?

LeMatte moved slowly down the slope. He had his flashlight in his left hand and what looked to be my Beretta in his right. He was about twenty yards away and moving on an angle. He'd probably end up behind us at this rate.

"Cut back toward your left, Paul," Flood called out. "They couldn't have gotten that far."

"Fuck you," I heard LeMatte say under his breath. "Why ain't you down here with us?"

My hands kept creeping over the dirt. I needed a weapon of some sort. Then it hit me. I had one. The handcuffs. I slipped them from my belt and put them together, threading my fingers through the spaces, giving me some makeshift brass knuckles. It would only take one good punch. But I still had to get in range to deliver that punch. LeMatte was angling our way, sweeping the flashlight over the bushes. The beam actually swung over us once, but I doubted that he saw us. As long as we stayed still for the meantime . . .

My fingers continued to search and I felt something smooth and long. Glass-like. An old bottle. I pulled at it gently, like caressing a lover's hand, and it came free of the entangling bushes.

Pressing my face close to Kris's ear, I said, "I need you to throw this as far as you can. Use one hand and flip it. Can you?"

"Yes." The word came between two rapid breaths.

"Okay, I'm going to move away, off to our right. Towards him. When I make a clucking sound, you throw it as hard as you can to your left and stay down. Got it?"

"But what if it doesn't work?"

"It's got to. Or we'll be dead a lot sooner." Regretting my word choice, I added, "It's our only chance."

She nodded.

I waited until LeMatte swung the beam away to slowly begin creeping in his direction. He was maybe fifteen feet away now, moving on a collision course with me. I stayed down, stayed still.

Let him come to you, I heard Chappie's voice telling me inside my head. Let him come to you.

No rush, I thought.

Flood's light swept closer to where I was, then moved back toward Kris and held firm.

"Paul, check over there," he said.

Great, I thought. Did he see her?

"Over where?" LeMatte called out. He was no more than six feet from me now and looking back up the hill toward Flood. It had to be now or never, I thought, checking the terrain that separated us. It looked like a series of small but tough bushes. They'd slow me down, but maybe the diversion would work.

I clucked. Nothing. Clucked again.

LeMatte started to turn toward me, then I heard the rustling sound behind me, off to the left. His gaze immediately shot that way, along with his light.

"What's that?" he yelled, doing some high stepping that closed the distance even more.

I shot up toward him, coming up on his left side and a little to his rear. Cocking my left hand, I swung with all my strength and connected with his left shoulder. He grunted in pain and I snared his right wrist. The Beretta discharged down into the dirt. He started to yell and I clubbed his face with the cuffs, once, twice, three times, feeling a spray of blood splash over my face with the last one. My hand closed over the slide of the Beretta, my thumb wedging into the trigger guard along with his finger. It went off again, the explosion lighting us up like a lightning flash.

I twisted him down to the ground. Out of the corner of my eye I saw Flood's big form running down the slope of the hill. I punched LeMatte's gut several times, each one eliciting a sharp gasp punctuated by a pitiful cry.

Wrenching the Beretta from his hand I was set to hit him again when I lost my balance and tumbled backward. My only thought was not to drop the gun. Something sharp poked into my back, and willowy fingerlike threads raked the side of my face. I heard the roar of the shotgun and a scream.

Kris?

No, LeMatte. His inert form dropped to the ground and rolled twice. I did a quick crouching run toward the nearest big-looking tree.

"Shit, you shot Paulie," I heard Harry say.

"Shut up," Flood yelled. He cocked back the slide and slammed it forward, chambering another round. How many did the magazine hold? Was it four or five? I tried desperately to remember.

"Is he okay?"

"Shut up," Flood's voice said again.

"Hey, man, this is nuts. I'm outta here."

I peeked around the edge of the tree trunk. Flood was close to where Kris had been. I hoped she'd had enough sense to move away. Had I told her to do that?

Harry began a loud and quick trek up the slope.

"Where you going, Norridge?" Flood yelled. "Get your ass over here now."

"No way, man. No way."

I saw Flood turn slightly and the night exploded again, the muzzle flash seeming to travel at least a foot and a half. Norridge's scream was brittle and pathetic as he fell.

I brought the Beretta up, ready to squeeze off a round at Flood, but my clear night vision had mostly vanished with the shotgun flash. The big man bent sharply and grabbed at something. The hollow, pale light from one of the cars illuminated him when he stood up. His left arm still held the flashlight, but it was angled upward, and the crook of his elbow was around Kris's throat.

"I got your girlfriend here, Shade," he called. "Why don't you come out real slow now, before I have to start causing her major pain?"

To emphasize his point, he did something to make her scream.

"That feel good, baby?" he said.

She screamed again.

I didn't know what he was doing to her, or even if he'd kill her eventually. I only knew that if I revealed my position now, he'd most likely get us both. Still, hearing her scream like that was turning my stomach.

"Please, Ron, help me," Kris called out. She grunted

and screamed again. Whatever Flood was doing, it sounded like it hurt. A lot.

I peeped one eye around the tree, as fast as a snake's head. Flood held her in front of him, facing in my direction. He didn't know where I was exactly, but he knew the general direction. The sawed-off, if he was using double-ought buck, and it had sounded like he was, would spray the area with so much buckshot I'd be torn apart. I held the Beretta down toward my leg and took a couple breaths.

Fight plan, I thought. Fight plan.

Kris screamed again. My fingers were still looped through the handcuffs. I cocked my arm and tossed them as hard as I could to the left, then edged around the tree, bringing up the Beretta.

The blast from the shotgun lit them both up, but Flood had fired off toward the handcuffs. He must have realized his mistake and dropped the sawed-off, trying to keep Kris in front of him as he reached for his pistol. She squirmed just enough to drop downward and for a split second Flood moved back, silhouetting himself against the glowing headlights of the Beater. It was all the edge I needed.

I squeezed off a shot at his head and I knew it hit because he jerked back like he'd taken a punch. Kris suddenly was able to drop free, but Flood brought up his arm and his pistol flared. I had no idea where the round went. I fired again, and again, concentrating on center mass.

Flood's arm suddenly lowered, and he turned and began walking up the slope, like he'd changed his mind and was going home. One step, two, his legs slowed and he staggered drunkenly. The pistol slipped from his fingers. His body listed to the left side, and he tipped over, flopping down in such a manner that I knew he was dead. But I still checked him anyway, taking my time to work my way over to him and using the lens of his flashlight to touch the open, vacuous eye that blankly stared up at me.

"Kris, you all right?" I asked.

"I think so," she said. "Is it over?"

"Let me check the other two and I'll let you know."

After doing the light touch to both LeMatte and Harry, I gave her the all-clear and headed up to the cars. The Beater was sitting with the engine off and the lights on full blaze. I reached in and shut them off, feeling a sense of propriety. Then I shone the light into the cars until I found my cell phone.

Kris slowly walked past me up the slope and sat down on the edge of the curb by the paved section.

I checked the battery and looked around. Woods, two pavilions, Porta Potties, and picnic tables. A real nice place for a showdown.

"Any idea where we are?" I asked her, dialing 9-1-1.

"In hell," she said.

"No, that's where *they* are," I said, figuring that the emergency dispatch center would probably have the telemetry to track my signal. "We're just in purgatory."

Chapter 23

George managed to clear enough red tape with the investigating Forest Preserve Police to spring me for the meeting I'd set up. I hadn't slept in over twenty-four hours and was running on pure adrenaline and bad coffee, but I still felt as fresh as if I was walking down to ringside. At 9:15 a.m., Rick, Denise, and I sat on one side of the polished wooden table in the Daley Center conference room looking at Todd Gooding, Mary Buckley, and the Great Gilbert himself. Gilbert seemed to glow with an aura of the guy who thinks he's just won it all.

"I'm very glad you've decided to settle on our offer, Rick," Gilbert said. He wore a gray, tailor-made suit, and his voice held that flawless bass quality that probably sent chills down the spines of juries everywhere.

"Actually, Mason," Rick said, popping open his briefcase and removing a sheet of paper, "we've got a counter-offer we'd like to present."

Gilbert raised his eyebrows as he accepted it, then slipped on a pair of half-glasses to read it. The ends of his mouth twisted downward.

"This is ludicrous." He took off the glasses but held them artfully, like he was posing for a picture. "Is it a joke?"

"No joke," Rick said.

"These terms are complete capitulation," Gilbert said. He slipped the glasses into his jacket pocket, next to a fine-looking silk handkerchief, and started to get up. "This meeting is over. You're going to regret this."

Rick glanced to me.

"Sit down, Gutman," I said in as rough-sounding a tone as I could muster.

"What did you call me?" Gilbert asked, his eyes narrowing in what must have passed for his "withering intimidation look." I wondered if he practiced those in the mirror.

"Gutman. Kasper Gutman," I said. "Sidney Greenstreet played him in *The Maltese Falcon*. You kind of remind me of old Sidney."

"Rick, please put your attack dog on a leash," he said, standing fully erect now. "Ms. Buckley, Todd."

It was Rick's turn to smile. He'd turned the corner all right.

The other two started to get up and then I used my follow-up punch.

"We got Kris Rand on ice, waiting to sing."

That stopped Gilbert. His eyes flashed for a brief second, then he slowly lowered himself back into the chair. It creaked slightly at the weight.

"LeMatte and Norridge ain't gonna be showing up either," I continued. I took a quick sip from my paper coffee cup and winked at him. "And Big John Flood's . . . kinda indisposed. Permanently."

"We know it all, Mason," Rick said, taking command now. "Either agree to our terms or face the consequences."

Gooding, who had a head about the size of a basketball, looked back and forth between Gilbert and Mary. His mouth dropped open and he began to look like he'd wet his pants.

"Mason, what are they saying?" he asked.

Gilbert laid a quieting hand on Gooding's arm and said, "Mary, would you excuse us for a moment?"

Ms. Buckley looked relieved as she stood up, gathered her purse and briefcase, and said she'd wait outside. I couldn't resist watching her butt move inside the tight skirt as she walked away. Maybe they were expecting Judge Foxworth to show up.

"We can go with half the settlement and no allocution," Gilbert said.

Rick grinned. "No way." He was smelling the blood.

"That loud, sucking sound," I said. "That's your license to practice law going down the drain."

Gilbert's lips tightened. He leaned over toward Gooding and whispered something. Gooding recoiled like he'd been scalded.

"That's nuts. I won't do it." He licked his lips and swallowed. "I'll be ruined. I'll lose everything."

"Not really," Rick said. "All the money will go into a trust fund for the kids. And we'll allow supervised visitation."

"Mason," Gooding said. "This is unacceptable. Make another deal."

The Great Gilbert glanced down at the table momentarily, then said quietly, "There is no other deal."

"I won't do it," Gooding repeated.

"And I will not lose my license to practice law," Gilbert said in his stentorian voice. He turned sideways and I realized that he'd grown the beard to cover the dollop of flesh that hung down under his chin. He seemed to relent a bit, placing another placating hand on Gooding's arm and leaning toward his client. "Todd, I'm afraid we really have no other choice."

Our victory party was sweet, tempered by the remembrance of the expressions on the faces of Laura's family when Todd Gooding stood up in court and stated his regret over the pain and suffering he'd caused. It wasn't as good as wearing a hair shirt for the rest of his life, but we explained to her mother and father that as soon as Kris Rand was finished talking to the specially convened federal grand jury, both Gooding and Gilbert would most likely be facing federal charges of insurance and mail fraud.

"That life insurance policy is going to prove their undoing," Rick said. "By admitting culpability here, Gooding opened himself up for the feds to get him."

"Plus," I added, "it seems the feds had already been looking at the Great Gilbert in connection with some shenanigans involving our favorite judge. Mark Shields went to them sometime back and started the ball rolling. They've been monitoring things. Now, they got his deputy by the short hairs, and as soon as he gets through playing 'Let's Make a Deal,' they'll go after the big fish."

"How did you do that?" Denise asked. "Figure that one out?"

She was actually starting to look at me in a whole different light, I'd noticed. And I kinda liked it.

"They traced it back to who ran my plate the night my buddy Ken was shot," I said. "Looks like he's gonna make it, too." I took the time to smile, then added, "Foxworth's deputy was the one who always accepted the payoffs for hizzoner. Flood went to him and practically strong-armed him to call dispatch and run my plate to get my home address after they figured I'd put it together about Mark Shields. And the rest is history."

I took a mock bow and straightened up. Denise was looking at Rick, and he was holding her hand. I was beginning to feel like a third wheel.

"Let's go celebrate," Rick said. "Everything's on the firm for this one."

It was obviously the biggest case of his career, and also

their moment. I took the opportunity to say thanks, but no thanks.

"Ron, why not?" Rick asked.

"Well, for one thing, I haven't slept in over twenty-four hours," I said. "Plus, I figured I'd go over to the hospital and tell Ken how things turned out. He's going to need a lot of rehabilitation, and George and I want him to know we're behind him."

"The company insurance gonna handle it?" Rick asked.

I shrugged. "Yeah, but they'll probably raise our premiums so high that Windy City Knights Security will probably be history."

"Well," Rick said, "if you need a good lawyer . . ."

He grinned and we shook hands. Denise came over and gave me a sisterly hug, and I watched them walk toward Rick's car.

I sighed. All's well that ends well, I thought.

Chapter 24

Friday, when I picked up the Firebird from Bob's Body Shop, he took particular pains to show me that he'd completely replaced the front seat and the tracking and glass for the window.

"Neat," I said, picking up one of those For Sale signs with the blank space for the phone number.

"You're selling her?" he asked.

I nodded. "Too many bad memories." I grabbed a Magic Marker and wrote my cell phone number in the space. "Besides, I still got the Beater."

"Yeah, right," he chuckled. "I'll keep my ears open for somebody wants to buy a nice ride."

I thanked him and pulled out on the street, heading nowhere in particular. The weather had cleared a bit and, despite the still-cold temperatures, it felt like a dash of spring in the air. Spring, when a young man's fancy turns to what? Romance? My romance meter was resting on empty after the way I'd let my ego override my judgment with Kris, with a K. I should have read the signals better . . . listened to what my instinct was telling me. Instead, I ended up looking like a chump.

My gas gauge beeped, letting me know that it, too, was sitting on empty.

Don't want to be more of a chump and run out of gas, I thought as I pulled into a nearby Gas City. Just as I was heading for pump number 11, this white Ford Escort cut right in front of me and stole the spot. I was set to swear at the other driver, and then I saw it was two babes. One had dark brown hair, and the other was blond. The driver, the brunette, covered her mouth with her hand as we locked eyes, and I realized that maybe she hadn't seen me coming for some reason. I nodded and swung over to the adjacent row of pumps, hit the release for my gas cap, and headed inside to pre-pay. A blast of wind, left over from January, seemed to come out of nowhere and cut through my clothes.

Early spring my ass, I thought.

I pulled open the door and saw this old guy standing in front of the solid glass window. The old guy was talking a blue streak, and the young girl behind the glass wall looked bored to tears.

I stepped up behind him, waiting for a break in his non-stop monologue so I could pay for my gas.

"And my son writes everything that he's done for that entire year on the card, and, boy, does he write good, too. And I take my time reading it so I'll know what he's been up to, so I really look forward to getting that Christmas card."

Still thinking about a Christmas card in March? I thought. Poor old guy.

He suddenly seemed to become aware of me standing there and stopped, stepping to the side slightly.

"May I help you?" the bored girl asked.

I told her I'd take twenty, passed her the bill, and turned around. The brunette from the Escort was right behind me and I almost bumped into her.

"Oh, sorry," she said. "Today just isn't my day, is it?"

She had a spray of brown freckles over her face, and one of the sweetest smiles I'd ever seen. Dark Irish, from the look of her.

"Sorry about almost hitting you," she said. "I was talking to my sister."

"No problem," I said. "I'm getting rid of the car anyway. In case you're interested."

Her head turned, showing me a long, very feminine neck and collarbone. The rest of her wasn't bad, either.

"Hmm," she said. "Nice car. I'll think about it."

"Well, in that case." I reached in my jacket pocket, took out one of my cards, and handed it to her. "That's me."

Her eyebrows rose slightly as she read it, then she reached in her purse.

"Here's mine," she said. "Maybe I'll be in touch."

I glanced at the name on the card. Alex St. James, Investigative Reporter, *Midwest Focus Magazine.*

"I read your magazine all the time," I lied. "It's great."

She smiled. "It's a TV show, you know, like *60 Minutes*, but I'm sure you meant you watch the captioned version, right?"

I smiled and nodded, saying, "You got it."

I slipped out the door to leave her to contend with the rest of the old man's Christmas card story and pumped my gas. As I got back into my car I watched Ms. Alex St. James walk over to her Escort, stop, and wave to me. She smiled, too.

Who knows? I thought, firing up the engine. Maybe it's gonna be an early spring after all.

About the Author

Michael A. Black graduated from Columbia College, Chicago, in 2000 with a Master of Fine Arts degree in Fiction Writing. He previously earned a Bachelor of Arts degree in English from Northern Illinois University. Despite his literary leanings, he has often said that police work has been his life. A former Army Military Policeman, he entered civilian law enforcement after his discharge, and for the past twenty-eight years has been a police officer in the south suburbs of Chicago.

The author of over forty articles on subjects ranging from police work to popular fiction, he has also had over thirty short stories published in various anthologies and magazines, including *Ellery Queen* and *Alfred Hitchcock's Mystery Magazine*. His first novel, *A Killing Frost*, featuring private investigator Ron Shade, was published by Five Star in September 2002 with endorsements from such respected authors as Stephen Marlowe, Sara Paretsky and Andrew Vachss.

Windy City Knights, the second novel in the Ron Shade series, came out in March of 2004. *The Heist*, a stand-alone thriller set during the freak Chicago flood of 1992, came out in June 2005, and another stand-alone, the wickedly humorous *Freeze Me, Tender*, debuted in March 2006. He has also written two nonfiction books, *The M1A1 Abrams Tank* and *Volunteering to Help Kids*, which were published by Rosen Press. *A Final Judgment* is Michael's fifth novel and the third in his popular Ron Shade series.

Michael has worked in various capacities in police work

including patrol supervisor, tactical squad, investigations, raid team member, and SWAT team leader. He is currently a sergeant on the Matteson, Illinois, Police Department. His hobbies include weightlifting, running, and the martial arts. He holds a black belt in Tae Kwon Do. It is rumored he has five cats.

Visit the author's website at www.MichaelABlack.com